Love You, Truly

By

Susan L. Tuttle

Candlelight
Romance
LOVE INSPIRED BY
HIS WARM GLOW

LOVE YOU, TRULY BY SUSAN L. TUTTLE
Published by Candlelight Fiction
an imprint of Lighthouse Publishing of the Carolinas
2333 Barton Oaks Dr., Raleigh, NC, 27614

ISBN: 978-1-64526-235-0
Copyright © 2019 by Susan L. Tuttle
Cover design by Elaina Lee
Interior design by AtriTeX Technologies P Ltd.

Available in print from your local bookstore, online, or from the publisher at: ShopLPC.com

For more information on this book and the author visit: www.susanltuttle.com

Brought to you by the creative team at Lighthouse Publishing of the Carolinas (LPCBooks.com): Eddie Jones, Shonda Savage, Linda W. Yezak, Jessica Nelson.

Library of Congress Cataloging-in-Publication Data
Tuttle, Susan L.
Love You, Truly / Susan L. Tuttle 1st ed.

Printed in the United States of America

PRAISE FOR *LOVE YOU, TRULY*

I fell in love with Susan's writing after reading her debut novel and *Love You, Truly* was quite possibly even better than that one! From the authentically flawed characters you couldn't help but love, to the romance that built at the perfect pace with almost-kisses that made me melt as much as the actual ones, to banter that had me laughing out loud. It all combined to make a beautiful story that I already can't wait to read again! Susan L. Tuttle is definitely an author to watch and she's already earned her spot on my favorites list!

~**Abbi Hart**,
book reviewer, *Adventures of a Literary Nature*

Love You, Truly by Susan L. Tuttle is romance novel perfection! Tuttle has created characters that are just magic on the pages! The characters in *Love You, Truly* provide fun and flirty dialogue, but each have their own vulnerabilities that really tug at your heartstrings and keep you rooting for them until the conclusion. I absolutely fell in love with this binge-worthy book and Susan L. Tuttle has solidified her place as one of my "must buy" authors!

~**Ashley Johnson**,
book reviewer, *Bringing Up Books*

Love You, Truly had me captivated from the opening page until the last. With a likable, no-nonsense heroine and a hero in much need of God's grace, *Love You, Truly* has it all—laugh, romance, and an intriguing cast of secondary characters. Susan L. Tuttle has a gift of creating a relatable story that has you wanting more. Best of all, *Love You, Truly* paints a beautiful picture of romance and the greatest love of all—God's.

~ **Toni Shiloh**
Author of *Buying Love* and the Maple Run Series

Love You, Truly will keep fans of reality TV romance flipping pages, eager for the next moment of sizzling connection or snort-out-loud humor. But in the course of the romantic conflict, this story also offers brilliant flashes of character motivations … the fractured thinking that holds us back in life. For example: "While others shone, she flickered, good enough to only go so far. But God needed someone to help fan into flame his larger plans. That was her role, and when she didn't hope for more, everything went fine." After this 'round-the-world adventure with Blake and Harlow, you'll be a new fan of Susan L. Tuttle, too!

~**Denise Weimer**

Author of *Fall Flip* and *The Witness Tree*

A fresh, riveting read from a superb storyteller! The sharp dialogue and romantic tension will pull readers in through the bachelor-style game show until the romantic conclusion, with every page a sweet indulgence. Tuttle proves herself an intelligent writer with this sophomore offering, a fantastic story layered with nuanced depth and humor, and readers will be eager for more!

~**Joanna Davidson Politano**,

Author of *A Rumored Fortune*

Love You, Truly is a delightful journey across the world and into the hearts of Harlow and Blake as they navigate finding love in the most unconventional way. By weaving together tender moments and witty dialogue, Tuttle builds the kind of storybook romance that's sure to leave the reader with a swoon and a smile.

~ **Janine Rosche**

Author of *The Wandering Heart*

Praise for *At First Glance*

It was a treat to read a romance novel featuring two characters who don't fit our unrealistic standards for beauty! I cheered for Penny and Jonah as they dealt with old scars, grappled with the meaning of worth, and fell in love with each other for all the right reasons. Heartwarming!

~**Becky Wade**
Christy and Carol Award-winning author of *My Stubborn Heart*

Susan Tuttle's debut novel, *At First Glance*, is a fun romance with deep undercurrents of truth. Tuttle gets to the heart of what we all really want at our cores—to be truly seen and loved the way we are. Through the story of two families with an inordinate amount of heartache, and a heroine with massive insecurities, Tuttle shows the ultimate healing of perfect love through her pretty-perfect hero, Jonah Black. Fans who enjoy a sweet combination of humor, heart, and the beauty of unconditional love, will find this story a wonderful addition to their reading list.

~**Pepper Basham**
Author of the *Mitchell's Crossroads* series

Susan Tuttle's *At First Glance* is such a refreshing read! Her unique characters tugged on my heart from the opening scenes and the plot moves along at a great pace. The underlying theme is one that will engage women of all ages: What is true beauty? And what happens when you find it in the most unexpected place … or person? Readers, get ready to make room on your bookshelf for Susan Tuttle!

~ **Melissa Tagg**
Author of *Made To Last.*

In *At First Glance*, Susan Tuttle creates true-to-life, flawed characters who sometimes look for love and redemption in all the wrong places—and the wrong people. Her debut novel is woven through with romance, honesty and hope—and not an ounce of sappiness. I'm looking forward to more from this new author!

-**Beth Vogt,**
Christy and Carol Award-winning author of *Somebody Like You*

Where do you search for your value? Woven with a powerful theme, laced with splashes of humor, and filled with fresh, witty dialog, Susan Tuttle's debut novel, *At First Glance*, will enchant romance readers of all ages and leave you with a sigh of pure delight! I can't wait to dive into more sweet romances by Susan Tuttle!

-**Dora Hiers**
Author of Heart Racing, God-Gracing Romance

Susan Tuttle's debut novel sings with wit and humor, but also an unconfined tenderness as it explores true beauty and self-worth. Tuttle's mastery to blend a palpable romance, characters layered with complexity and heart, and meticulous attention to details, results in a stellar love story, proving she's one to watch in the contemporary romance genre.

-**Jessica R. Patch**
Author of the *Seasons of Hope* series and *Unleashing Love.*

ACKNOWLEDGMENTS

Writing this book didn't happen alone, and right here is where I have the privilege of thanking everyone involved. I start with Jesus. He is the author and perfecter of my own personal story. Any good thing that comes out of me is because of him, and he will always receive the glory for every drop of it. And my eternal thanks.

Next, I'd love to thank my writing friends who step in at a moment's notice to offer advice, brainstorm, or simply talk me off a cliff. Dawn Crandall, Joanna Politano, and Jessica Patch, I honestly don't know what I'd do without you ladies. You enriched this story in so many ways. Thank you!

To my amazing agent, Linda Glaz. Thank you once again for believing in me and for finding a home for this story. I am forever grateful for how you champion me.

To my editors, Jessica Nelson and Linda Yezak. Thank you ladies so much for loving this story in its early state and then pushing it to become even better. Your comments, catches, and encouragement along the way helped more than I can say. I'm blessed as a writer to have you both.

Lastly, to My Love and to my kiddos. Thank you again for believing in me, championing me, praying for me, and loving me. Chasing dreams is a tough job full of failures and successes. I couldn't do this without you all in my corner. You four are my greatest success story of all. Love you more!

DEDICATION

For Dad and Mom. Thank you for demonstrating true love to me on a daily basis. Even more importantly, thank you for ensuring I knew the One who is love. That's the best gift you ever gave me.

Chapter One

If Harlow Tucker had an ounce of self-preservation in her, she'd move to a state that at least pretended to cooperate with its seasons. But that would mean leaving her parents and her sister, Mae, and that was about as likely to happen as Michigan being consistent with its weather.

"You okay?"

Harlow winced as she righted herself from where she'd wiped out on the sidewalk. A bitter wind whipped the bangs from her eyes as she looked at the wrinkled, dirty hand extended to her and then up into the lined face of Chet, an old homeless man she'd seen on more than one occasion during her nursing shifts in the ER. Hadn't seen him last night though, but work had been slow. So slow that as the sun began to tip this morning's sky, her boss told her to go home early. Instead, she spent her found time strolling the downtown streets of Abundance, Michigan, with her camera in hand, eventually wandering a few blocks from the ten-story hospital which claimed the title of tallest building in their small city. That's how she'd discovered the patch of ice that had recently bested her.

She grasped Chet's hand and allowed him to think he helped her up. "I'm good. Just didn't expect ice in the middle of April."

He bent. "This here your phone?" He handed it to her.

Another cracked screen.

"Yep." Cheaper to fix than her camera lens, which she'd managed to save, thank goodness.

Harlow pocketed her phone and rubbed her sore hip.

"Sure you're okay?" Chet motioned to her side, the stinging cold seemingly not affecting him.

"Yep." In the distance, Victorian houses perched at the top of rolling hills that lifted sections of town while Craftsman style homes created a picturesque perimeter. But right here, running through Abundance's center, one long street of brick buildings formed a shopping district currently being revitalized. It was the people in this area that so often grabbed her attention. She nodded to the young boy walking down the street whom she'd been focused on when she wiped out on the slippery pavement. "You know him?"

"Keenen. His mama worked the overnight at the gas station. She's probably finishing her shift. I suspect she thinks he's home in bed. I'll see he gets there."

The boy appeared about five. "No one's watching him?"

"He's got an older brother, probably still asleep himself." Chet squinted at her. "Hospital let you off early?"

"It was a quiet night." And she'd been unable to resist capturing the rising daylight softly glowing through swollen gray clouds. The way beams of light escaped to illuminate the darkness captivated her. Another whip of wind stole her breath. She regarded Chet. "Where'd you stay last night?"

He grinned, wide and near toothless. "I got me a bed and new blanket under the bridge. Slept like a bug in a rug."

She swallowed back prodding words meant to get him to a shelter. He'd ignore her anyway. Always did. Funny, he was comfortable chatting up the nurses with his almost nightly visits to the ER, but trying to convince him to spend the evening indoors was as futile as using fingers for a glass. He'd slip right through the doors.

Chet hurried off, and Harlow raised her camera to her face. Sure enough, he grasped the boy by the hand, and she snapped away as they toddled down the broken cement sidewalk.

Found.

The caption came easily. She could blur the few cars and people moving around Chet and Keenen, then bring the two of them into sharp focus. Hitting the play button on her Nikon D750, Harlow scrolled until she found the shot of Keenan gazing up into Chet's face as they linked hands.

So many people had no clue this other world existed. On several streets the crumbling buildings and boarded up homes were being repaired, but the families who lived two blocks over from the renovations remained overlooked. Lately, God had opened her eyes to see these forgotten and others as well. Through her camera and the nonprofit she was helping her sister with, she saw even the patients revolving through the ER.

Perhaps because she felt unseen herself.

No. Her mind didn't need to travel that way this morning.

She caught one more still as Chet and Keenan strolled under the streetlight shining in the hazy morning, its yellow glow lighting the swirls of tiny snowflakes that floated on the breeze.

Snowflakes. In April.

Harlow's camera hung around her neck as she slipped her phone from her back pocket. Please still work. Sliding her finger over the glass, she held her breath until it lit up—with five missed calls. Three from Mae, one from their lifelong friend, Jack Townsend, and one from Charity Lewis, who was like a second sister.

Her phone worked, but darn it all, she'd forgotten to take the thing off *do not disturb*.

Hurrying down the sidewalk, she dialed Mae, who picked up after two rings.

"Finally. I called you three times in the last hour, Harley."

Only Mae got away with that nickname. "I saw. What's wrong?"

"Nothing. Except Jack had to move the meeting up."

She stumbled. Checked her watch. Nearly eight. "I can be there in ten minutes." Not showered, still in her dirty scrubs, and sweaty from the now near jog to her car, but she'd be there. Had to be. Jack was their "in" with his family agency—the last hope at starting Wheels on the Ground, the nonprofit Mae had dreamed up and Harlow had jumped on board with.

"He already left."

Air puffed from her lungs. She'd missed the meeting. "I'm so sorry, Mae." Beyond sorry. "I should have come straight home when I got out."

"It's not like you could have known he'd need to rearrange his schedule."

"But I should have turned my ringer back on once I left work. I was distracted." Focused on grabbing more pictures while the light was perfect. All noble and good, but her camera and those shots would always be here. Mae wouldn't.

Harlow's Honda sat in the staff lot. She clicked open the locks and jumped in. "Did you at least have a chance to talk with him about the grant?"

"Of course." Mae's voice tightened. "It's my legs that don't work, Harley, not my brain or my mouth."

And recently, her heart, but they were avoiding that. Muscular Dystrophy had taken so much from Mae already. It didn't seem fair that it may steal her future too.

Harlow flopped her head against the headrest and squeezed her eyes closed. "What did he have to say?"

"The board likes our idea."

Hope swelled.

"But they're not ready to give us the grant yet."

And crashed.

Her sigh fogged the window. She started the car to let it heat up. "Why not?"

"They want us to put together a business plan and run some numbers for them." Outside, the wind rocked her little SUV. "Jack also mentioned we might need to put in our own seed money before they're willing to invest."

Might as well ask them to scale Kilimanjaro too while they were at it.

Sucking in a deep breath, Harlow threw a smile into her voice. "All right. There's got to be a computer program I can purchase that will help me make a business plan. If not, I can research it on the Internet. How long until they need it?"

"He didn't say, and I didn't think to ask because he was in a hurry. He and his dad want to help, but they need something more concrete for the board."

"Helping children who can't afford a wheelchair obtain one isn't concrete enough?"

"Our mission statement is good, but our business plan isn't." Mae's own wheelchair whirred in the background. "I took notes, and Jack offered to help me put one together."

"You don't need to sink your energy into that, Mae."

"I want to."

Because she wanted to see this nonprofit up and running before …

Harlow shook her head. Not going there. Which meant she needed to do everything she could to keep Mae strong. She'd been doing that her whole life, but now the weight of its importance pushed into her.

"I'm really sorry I missed the meeting."

"It's okay." Knowing Mae, she meant it. "You can make it up to me though."

"Anything. Name it."

"Watch the *Gamble on Love* finale with me this morning. I DVR'd it last night."

4

Harlow groaned. "I loathe that show, and you know it."

"You already agreed to anything."

Because there was nothing she wouldn't do for her big sister.

"Fine. I'll be there."

"Well hurry, because I'm ready to see who he chose, and I need a nap before Charity's surprise party tonight."

"You're sure about going?"

"Wouldn't miss it."

"All right. Give me an hour."

"Thought you said you could be here in ten."

"That was when I thought it was for something important." *Gamble on Love* didn't even come close. "I need coffee and a shower. You'll thank me."

Mae giggled and hung up. Harlow pulled into traffic, a chill making its way into her bones even with her heater on full blast. Wheels on the Ground was a good idea, meant to help children who couldn't help themselves. Children who blended into the fabric of their world, unseen because they were unable to contribute. So why couldn't she convince the Townsend Agency to get on board?

She would. For those kids and for Mae. She'd just have to try harder.

And keep her phone turned on.

Dodging a bad mood, Harlow cranked a left and drove toward Starbucks. They were putting out a new brew this morning. Something from Africa, which meant she'd get another pin on her map at home. She was almost done researching the continent and had an entire scrapbook of photos printed off the Internet. After today's coffee, she could complete the book and move on to another location.

She pulled into the Starbucks lot and climbed out of her car.

Inside, there was a long line of customers ordering specialty drinks, but Harlow only needed the fast line—self-serve with the new African blend. Her eyes centered on the carafes in the corner. The far left one read Burundi, and only two people were in line.

She joined them right as the morning barista, Allen, waved. She spun, returned the wave, and brought her focus back to her line ... or what was her line. Only now a large man stood in front of her. A large man who hadn't been there a moment ago.

She cleared her throat.

He couldn't have missed her. She wasn't that short.

5

Clearing her throat with a little more gusto still didn't gain his attention. Rude.

He grabbed a paper cup and studied each carafe. Slowly. His hand wavered over the hazelnut blend but didn't press the button. She'd never been a violent person, but if he didn't move soon, she was liable to unleash her inner warrior.

Harlow tapped the toe of her black sneaker against the faux wooden floor of Abundance's one and only Starbucks. The mocha-haired brute in front of her didn't move. Ha. Mocha-haired. Oh boy, she needed her coffee. She tapped harder.

The man turned enough for her to see his cheek, covered in early-morning scruff, pull up with a smile. With eyes hidden behind aviator sunglasses, it was about all she could see. That and the small curls that escaped from under his Michigan State baseball cap. "Need your morning fix?"

That was putting it mildly. Harlow punched down her frustration and simply smiled.

He finally made his decision. The Burundi. After three long pumps he tapped the button one last time. "Hope you weren't going for this flavor. I just used the last."

Heat built behind her eyes.

Not only had he cut in front of her, but he'd stolen the last of her coffee?

Sure, there were three other carafes. Coffee still readily available. But he finished the reserve blend they'd put out for the day—Burundi, Africa. No pin for her map.

Her smile grew stale. "Seriously?"

Mocha Man turned to look at her. Dark eyebrows rose behind his sunglasses, and he quickly returned his stare to his coffee. "Seriously." He reached for a packet of sweetener, blocking her way even if she wanted the other options. Which she didn't.

But she needed the caffeine. She'd been up too many hours, and the idea of staring at a business plan could put her to sleep just standing here. Then there was her promise to watch that stupid show with Mae.

Oh, she needed a Venti.

She stepped closer. "Can I get in there?"

He didn't even pass her a glance, simply slid his cup full of Burundi down the counter. She held hers under the regular and pushed. Nothing happened. She pushed again. And again.

6

Mocha Man chuckled. "Guess you're having a bad morning."

Her eye twitched.

He stuck a lid on his cup. "There's always hazelnut." His focus remained on his coffee as he added a sleeve. "Decaf too, but I'm sensing you like your caffeine."

"I do." Across the room, the ever-growing line of specialty drinkers grew. "But I'm allergic to hazelnuts, so I tend to avoid them."

"Don't worry. I'm sure they'll bring more out in a minute." He sipped on what should have been her coffee and wrinkled his nose. "You're not missing much though." With a shudder he dumped his into the trash. "I think I did you a favor."

She held her hands against her sides to stop from throttling him.

He grabbed another cup and stuck it under the hazelnut, still not looking at her. "Not allergic." Again, he added a packet of sweetener to his drink. "Hope you get your coffee."

Then he turned and strode away.

She mentally counted to ten. Then twenty before her fingers started to uncurl from their fists. Could people really be that self-centered?

"Hey, Harlow!"

She gritted her teeth and turned to Allen who was motioning from behind the counter. She slid past the line of customers and over to the opposite side of the store. "What's up?"

"I've got something for you." Hands busy with the steamer, he used his upper arm to scratch his nose. Then he nodded to a twenty-ounce cup sitting beside him. "Burundi, black."

The man had produced a morning miracle for her.

"You are my favorite barista." She dropped a five into the tip jar beside him and grabbed her cup before returning to the freezing cold wind outdoors.

Crossing the parking lot, her phone dinged a text, and she dug into her purse for it.

"Look out!" A voice boomed behind her as a horn and squeal met her ears.

Her gaze pulled up in the same instant. She jerked her hands out to stop the white Cadillac Escalade barreling straight for her. Time stitched into slow motion as she heard people—or herself?—screaming. She closed her eyes and prepared for impact.

It didn't come.

A car idled in front of her. She peeked her eyes open. Its fender parked an inch from her knee cap with her coffee splashed across the windshield and sparkling white hood.

Wiper blades turned on, sloshing away the liquid, and behind the glass sat Mocha Man.

*

Blake Carlton slowly released the iron grip on his steering wheel. Letting out the breath he held, he flicked on his wiper blades to clear the coffee smeared across his windshield. As the liquid slid away, that woman from the line inside came into view. He knew her name—had read her folder again in his hotel room this morning—but couldn't call it to mind for anything right now. All he could think of was Red, like her hair. And her cheeks. Of all the people in this small town, the one woman he'd come to surprise, and thus the one woman he was supposed to avoid, he'd run into. Almost literally.

Apparently she'd found her cup of coffee.

And lost it again.

He stifled a grin. Nerves always brought out laughter in him at inappropriate times.

He slid the car into park and stepped out. Red looked nearly as angry as she had inside when he took the last of the African blend. A few bystanders gawked, one asking her if she was all right. She nodded at the woman, then returned her hot stare to him.

"You sure you're okay?" He used the voice he'd perfected from years of talking Mom out of her moods.

She wasn't having it. Her clear blue eyes narrowed another notch, but her voice remained steady. "I am."

Did she ever soften that sharp edge? "Sorry about your coffee. Again."

She glanced at his hood and then back at him. "But not about practically running me over?"

"That too."

With a long sigh, Red scooted out of the way of his car, and the edge in her eyes actually dulled. If he removed his hat and sunglasses, allow her to recognize him and then reveal he'd come to town for her, would it disappear for good?

He bit his tongue—too costly of a theory to try. Too many people with phones stood nearby. Word would immediately spread that he was here, tonight's event would be ruined, and his production crew—along with the network—would be less than pleased, to put it mildly.

"It's my fault." She brushed a hand against the purple scrubs she wore, a slight tremble running through her fingers. "I should have watched where I was going. Glad one of us was or I'd be under your car."

Blake smiled. "I'm glad you're not."

"Me too."

"Can I buy you another cup?" He nodded toward the store. "Maybe this one you'll actually get to drink."

Red gripped her phone. "Thanks, but I've got to get home."

Most likely to help her sister. She'd been the one to supposedly nominate her for this evening's little surprise.

"Well, I hope your day gets better."

"It can only go up from here." She absently waved and crossed to her silver Honda CR-V.

Blake watched until she'd turned out of the parking lot and headed up the street. Toward her home, he guessed. He hopped back in his Escalade and drove the opposite direction toward the Tipton Hotel.

The city was small, but it possessed its own character. Throughout the downtown area, the homes were older and varied in style. What he really enjoyed, though, was how artists used several of the brick businesses as blank canvases, covering their sidewalls with some pretty amazing murals that livened up the place. A must-have if their winter and spring were always this cold and gray. He'd overheard people talking that it had been nearly a week since they'd seen a full day of sun—and that it wasn't unusual. Would Red enjoy her upcoming vacation to someplace warmer and brighter?

He tried again to tug her name from the back of his mind. Whatever it was, he knew it was a contradiction. Her first name conjured up glamour. A would-be platinum blonde with regal height, perfect lips, and an old movie-star air about her. While her last name made him think of ponytails and flannel. But no matter how hard he hunted after it, the name eluded him, as names often did.

Either way, she seemed better suited for the second half of her missing name.

The top of her head didn't even touch his chin. Hospital scrubs and tennis shoes hid any curves she might have. Her long hair was in a loose ponytail, and it held more red than on her audition video. Then there were her eyes, a shade of blue he doubted even the HD cameras could pick up—her iPhone video surely hadn't. Even with frustration lining her words and face, her voice was softer and her skin a shade paler than he'd expected too. She'd probably sprayed on fake tanner before shooting the video—even though her sister claimed to have nominated her without her knowledge. He wasn't buying it.

But America would. At least that's what Mom and Dale Edwards—their producer—were betting on.

Blake parked at the hotel and walked across the lot. Everyone played tricks to get their fifteen minutes. Using a disabled sister wasn't unheard of, but it still turned his insides. Fortunately for Red, the combination of good looks, small-town-girl status, poor luck in love, and so-called nomination by said disabled sister was one that spelled viewers. Mom and Dale had cast Harlow without a second glance.

Speaking of Dale—he erupted from behind the hotel's sliding glass doors. "Where have you been?" he hissed. Wouldn't want anyone overhearing them.

"I needed coffee."

"The hotel has coffee."

Blake swished his green and white cup in front of the producer. "Not this they don't."

"That mocha was worth blowing our cover?"

"It's not mocha, just real coffee." Blake brushed past him. "And relax, no one expects to see me in the middle of Tinytown, USA."

Dale trailed him into his hotel room. "No one saw you?"

"Of course, people saw me. I'm not invisible." Blake dropped his keys on the small table and removed his baseball cap, waving it. "But thanks to this and my sunglasses, no one recognized me."

Dale's face tightened. "If anyone discovers you're here before—"

"Relax. No one's on the look-out for us. We're a new show."

"Except last night they promoted our show on the *Gamble on Love* finale." Dale ran a hand through his nearly non-existent hair. "The few people who happened to not know you before surely will now. You're officially on America's current radar."

Apparently, Red hadn't gotten the memo.

"We're in Abundance, not Hollywood. It's fine." He perched on the edge of the dresser. "What time do we start today?"

Dale glanced at his watch. "We meet here with Jace and the crew at noon to go over what I want for the Tucker reveal. Darcy will be down soon for your wardrobe choices."

Tucker. That was her last name. He'd check the file for her first and hope this time it stuck. Thanks to his mother's once-upon-a-time popularity as darling of Hollywood, Red would definitely know his name. Should guarantee him a warmer reception this time around. Something he looked forward to because, for whatever reason in their short interaction, she'd snagged his interest more than any of the other contestants he'd already invited onto his show.

"What time do we meet Tucker?" Blake leaned forward.

"The fake surprise birthday party is scheduled for five. Harlow thinks her job is to get her friend there." Dale stood. "Her parents and sister will meet us around two at the banquet hall we've reserved downstairs. That gives us plenty of time to set up and be ready for her and get in an interview with the disabled sister."

Of course, Dale wanted that. Better ratings.

"By the way," Dale said, "I know you wanted Charlie Banks, but I brought in a second cameraman too. Name's Tad Guthrie. He's worked with your mom before."

Didn't bolster any confidence. "But not with me." He didn't trust cameramen—at least not any except Charlie, who needed this job.

"Your mom vouched for him, that's good enough."

"Fine. Whatever."

Dale paused at the door. "I'll see you in my room at noon."

The door closed behind him. Blake pushed off the dresser and walked over to the window. He opened the heavy, forest-green curtains and raised up the glass, allowing an icy breeze in.

Another hotel.

Something he swore he was through with, yet already this month he'd seen four. Now the next few months stretched ahead in an endless connection of empty rooms.

Below, a minivan pulled into the parking lot. A family of five stumbled out. Why on earth would anyone visit Abundance? The mom rolled back one of the doors and unstrapped a baby, smothering its chubby cheeks with kisses.

He closed the window and moved away. Maybe Charlie wanted to play cards for a bit. Hated cards, but it was better than staying in here. He snagged his phone and room key and went to find him. To find any connection.

He was so tired of being alone.

Chapter Two

Harlow parked in her small garage and grabbed her things. Exhaustion yanked at the edges of her brain. No time for a nap, though. Mae waited across their joined yard in the home she shared with their parents. A disgruntled meow greeted Harlow as she entered her house. Hanging her purse on its hook, she placed her camera on the black laminate—wannabe granite—countertop beside a pile of mail, then bent down.

"Hey, Ansel." She rubbed his thick gray fur. "You have a good night?"

Purring, he jumped on the counter while she opened a cupboard and grabbed a can of food. She shooed him off. "I love you cat, but you aren't allowed up here."

She poured his food in a bowl and placed it on the bright yellow mat beside the door.

Shuffling into her small family room, she sorted out the mail, then began placing it into the labeled trays on her desk in front of her large bay window. The third envelope was square, white, and thick, with embossed gold lettering across it.

Wedding invitation for one Opal Berry to Peter Eisler.

Nothing like your fiancé dumping you for one of your best friends. How incredibly sweet of them to send her an invite—not. She tossed it into the trash, then hurried upstairs to her bathroom to toss her scrubs and bad memories. After the world's fastest shower, she tugged out the knots in her hair, donned her oldest pair of sweats and her Uggs, then snuck out the side door, doing her best to ignore Ansel's scowl. She'd owe him some serious cuddle time when she returned.

A light dusting of snow covered the arbor that separated her guest house from the main house where Mom, Dad, and Mae lived. She ducked under the arbor, following the stone path to the back stairs. On the white-washed porch, two large black pots overflowing with flowers flanked the matching black door. Mom should have brought in the purple and white pansies last night. One week ago it had been in the upper sixties. Last night dipped below freezing.

Only in Michigan.

She stepped inside, the aroma of Mom's banana bread swirling through the air. "Mom?"

"In the kitchen."

Harlow kicked off her boots, lined them neatly against the wall, and slipped into the kitchen. Mom sat at the table, a mug of coffee and small plate with a few crumbs in front of her, sunshine highlighting her light blond strands void of any gray.

She set down her paper. "Hey, darling."

"Morning." Harlow kissed her cheek and went for the bread. "Smells wonderful."

"Help yourself. Coffee's warm."

Harlow cut a thin slice and nibbled it slowly.

"I brought your mail in for you. Saw you hadn't gotten it before your shift yesterday." Mom studied her.

So much for ignoring her painful past—or forgoing the mug of coffee. "I saw it."

She might have been able to trash the wedding invite, but it didn't erase the fact that Peter had chosen Opal over her. He'd lined the two of them up, and Harlow had fallen short. Of course, it would have been nice to know she was even in a competition—she'd have kicked his butt to the curb rather than him dumping her.

They'd both said they were sorry multiple times and apparently figured her silence meant everything was hunky-dory. Least that was all she could come up with as a reason for that invite sitting in her trash at home.

Pouring more liquid strength, Harlow focused on her mom. "It's all good."

"Really?"

"Really."

Mom settled back against her seat and allowed for a few quiet moments before thankfully moving past Peter. "Mae said you were taking pictures this morning." She held out her own mug for Harlow to refill. "How are things going with your photography?"

"They're not." The latest rejection letter in her inbox testified to that. "But it's fine. Photography needs to remain a hobby for now while I focus on this grant."

"Have you ever thought about letting Mae take over the process so you can make photography more than a hobby?"

Harlow brushed her hand through the air. "Mae needs rest, especially after the last doctor's appointment." The one that said her heart was growing weaker, while Harlow's beat effortlessly. "I can handle it."

Mom opened her mouth, then shook her head. "She's waiting for you. Apparently you promised to watch some show with her?"

"Ugh. Don't remind me."

"I don't need to. She's not likely to forget."

"I can dream."

"Never stop."

Leaving Mom to finish reading her paper, Harlow went to find her sister. Dark walnut floors flowed from the kitchen down the long hallway, and she followed them to the last door on the right. Mae's room stretched virtually the entire back length of the house. It had taken every penny of Harlow's savings and—she suspected—her parents', but when Mae finally succumbed to needing a wheelchair full time, they'd added on the room, fixed the kitchen, and put a ramp on the front of the house.

In the past five years, her muscles had only grown weaker. Now it was her heart, but the doctors could offer no timetable. Could be a year, could be another five. There was no way to predict.

Harlow shook off the thought and tapped on the door. "You awake?"

"Of course."

Inside, Mae's golden hair spilled over her white pillowcase. Though Dad's eyes were nearly as dark as the floor, his daughters had both inherited Mom's brilliant blues. Mae's sparkled this morning. "Hey, sis."

At least the disease hadn't stolen her beautiful smile.

Harlow placed a kiss on her forehead. "Glad to see you're smiling at me. I'm really sorry about this morning."

"I got that after the first three apologies." Light laughter coated her words. "And I forgave you before the first. Wasn't your fault."

They'd have to agree to disagree.

Her job was to watch out for Mae, make sure she had what she needed, wanted. It was a job done from the sidelines, but hers nonetheless. She hadn't failed yet, and she wouldn't. Especially now with Mae growing weaker.

She motioned to the mug in Harlow's hand. "I thought you stopped for coffee on your way home."

The memory of Mocha Man filled her vision. "Let's not go there."

"Why? What happened?"

"Long story involving a self-absorbed man who almost hit me with his car."

Her sister's eyebrows lifted along with her lips. "This I need to hear."

"Another time." Harlow scooted into bed beside her. "Tell me what Jack said this morning. Where are we?"

Mae looked like she wanted to ask more, but let it drop. "Pretty much what I told you on the phone. He and his dad love our idea, but it's only that, an idea. They pushed us through to the second round, but if we want them to choose us, we need a business plan to bring to their board."

Harlow didn't know the first thing about business plans. Giving someone a trach, stopping a bleeder, grabbing a BP, no problem. But charting numbers and predicting expenditures? None of that was taught in nursing school.

She'd figure it out, though. Failure wasn't an option. Wheels on the Ground would happen.

"Well then, I better get started."

"*We'd* better get started. But not before *Gamble on Love*."

"I hoped you'd forgotten."

"Right." Mae nodded toward the forty-two-inch TV mounted across from her bed. "Grab the remote and put it on."

Harlow plucked the remote from the bedside table. The reality dating show was beyond her. She still harbored bitterness—sorry, Lord—over Peter cheating on her. She wasn't one to share her fiancé—or boyfriend for that matter. Why would anyone knowingly put themselves in a similar position?

"You're really going to make me watch this?"

"Yes."

Better get comfy then. She grabbed an extra pillow from Mae's closet, then climbed back in the double bed. "You know it doesn't matter who he picks. They won't last."

"You're so cynical."

"I prefer *realist*." She pointed to the TV. "In what world would you want to be one of twenty women dating the same man?"

16

"He narrows it down."

"Oh, then it's all okay."

"Shush." Mae nodded at the TV. "It's starting."

They watched the intro, and Harlow gagged. Two long hours later, hours filled with the two final women fighting over the same man—who was a total player—and the show finally ended. No way she'd have made it through an entire season of this. Her sister, however, ate it up.

A long sigh escaped Mae's lips. "I knew he was going to pick her." She placed her hand over her heart. "They're perfect together."

The tall blonde in her emerald evening gown and fresh, glittering, two-carat, oval diamond ring clung to the arm of the baseball player.

"Sure." Harlow shook her head. "Perfect until tomorrow's headlines." She stood.

"Where are you going?"

"Home."

"Sit." Mae patted the bed. "The follow-up show is coming on."

"I never agreed to that."

"It's all part of the finale."

"You're stretching it."

Mae patted again and batted her eyelashes. "Please, Harley?"

"You'd think you were the youngest." She groaned. "How long is this after-show?"

"An hour."

"Fine. But I'll need popcorn." Harlow made for the kitchen. By the time she returned, the show had already started.

Mae peeked into the bowl. "You are the most boring person."

"I like my popcorn plain. Sue me."

Nearly forty-five minutes in, the host, Jace Kincaid, turned from the happy couple. "And now we've got a little treat for everyone. Something you've all been waiting for." He leaned forward. "We told you about a new dating show filming this spring and asked you, America, to send us your applications and videos. Tonight we'll reveal the bachelor." Jace switched his stare to another camera. "He's an old friend who's ready to settle down, but his track record in love needs some help. So he called us. What birthed was the reality show we're about to start filming. From the producer of *Gamble on Love*, we bring you *Call for Love*."

"*Call for Love*?" Harlow chuckled. "Sounds like it belongs on the nature channel."

"Shush."

Jace's face filled the screen. "*Call for Love* will follow our new bachelor as he gets to know several women. A smaller filming crew. More one-on-one dates. No elimination ceremonies. But all of the amazing romance you've come to expect as our bachelor goes on a quest to find his true love. Take a look, America."

"Like slapping lipstick on a pig." Harlow tossed a kernel at the screen.

"Tell me how you really feel."

The shot faded to a pre-recorded one focused on a beach. A dark-haired man strolled the surf's edge. The camera zoomed in on his face.

"Blake Carlton." Mae grinned. "He is hot."

"Mae." She couldn't put much censure in her words though. Blake Carlton was hot. Of course, his mother, Summer Carlton, wasn't short on looks either—a fact that kept her as one of Hollywood's most sought-after actresses even in her early fifties.

At least Harlow assumed. It'd been a while since she'd seen her on any screen.

The camera shot widened, showing off Blake in khaki cargo shorts and a gray v-neck, muscles clearly visible as he waded through the shallow water rolling onto the beach. His dark, wavy hair schooled to perfection, it lifted slightly on the breeze as the camera zoomed in again for a close-up of his perfect smile and tanned face. Harlow half expected a burst of light to come off his teeth like in those gum commercials.

"You don't think he's cute?" Mae asked her.

"No. He's cute." Something about his smile tugged at the back of her brain. "Problem is, he knows it. Check out that cocky grin. And isn't he the one who's always calling women sweetheart or darling or anything other than their names?" It grated on her nerves.

"Everyone has annoying habits." Mae shrugged. "How do you know he's not a perfect gentleman?"

Harlow scoffed. "I just know." She'd run into men like him before. Probably why he seemed so familiar.

Mae grew quiet as Blake's deep voice floated from the TV. "America may see me as a player, but I want to find love like everyone else. Between that desire and the matchmaking skills of the crew from *Gamble on Love*, I hope to find it."

Harlow laughed. "Right. He's just run out of women dumb enough to date him."

"Harlow Ruth." Mae shook her head and refocused on Blake who was speaking again.

"I know the right lady is out there for me, and I can't wait to finally meet her."

The screen faded to black, and Jace faced the camera again.

"You heard him, America. Blake Carlton is searching for love, and we're in the process of inviting fifteen women to meet him in Malibu."

The audience clapped.

"Cattle call," Harlow muttered.

Mae glared at her.

Jace droned on. "After Malibu, Blake will narrow the girls down to eight possible love matches. From there the group will leave the limelight of Malibu and travel to a romantic destination, where each woman will have her first private date with Blake. When he arrives back in the States, only three women will remain. Blake will travel to their hometowns and spend a week with their families and friends, getting to know each woman better."

"Oh, in their natural habitat. Told you it should be on the nature channel." She tossed more popcorn.

Mae didn't even look at her. "You know you have to clean that all up."

The shot widened. "By the end of six weeks, the two remaining women will travel with Blake to his family estate in Catalina, California, where he will propose to one lucky lady."

"Lucky lady." She scoffed. "I'd like to see the woman who'd fall for his lines. Now that finale I'll watch with you."

Mae shifted in her bed.

"Are you uncomfortable?" Harlow set down her popcorn bowl.

"No. Simply tired. Ready for my nap I guess."

Harlow studied her. Looked more like worry lines running across her forehead. "You sure?"

"Positive."

They didn't need to be wasting their time on some stupid show. What they needed—she needed—was to get the business plan set so Wheels on the Ground was a go.

Harlow scooped up their dishes. "Get some rest. I'm heading home to figure out business plans."

"You're the one who needs rest. You worked all night, and you have to help with Charity's surprise party tonight. It's your job to get her there, you know."

"I know." She halted in the doorway, her day growing fuller by the minute—not that she'd miss her best friend's birthday for anything. "I'll catch a couple of hours, but first I want to nail down a few things and talk to Jack."

"I told you he offered to help me with it."

She tightened her grip on the dishes. "I'm sure he meant well, but he's a busy man. I have the time."

"So do I. Loads of it in fact."

"Good. Use it to rest and keep up your strength." Because a future without her was unimaginable. "Now I need to move if I'm going to get some research done and a few hours of sleep in before tonight."

Mae fiddled with the fringe on her blanket. "Think Charity suspects anything?"

"Since she's had Amaya, she's too sleep deprived to even remember her birthday's coming."

"I can't wait to see her face."

"Me too. Wish I could catch it on film."

"Mom and Dad will have their camera."

"I'm sure they won't be the only ones."

Mae's grin grew. "I'm sure not."

Huh. She seemed pretty excited for a surprise birthday party.

Harlow trekked down the hall and dumped the dishes into the sink. Snuggled in a chair across the room, Mom dozed by the gas fireplace—a splurge for the house Harlow had included during the kitchen remodel. Mae always seemed so cold.

She stared at the flames. So many little fixes she'd been able to make for Mae since starting her job in the ER. Could she fix this? She didn't even know where to start when it came to a business plan.

But she'd tackled science classes she'd never thought she'd pass to obtain an associate nursing degree. Remained on the Dean's List while working and obtaining her bachelor's degree. If she could figure out bio chem, she could figure out how to fill a spreadsheet. She'd yet to hit an insurmountable wall where caring for Mae was concerned.

This time could be no different, because one thing being an ER nurse taught her on a daily basis was that time was a precious commodity.

And she didn't know how much more of it she had with Mae.

Chapter Three

Blake slipped into the Diesel jeans, blue plaid shirt, and camel suit coat that Darcy London had brought to his room moments ago. He'd spent the afternoon playing cards with Charlie. Hard to believe that up until a year ago, he'd never met the man. Now he was someone Blake actually considered a friend. The only other person to truly hold that spot was Darcy—Charlie's girlfriend.

She also happened to be Blake's best friend. People said men and women couldn't be "just friends," but he and Darcy had maintained their strong bond without ever crossing that line. No, if he was honest, they'd actually shot past that line long ago. Darcy was something more. She was the little sister he'd always wished for, and he'd been happy for her when she started dating Charlie—until he checked into his past. He'd partied hard. Shown up drunk or high to so many jobs in the film industry that no one would hire him anymore. So when Darcy claimed to have met Charlie at her church, Blake knew something didn't add up.

Until he met the man himself. Not a tremor to his hand, full cheeks instead of sunken, and crystal clear eyes that sparked life. Charlie claimed he'd found God. Darcy, having made the same claim years before, believed him.

Blake had figured he would hang around to pick up the pieces when Charlie broke her heart. Instead, in the past year, he'd gained another friend.

His door popped open. "Decent?" Darcy's hand covered her eyes.

"You can open your eyes." He tugged the door from her hands and opened it wide. "How'd you get a key?"

"You had an extra on your dresser."

"Klepto."

She pointed to the chair in front of her. "Sit." At five-foot-two, the only way she was reaching his hair was with his rear-end in a chair. "You okay with the clothes?" She circled him and snapped her gum.

"Yes. You dressed Ken fine."

"You're not my personal Barbie doll."

"Sure I'm not." He folded himself into the chair. He'd been her personal Barbie doll ever since she showed up with her handy bag of tricks to cover his scar. She'd done more than cover up his injuries, she'd offered him a measure of stability.

Darcy squirted pomade into her hands and ran her fingers through his hair. "Women would die for this hair."

"Thank my mom."

She'd passed on her looks. It was about all she'd given him.

"You ready to meet Harlow tonight?"

Harlow. He ran it through his mind several times. "If I can remember her name."

"You'll have an earpiece."

"True."

"There's something I like about this one."

"You haven't even met her."

She leaned back and eyed each lock of his hair. "I have a gut feeling. I'm good with those."

She was, but he wouldn't tell her that. If he kept the conversation going in this direction it'd end up on God. Always did with Darce.

"My hair done?"

Again, she circled him. Gave another pop of her gum. "I'll drop it."

"Thanks."

One more twist on the wave at his forehead and she pronounced him ready. A knock on the door and Charlie peered in, his curly brown hair edging close to the clown side. "Looking good." All six-foot-six of him entered the room. "Met Harlow's family. Real nice group. Dale's down there now with Tad, grabbing some set-up shots of the space. I need a few of you." He tossed a mic pack at him. "Thatcher said to give you that."

"Thatcher?"

"Alex Thatcher." Charlie returned Blake's blank stare. "The sound guy?"

"Oh, right." Blake held up the mic. "I've finally got his first name down, but I can't seem to keep his last."

"Wish I'd known that. I only wrote his first name across his forehead in permanent marker for you." He opened the door. "I can always add the last, but he's got a pretty small head."

"Funny." Blake threaded the wire down through his shirt and clipped the mic on, then followed Charlie and Darcy into the hall. Her stride half of his, Darcy's black hair swished in its ever-present ponytail as she half ran to keep up.

Charlie spoke over his shoulder. "Remember her sister sent in the video. Her name's Mae. Mom and Dad are Diane and Glen."

Diane, Glen, Mae. Diane, Glen, Mae … Diane may take a walk in the glen.

"You good?" Charlie asked.

"Hope so." They would give him an earpiece for tonight. Right now, he was on his own.

Diane, Mae, Glen …

They hustled down the steps and toward the banquet hall.

Dale stood outside. "I'm excited about this one." His white teeth gleamed against his bronzed skin. Five bucks said he had hit the spray tanner and dentist before coming here this week. "Couldn't have cast America's Sweetheart any better—you can't write this stuff. She's someone the women watching at home will love, and the women on the show will hate. Definitely part of our top eight, possibly top three."

Blake held back his eye roll. And America thought this was all real. There was nothing real about it. But he could give them their fairy tale if it meant preventing him from making the same mistake with Mom that he'd made with Dad. She needed this show. The memory of her passed out on her bathroom floor melded with the memory of Dad …

This time the outcome would be different.

Out of sheer desperation, he'd pitched this idea to her and the networks had jumped at it. Their reaction reawakened the old Summer Carlton, catapulting her back to the land of the living. And she was going to stay there—even if it killed him in the process.

"Are they ready for me?" Blake pointed to the door.

Dale nodded and opened it. Dead center of the room stood three people. Well, only two of them stood. The third was in a hot pink wheel chair. Her blond hair hung in curls, and she beamed with a smile that ran straight through him.

Same smile she shared with Red. They'd beat out Julia Roberts in a competition.

23

Blake crossed the floor, grasping for the sentence he'd stored their names in, but with each step it receded farther into the cloud called his brain. Plan B. He shook the dad's hand, swallowing his ever-present nervous laughter. "Blake Carlton." Offering his name was a surefire way to hear theirs.

"Glen Tucker. This is my wife, Diane." She took his hand as Glen placed his on their daughter's shoulder.

"And this is our oldest, Mae."

She shared the same clear blue eyes too.

"Nice to meet you Glen, Diane, and Mae."

"Our pleasure."

The girls had gotten their warm smiles from their mom.

"So, Re—" He cleared his throat. "Uh ... your daughter has no idea this is all for her tonight?"

"None."

Of course they didn't supply her name.

"And Mae, you're the one responsible?"

He'd heard the term *twinkling eyes* before, but this was the first he'd seen them. "I am."

No nervous chatter, shaking hands, or shifting glances. Mae's voice rang strong and clear in a matter-of-fact tone. So maybe this *was* all a surprise for Red, no gimmicks.

Interesting.

Blake held Mae's steady gaze. "I have to say the video you sent us really caught our attention. Your sister appears to be an amazing woman."

"She is. I hope you see that in her."

"I already have. It's one of the reasons I picked her." More like Dale and Mom saw potential ratings in her, but that didn't quite roll off the tongue as nicely. "I look forward to getting to know her well."

Mae's smile held, her eyes still twinkled, but now with an edge. "Not *too* well, right?"

"Definitely." Big sister played her role to the nines. He glanced at his Tag Heuer. "My time's up. I'll see you in a couple hours for the surprise."

"Can't wait."

The new cameraman—Tanner, Ty, who knew?—and Alex stayed with the Tuckers while Charlie filmed his exit. The door to the room closed, and Charlie lowered his camera. "She's a spitfire."

"Just wait until you meet the sister."

"You have?"

No way he was divulging that little unplanned meeting. At least she hadn't recognized him.

"Blake?" Charlie's deep voice pressed him.

Blake's phone rang, and his mother's perfect face lit the screen. He held it toward Charlie. Wiggled it. "Gotta take this."

"Lucky for you."

First time he'd qualify a call from Mom that way, but right now it fit. Blake stepped away. "Hey, Mom."

"Your promo last night should have been longer."

"Just a sec." He placed his hand over his phone and faced Charlie. "I'm going back to my room."

Charlie pointed at his camera and then down the hall. Must need a few extra shots. Blake nodded, turned, and strolled to the stairs. "You saw the promo?"

"Of course I did. Though with an hour show, they could have afforded you more than two minutes."

He exited one floor up. "I'm going to have an entire season. I'm sure it will all even out."

"See that it does." Her tone brooked no argument. "Tonight's the final girl, right?"

"Yes." His swiped his key and shut the door behind him.

"You'll be in Malibu tomorrow?"

"In the morning."

"I'll reserve you a room at The Four Seasons."

"I'll get my own room." At a different hotel.

She sighed. "Stay where you want then, but give me a call when you get in. I'd like to have dinner."

Strange. She never wanted—

"We need to go over which women will make it past Malibu and who the front-runners are. It'll determine camera time and who goes on which dates." She sipped something. A Bombay Sapphire martini, two olives, if he had to wager a guess. "I spoke with the network today, and they love the idea of bridging our shows with a wedding." The determination in her voice was a welcome sound.

"They picked up your reality show then?"

"Not yet, but they're very interested." Another sip. "They're waiting to see how you premiere. Your numbers are key."

Not him, just the numbers.

Blake shrunk back from that line of thinking. Couldn't grow something that didn't exist. Love wasn't real, and no amount of wishing or playing make-believe would make it so. But numbers? Those were tangible, and they'd keep Mom safe from the depression dogging her heels.

"I'll make us reservations at Nobu for the night you return. It'll be good to have us seen together." Another long drink. She must have used her large shaker tonight. "You're meeting that young woman with the disabled sister tonight, right?"

"Yep."

"I like this one. That backstory will drive up early viewership, and with the right conflict we'll maintain those numbers. I'm not convinced she's who we'll want at the end, but I could see her in the final two."

Shouldn't be too hard. Red definitely held his interest this afternoon. So if Dale and Mom said she'd bring ratings—and ratings were what Mom needed—he was game.

Darcy snuck into the room. "Touch-up time." She wheeled a black case behind her.

Because he didn't have enough makeup and hair gunk on already.

"I've got to go, Mom. Send me our reservation time. I could pick you up too. If you'd like?"

"No need. Colburn will drive me, and he'll text you the info."

Right. No need. She had it under control. Because Colburn—her long-time driver who'd practically raised Blake—ensured things were taken care of. "I'll watch for it."

Mom hung up without a goodbye. She'd never had a problem with the action, only the words.

"Everything good?" Darcy unpacked her brushes.

He dropped into the seat. "Everything's great."

She picked up a bushy black one and a vial of powder. "At least it will be once I help cover things up, right?"

He held in his retort.

"Of course," she said, dabbing on the powder, "I actually prefer the real deal. Funny, right? Seeing how I'm the makeup and wardrobe person. But really, do we all have to hide under layers?"

"Subtle, Darce."

She snapped her gum. "Want me to be blunt?"

"Nope." He closed his eyes while she batted that brush across his face again. "I want you to spit out your gum. And hush."

"So, *you're* being blunt."

"If I was being blunt, I would've chosen different language."

"Thanks for protecting my innocent ears."

He cleared his throat with a laugh. "Known you too long to buy that line."

The brush stopped. He opened his eyes to find her staring at him. "Yeah. Which is why you've seen the change and why you held your tongue." She tapped his nose. "Means I'm making progress."

He let out a curse just to prove otherwise.

She didn't even flinch. "Nice try." Another snap.

Charlie entered the room and leaned on the wall. "Colorful. You planning on using that mouth to sweet-talk the ladies?"

"Never worked on Darce."

"Because she's got too good of taste." Charlie ambled over and smacked a kiss on the top of her head. It was like a raven-haired Goldilocks and her bear—the only fairy tale his mother ever read him as a child—and he liked this version better.

Darcy squeezed him, then resumed Blake's touch-ups.

Charlie frowned and glanced out the window. "I'm over cold-weather locations."

Blake leaned his head back as Darcy blended something down his neck. "Should have bought a coat like I suggested."

"Should have picked women from warmer climates."

Blake chuckled.

Darcy capped whatever makeup she was using and packed. "You're good as long as you don't start to sweat."

"Never do."

"Of course not." She clicked the locks on her case. "I have to do the family. Good luck tonight."

"Because I'll need it."

"Your ego's definitely intact." Waving, she left.

Charlie somehow managed to settle his huge frame into the tiny chair in the corner. "How was your mom?"

"Perfect as always." He eyed his friend. "How about yours?"

Charlie's mom was failing with Alzheimer's and needed around-the-clock care but didn't have the bank account to support it.

Charlie rubbed the back of his neck. "Not so great, but I'm holding on to the memories for her."

"If you need—"

His hand went up. "You've done enough already. I'm not so naïve to think Dale wanted me on this show. I killed my reputation in this industry. If it weren't for you, I wouldn't have this chance."

"Packaged deal." Blake grabbed his key off the table. "I take care of my friends."

"And I appreciate it, but you're not my personal ATM. My mom's care could stretch out for years, and I'd like to actually put a ring on Darcy's finger while Mom's still around." He sucked in a deep breath. "You got my foot back in the door. I'll take it from here. God hasn't let me down yet."

They stepped into the hall, and Blake kept his mouth shut. God was about as real as the idea of love, but Charlie had drunk the Kool-Aid and believed in the same fiction as Darcy. They kept tempting him, but he wasn't caving. Not that believing in God was bad, but he'd had enough of fake things in his life.

*

Harlow turned into the parking lot of the Tipton Hotel, bone tired and nearly cross-eyed from staring at business plans and spreadsheets all day. She was nowhere closer to figuring it all out, but tonight was about her best friend.

She swiveled and faced Charity. With her baby face and that small figure wrapped in skinny jeans and a chunky sweater, Charity looked more teenager than new mom. Actually, she always looked like a teen—a fact that irked her to no end. "Thanks for coming with me to check this place out tonight, Chare. I really hope it will work for Mae's birthday party."

"No problem."

They entered the lobby.

"I haven't been here in years." Charity peered up at the large new chandelier in the entrance.

"Beautiful, isn't it?" Harlow shook off the spring chill. "They're remodeling. The entrance, banquet halls, and restaurant were recently completed."

She led Charity through the lobby. "How about we check the space in the hall first? If it's big enough, then we can sample the food from the restaurant. I'd have them cater the meal."

"Sure." Charity nodded her head of chestnut curls and followed Harlow.

Harlow's heart pounded as they neared the double doors. Charity's husband Mark had worked so hard on this party. She didn't think Charity suspected anything, and she didn't want to ruin it.

Charity slowed as if to allow Harlow through the door first, so Harlow grabbed the handle, swished open the door, and stepped back, forcing Charity to enter ahead of her.

The awaiting crowd erupted. "Surprise!"

Sweet success.

She grinned at Charity, but rather than Mark stepping forward, Harlow's parents wheeled Mae out of the throng of people, a cameraman with them. Another materialized inches from Harlow's face, and a huge fuzzy mic on a stick appeared over her shoulder.

Had Mark hired a videographer for the night?

Something was off. Harlow swept her gaze between her family and Charity, catching the excitement on their faces directed toward her. "What's going on?"

Charity gently shoved her toward the crowd, which parted to reveal two men in the center of the room. She caught her breath. Jace Kincaid, host of *Gamble on Love*, and ... Blake Carlton?

Chapter Four

Harlow tripped but quickly steadied herself.

Blake stepped forward and offered her his hand. His other touched his left ear, and his lips thinned for one quick second before switching to his trademark smile. His deep voice filled the room. "It's a pleasure to finally meet you."

She had to be in a dream. A very, very strange dream.

He led her to center of the room where Jace now stood with her family.

"We've spent some time talking with your family and getting to know them"—Jace motioned their way—"and your sister has something to tell you."

Mae's grin was so huge, Harlow wasn't sure she'd be able to talk. "Remember that video I shot of you a few months ago?"

"The one you did as a project because you were bored this winter?"

"Yes, that one. Except it wasn't for me. I sent it to *Gamble on Love* and nominated you for their new show, *Call for Love*."

"You what?" Surely she'd heard wrong, because there was no way her sister would nominate her for a show she found painful to even watch.

But Mae's smile only grew. As did Dad's and Mom's. Charity leaned toward her ear. "In case you missed it, I was actually stalling you, not the other way around."

Sweat pooled along the small of her back. The room began to close in. Blake stepped closer. Blake Carlton.

Hollywood socialite.

Player.

Regular in *People*'s "Sexiest Man Alive" editions.

"Hey, sweetheart." He opened his hand to reveal a plane ticket. At least she thought it was. She'd never actually seen one before, and too many black spots danced in her line of vision for her to be sure.

31

Her breath stilled in her lungs, and the black spots grew. She turned and ran before she splatted all over the ground. Shoving open the double doors, she escaped through the nearest exit. Fresh air blew over her face, and she palmed the scratchy brick wall, gasping in lungfuls of sweet air.

Ever so slowly, reality settled in. Crazy, unbelievable, reality. Blake Carlton stood inside those doors. Waiting. For her.

She'd entered another dimension.

The cold from the brick seeped into her skin.

Another dimension that contained Blake Carlton.

His name ping-ponged in her mind, refusing to settle. The entire idea was impossible. That thought mixed anger and anxiety in her gut. Out of all the things she'd wanted in life, God had finally chosen her for something. A reality TV show starring a Hollywood player and his harem.

It was a joke.

A cruel joke.

Then it hit her. No, it wasn't a joke. The answer was so much simpler. She lifted her face toward heaven. Scoffed. "It's because Mae asked, isn't it?"

"I'm sure that played into it, but your profile and video are what piqued our producer's interest."

Harlow jerked her focus around. Blake Carlton leaned against the doorway, barely concealed amusement lighting his face. He probably thought she was crazy. Running from him. Talking to the sky. She turned her back, that stinking smile of his grating her nerves like she'd seen it before.

She gasped and slowly swiveled to meet his cocky expression. "Mocha Man."

His grin flatlined as his eyebrows lowered. "Excuse me?"

"You took my coffee this morning."

And then it returned. "You recognize me?"

"I recognize that smirk." She fisted her hands on her hips. "I wanted to knock it off of you."

He chuckled and stepped outside, the metal door closing behind him. "You're pretty serious about your coffee."

"That coffee I was."

"Special brew?"

She clammed up. The conversation only made her appear crazier.

"You should know, I can only hold the cameras back for a few more minutes, if I'm lucky." Blake stood like a sentry at the door. "Dale Edwards, our producer, sent me out to speak with you. I told him I'd need a minute alone, and it's been over two. I don't think our luck will keep holding out."

"Don't you mean *my* luck? Pretty sure you're used to the cameras."

His eyes hardened, but only for a split second before softening again. Not that she trusted for one second that his gentleness was authentic. "Nope. Because if I can't convince you to come back in there and say yes, I'll have to deal with his tirade."

She held up one finger. "I need a minute to process."

"What's to process? There's a handsome man who wants to date you, darling, so just say yes."

Was he for real?

"Handsome goes a lot deeper than looks in my book, Mr. Carlton. That may work on the other countless women you've propositioned, but it's not working for me. Especially when you can't even remember my name." She started toward the parking lot. Her keys were in her pocket. She could leave. "Have fun dealing with that tirade, because I'm out of here."

*

She'd walked away from him.

He blinked at Red's retreating form.

Because he'd called her darling? Most women loved that word rolling off his tongue. He'd even broken out his smile.

He had half a mind to let her go. She'd be the one regretting it in the morning.

But so would he once Mom found out they'd lost her.

"Hey!" he called.

She kept walking.

"Be real nice if someone could supply her name right now," he muttered. All he saw when he reached for it was Red.

His earpiece emitted another squeal, and he forced himself to keep it lodged in place. Hopefully the tech guys would get the feed going and supply her name, because no way it was coming out of the cloud called his brain. Till then, he was on his own.

She'd nearly cleared the building. Time for Plan B.

""All right. So we agree my good looks aren't working for you," he called after her. "How about your sister then?"

Red stopped. Turned. "What about her?"

33

"Do you have any idea what this means to her? Why she nominated you?"

"I haven't a clue."

He pulled out his phone. "Then let me show you the video she sent in."

Red held her ground. "I was there when she made it. I wouldn't have said or done half the things I did if I'd known what it was for."

"Sorry to hear that," he teased, "because your dancing was one of our favorite things."

Pink tinged her cheeks. "Thanks, I work hard at it." She delivered the words straight-faced and without even a blink. Bold, considering her dancing had been awful.

She still didn't move, so he took a step forward, leaving only a short gap between them. That was hers to fill. "And as much as I liked it, I'm not talking about your part. Mae had to let us know why she was nominating you."

Red hesitated, tapping a nail against her teeth. After one very long moment, she stepped closer. "She did?"

"Yep." He pushed play, hoping to kill two birds with one stone. Get her to agree to join the show and hear her name.

Mae filled the tiny screen. "So you've seen my amazing sister, and I can't imagine you not wanting her, but I'm supposed to film this part too, so here goes. She's taken care of me for years. She attended college here, moved into our parents' guest house, and even took a local job. She's spent all her money and time helping our parents care for me, making our home easily accessible to me, even helping pay for my medical bills. She's had barely any time to play or see the world—which is one of her dreams, even if she won't come out and say it." The video panned out, showing a map with tiny push pins on several continents.

Red gasped. "She's in my kitchen." Her hands grabbed his screen and pulled it—and him—closer.

Man, she smelled good. He leaned down, his nose brushing against her hair. Too consumed by the video, she didn't notice.

Mae kept talking. "All those pins are places she's traveled by way of pictures, documentaries, books, or the Internet." Mae leaned in close. "She picks them based on the coffee she's drunk."

He played it smart and stayed silent.

"Then there's her love life—"

"What? No!" Red's finger swiped at the pause button, but he stretched his arm, preventing her from reaching it.

"Not like I haven't already seen this." He looked down at her. "And whoever he was, I can say with complete confidence that he was an idiot."

"Always working the charm angle, aren't you." Sarcasm might edge her voice, but he didn't miss the pain on her face.

"Is it working?" he asked.

"Nope."

She focused on her sister, who finished recounting how some jerk dumped Red for one of her friends. The man was worse than an idiot. Blake didn't have the best track record with women, but even he knew you didn't go after your fiancée's friend.

He pulled the phone close again as Mae's face filled the screen. "It's my turn to give something to my baby sister while I have time left to do it. She deserves to see the world. To fall in love, be happy, and find someone to take care of her the way she's always cared for me. Whoever the bachelor is on *Call for Love* would win big time if he wins my sister's heart."

The screen went black, and Red—Mae couldn't have said her name even once?—swiped tears from the corners of her eyes. She seemed legit, but he wasn't ready to bet on it. Still, if even a small part of what Mae said was true, Red absolutely deserved the show's perks.

"I never told Mae I did all those things."

"The people we love figure out what we do sometimes without us telling them." A lesson he'd learned the hard way.

But he wasn't here to give advice on love. His job was to move her through those doors and onto his show.

She ran a hand through her hair. "I never did them to make her feel guilty or indebted to me."

Blake rubbed his chin. "She didn't seem indebted. More like she wanted a chance to be the provider once. It's probably a role she can't take often. By saying yes, you'll give her that." He crossed his arms. "A win-win situation."

"Do I have to say yes today?"

"'Fraid so. We're on a tight schedule."

She hesitated. He snuck a peek at his watch. They needed to get inside, or Dale would move the party out here. Amazing he hadn't already. Yet waiting her out was the best chance at obtaining the answer he wanted.

After a moment she spoke up. "Why are *you* doing this show?"

Okay. So she wanted more than time, she wanted reassurance. Easy. He pulled his trademark smile out and the answer every lady desired. "To find love."

Red crossed her arms and sized him up. "Try again."

Maybe not so easy. "To fall in love?" He shrugged. "Not really sure what verbiage you're looking for, but does that one work?"

"It would if I believed for one second you're interested in love and marriage."

"Look, sweetheart—"

She came alive. Stalking over to him, she thrust her finger toward his chest. "It's Harlow. Harlow Tucker. Not sweetheart, darling, cutie, or any other adjective you come up with. Got it? If I'm going to be on your show, the least you could do is get my name right."

He captured her hand. "To be fair, I never use the word cutie. I prefer beautiful." And she was.

She tugged hard enough to stumble back when he finally released her. "This will never work."

"Not like I'm proposing marriage right now."

"Not like I expect you to at all."

"Then what are you afraid of?"

She crossed her arms. "Nothing."

"So you'll do the show?"

Harlow sighed. He couldn't remember ever having to work this hard to get someone to date him. He started wondering if she was worth this effort. Then her eyes caught his, the kind of green-blue he'd find in beach glass, the outer rim nearly as indigo as the ocean depths itself. Her pictures hadn't captured what he discovered standing a foot from her.

Charlie popped his head outside. "Time's up, and seeing how I'd like to keep my job …"

She waved her hand through the air. "It's fine. We're through."

As in, she wasn't going to do the show, or she was through with the conversation? He didn't have time to ask before she marched inside and down the hall. Blake shrugged at Charlie as he passed him.

Harlow entered the banquet hall before he caught up, and the room stilled as he stepped in behind her. Women's eyes followed him. Everyone's but Harlow. She sought out Mae.

"What were you thinking?" Her soft voice reached him as she knelt by her sister, oblivious to the filming cameras or the boom mic above her.

"That I'm the big sister and for once I wanted to take care of my little sister." She patted Harlow's hand. "You should have a scrapbook full of places you've actually been to, not simply researched."

"Then buy me a plane ticket. Why sign me up for a reality show?"

Mae's face tipped down. "You know I can't buy you a plane ticket."

"And you know I can't leave. Not now. Not with all the work I need to do to get Wheels on the Ground up and running."

As if something sparked in her, Mae's chin lifted. "I can handle it."

"We're not talking a day or two. We're talking nearly a couple of months." She shook her head. "I can't do that to you." Or leave her for that long.

"Did you even watch the promo this morning after *Gamble on Love*?"

"I hate the show. I may have made space in my brain for more important things once it was done."

"You'll only travel about three weeks, then you'll be back home for a while before a week in Catalina—if you make it to the end."

Harlow peered up at Blake. "That true?"

"Yes. Is it true you hate the show?"

"Yes." Back to Mae. "This is important to you?"

"Incredibly." She fiddled with her wheelchair. "It could even help us with Wheels on the Ground, Harley. With your name out there, it may give us a platform to get the word out."

Harlow held Mae's stare and tapped a nail against her tooth. Finally she stood, then gazed around the room, stopping at Dale. She walked over to him. "You're the producer?"

"Yes." He held out his hand. "Dale Edwards."

She shook it. "If I say yes, can I maintain contact with my family?"

"We could work something out. Blake and I would both like this show to be as natural as possible, and we're making a lot of allowances to see that happen. This won't be your typical dating show."

She hesitated. "And you want me to take the spot of a woman who actually wants to date him?" She jabbed her thumb toward Blake.

Dale chuckled. The whole room did. "The spot is yours to take. Though I admit, it's a first in my history of filming dating shows to have a woman who doesn't want to be there."

It was a first for Blake too.

Harlow swallowed. "Fine. I'll come."

"Don't let anyone force you." Blake bristled.

"Trust me," she said, her shoulders squaring. "No one can force me to do anything I don't want to."

Her message came across loud and clear. Harlow Tucker had no interest in falling in love with him.

The thought shouldn't bug him. It shouldn't. And yet it buzzed around him like a tiny gnat, large enough to bother him, yet too small to catch.

It wasn't until he watched the room engulf her in a hug that an even bigger thought took flight in his mind.

For this moment, at least, he'd remembered her name.

Chapter Five

Harlow snuggled deeper into her fluffy white comforter. Sunlight tried to penetrate her wooden blinds, but she ignored it. Last night ...

She sat up straight. Wait. It was morning. Maybe, just maybe, it had been a dream.

She nabbed her phone off her bedside table and nearly dialed Charity until she noticed the sweater she'd worn to the party crumpled on the floor beside her bed. Either she'd worn it in her sleep, or last night was her crazy new reality.

Her pillows swallowed her as she fell back against them, one arm bent over her forehead. She, Harlow Tucker, was going to be on *Call for Love*.

Ugh.

She needed coffee and her camera.

Possibly a shower too.

One half hour, one hat, and one thick coat later, Harlow locked her front door and started for downtown. She had finagled the entire weekend off and by the end of it she wanted a new series of photos to play with. Lately an idea niggled in the corner of her mind to create a collection that showed more than scenery. Pictures that told a story, even in one word, like how she'd seen Keegan and Chet the other morning. They could make a beautiful book, even if she was the only one to ever see them. Stringing them together would definitely help balance out the boredom of staring at spreadsheets, while also easing her anxiety over the finality of last night's decision.

Any luck, and Blake Carlton would toss her off in California. She'd have made Mae happy and could return home with plenty of time to focus on the business proposal for Jack.

Harlow parked in the center of town, slipped on her gloves, and started down the sidewalk. The shops were opening for the day, but she headed three blocks up to Ford Square, one of the first spots the town had rejuvenated. Two winters ago they began flooding the square with water, turning it into a skating rink. And in summers, the space overflowed with people attending small concerts and outdoor movie nights. With it being early spring, things might be quiet this morning, but she'd take the chance. but she'd take the chance. Starbucks sat close by, so she could people watch, grab a few snapshots, and enjoy a coffee all at the same time.

After snagging her warm drink, Harlow slipped along the edges and settled onto a chair. She knotted her thick purple scarf tighter and tugged the matching crocheted beanie lower to cover her ears. The chill in this morning's air promised she wouldn't last all that long, but there were enough people milling around for her to snap a few frames.

She picked up her camera and, eyesight glued to her telephoto, scanned the area. Motion to her left drew her like a homing pigeon. An old woman, bundled in what had to be at least twelve layers of heavy fabric, pushed a cart through the square. She stopped at the trash barrel to dig out pop cans. A bright yellow bandanna held up her coarse hair, and Harlow zoomed in on her lined, dark face. Hazel eyes stared back. Eyes that danced with a spark Harlow recognized.

Light.

Blessed are those who have learned to acclaim you, who walk in the light of your presence, O Lord.

She clicked away, zooming in tight on the woman's face, capturing each line, each leathery pull of her skin that framed those joy-filled eyes. People walked past the old woman, never even acknowledging her presence. Never realizing she likely had more life in her than many of them did.

No one saw—

A dark blue T-shirt blocked the end of her lens. She peeked from behind her camera even as Blake Carlton's rumbling voice reached her. "Does that woman"—he thumbed behind him—"know you're taking her picture?"

She could almost see the flames shooting out from behind his eyes despite his sunglasses. Only this time they were some sort of sports glasses, and in place of his baseball cap was a black neoprene beanie.

Harlow lowered her camera. "No."

He crossed his arms in front of him, his navy T-shirt pulling snug across his perfectly toned chest. Ear buds hung around his neck. She looked down to his fitted running pants which hid nothing. Not like he had an ounce of fat on him. The man was all muscle.

"Invasion of her privacy, wouldn't you say?"

Funny he could say that when he was wearing those pants. She tipped her head up to see his face. "I'm in a public place, so is she."

"And that makes it all okay." Disgust coated his words.

Harlow pushed back her chair and stood. She didn't need to explain herself to him. That she saw the world more clearly through this lens than with her very own eyes. That each time she picked up her camera, it felt like what she was made to do. "Did you need something?"

Blake used his bicep to swipe at a bead of sweat trickling down his temple. "I had no idea you were a photographer. Convenient how that was left out of your video package."

As if she'd had any clue she was even making a package. "Because my hobbies matter to you?"

"They do when it's this one." He flicked a finger against her camera. "I have a strong dislike for the paparazzi."

Ugly word. She stepped back. "Unpaid photographer. Big difference."

"Unpaid photographer who's taking a picture of someone without her knowledge." He shrugged. "Paparazzi."

Harlow stuffed her Nikon back in its bag. "If my hobby is going to be a problem for you, how about you send me packing right now?" Easy solution to both their issues.

"Wish I could, sweetheart."

Her hand stilled on the bag's zipper. Sucking in a deep breath, she jerked it shut. "Again. I know it's hard to remember the name of a woman you plan to date when you've asked out so many, but it's Harlow."

"Harlow." Blake nodded. "We're stuck together for now. Dale would have a coronary this close to production if I messed with his numbers. Show starts with fifteen, he'll have fifteen."

"Nothing like a cattle call." Mumbling, she grabbed her coffee cup and started walking.

"Moo."

She stopped.

Blake stood, hands on his hips, rocking back on his heels with that insufferable grin on his face. Was he trying to give her whiplash?

"Excuse me?" she squeaked.

Again with the shrug.

She sighed and turned. "I'll see you in Hollywood. Lucky me."

*

It was freezing out here. Had he kept moving, he'd have been fine. Stopping allowed the sweat to chill him, but seeing her with a camera slung around her neck had acted like a red light he couldn't blow past.

Photographer.

Why'd she have to be a photographer? They'd had a hand at running his dad into the ground. Ever since, other than Charlie, he'd never met one he could trust. Wasn't sure he was open to even trying. Even if she did stand up to him, had an incredibly pretty face—and walked away from him for the second time in less than twenty-four hours.

Not that her retreating form was all that bad.

He shook his head and followed. "Wait up."

She turned. "What? No sweetheart? Darling? Beautiful?"

He deserved it. Faces he remembered. It was names he struggled with. Got him in trouble his whole life. How did you explain that you remembered someone, just not their name?

"Nope." He shrugged, covering his frustration as he sifted their earlier conversation through his mind. She'd said her name again. It lingered along the edge, teasing him. He could feel the heat in the word as she'd thrown it at him, touch the tone, but her name slipped back into the fog. He thought he'd had it stored last night, but then Dale had shoved all the ladies' files in front of him this morning. "I've come to realize terms of endearment bother you."

"When used by a practical stranger, yes." Arms crossed, she tapped one foot. "Silly me would prefer the use of my name."

So would he, if he could remember it.

"I see you finally got your coffee." He pointed to her Starbuck's cup.

"I did." She sipped, then started walking again.

He matched her pace. "That mean you'll put a pin on your map?"

Red eyed him. "You think it's funny that I explore the world based on my coffee selection."

"I think it's funny you believe you've explored the world based on your coffee selection."

Her jaw jutted out. "Not all of us have bottomless bank accounts."

"You don't need a bottomless bank account to travel. Fly economy. Take the local transportation. Stay in three-star hotels."

Her lips parted, and she laughed, only it sounded more like a snort. She stopped so quickly, he couldn't be sure.

"Didn't realize I was a comedian." He swiveled to see if people were watching.

"No. I doubt you did."

"What exactly was so funny?"

Red slowly rolled her eyes. "If you don't see it, I can't explain it." She took off. "I'll see you in Hollywood, Hollywood."

"Was that a stutter or you trying to tell me something?"

She waved without looking back.

"And for the record," he called, "we're going to Malibu."

She kept walking.

Her silver coat was tucked in around her tiny waist, her long red hair hung in curls down her back, and her hips swayed slightly with each step. Not an intentional movement. He'd seen enough to know she wasn't putting on a show, even if he was enjoying watching it. Her laughter moments earlier trickled through his memory, igniting a spark of physical attraction.

She might as well have beckoned him to follow.

He hustled and caught up with her.

They walked nearly half a block up the street before she slowed. "Any particular reason you're following me?"

Because she captivated him.

"To ensure you make it to your car safely."

"This is Abundance, not Holly—Malibu. I think I'll be fine."

He nudged her shoulder. "Says the woman I just startled in the park."

"Because I was focused on a shot."

"And not on your surroundings." Each step closer, he'd expected her to notice him. It took getting in her frame before she realized he stood two feet from her. "Not a safe thing." And yet another reason he didn't like photographers. They could care less about the world around them, including the safety of themselves and others.

Her cheeks darkened. "I was in a public place."

"Because crimes don't happen in public." He didn't bother to rein in his sarcasm.

She didn't bother to hide her glare.

"My mother didn't teach me many things," Blake said, "but she did teach me how to be a gentleman." Actually, it was more like the leading men in her movies, but he'd learned the lesson from watching her nonetheless, even if it was on the screen. "Or should I save the chivalry till I get to know you better too?"

They stepped aside for a couple of teenage girls to pass. One gave him a long look. He turned to stare at the building beside him.

"Fine." Harlow acquiesced. "Accompany me to my car."

Most women couldn't wait to get him in their car and in their beds. This one barely even wanted him walking beside her. He couldn't remember the last time he had to honestly chase a woman.

He couldn't remember the last time he'd wanted to.

Even if she was playing a game, it definitely made it more interesting.

They walked in near silence to her silver SUV. She dug in her pocket for her keys, and he was ready. The click of her locks releasing sounded, and before her hand reached for her door, he had it open.

"Thanks."

"Don't mention it, swee—" That was going to be a hard habit to break.

Her eyebrows drew together. "Nice save."

"I try." Her disbelieving grunt in response amused him. He waited for her to climb in. "Are you meeting with Darcy today?"

"Darcy?"

"She hasn't called you?"

"Who's Darcy?"

"Our stylist. She's taking you shopping for your wardrobe."

Lines deepened across her forehead. "Shopping? For me?"

"You don't have to pay for it. You have a clothing allowance."

"I also have clothes."

"I'm sure, but the show wants to buy you new ones. I thought ladies loved shopping and primping. It's why I insisted on a wardrobe and makeup person." That, and he'd missed his friends. Having Darcy and Charlie along filled the hollow parts, but he wasn't about to own that in front of Red.

She watched him. "You have a lot of preconceived notions, don't you?"

"What?"

"Nothing." A short moment passed as she studied him. "So this Darcy will be calling me?"

"If she hasn't already, then yes. She planned on you shopping today."

With a nod, she closed her door and then rolled down her window. "You going to finish your run now?"

"Nah. I'll head back to my hotel and maybe swim a few laps, then shower. I have a local TV interview and then an afternoon flight."

"*Take Five?*"

"They called you too?"

She nodded. "Want a ride to your hotel?"

"If you're offering."

"Just did."

He walked around to the passenger side and climbed in. "I'm actually staying at the Tipton."

"Sorry we don't have a Four Seasons here."

He wouldn't have stayed in it even if it was the only hotel in a hundred-mile radius. Too many bad memories. "No problem. A bed's a bed."

"Right." She smirked. "I'm sure their mattress compares to whatever you sleep on every night."

"Now who's got the preconceived notions?"

Her wide eyes found his. He grinned.

She chuckled.

Within minutes she was at the hotel.

"Guess I'll see you on *Take Five?*" Blake hopped from her car.

"Sounds like it." She waved and was gone.

He hadn't anticipated an interview this much in ages.

Chapter Six

Not even five minutes. He'd been in her car less than five, and yet somehow his scent permeated every nook and cranny. A little bit of sweat mixed with spice and a hint of something citrusy. *She* worked out and she stunk. Mr. Hollywood went running and smelled great.

Figures.

Palming her phone, she slid her thumb over the screen to call Mae and noticed three missed calls. Huh. Flipping it on its side revealed she'd forgotten again to turn on the ringer this morning. Nice. Jack's name showed along with two calls from a number she didn't recognize, which meant it was most likely Darcy.

She dialed Jack's number first.

"Morning." His tenor reached her ears. The man practically sang through life.

"Hey, Jack."

"Your feet back down on the ground since last night?"

They'd never left.

"Somewhat." She attempted a laugh. "I saw you called."

"Sure did. Wanted to fill you in on my breakfast with Mae yesterday. Sorry I had to leave before you got there."

"I understand, though I wish Mae could have reached me."

"Things actually went fine. She's got a great head on her shoulders."

"I know she does, but she needs to be resting not worrying about all this."

"Which is why I didn't tell her everything, but I also didn't think last night was the time to share with you."

Her stomach knotted. "Go ahead."

"I assume she told you that the board met, and you made it to the second round?"

"Yes. That's good, right?"

"Definitely." He sighed. "But Harlow, you made it because Dad and I pushed you through. I won't lie, your proposal wasn't a strong one. No business plan, no numbers or money saved that we could see. Basically, all you have is a mission statement."

"That you believe in."

"Yes."

"And you've been friends of ours for years."

"Which is why you made round two." Something tapped across the line. Most likely Jack's pencil on his desk. "But the board will need more than our friendship to give you the grant money."

"Please don't say no, Jack. You're our last hope."

"We're your only hope, right?"

She bit her lip. "Pretty much."

"Wheels on the Ground makes sense to Dad and me. I—we—love Mae. I know what it would mean for her to see this charity take shape, but the board has asked for two things before looking at it again."

"A business plan and money. I know. You told Mae."

"Yes, but I didn't tell her how much. Or the time frame."

The knot in her stomach tightened. "How much?"

"Even a base model, indoor/outdoor electric wheelchair would take nearly two thousand dollars. That's not even the cost to get it to the regions you want."

"How much?"

"And your mission statement says you want to supply one hundred wheelchairs per year. So what we feel we're asking you to invest is merely a drop in the bucket."

"Tell me the amount."

"Fifty thousand."

The knot squeezed out her breath. "Come again?"

"Fifty thousand, Harlow. We need you to show that amount along with a business plan for the board to even consider you in the running against the other two requests. The board calls it a good-faith effort. They want to make sure you're serious about this."

"I am. You know me, Jack."

"I do, but you're asking the board to invest a substantial amount of money. You can't ask that without putting in something yourself. I'm sorry."

It was evident in his voice. He didn't want to bear the bad news, but someone had to. Fifty thousand may as well be the entire two hundred thousand. No way she could produce that money this year. Not even in two years' time.

Except Mae might not have two years. Her sister depended on her to see her dream fulfilled. Those kids depended on her for someone to notice them. There was no way she'd let any of them down.

The knot loosened enough for her to pull in a breath. "I'll start working on the plan. God will provide the money. Somehow."

"I pray he does, Harlow. We're making the decision before the end of our second quarter."

"That gives me three months." She kept the wobble that attacked her faith from her voice.

"I know." He was silent a moment. "When do you leave for California?"

"Two days." Except, how could she leave now? "I have an interview with *Take Five* this afternoon, and apparently I'm supposed to do some shopping." An idea took shape even as the words flowed past her lips. "I've got to go."

"Oh. Okay."

Before he could say goodbye, she hung up and dialed the other number on her recent calls list. Two rings and a woman picked up. "Darcy London."

"Darcy, this is Harlow Tucker."

"Oh, hey, Harlow. I was trying to reach you."

"About shopping?"

"Blake said he ran into you."

"You saw him already?"

"He was just in here." She snapped gum. "Sorry. Awful habit."

"It's all right."

"Can you meet me at Renee's on Eleventh Street in an hour? I've already spoken with them and pulled a few outfits for you. They have a little of everything, but I want to make sure you have an interview outfit for today and a gown for the party in California. Maybe one more outfit for diary recordings. If you make it past California, I'll flesh out your wardrobe then."

"About that." Harlow pulled into her driveway. "What is my clothing budget?"

Darcy didn't answer immediately. "Enough to cover anything you'll need today."

"I'm not trying to be nosy, but I was thinking. I have a closet full of clothes, even a pretty dress from our hospital's Christmas party last year. I'd like to wear those things and donate my clothing budget to a charity I'm working to start called Wheels on the Ground."

Complete silence met her.

Then Darcy cleared her throat. "Um, it doesn't exactly work that way, Harlow."

"Just because it hasn't, doesn't mean it couldn't."

"Unfortunately it does. We can't cut a check to your charity of choice without the network's permission, and they're not going to give it. I'm sorry."

"But—"

"Not to mention, they require that each woman is fitted for a wardrobe that they approve. We can't have you wearing a label that competes with one of our sponsors."

Harlow's heart sank.

"So can you meet me in an hour?" Darcy's voice was soft.

"I'll be there."

*

The side door to the *Take Five* greenroom opened, and Blake did a double take. First thing he'd done when returning to the hotel was locate Harlow Tucker's file. Then he'd spent the afternoon spinning her name through his mind. She nearly tore it from him with her entrance.

Her toned legs peeked out from beneath a short white number. The rounded neckline revealed her creamy skin but remained modest, while some sort of emerald lace created an hour glass effect along the sides of her dress. Either that or it was the thin belt cinched at her tiny waist. Darcy had put Harlow in a pair of those ankle boots on spikes which made her legs appear longer. Then she'd taken her red hair and pulled it into a loose, wavy braid and tossed it over her shoulder.

She took his breath away.

"Harlow."

He picked up the coffee he'd grabbed on his way over and offered it to her. "I stopped by Starbucks, and they had out a new brew, Yirgacheffe. I'm sure I'm slaughtering the name, but it's from Ethiopia." He shrugged. "I figured you could add another pin."

He hoped for a smile and was rewarded with a wide one.

"Thanks." Her fingers brushed his and she sipped, peering up at him over the lid of her cup. Even in those heels, she was still a good six inches shorter than him.

Her smile still held as she set down her coffee. Genuine. Real. Not asking for anything. And it warmed him in a way nothing else had for a long time.

"You look beautiful."

She fidgeted. "All Darcy's idea. I'd never have paid this much for a dress."

"Don't say that on camera." Darcy scolded before Blake could.

"Why not? It's the truth."

"Because Renee's gave us a discount hoping for increased traffic once we say where your dress is from. They wouldn't be happy if you also say it's too expensive."

"But it is."

"Yet once people see you in it, they'll buy it."

"Only because I wore it?"

"And stood next to Blake?" Darcy nodded. "Yes."

"Good to know."

The lines crinkling her forehead snagged his attention, and he stepped close. "Ready for your first interview?"

"I think I am." She tapped her teeth. "Can I speak with you privately for a moment?"

"Sure." He took her by the elbow and led her to the corner of the room. "If you're nervous, don't be. I'll field the questions. I'm used to it."

"That's not it." Her distracted gaze cleared and then focused on him. "I have a favor to ask, but you can say no if it makes you uncomfortable."

A favor.

Of course.

"Go ahead." He pushed back the disappointment.

"I'm working to start a charity called Wheels on the Ground, but I need some seed money."

He'd read her and that *genuine* smile so wrong. Already she was hitting him up for money.

"Sorry. I'm not a bank."

It took a moment for her low response. "Wow."

The chastisement in her voice sent waves of heat through him. "Yeah. Wow. You've known me less than twenty-four hours, and you ask me for money?" He raised a brow. "Couldn't have said it better myself."

She sniffed. And it wasn't a lady-like sniff. "Did I actually ask you for money? Because I'm pretty sure I didn't."

He slid his hands into his pocket. "Oh. I'm sorry. I didn't give you the chance. Go ahead." He leaned down until his face was in hers. "But don't expect my answer to change."

Her blue eyes narrowed into ice chips. "You're a real jerk."

"Because I won't open my checkbook to a stranger?"

Tears built behind that ice. Blake straightened, his frustration slipping away even as she angrily swiped at the wetness spilling over her soft cheeks. He started to speak, and she held out her palm. "Uh-uh. These aren't tears for pity. The angrier I get, the more I cry, and you just royally ticked me off."

That stopped him cold. "I ticked *you* off?"

"I didn't want your money. I wanted your help."

"My help?" That was a new one. And the possibility actually made him want to listen.

"Forget it." She brushed past him.

He snaked an arm around her waist and stopped her. "Hold up."

"Let go."

Frostbite came with her words. He dropped his hold, and she straightened the hem of her dress. Silence hung for a moment.

"How can I help you, Harlow?"

She sucked in a long breath and placed her hands on her hips. "I'd like your clothes."

"Um ... come again?"

"Your clothes." She waved her hand from his head to his toe. "And anything else you'd be willing to donate. I'd like to do an auction when the show is over. I'll throw in my clothes, but I bet yours will go for more. The money would go to—"

He spat out laughter. "Help, my—"

He stopped before curses spewed from his mouth. Didn't need to give more of a show than he already was. Harlow Tucker didn't want his help, she wanted what everyone else did. A piece of him.

"Sorry, sweetheart, but you're not getting my money, my clothes, or one single piece of me."

Ignoring her huge sea-glass eyes and trembling lip, Blake spun on his heel and stomped toward the set. She had the same skin to get happy in that she got angry in. He owed her nothing. He'd been twisted and squeezed by enough big eyes and pouty lips in his life. Given all he had and never gotten what he wanted in return—for one person to actually want *him*.

He tore a hand through his hair, messing it. Darcy would kill him, but he really didn't care. He slumped into the corner and waited for the crew to call him. Served him right for even treading beside the possibility that Harlow was different, but something in her gentle stare had teased him to believe love could be real. Or something akin to it. Spending time with a person because you wanted to, not because you could gain something from them. Giving simply to give, not to get.

Right.

Now he was chasing fairy tales.

Because he was after something he'd never seen, something the rest of America actually believed in. Come summer he'd deliver it to them in a neat little package every Monday night. They'd never realize he was spinning something he didn't even believe existed—only hoped.

And that hope was growing dimmer by the minute.

Soft footsteps tapped toward him; a production assistant led Harlow his way. A few strands of her wavy red hair escaped the braid and curled around the gentle curve where her neck met her shoulder. She certainly had no trouble in the looks department. And as much as he'd hoped that went farther, apparently he'd been wrong.

Her gaze landed on him, and she turned the other way.

Ought to be a fun interview.

Good thing he'd learned from the best pretender in the world.

"Mr. Carlton, they're ready for you." The crew member waved for him to join Harlow, and he followed her on set.

No audience, just a small set with a white bistro table and a host with big hair, big smile, and most likely a huge reputation in this tiny town.

"I'm Marla Mapleton." The brunette unfolded her tall, rail-thin body from her chair and offered him her manicured hand. Luckily, the coffee mug in front of her had her name sprawled across it, so he didn't need to chant it to himself a hundred times.

"Blake Carlton."

She held for a moment longer, leaning in. "Oh, I know who you are." Her fingers wiggled in his palm before thankfully letting go. He took a step back from her rose perfume, which was nearly knocking him out.

Marla turned to Harlow. "Miss Tucker?"

"That's me." Harlow took Marla's outstretched hand next.

"Everything okay?" Marla tilted her head. "Your eyes are watering."

"I'm good." Harlow swiped at her nose.

Still playing for his sympathy. He'd underestimated her.

"Why don't you two take your seat? We'll record your segment, and it'll play later tonight."

Beside him, Harlow eyed the tall chairs and fiddled with the hem of her short skirt as Marla nodded to the camera man to begin the interview.

"Welcome back, Abundance," she greeted her viewers. "As promised, Blake Carlton and our very own Harlow Tucker have joined us."

Not missing a beat, Harlow turned and faced the red light, a slight tremor in her fingers which rubbed the arm of the chair she was supposed to be sitting in while her voice remained confident and sincere. "It's good to be here, Marla."

"Thanks for inviting us." Blake matched Harlow's warmth. He'd done this too many times to let her outshine him.

Marla took her place, then motioned to them. "Go ahead and get comfy."

Harlow shifted her weight from one high heel to the other.

Modesty wasn't something he was used to. But if she wanted to play the game …

With a sigh, he grabbed her around the waist and plopped her in the chair, standing in front of her while she adjusted her skirt.

Pink rolled across her cheeks. "Thanks." She aimed her smile at him, but he let it fly by. He refused to let the subtle ploys of this woman work on him.

"You're welcome." He sunk into his own seat.

Marla fanned herself with her note cards. "Don't know about you, West Michigan, but it seems like we've already got chemistry rolling through here." She leaned in toward Harlow. "He's not only handsome, but quite the gentleman. You're one lucky lady."

Harlow snatched a Kleenex off the table. "I can't deny he's handsome." She swiped at her eyes. "As for the gentleman end, I don't know him well enough to say."

If she kept this up, she wouldn't. Mom might want her on the show, but that didn't mean he had to give her the time of day.

He turned on the smile that Mom had poured thousands of dollars into. Each time he broke it out, it paid huge dividends. "Trust me, despite what America thinks, I'm a perfect gentleman."

Marla focused on him. "And you're finally ready to settle down?"

"I wouldn't be doing the show if I wasn't." He leaned back and crossed his arms.

"Ready to give a piece of yourself?" Harlow raised one slim eyebrow.

Blake clenched his jaw.

"A piece of himself?" Marla questioned.

"Yes." Harlow's smooth facade didn't even slip. "I mean"—she broke his gaze and turned to Marla—"isn't that what love is? Giving your heart, a piece of yourself really, to someone else?" She spun back to him. "I have it on good authority that you might not be ready to do that."

So. She wanted to play.

He leaned in. "Oh don't worry, sweetheart, I'm more than ready to give myself to a genuine woman. It's the fakes I turn down."

Harlow dabbed at her eyes again. She could go on and try the tears. It wasn't doing a thing for him.

Marla patted Harlow's arm. "Sounds like you've got nothing to worry about then. He chose you for the show, he's ready for love. And there's no denying the sizzle you two bring to a room. I'd say the other women need to be worried." She pointed to Blake. "So can we assume you'll keep Harlow around for several episodes?"

"You'll have to watch the season to see." He relaxed in his chair. This was his territory.

They chatted for a few more minutes, Harlow doing her part to plug Renee's and this season of *Call for Love*. Blake went on autopilot, the questions the same as they always were. Finally Marla began closing up the segment.

"Can I add one more thing?" Harlow asked.

Marla nodded. "Sure."

Harlow smiled directly at the camera. "I wanted to let everyone know that I'm working on a charity called Wheels on the Ground that will bring wheelchairs to children all over the world who need them. To help with our start-up, I will be auctioning off all the clothes I wear on *Call for Love*. I hope it will be a win-win for both sides. The buyer gets a designer piece of clothing that's been worn only once for a huge discount, and our charity—and children nationwide—benefit."

Marla clasped her hands. "Great idea! When and where can we expect the auction?"

"Um … I don't have all those details worked out yet, but I will once the show is finished filming."

"And what about you, Blake? Will you be tossing in your clothes too?" Marla inhaled deeply. "If you are, don't wash them. You smell delicious."

Only years of practice allowed him to bite down the answer that wanted to escape. "I'm afraid right now I won't be adding mine in, though I wish Harlow the best. As you mentioned at the top of the show, her older sister is in a wheelchair, so I know this charity is near and dear to her heart."

"It is." Harlow's large smile focused on his. "Thank you."

Marla tapped her cards against her desk. "I know I'll be bidding for sure." She faced the camera. "So get out your checkbooks, West Michigan. Let's help Harlow with this wonderful venture."

The red light on the cameras turned off, and Marla scooted from her chair. "Really great idea. Please come back by when you have the details worked out, and you can announce it on air." She hugged Harlow.

A round of sneezes exploded from her. "Excuse me." She reached for another tissue. "I'm so sorry, Marla, but I'm allergic to your perfume. Roses, right?"

Marla took a large step back. "Oh dear, I'm so sorry. I don't typically use any scents, but my hands were so dry this morning I grabbed something from the green room."

Harlow dabbed at her eyes. "I'll be fine once I get outside." She took a step back. "It was so nice to meet you. Thanks for having me on your show." She glanced at Blake—"Mr. Carlton"—then hustled past him.

Had her watery eyes been from the perfume and not some on-camera ploy? His thoughts swirled. He honestly didn't know anymore with her.

"Marla, great to meet you." He skipped the hug and shook her hand, then hurried after Harlow. "Harlow?"

"Yes?" She turned.

"Nice job on the interview." He shoved his hands in his pocket. "And sorry about my earlier attitude. I hope you understand, it's not personal. I simply can't help. I get too many requests, half of them not legit. I learned the hard way I can't trust my name to just anyone, so I don't put it out there anymore."

Her smile picked back up but didn't reach her eyes. "Most people spend their entire lives hoping to have what you have, money and influence." She nibbled her lip, then released it. "Sad that you have it but won't use it."

"It's not that I won't. Like I said, it's that I can't."

"I know the meaning of the word can't, Blake. I see it every day in my sister's life. Can't means you don't have the ability, even when you have the desire." She stepped past him. "You don't lack the ability."

"I'm sorry." He didn't know what else to say. He didn't want to examine her words, but he didn't want her upset with him. That thought bugged him nearly more than her answer had. Another fact he didn't want to examine.

Chapter Seven

Blake slammed his suitcase onto the bed. Harlow Tucker had invaded his dreams, making it an awful flight to California. She'd burrowed under his skin the moment he met her, and only irritated him more every minute she stayed there.

He'd met pretty women before, but none that challenged him. She certainly wasn't taking the normal route to snag his attention—sucking up to him to get what she wanted. No, for some reason she thought irritating him would do that.

A chuckle escaped, and he clamped down on it. He would not be amused by her. She wanted the same thing as everyone else, even if she was going about it in a different way.

Unzipping his suitcase, he grabbed the first shirt he saw, a clean pair of cargo shorts, and his toiletry bag. He'd need to have the maid unpack and take his clothes down to be laundered, but until then, this would have to do. Dinner with Mom wasn't for several hours, and he wasn't staying cooped up in here until then.

A knock at his door pulled him around. "Coming."

He peered through the peep hole. No telling who knew he was here.

A petite female version of himself stared back, hardly any wrinkles to note her age.

Mom.

Blake opened the door. "You're early. I thought we weren't doing dinner until eight."

"Yes, well ..." She breezed into the room. Her jet black hair hung in a new short, smooth bob that was slightly shorter in the back and longer in the front. She had on her trademark high heels—he swore she'd been born in them—and a fitted dress. America's Darling had to keep herself in perfect shape. Amazing she'd let herself get pregnant with him.

Blake shut the door and leaned against it.

"The Peninsula is nice, but not as nice as The Wilshire." She ran a hand along the back of one of the chairs. "Why didn't you book there? You loved staying there as a boy."

The Wilshire was owned by The Four Seasons. And it wasn't him who loved staying there. She had. A little too much.

"You look nice, Mother." He strolled toward the minibar. "That cut suits you."

"I have another meeting for my show, and I want to put forth my best." She sat. "Kris Jenner and her girls have had their share of the limelight. It's our turn."

He'd always been her stage prop. But at least this time he was legitimately helping her—even if she wouldn't admit it. Six months ago, she'd been dropping off the far side of depression. Three shows and one movie had passed her over for another actress, something she had never experienced. Add to that, husband number four had left her.

When Blake found her passed out on her bathroom floor, he'd committed to helping her. He'd been unable to save Dad from himself—been responsible for the start of his father's downward spiral—no way he'd lose another parent.

He was her salvation. Doing *Call for Love* would thrust him into the light and tug her out of the shadows. The thought of filming a reality show based around him, his soon-to-be fiancée, and Summer Carlton was enough to make the network sit up and take notice. Even if it did make him cringe.

But she'd be healthy. Safe.

"What is the meeting for? I thought they were waiting for numbers, but it sounded like a done deal."

She inspected her manicure. "They are, but I want them to know in the meantime I'm shopping other networks."

Meaning she wanted more money.

There was always an angle.

Blake poured a water and handed it to her. "So, did you want me to come with you to the meeting, and then we can grab a bite?"

"Sorry, darling, but you'll have to eat alone tonight. Carl Sweeny invited me to dinner. Starting a relationship with him would be a great pairing for my show."

Carl Sweeny was big right now on the small screen and rumor had it he'd recently wrapped a movie that would be his first major hit on the big screen. He was also fifteen years Mom's junior, a fact that played into her desire to be seen with him, no doubt.

That was his mom. Always filling her life with everyone and everything else. Always reaching for something to fulfill her—anything, apparently, but her own son.

"Sure. I understand."

"I knew you would." She stood and walked to the small table where several files sat. "Are these the ones we were going to peruse?"

"Yes."

She flipped open the top one and gave a low laugh. "You approved this mess?"

Blake joined her, peering over her shoulder. A curly haired brunette stared up at him from her contestant sheet, her name lost in the ever-present fog. He scanned the sheet: Samantha Diggs. "She was nice."

"She's plain. Cut her." Mom tossed aside that folder and grabbed another. "Tarynn Knoxville." She paused. "Not one of my top two, but definitely pretty enough for the top eight. Plus she's an Oilers cheerleader. Built-in fan base, which means numbers. Keep her."

He slapped his hand on the next file she reached for. "Mom. If there's one thing I know, it's women. I can pick the right ones. Let's go grab a drink and catch up."

"Blake, darling, I let you pick the first few. That's how we ended up with that." She jabbed her French tipped nail at Samantha's file.

"She's a nice girl."

"Who won't hold anyone's attention." She tugged, but he held firm. "Honestly, Blake."

"Let me pick." If he was going to be stuck in their presence for almost two months, he at least wanted women he could stomach.

Mom rubbed her lips together and sniffed. "My show's at stake here, Blake." Another sniff. "And I need this."

The file under his fingertips grew warm as she battled tears beside him. Was she playing him, or was she still that fragile?

He wouldn't take the chance.

"Fine." He sighed. "I'll take your thoughts into consideration when choosing who stays and who goes."

Her lips revealed perfect teeth that must have been whitened, again. "Thank you, son."

Blake removed his hold from the pile and stepped back to the minibar. "How about you settle in, and I'll brew us some coffee? We can start to go through the names, and I'll make notes."

"Oh, I'm not staying."

He turned.

She'd flipped open the file he'd had his hand on. "Now this woman, I like." She held it up.

Harlow Tucker.

He swallowed.

"My gut says top two at least, but only time will truly tell. America loves the sweet ones, but sweet can sometimes swing toward boring. I'll chat with Dale to ensure we counterbalance that." Mom closed it and scooped up the remaining ones.

"You're really leaving?"

"I told you, I have plans." She sauntered to the door. "I only needed to pick these up. I'll page through them before meeting with Dale, and then he'll help you narrow it down to the eight you keep tomorrow night."

His hand stilled on the granite countertop beside him. "But I thought ..." He shook his head. He knew better. "Sounds good. Enjoy your night."

"You too, darling."

His phone rang as she slipped through the door. He grabbed it from the counter. No face came up with the number, but he recognized it anyway. He'd had the contact stored too long not to, even if he'd eventually deleted it.

He stared at the screen through four rings. One more and voice mail would pick up. His finger slid across the screen instead. "Bianca."

"I wondered if you'd answer." Her voice still hit all the right low tones, smooth and caramelly without a hint of actual sweetness.

"Me too."

Her laughter brought out good memories. "I heard you're in town."

"Doubt you could've missed it."

"You're really going to do that show?"

"I am."

"You have tonight free though?"

He hesitated. Looked around his empty room. "I do."

"Mind if I come over?" Her warm tone coupled with the invitation brought out even better memories. "Maybe exchange a favor for a favor?"

Her proposition eclipsed the better memories with bad ones. His grip tightened on his phone. Bianca had taught him many things. One of which was pleasure could still hold emptiness. And he was through being empty.

"Afraid I'm all out of favors, Bee."

"Bet I could change your mind. Even if I didn't, you'd certainly have fun while I tried."

No doubt he would, for a moment. But it never lasted and only left a bigger void. "Not tonight."

Her voice tightened. "Blake, please. I've got an audition with a director who worked with your mom. She could put in a good word for me if you asked her. I'll make it worth your time. I promise."

"Get the part because you're good. Not because you slept with me." He hung up on her shrieks, strolled into the bedroom, and fell on the thick mattress. Maybe it would swallow him whole before the emptiness bubbling inside did.

He rolled over. The outfit he'd worn on *Take Five* lay crumpled at the top of his suitcase. Images of Harlow Tucker floated through his mind. He'd felt a connection to her in the first moments of meeting her, but really, she'd turned out to be no better than Bianca.

He sat up, then grabbed his keys. There was a great sushi place down the street. Maybe Charlie could meet him.

As for Harlow? Didn't matter. She wasn't the only woman showing up tomorrow. In fact, fourteen other women were on their way to California right this moment. There had to be at least one who'd fill all his voids.

Whoever it was, she definitely wasn't the redhead who kept trying to push her way into his thoughts.

*

Harlow grabbed the dash as Charity's cherry-red Mustang hugged a curve.

"You sure we have time to stop?" Charity spared her a glance.

"Eyes on the road!" Sure, she didn't want to go to California, but she didn't have a death wish either. "With as fast as you're driving, I think we can spare a minute."

"I don't know." She whipped down the street. "Your flight leaves in just over an hour."

"Mae's health is declining, and I'm flying to California to go on a group date with a man I'm not even sure I like." Harlow pointed to the green sign quickly approaching. "Make time."

With a laugh, Charity pulled into a spot and kept the engine running. "Hurry it up then."

Harlow leapt from the car. Thank goodness the line was short.

"Hey. I thought you were already gone." Allen grinned from behind the counter.

"Charity's bringing me to the airport now."

"Not your parents?"

"Mae had a hard night, so they're home with her."

Guilt for leaving slammed her again. The only thing that had her climbing in the car this morning was the bigger guilt if she didn't go. This meant the world to Mae.

Not to mention they'd both agreed it provided a good springboard for Wheels on the Ground. The auction was a sound idea. Right now, it was their only idea. They definitely had the local publicity behind them, and hopefully after her stint on *Call for Love*, it would reach to a bigger level. Not her comfort zone, but she'd do it.

"I hope she's feeling better soon."

"Me too." Harlow grabbed her coffee and waved goodbye. A middle-aged man whose hair appeared to be colored with black shoe polish held the door for her as she approached. "Thank you."

"Harlow, right?" he asked as she stepped past.

She faltered, scrutinizing him more closely. He wasn't someone she'd met before. No way she'd forget his short stature, paunch, and comb-over. "Um, yes. And you are?"

He held out his hand with a business card in it. "Marty. Marty Pontelle with *Star Magazine*."

She ignored the card. "Nice to meet you, but I'm in a bit of a hurry."

"You're flying out to be with Blake Carlton, right?" He followed her, and she quickened her step. Unfortunately, he kept up. "I'm not stalking you, Harlow. I saw you on *Take Five*."

"And happened to bump into me here?"

"I made a few calls. It was easy to find out this is one of your hangouts. I figured I'd see you here one morning."

"But you're not stalking me." The man creeped her out.

"Nope. I'm offering you a way to make the fifty K you need to start up your charity." How'd he know the amount? She hadn't mentioned it on TV. He waited for her to turn before continuing with a slimy grin. "Much faster than trying to sell clothes on eBay and much more lucrative. In fact, you'll probably be able to make enough you won't need to rely on any grants."

Harlow opened her car door. "I think I'll pass."

"You haven't even heard my offer."

"I don't need to. Thank you." Something about him felt off. Especially the way he'd tracked her down.

Charity rose from her car. "Everything okay?"

"Charity, right?" Marty asked.

He knew her name too?

Charity tossed her a wary look.

"It's fine, Chare." Harlow faced Marty. "Like I said, I'm good."

He pushed his card at her again. "If you change your mind, let me know. From what I hear, you're a photographer. You'll be in a position to get some great shots of Blake—hopefully in some creative positions." He winked. "Think about it." Then laid the card on top of her Starbucks cup and strolled away.

"Are you kidding me?" Charity's voice squeaked.

"And yet another reason I have no interest in this show. Not when that's the kind of attention it draws."

They both climbed in, and Charity started down the street. "Do you think that's what Blake has to deal with every day? Freaky people knowing where he's at? Knowing who he's with?"

If so, it explained a lot.

"I don't know. If it is, I feel sorry for him." And she probably owed him an apology. People really did want a piece of him.

Charity maneuvered the car through the heavy traffic like the race-car driver she'd always wanted to be. She glanced at Harlow fidgeting with the business card. "You're not planning on taking pictures for that man, are you?"

"Absolutely not." Not even a question in her mind. She shoved the card into her jeans pocket. "Just wondering what I'm getting myself into."

"Maybe the best thing you've ever done."

"I'd rather shoot for something a little loftier. Like, I don't know, getting Wheels on the Ground started."

Charity shifted gears and slowed, turning into the airport. "Good thing God's plans for us are always higher than our own."

Chapter Eight

The light scent of rain still filled the air as Blake walked to the end of the red carpet production had rolled out. It led to the massive stone house behind him where the evening's cocktail party was about to take place. Fifteen women had primped and squeezed into their evening gowns hoping to snag his attention before the night was through.

One already had.

Even if he'd spent the last two days fighting it.

Red hair, giant blue eyes, creamy skin, and a name that had finally implanted into his brain. Though he wanted to throw a *sweetheart* at her tonight just to get under her skin. Her fire was nearly as enticing as her calm. That heat hinted at other passions, ones he wondered if he could pull out.

His foot slipped on the wet brick of the driveway, jarring him back to his senses.

He should have scuffed up his new shoes before standing on these slick bricks.

Not that he didn't need a good knock on his noggin. One hard enough to jar Harlow Tucker right on out.

"You ready for all these women?" Jace strolled out from behind the fountain, hands casually tucked into the pockets of the tailor-made suit he wore. "Because they're ready to meet you."

"More than ready." Blake repositioned his footing. The sooner they got started, the sooner this whole show would be over.

Jace clapped a hand on his shoulder. "Good. The first limo is here."

A black stretch SUV pulled up and stopped a short distance from Blake. Charlie took his spot a few feet away, while Alex extended his boom mic. Jace disappeared around the corner as the driver exited and opened the rear passenger door. One long tanned leg stretched out from the back seat, a strappy silver heel attached. The driver offered his hand to whoever was owner of those legs, and the black-haired beauty he'd invited from New York stepped out. A year ago his pulse would have jumped. Now he fought boredom.

The woman's smooth stride ate up the five steps between them. She wrapped her arms around him and purred, "Hope you didn't forget me."

"Of course not …" He waited for her name in his earpiece. A hint of annoyance flashed across her face as she released him. "Carmen."

"Carmen Delgado." Dale's voice came through at the same time.

A lot of help he was.

Blake held out his hand, but she dodged it and kissed his cheek. "I don't do handshakes, but you can squeeze me whenever you want."

"Good to know, Carmen." She still had her fingers wrapped around his arm. Blake pried her off. "Why don't you step inside. I have a few more women to greet."

A small fire played behind her eyes. "But only one who made a first impression. You won't forget me now." She pointed to his collar. "I branded you."

He looked down. Bright red lips marred the white fabric.

She touched his arm again. "Come find me tonight, and I'll make sure the next one hits dead on." Her fingers squeezed, then she sauntered inside.

It was going to be a long night.

Ten women later—one with a tattoo of his name, one with a wedding band around her neck that was "his for the taking," and countless others who'd offered him more than a handshake—and he was ready to call it quits.

Knowing he could have any one of them bored him. Took the chase out of the game—a game he'd conquered too many times with nothing to show for it.

The last limo pulled up.

"Dale?" Blake spoke into the microphone attached to his lapel.

"What?" his voice buzzed through the earpiece.

The car door opened and another blonde stepped out. He remembered her from Colorado, but couldn't recall why he'd okayed her for the show. "I'm only allowed to cut half of them tonight?" His count was already beyond that.

"Blake Carlton!" The woman and her nasal voice wrapped around him.

Way beyond.

"Seven. That's it."

Blake covered his groan with a cough. His gaze stayed glued on the limo door. Harlow had to be in there.

No surprise, she was the last one out, exiting fluidly from the limo without any theatrics. Her lilac gown covered all the places the other ladies' hadn't, but showed off some very feminine curves.

All Harlow, no trace of Tucker tonight.

Her red hair was swept softly off her face. Thin silver earrings rode the curve of her neck and stopped nearly at her shoulders. Light makeup enhanced her translucent blue eyes, making them stand out even without any sparkle in them. No. In fact she barely graced him with a glance. Nerves? Or was she still disappointed in him?

She stepped up and held out her hand, a slight tremble there. "Good to see you again, Blake." She still refused to meet his stare.

So unsure of herself for someone who'd had no trouble putting him in his place last time they were together. Where was the fire?

Blake brought her hand to his mouth and placed a small kiss there. "Glad you made it here safely, *sweetheart*."

There it was.

He didn't bother to hide his grin as she pulled her hand back. All her motions remained polite, but her jaw slightly tightened. "Why I ever thought I should apologize ..." She gathered her skirt and made for the door.

Apologize? "Harlow, wai—"

She hurried for the carpeted path to the house, but her pace and spikey heels were no match for the slick bricks. Her foot slid out from under her, and she toppled toward the pavement. Blake reached for her, catching her in both his arms, and swung her back up to a stand. Her pulse beat in her throat. His did too, but not from the scare.

Her silky skin was warm beneath his hands. There was a slight hint of jasmine under whatever fresh scent she'd sprayed on, and her curves molded into him perfectly. The woman felt good in his arms.

Laughter escaped him.

Charlie panned in close, and Harlow disengaged herself from Blake's arms, glaring up at him. "Glad my nearly wiping out is providing you with a laugh."

He snapped his mouth shut.

She stepped onto the carpet and smoothed her dress with shaky hands.

"I laugh when I get nervous." It was out of his mouth so quickly it surprised even him.

She glanced up. Watched him through slightly narrowed lids before tipping her head. "So I make you nervous?"

He shrugged. He'd already made himself vulnerable enough with the last confession. What was it about this woman that pushed past his defenses? He doubted she was even aware of it, much less trying to gain ground on territory he'd walled off years ago.

"That was my attempt at a joke." Her shoulders relaxed and her warm smile reappeared. "This whole situation makes me nervous, so I can't blame you for being a bit anxious tonight too." She nodded to the bricks. "Thanks for catching me."

"You're welcome." He pocketed his hands to avoid touching her again. Long black lashes blinked, one sticking to her cheek. His fingers twitched to brush it away, but he kept them hidden. "Now what were you saying about an apology?"

"That you make it nearly impossible to give you one." She placed her hands on her hips, her smile turning to more of a smirk.

He matched it. "But you think you owe me one?"

She tapped a fingernail against her teeth, then nibbled at the tip of it. After a moment her eyes met his, their edges softening, and she lowered her hand. "You really do have people hitting you up for stuff all the time, don't you?"

"I do."

Alex swung the boom mic in closer, and Charlie moved around to zero in on Harlow's face, but she didn't drop the stare they shared. "Then I truly am sorry for being one of many. For having expectations of you without getting to know you. And for being angry with your response when it was perfectly understandable—even if it was a bit overblown."

Blake raised one brow. "Good apology until that last bit."

"Honest apology, even through that last bit." She tilted her chin up and matched his raised brow.

"Fine. I may have overreacted a little, but it was a knee-jerk reaction."

"Understandable. But one you might want to learn how to control. Love it or hate it, you are a public figure and people are going to ask you for things."

"With great power comes great responsibility and all that jazz?"

70

"Something like that."

"Well, I'll take the responsibility and offer an acceptance of your apology." He leaned toward her, hands still caught in his pockets. "You're forgiven."

"Thank you." Her grin softened her face and sent the fire from her eyes straight to his middle.

And he'd always loved playing with fire.

He pointed to her feet. "So. New shoes?"

"How'd you guess?"

Blake lifted his foot and showed her the bottom of his. "I nearly took a spill too." He clasped her elbow and shifted her slightly so Charlie could get a good angle. "How about we scuff them up together?"

She hesitated but let him lead her to the edge of the carpet. Then, he stood on the bricks and started swiveling back and forth. "Come on. I'll make sure you don't fall." Her lips twitched, and she shook her head but stepped onto the brick too. He held her hands as they twisted back and forth like they were listening to Chubby Checker's *The Twist*.

"This is gold, Blake." Dale's voice startled him. For one long moment he'd forgotten Dale was there. "People will eat this up. You are a pro."

Blake stopped.

Harlow did too. "All broken in?"

More than he cared to admit. "Yeah." He swallowed the sudden lump in his throat and then offered her his arm. "Can I walk you in?"

She cast a quick glance at the cameras, hesitated, then nodded. "Sure."

"Blake," Dale spoke into his ear. "You're supposed to meet with Jace and give a recap of which ladies stood out, not walk this one inside."

He ignored Dale's voice. He'd heard enough for tonight.

The cameras followed them. Harlow remained quiet.

"Did you have a nice flight?" Unable to stop himself, he placed his hand over hers where it lay on his arm. "It was your first, right?"

She nodded. "It was fine. Uneventful." She scrunched up her nose.

"And?"

Her head tipped up to him. "And I felt like I was packed into a sardine box."

"Not quite what you were expecting?"

"Not at all."

He'd heard economy was like that.

71

"Did you find a Starbucks in LAX?"

"Like a homing pigeon." Her eyes twinkled. "They were brewing Burundi."

"I saw." And thought of her. "I'm glad you got another cup."

"I did. No thanks to you." A smile softened her words.

"So you got to add a pin to your map then?" He directed her down a path that wound around to the back of the large house.

"I did."

Inside he could hear the cocktail party in full swing. He wasn't ready to exchange this quiet conversation for that loud one. He wasn't ready to let go of his hold on her. Or maybe it was her hold on him.

"Wrong way, Blake." Dale's brittle voice interrupted. "Go back to the front entrance. Send her through and head over to Jace."

Blake continued like Dale's voice didn't exist. "Will you put a pin on California now?"

"I suppose. I hadn't actually thought about it."

"Really?" They rounded the corner of the house. "You need to do something special, since you've actually been here."

"But I haven't *actually* seen anything." Lines crinkled her forehead. "Um, aren't we supposed to be going inside?"

"It's my party." And it was growing louder by the minute. "I'd rather spend it with you."

Dale yelled in his ear. Blake opened the patio gate, turning down the volume on his earpiece as Harlow slipped past. He directed her to the small pool house, and then slid open its large glass door, keeping the lights low in hopes no one would know they were out here. The back of a gray sectional faced them from a few steps away, its large cushions inviting. Not to mention the quiet of the room.

Harlow stilled in the doorway, her stare landing on the couch. "You're kidding me, right?"

Blake stopped, his hand on the small of her back. "Excuse me?"

"I'm not going in there with you." Her muscles tensed beneath his palm. "I'm not making out with you. I'm not going to be your first conquest of what I'm sure will be a long line this season."

Words deserted him.

So did Harlow. She turned and stalked toward the large house. Charlie's camera stayed on Blake's open mouth even while he informed the other camera guy that Harlow was moving his way.

Utter disbelief engulfed him.

First. No woman had ever turned him down. Ever.

Second. She couldn't have been more off base if she'd run them backwards.

He took two steps after her and Dale appeared, red faced. "Get in that house."

The man did *irate father* well.

"I'm going."

He needed to set Harlow straight.

*

Harlow walked through the back door and stopped.

"Why are you coming in that way?"

One look at the woman who voiced the question and her name immediately came to mind. Carmen. Raven-haired, stick-thin everywhere but on top, and spilling out of her sparkly red gown, Carmen's wobbly steps hinted at the number of cocktails she'd already consumed. With open bottles and empty glasses littering most surfaces, it appeared the alcohol flowed freely—a gift from Dale the producer, no doubt.

"I got a little turned around." Harlow tried to step past her, but Carmen didn't budge.

Behind her, a draft ruffled Harlow's skirt.

Carmen's eyes narrowed. "Turned around. Right." She lifted her chin.

Harlow peered over her shoulder to find Blake in the open doorway. The same door she'd come through. With that lopsided grin, he wasn't helping matters at all. She swung her gaze to Carmen only to find more girls lined up beside her, hunger on their faces.

And she stood between them and their dinner.

She cleared her throat. "I think I'll go find some water."

Carmen wiggled her fingers—"Bye"—and slinked to Blake's side.

Harlow left him to the feeding frenzy. He'd probably enjoy it.

She found the kitchen and a bottled water, but refused to join the main room which currently held a group of girls, most of them already the victim of too much drink and not enough dinner. What she needed was a little peace and quiet. She scooted down a narrow hallway and tried several doors only to discover they were locked. Trying one last door, she sighed sweet relief as it pushed open. Inside was a gorgeous library. Except it wasn't the books that caught her attention. It was the beautiful photography lining each wall.

She walked to the first portrait, a black and white close-up of a little old man. He was a stranger, but his face held a lifetime of stories. Photos like this captivated her. After listening to his tales, she strolled to the next picture. It took her a moment to figure out what it was, then it clicked. The photographer had used a macro lens to get a close-up of the Eiffel tower from underneath, distorting the iron as it climbed upwards and together.

"Great picture."

She swiveled around, recognizing the voice even though it lacked the caramel. Blake stood in the doorway, minus the cameras.

"How'd you manage to ditch your entourage?" she asked.

He nailed her with his charming grin. "My mom's taught me a thing or two over the years about avoiding cameras." He stuck his hands in his pockets and shrugged. "One of the only useful things she did teach me."

She didn't dig into the comment even though she wanted to unearth what was under it. Instead, she returned her focus to the photos. "I thought you didn't like photography."

"Never said that." He strode over to her, his long legs eating up the distance between them in three steps. "What I said was I don't like people taking shots of others without their permission." He reached over her shoulder to tap the photo of the Eiffel Tower. "This is a beautiful piece."

His arm warmed her skin. His scent filled the air around her. The same cologne that still lingered in her car from the five minutes he spent in it. She'd yet to place it. Had even smelled her way, purely to kill her curiosity, through the mall at home—though the biggest store in Abundance was a Kohl's.

He leaned against the wall, still close. His finger lingered on the photo. "You like?"

"I do."

He might be pointing to the shot, but she had a sneaky suspicion he referred to himself. He'd invaded her space and focused squarely on her.

She stepped to the next photo. "They're all great."

"They are." He followed. "Some are better than others, though."

He reached out to brush her cheek.

She leaned back. "Seriously?"

"What?"

"Does this ever really work?"

"Do you ever really relax?"

74

"Agh!" She stomped to the door only to find a camera man filming them. Behind him, another man stood with a long pole and mic attached.

"Apparently your stealth mode didn't work." She brushed past them both and out the door. At the end of the hall she ran into some blonde who'd spent most of the past twenty-four hours since they'd all arrived attached to Carmen's side. The woman smiled, then her eyes widened. No doubt she saw Blake exiting the same room she'd witnessed her coming from.

The woman's mouth dropped open, and she hurried into the next room.

Great. The entire group would think she'd been making out with Blake already. Ha. If they only knew she had no intention of kissing him at all. With the stilted interactions they'd had, she'd be lucky to even survive the night. Blake was sure to axe her come midnight.

She'd rather be home anyway. And Mae couldn't say she hadn't at least tried.

Harlow escaped the opposite way of the blonde and found herself at another door that opened to the large backyard. She stepped into the warm Malibu night and wandered the stone patio. A few feet away, lights shone through the living area, illuminating it. Blake stood in the center of what appeared to be more than half of the women here tonight. One snagged her arm around his and led him away.

More power to her.

A slight breeze stirred, much nicer than the stale air inside. Since arriving here, Harlow hadn't made any friends. They'd shared meals together yesterday, but she was so different from all of them. They were all focused on Blake. Centered on how they looked. And based on conversations she'd overheard, willing to do anything necessary to win him.

It was one reason she hated being here.

She wanted to be pursued, not the other way around. Peter had pursued her. Problem was, he'd pursued Opal too—and chosen her in the end.

Blake Carlton was no better. And while Peter had snowed her, she knew full well Blake was a player. He'd get what he wanted and then move on to the next conquest.

Harlow had no intention of adding her name to that list.

Light shone up from the dark blue depths of the pool. There was a slide built into the rock on the opposite side and a hot tub in the shallow end. At twelve feet, it was one of the deepest pools she'd seen, not that she'd be getting in. Thirty years old and she didn't know how to swim.

"For a woman who voiced such little interest yesterday, you sure cozied up with Blake every chance you got tonight." Carmen's hard voice came from behind.

Harlow peeked over her shoulder. "Good evening to you too, Carmen."

Her footsteps closed in. "Why's he so interested in you?"

"He's not."

"Right."

Before Harlow even realized the need to react, Carmen bumped into her, tossing her off balance.

She flailed her arms in the air, but there was no place to grab. She fell backwards, and the water swallowed her whole.

Chapter Nine

How much longer was this night?

Blake had lost count of how many women he'd spoken with throughout the evening. They all blurred together, all except the one who seemed to have no problem walking away from him.

Unlike Nikki who'd sought him out. Stolen him from the one with black hair—Carmen, he thought—mid-kiss. They had barely landed on the outdoor sofa before Nikki launched herself at him. As expected, he wasn't the only one playing a game.

Lucky for him, his game came with an earpiece, or he'd never remember these ladies' names.

Nikki grabbed his lapels and snuggled in closer, a soft sigh emitting from her. He couldn't remember the last time his brain had stayed as engaged in a kiss as his lips had. Certainly not tonight. Definitely not right now.

At least he'd filled the quota Dale had pushed for. He tilted his head to allow the camera a better angle. Nikki would get thirty more seconds, and then he needed to find a way to disengage. Take a break before the next woman grabbed at him.

She came up for air. "Ummm … you're a great kisser."

It wasn't anything he hadn't heard before. He ran a hand along her cheek. "You're not so bad yourself."

She giggled, and he held in his wince.

High heels clicked across the cement toward where they sat. "Sorry," though the voice held no remorse, "but I'm going to steal Blake from you."

He turned to see a redhead in a short, sequined, emerald dress paired with three-inch heels. He was beginning to feel like the main entrée at a dinner for people who hadn't eaten in a year.

Nikki stood. "I guess I have to share. Tonight anyway." She ran a hand along his arm. "Catch you later."

The redhead twisted a lock of her hair around her finger. "Should I sit?"

Blake stood. Touched his ear.

"Melanie," Dale supplied.

He internally repeated the name, not that it mattered. Melanie could bat those eyes and sway her hips all she wanted, but she was no match for the other redhead who'd consumed his thoughts all night. Would she believe him if he said he needed to use the restroom?

"If you don't mind, Mel—" A splash interrupted him.

What woman had decided to jump in to the pool to gain his attention? He wasn't sure if he was impressed or worried. At least it wasn't as bad as a woman tattooing his name on her arm. "Let's check out the pool." He offered his hand to ... and it was already gone. He tapped his ear again.

"It's Melanie." Dale didn't sound amused.

Melanie put her hand in Blake's and leaned her cheek against his shoulder, her lower lip pooching out in a pout. "We didn't even get a chance to talk."

"The night's not over yet."

"I'm holding you to that."

To what, he wasn't sure. He hadn't promised anything. And since he forgot her name in under fifteen seconds—pretty sure a new record—he wasn't going to promise her anything.

He arrived at the pool right behind Charlie and the other cameraman, both focused on the deep end where someone floated under the surface. Alex trained his mic in the center of all the action. Pale lavender fabric lifted toward the top of the water. Blake stilled.

Lavender.

Harlow had jumped in the pool?

Apparently she was full of surprises.

"Is that the Tucker girl?" Dale asked in his ear. "Get a close up." He chuckled. "It is. I knew she'd be good for ratings."

Blake stepped to the edge of the pool. Harlow wasn't coming up. His heart started racing, but the cameras continued filming. Was he the only one who thought this was strange?

A few bubbles escaped her mouth, and then her wide eyes looked up.

Panic.

Blake tore off his mic and dove in. Harlow's arm reached for him, and for a split second he worried she'd claw him to the bottom with her, but she controlled the fear he saw behind her eyes and clasped his hand. He tugged her to him, pulling her to his chest. As they broke the surface, she rested her head on his shoulder and coughed.

He leaned his lips to her ear, his pulse racing. "How does a thirty-year-old woman not know how to swim?" She tensed under him, and he dragged her to the ledge. "Do you really want camera time so badly you'd pull a dangerous stunt like this?" A hard lump dug into his abdomen from where she rested against him. Seriously? "You didn't even take your mic off."

She grabbed the concrete edge, a familiar fire flaring in her gaze. Once again he wondered what it would be like to have her heat directed at him, not through him. She shoved him away. "Why, yes, I'm fine. Thank you." Then tried to haul herself out, but her limbs were shaking and her dress had to weigh a ton. Her body dropped back into the water.

Fourteen pairs of heels pointed at them from the pool deck. Several gasps, a few *are you all rights* and countless *what happeneds* filled the air.

Beside him, Harlow attempted once more to haul herself from the pool and failed. The woman was stubborn enough to try again if he didn't intervene. She gasped as he swept her close, but at least she didn't fight him as he swam her to the shallow end. The moment her feet could touch, however, she broke free.

He snagged her wrist, stopping her. "Really. Are you all right?"

She glanced from his hold to his face. "I'm fine. Embarrassed. But fine."

"You know, there were plenty of other ways to get my attention."

"Your attention is what landed me in that pool to begin with." She pulled away. "I'm glad I came out to Malibu and all, but I think I'm done. We both know I'm not your type."

The women all congregated at the top of the steps, Carmen at the front, holding a towel for Harlow. "Harlow! Are you okay?"

Harlow's jaw tensed.

Jealousy rolled off Carmen, and he replayed Harlow's words. He didn't like the picture they painted.

Easy fix.

Blake hauled himself out of the water alongside Harlow. Jace stood in the group of women, and Blake found his stare. "I'm ready to hand out the phones."

"Then let's get you some dry clothes."

"Not unless you have a set for Harlow."

"We'll find something. We need you both miked again, and we can't do that with you wet."

"Good. I'm going upstairs to change. I'll come down once you let me know Harlow is dry." He didn't wait for a response but brushed through the group and into the house. Dale was waiting for him in the upstairs master bedroom and handed him a towel.

Blake pulled off his soggy tie and suit coat. "What do you want?"

"Noticed we had some mic trouble tonight."

"I took it off to dive in." He scrubbed his hair dry.

"Before your little swim." Dale raised a brow.

Right. He'd turned it off when he followed Harlow into the library. Unfortunately, hers had still been on. It was how they'd found them. He might be used to cameras, but he wasn't used to the mics. He'd figure his way around them though. Always did.

Dale leaned against the wall. "I'll brush it off as a malfunction. Make sure it works from here on out."

"Technology can be testy. Can't promise it won't happen again."

"Fine. Have your fun, Blake, it only makes for good conflict, and—like tonight—the right conflict is good for my show."

He stilled. "You're saying Harlow didn't jump in? She was pushed?" It's what he suspected, but Dale confirming it would only solidify his decision to send Carmen home.

The producer shrugged. "Heard the audio. It could go either way."

Blake worked his jaw. With Dale, that was as close to a yes as he'd get. Carmen was through here.

"I'm on board with you having fun," Dale's voice grew as firm as his stance, "but the moment it interferes with my show, I'll put a stop to it. You signed a contract, and I'll have no issue enforcing it if need be. Are we clear?"

"Crystal."

"Good." Letting out a long breath, Dale nodded toward the door. "Ready to hand out the phones?"

"More than."

"Planning on giving Carmen one?"

"No. She's trouble." He tossed the towel and grabbed a dry T-shirt. "I don't need that kind of drama."

Dale crossed his arms. "You just outlined every reason we're keeping her."

Blake stopped, his dry T-shirt halfway over his head. He slowly pulled it on the rest of the way. "Come again?"

"I get veto on who you're kicking off, or have you forgotten?"

He had. His gut tightened. "I'm not keeping Carmen."

"Yes. You are." Dale straightened. "Don't mistake my willingness for you to have a little fun as you being in control. This is my show. Carmen stays. Get dressed and pick the other seven." He slid out the door.

Blake resisted the urge to punch something. Already he felt trapped. These women were here for a meal ticket, not to meet him. And Dale wanted to keep the hungriest of them all.

Then there was Harlow. Still wasn't sure what to make of her. Was she honest, or another good player? It had been a long time since he couldn't read someone. Could make for an interesting season.

Could make for heartbreak.

The thought stopped him cold. Heartbreak implied he believed in love.

How could he believe in something he'd never truly experienced?

Gah. He needed to pull his brain out of whatever clouds it had ascended into.

After changing his clothes, he quickly flipped through the files and scribbled down the names of the women he wanted to keep. Just as he finished, someone knocked on his door. He opened it to find Charlie and Darcy waiting for him.

"Let me touch up that shine." Darcy came at him with her makeup sponge. "Nice save, by the way. Completely swoon-worthy." The scent of peppermint washed over him as she popped a bubble.

Charlie handed him his mic pack and helped him reconnect everything, attaching the receiver to his camera. "Thanks a whole lot, buddy. Make my girl swoon over you."

"You could have jumped in."

"I thought Harlow was playing."

No one could manufacturer that look of terror. It still sliced through him.

They started downstairs, meeting Jace who waited at the bottom of the steps. "I've got the ladies in the other room. Do you have your list of names for Dale to feed you?"

Blake handed it to Darcy and then tightened his tie.

She scanned the list. "Whew. Sure you can handle the reaction from the ladies not on this?"

Jace laughed and slapped him on the back. "Course he can. He's an old pro."

What a sport to be a pro at—skirt chasing. He wasn't so sure he wanted the title anymore.

"Did you find a dress for Harlow?"

Jace met Darcy's gaze and grinned. "Yes." She shrugged. "I only had one she'd fit into. Might not be her style, but I have a feeling you'll appreciate it." With a quick kiss on Charlie's cheek, she left to deliver the list of names to Dale.

Curious, Blake turned back to Jace. "Lead the way."

Jace guided them down a long hall and stopped short of an arched opening. He held up his hand for Blake to wait and then walked through.

"Ladies, Blake is ready to issue his invites." Jace paused until the excited squeals quieted. "If he asks you to stay, he'll hand you a phone. Now these phones are only good for receiving calls from Blake. Much like any other dating relationship you start, after each date—if he feels like it's going somewhere—he'll call you for a second one. If he calls, you have the option to not accept and instead return home, but this goes both ways. If you don't hear from him by the end of the next day, you'll know he wasn't feeling enough of a connection to continue pursuing a relationship." Jace motioned to the doorway. "Blake?"

He entered the room, following Charlie who walked backwards with his camera pointed straight at him. Tim ... no it was—scratch that. Didn't matter. Whoever he was filmed the women. Alex, sound pack strapped across his chest, held his boom mic in their direction. A few other mics dipped low from the ceiling, while others were hidden around the room.

Blake was used to being a bug under a microscope, just not *being* bugged.

"Whenever you're ready, Blake." Jace motioned to the women, then exited the room.

Blake met each woman's eyes, his gaze slowing as it rolled past Harlow. Amusement bubbled. Darcy had put her in a short black number with a deep V in the front and fabric that clung to all her curves. And she had plenty of curves. They'd stayed hidden in the soft lilac dress she originally wore tonight. He'd noticed how tiny her waist was while hauling her from the pool, but now he could appreciate it. Even more so as she wiggled to tug down the hem.

Darcy was right in the fact that it wasn't Harlow's style, but wrong when she thought he'd like it. Sure, she was beautiful in it, but he liked how she'd stood out from the crowd with her own subtle style.

Blake offered her a conciliatory smile and confronted her glare. Apparently he'd stared too long.

He glanced over all the women again.

"Amber. She's the brunette in the blue dress in case you don't remember." Dale finally offered a name. Clenching his jaw, he waited another thirty seconds before focusing on the petite brunette in the front row. "Amber."

She gasped and stepped forward, sashaying over to him.

"Amber," he said, handing her a phone, "would you be willing to take a call for love?" He nearly choked on the cheesy line, and he had to say it seven more times.

"Of course." She took the phone and deposited a kiss on his cheek.

The whole process went faster on TV with the melodramatic music playing in the background. As it was, five very long minutes later, Blake was down to two more phones. Carmen's gaze skewered him while Harlow's focused on her toes. Two women whose names he remembered for very opposite reasons.

One who'd chase him down, one who'd run the other way.

One he had to keep. One he wanted to keep.

"Carmen." Dale supplied the name next.

Not that he needed it. Blake looked at her. "Carmen."

She emitted something between a growl and a purr before ramming into Harlow's shoulder on her way to him. "You don't even need to ask. I'll take anything you have to offer." She slid the phone from his hands and kissed him, then turned and smiled at all the ladies.

Blake cleared his throat as Jace stepped into the room. "Last phone of the night."

Because that wasn't totally obvious.

Blake picked it up and tapped it against his chin, waiting for Harlow's blue eyes to find him. She kept her stare on her silver shoes.

Unable to wait any longer, he gave in. "Harlow."

She looked up. "Me?"

"You don't want to date me?" he challenged.

"You invited seven other women before me, so I'm not too sure." Innocence coated her words and face but missed her eyes.

"Refreshing." Charlie's voice came from behind Blake so quietly he nearly missed it. He glanced over his shoulder.

Judging by his friend's face, Harlow had already charmed him. Probably why Dale wanted her. She'd charm half of America with her sweet words and so-called honest ways.

83

Question was, how honest was she?

He didn't know. But he wanted to find out.

Which meant he needed to give her a little push.

He closed his hand around the phone. "I'm sorry, but I thought Mae had explained all this when she nominated you. You don't get me alone unless you make it to the end, which is kind of the point of the show."

The other women around Harlow smirked. Except for the seven who still stood empty handed. They sent her daggers.

Harlow aimed hers at Blake. "I thought the point of the show was to find love."

"Which won't happen unless you take this phone." He held it up. "Or is Mae the only sister willing to take risks? She took a mighty big one nominating you for this show." He lowered his voice. "I think she hoped it would pay big dividends."

Harlow narrowed her eyes, watched him for a long moment, then sighed. She actually sighed. Either she was aiming to be their most memorable bachelorette, or she really wasn't excited. He truly couldn't tell which one. Her tight smile made him think the latter. "She did, and you're right. I need to take a cue from her." Stepping forward, she held out her hand. "I'd be happy to take your call for love."

Only he didn't think she meant it like the other ladies had.

This would be an interesting season.

He placed the phone in her hand, running his fingers over her palm. Beneath his touch, she trembled, then quickly tensed and jerked away.

Interesting, indeed. Because Harlow Tucker was laying the perfect trap. Boredom, anxiety, and innocence mixed together in perfect proportions only enhanced by the charity and sick older sister which were the reasons she'd agreed to do this show.

Of course Dale wanted her. America would fall right into her little concoction.

Blake was already teetering on the edge.

Chapter Ten

Harlow stepped to the corner of the room while Blake escorted the seven phoneless women from the house. She needed to catch her balance. Blake was throwing her off kilter, and she couldn't figure out why.

She tugged down the short elastic hem of the crazy dress Darcy had found her. Her soggy gown would have been more comfortable than this thing. Unfortunately, the crew insisted she change. Thinking she only had to last through the ceremony, she'd agreed. And now she still stood here, wondering what else she'd agreed to.

Why had Blake even asked her to stay? After the way they'd clashed all night, she expected him to send her packing.

Across the room, Carmen leaned in toward a blonde, Jillian, and whispered. They watched Harlow, their eyes narrow slits.

This was going to be a fun couple of weeks.

Harlow surveyed the room. In a group like this, she typically blurred into the background, but somehow he clearly saw her. His focus massaged the painful places still raw from Peter.

No, no, no. She could not let that happen. This situation too closely mirrored that one. She was here for her sister. For Wheels on the Ground. If she kept her mind there and steeled her heart from falling for what she couldn't have, then she'd survive. Which meant ignoring the warmth Blake stoked when he'd called her name.

"Ladies." Jace strolled into the room, snagging her attention. "Blake's about to rejoin us. Grab your champagne goblets and come to the center of the room, please."

Blake returned inside, and the women swarmed him. He held up a bottle of bubbly and filled everyone's glass until he reached her empty hands. "Let me guess, you're not a drinker?"

"I drink." She injected amusement into her voice, matching his.

"Need a glass then?"

"No, thank you."

Carmen pushed hers in front of him, her other fingers wrapping around his upper arm. "More for me."

He hesitated a moment and then refilled her glass before moving to another brunette in a cream-colored dress. Peyton. Her form was as sporty as her name. She'd spent most of her time in the gym since arriving. Harlow had barely shared two words with her.

Around the circle, Blake *sweethearted* or *darlinged* each woman as he filled their glasses. Someone really needed to tell him that trademark wasn't one he wanted to own.

Once all the goblets were full, he raised his. The cameramen edged in close.

"Ladies." Blake turned around the circle. "I want to thank you for making the trip out here and joining me on this adventure. I'd love to get to know each one of you, and we'll begin that journey in …" he held the word while his gaze rolled past each of them. Finally, his eyes rested on Harlow. "Budapest."

Squeals nearly split her eardrum. Her heart pounded. Budapest. She was going to Budapest? Blake removed himself from the middle of the commotion to join her. "Think Mae will be happy?"

And then it clicked, allowing her earlier resolve to strengthen. He didn't see her, he saw Mae. This entire plan was her sister's wish, and he was doing his part to ensure its success—exactly like she was. That fact melted her heart and cut it all in one swoop.

"She will be." That small thought soothed the part that hurt. "Thank you."

He smiled and faded into the crowd. Harlow crossed the room and exited out the set of french doors to a tiled balcony overlooking the lights of Malibu. She slipped off her heels and let the cool floor massage her feet.

She needed to regain focus. Nothing was different here. Her entire life she'd worked from the background, watching as everyone else around her was picked for the big things. There always seemed to be a wall when she tried for more. While others shone, she flickered, good enough to only go so far. But God needed someone to help fan into flame his larger plans. That was her role, and when she didn't hope for more, everything went fine.

Problem was, for one split second tonight, for whatever crazy reason, she *had* wished for more.

The door opened behind her. She didn't have to turn to know it was Blake. Already that spicy scent with the citrusy undertone was embedded in her brain. A fact that bothered her *because* it bothered her.

"Sorry you got tossed in the pool because of me." He leaned against the iron railing, sincerity lining his words.

She peered up at him, noting he was once again without a cameraman, and smiled. "And you think coming out here for some one-on-one time is going to stop it from happening again?"

He chuckled. "Now that you mention it …"

She raised both brows. Honest laughter looked good on him.

A few dogs barked in the distance and more lights sprang on. "Thanks again for doing this, Blake." She swallowed. "Mae will be ecstatic."

"I didn't do it only for her."

That answer and his soft tone surprised her. It nearly sounded like he wanted her around. "You didn't?"

He brushed a lock of her hair from her cheek, his touch snapping against her nerves in ways she'd rather ignore.

It took her a second to realize he'd leaned in, and she hadn't leaned back. No, she'd stretched forward.

What was wrong with her?

She stiffened and stepped away before she stepped into a world of hurt.

A low chuckle reverberated through his chest. "You're attracted to me."

His cocky grin was the splash of water she needed.

"Even if I was, your attitude is pretty good at killing it." She gained more space between them. "Along with the fact you're dating seven other women. Like I said, I don't date men who play around."

"All part of the game you signed on for."

She picked up her shoes from the tile floor. "Kissing you was never part of the deal." Nor was giving him her heart. Neither one was going to happen.

He pushed away from the railing. Came closer. "So you're saying you didn't want to kiss me just now?"

Her words stuck in her throat.

"Awful quiet."

"Fine. For one split second I wanted to kiss you. It must have been the night air and the beautiful scenery. I got caught up."

"It had nothing to do with me?"

She turned. Better not to answer than to lie. "If you'll excuse me, it's late and I'm tired."

His laughter followed her. "That's all right, Harlow. Your inability to answer tells me all I need to know."

She growled under her breath but kept moving. No way Blake Carlton was getting farther under her skin than she'd already let him burrow.

*

Blake dropped on his bed. Longest night of his life, and he'd had a few doozies. But one small thank-you from Harlow had made up for it. He couldn't remember the last time someone had said those words to him and meant them.

Knowing she wanted to kiss him only sweetened the evening.

That she refused to give in to it intrigued him. All the other women had thrown themselves at him tonight. She'd run the other way. Maybe she was the one person who didn't want something from him.

Someone knocked on his door, and he groaned.

"It's just me," Jace said from the other side.

Blake bit back another groan. "Come on in."

He'd known Jace for years. They'd run in similar circles ever since Jace arrived in Hollywood. The man tired him out.

"So how'd you think it went?" Jace pulled out one of the club chairs and sat.

"You were there."

"I was," he chuckled. "And you've got your hands full."

"That's putting it mildly."

Propping his ankle on his knee, Jace eyed him. "Dale make you keep Carmen?"

He tugged off his suit coat. "How'd you guess?"

"This isn't my first run. Better get used to her because if I know Dale, she'll be here for the long haul."

"Great."

"So what'd you think of the other ladies? See any potential?"

Blake shrugged. "Who knows. Time will hopefully tell."

"And Harlow?"

"What about her?" No way he was putting his foot into that trap.

Jace stared him down, but he didn't flinch even when his friend's grin grew. "All I needed to know."

"Don't start."

"Hey. She's not half bad. You could do a lot worse."

"Drop it," Blake growled.

Most men might pass Harlow over for someone like Carmen at first glance. But he was growing tired of being most men.

"That's an even better response."

He stood and walked to his bathroom. "I'm taking a shower and going to bed. It's been a long day."

"I'll see myself out."

By the time Blake pulled back his covers, Jace's laughter had firmly implanted in his mind. He should laugh. The thought of someone like Harlow with Blake was like the old comedy his mom had starred in—and found her third husband from.

He knew all too well how that relationship ended off screen.

All the more reason not to start one with Harlow.

Because real life never ended with a permanent happily-ever-after.

Chapter Eleven

Whoever made flights this long ought to be shot. Nearly ten hours squeezed into the middle of five seats with a baby screaming to her left, Carmen snoring on her right, and the man in front of her fully reclined—all her years spent dreaming of overseas travel, and Harlow never pictured this.

"Seats up, please, sir." A flight attendant leaned across the row and nudged the man. Finally he put his seat forward. Harlow stretched her legs, massaging the cramp that had formed.

Ten minutes later the plane bumped across the tarmac. "Welcome to Germany," the captain's voice announced over the speakers.

Carmen stirred and pushed up her sleep mask. "We're here?"

"Seems like it." Harlow smiled, hoping to maybe elicit one in return. No such luck. She'd even tried chatting their first few minutes aboard, but Carmen had stuck in her ear buds and focused on the TV screen in front of her until she'd finally nodded off.

Harlow had grown tired several hours into the flight, but the man behind her apparently enjoyed the touchscreen game attached to the back of her chair. She'd spent most of the flight with him punching it, sending her chair into convulsions.

Within twenty minutes of landing, they were off the flight, and Harlow congregated with the other ladies around Dale, who looked fully rested. Having seen the space in first class, she wasn't surprised.

"Ladies, we need to go through customs together. The production crew will keep an eye out for you." He smiled. "We want to make sure no one gets lost. Blake would be sad."

The women around her laughed.

The line at customs filled three-quarters of the room. After nearly forty-five minutes, Harlow stepped forward. This was it. Her first stamp in her passport.

She stood at the glass. Offered a smile. And, with the same level of excitement she put into folding her socks, received a stamp from the man sitting behind the glass.

That was it?

She pocketed her passport as they ushered her along. Customs needed to do something for first time stampers, because that was a complete letdown.

Or maybe she was exhausted and grumpy.

Following the rest of her group, Harlow practically sleepwalked to the gate for their flight from Germany to Budapest. She eyed the benches and their black plastic padding, contemplating a nap.

"Some of us are going in search for coffee." The only chestnut-haired woman in the group walked over. Pretty sure her name was Tarynn. With that grin and bubbly personality, it was no surprise she was a cheerleader.

It was too early for bubbles.

"I think I'm going to hang here."

"You sure?"

"Yes." Dead on her feet. She was sure.

"Okay."

The group left, and Harlow made for one of the open benches.

"You look beat." The bear of a cameraman walked over. With his head full of blond curls, face full of scruff, and trademark yellow T-shirt, he was a landmark of their crew.

"I am." She held out her hand. "Charlie, right?"

"Yep." He settled across from her. "Go ahead and lie down if you want. I'm on gate duty, and I'm not going anywhere. I'll watch your bags."

The offer was too tempting to resist. "Thanks." She propped her travel pillow on top of one end of the bench and laid down, relishing the fact she could finally stretch. Four hour layover. Charlie the cameraman watching over her. She was set. Relaxing her muscles, she closed her eyes.

And someone wiggled her leg.

She pulled herself from the fog surrounding her and peeked open one eye. Had she actually slept?

Tarynn stood over her. "You might want to wipe your drool. People are starting to stare." She leaned in and whispered, "Plus you were snoring."

Heat flamed her face. Her cheek was stuck to the plastic chair, making a lovely noise as she sat up and wiped wetness from her face. Charlie's lips twitched. She pushed her hair off her face. At least Blake was nowhere in sight.

She shook her head. Why on earth would that even matter?

"Thanks." She rubbed her eyes. "What time is it?"

"Four a.m. We've still got a couple hours until we board." Tarynn flipped the pages of her magazine, an empty coffee cup beside her.

"How far to the coffee?" Harlow stood and stretched.

"It's up and around the corner; about a five minute walk."

She reached for her wallet. They'd each been given a stipend for their travel. "Think I'll grab some."

"I'll go with you." Darcy stood from her seat. She'd accompanied the others too. The production crew didn't seem too keen on letting them wander around alone.

"Sure." Not that she really had a choice.

Darcy fell in step beside her.

"I've been meaning to ask, how's your sister doing?" Kindness mixed with her curiosity.

"All right. All things considering." Really only one thing, but it was a biggie. "Starting to have problems with her heart muscle, but we're praying the Limb Girdle stays away from that."

"Limb Girdle? I thought she had Muscular Dystrophy."

"Limb Girdle is a form of that." She was too tired to be more detailed.

"I'll add her to my prayer list."

Even better than not digging farther into Mae's disease right now, Darcy seemed sincere.

They walked a few more steps before Darcy spoke again. "Pretty neat what she did, nominating you for the show and all."

"That's one way to put it."

She chuckled. "That's right. This isn't your favorite show."

"Not exactly." Harlow dodged a young man with spiked hair and chains. "But Mae knows I always wanted to travel, so she thought she was helping."

"Pretty big long shot."

"She doesn't believe in the word impossible."

"But you do?"

Harlow shrugged. It was far too early for this conversation. Or too late. She couldn't remember anymore. The coffee shop sign came into view, and she sniffed the air.

"What do you think of Blake?" Darcy asked.

Harlow stopped. Turned. "Um." She needed that cup of coffee. "I'm going to order. Do you want anything?"

She waved her hand. "No. I already had a double. I'll wait over here."

Harlow stepped into line, beyond exhausted. This wasn't how she'd envisioned her first jaunt onto foreign ground. Mae would be with her. Or at least someone she loved. She'd be put together. Hair combed. Makeup done. Maybe a pair of skinny jeans and cute flats, a long sweater.

Okay. She'd gotten that part correct, except for all the wrinkles. Not to mention she should have packed a toothbrush and deodorant or at least body spray in her carry-on.

The man in front of her stared at the board. She wished he'd hurry up and order. But no, he needed to read every word on it.

She tapped her foot.

The man turned.

And smiled.

Of course.

*

Blake held in his laughter. This wasn't Harlow behind him. This was Tucker. And even with sleep still lining her eyes, her hair in long red strings, and her clothes full of wrinkles, she still caused him to suck in a breath.

Not one other woman in his life would ever be caught dead looking like that. He'd be scared to get caught like that—not with cameras constantly trying to catch him in an embarrassing moment and tear him apart.

Her comfort with being real made her even more beautiful.

"Long flight?"

She dipped her chin and raised an eyebrow. "What gave you the first clue?"

"Sir?" The barista gained his attention. "Can I take your order?"

"Double espresso along with a chocolate croissant," he said, moving aside, "and whatever the lady would like too."

Harlow didn't budge. "Is that even legal?"

"Legal?"

"Show rules and all?"

"It's fine." He motioned for her to order.

She still hesitated.

"It's on the show's dime either way, so let's put it on one transaction and let the nice people in line get their coffee a little faster." He leaned down beside her and lowered his voice. "Unless you'd like to make the large German man behind you wait longer."

She turned her head, her nose brushing his cheek in the process. Her eyes widened. He let himself believe it was from their brief contact and not the size of the man behind her. She stepped up and ordered. "Double espresso, no cream, no sugar."

"Anything to eat?" Blake pointed to the pastries in the glass case.

"No, thank you."

No cream or sugar in her coffee, and no pastry for a treat. She'd walk around the airport looking like that, but then she cared about what she ate? He couldn't figure her out, and it intrigued him even more.

"Suit yourself." Blake paid and followed her. He spotted Darcy smacking away at her gum. Of course, Harlow had a babysitter. He met Darcy's gaze hoping she'd stay put. She narrowed a glance at him but gave a short nod.

He stood beside Harlow at the end of the counter waiting for their coffees. "The next flight is pretty short."

"You've been to Budapest before?"

"Nope." He leaned against a post. "Looked at my ticket."

Laughter escaped her lips. "Suppose I could have done the same, though I'm so tired I think my eyes would have crossed." She leaned on the opposite post. "All these years I've heard people talk about flying and thought they were exaggerating, but they really do squeeze you in tight. I didn't mind it so much flying to Malibu, but this one was tough."

"I'm taller than you and always have plenty of room."

Harlow snorted. "Seriously?"

He took his time scanning from her legs all the way up to her face. "Very."

"Not that you're taller than me." She planted a hand on her hip. "The fact that you honestly think how you travel is how the rest of the world travels. Have you even seen what economy's like, or do you never make it past first class?"

His cheeks heated. He'd never had a reason to look beyond that curtain.

"Right." She closed her eyes. "Since you slept like a babe, how about you wake me when my coffee is ready?"

The heat traveled from his cheeks to his blood. "Sorry that my life is such a turn-off to you."

She didn't even peek open one eye. "Not your life, but your attitude."

The barista called out their drinks, and Blake stalked over to them, thankful they had a lid on or he'd have a burn. He stepped back over to Harlow and thrust hers at her. "Enjoy your flight."

She opened those pale green-blue eyes of hers and stared at him. No edge there. "Listen. I'm tired and a tad grumpy, but it's not fair of me to take it out on you." She reached for her cup. "Sorry."

He held it, her fingers touching his, and he searched for the angle on her apology. There was always an angle.

Then again, her last apology had been angle-free, something he was still wrapping his mind around.

Her stare pushed into him and softened. "I really am sorry."

He released her cup. "Forgiven."

"Harlow?" Darcy stood a few feet away. "We should get back."

"I'll see you in Budapest?" he asked.

"Pretty sure that's what my ticket says."

Darcy and Harlow disappeared down the long hall, and Blake returned to his gate. They weren't on the same airline, and he had no idea what one the women were on. But he could find out.

He picked up his phone and dialed Charlie.

"Hey, where you at?" Charlie's deep voice boomed.

"Same airport as you."

"Really? Where?"

"A little coffee shop where I happened to run into your girlfriend and Harlow."

"Happened to, huh?" Charlie laughed.

"Actually, they ran into me."

"Sure."

Blake ignored the disbelieving tone. "Listen, they're coming back your way, and I need a favor."

"Name it."

"What airline are you on?" He grabbed a pen.

"Why? You planning on joining us?" Charlie's disbelieving tone turned to one of pure interest.

"Just tell me."

"We're flying out on Lufthansa."

He jotted it on the sleeve of his coffee cup. "Thanks."

"Hey, hold up."

Blake stuck the phone back to his ear. "Yeah?"

"What time are you getting in?"

"Nine local time."

"I beat you by a little over an hour." Charlie yawned. "I plan on laying low for a bit, getting settled, and Dale has me in an afternoon meeting, but do you want to meet Darce and me for an early dinner?"

"Sure. Give me a call when you get in."

"You got it."

They hung up and Blake called Lufthansa.

Five long hours later his cab pulled up in front of his hotel. Blake cursed. The Four Seasons.

He was too tired to deal with this.

He got out and paid his cabby. If his clothes hadn't already been delivered to his room, he'd ditch the place. But he wanted a shower and a bed too badly. Mainly the bed for now. He'd deal with Dale later. The man was fully aware of how Blake felt about this place.

He didn't even pause, stalked straight to his room, and fell onto the bed. He woke to a knock on his door. Stumbling over, he checked the peephole, then opened up.

Jace brushed past him. "I know you love The Four Seasons."

"You're way too awake."

"Hyped up on caffeine."

And who knew what else.

"What time is it?" Blake opened his dresser. Someone had filled it with his clothes before he even entered the room.

"Three. But we're all starved."

"Give me a minute." He pulled out a T-shirt and pair of khakis. "I'm gonna grab a shower. Make yourself comfortable."

"I think I will. Your suite is larger than mine."

"I'd be happy to switch hotels and let you have this room."

Jace snorted. "You really do hate this place, don't you?"

"Drop it." Blake walked to the bathroom. "Did you need something, or can I take my shower?"

"Darcy said you ran into Harlow at the airport."

Blake slammed the bathroom door. Unfortunately, Jace's laughter still seeped through it with ease. Only reinforced his belief that for all the fancy decorations, The Four Seasons was still cheap. Or maybe it was the owner.

Flipping on the water, he cranked it to near scalding, hoping to burn away his memories before they chased too far. Fifteen minutes later the bathroom was steamed, but Blake was cooler.

He towel dried his hair and pulled on his clothes, ready to get out of this hotel. Filming started tomorrow. They'd begin with a few shots at certain sights around Budapest, and then he was scheduled for a date. His first one-on-one.

Who stayed was up to Blake, but the order of dates was all Dale.

Which meant tomorrow constituted a blind date.

As Blake walked through the large sitting room, Jace flipped off the TV. "About time. Nothing on here to watch, and I'm starved."

"Where's the other two?"

"They're waiting in the lobby. We want to find a little café and have dinner."

"All right. Let's go."

His phone rang before he made it out of his room. He snagged it, and Mom's grin greeted him. At least he pretended the smile was meant for him. Following Jace into the hall, he slid his finger over the screen. "Hey, Mom."

"You were supposed to keep Natalie."

Blake searched for a face to go with the name but came up short. "The women I kept are fine."

"Fine?" She sipped on a drink. "I expect more than fine. So do viewers. And so does the network."

He held his silence.

"I need this show, Blake."

And he wanted his mother to be healthy.

He sighed. "Don't worry, Mom. You'll have your show."

"Then listen to Dale. The man knows what he's talking about."

"Fine." They met Darcy and Charlie in the lobby. "I've got to go. Dinner is waiting."

"Nothing fattening. And nothing that would make a bad picture."

"No one's taking my picture out here."

She laughed. "Always believe you're on camera, Blake."

A motto that drove her happiness while grinding his to a stop.

Mom hung up, and Blake looked at his friends. "What's on the menu?"

"Goulash." Darcy rubbed her hands together.

Charlie tugged her close. "Soft and warm, just like me."

Groaning behind her huge grin, Darcy leaned into him, and they walked out to the street.

What would it be like to have that?

Jace stopped, casting a glance over his shoulder. "You coming?"

"Sure."

Only he worried he'd never really get there.

Chapter Twelve

Harlow dropped onto the bed and every muscle relaxed. Who knew they made mattresses so soft? Tarynn flopped onto the queen size across from her. They arrived at The Four Seasons a few hours ago, but there'd been a meeting in one of the banquet rooms downstairs. She'd nodded off a few times during it, but who could blame her? She'd been awake more hours than she could count.

Finally, they'd assigned the rooms and sent them off with a free schedule for the rest of the day. Not that she needed the freedom for anything other than sleeping at this point.

Luckily, she was paired with Tarynn as a roomie. Of the women left, Tarynn was the one she felt most comfortable with. They'd come up to unpack, something that appeared would take Tarynn all day.

"Still can't believe you gave up your first class seat on our last flight." Tarynn lugged her suitcase onto her bed.

"That woman needed it more than me. I wasn't even supposed to have it in the first place."

Tarynn unzipped her bag. "I know. How'd you get so lucky, anyway?"

Harlow still wondered herself.

And half-suspected. But didn't dare guess.

Her roommate slipped into the bathroom with the largest toiletry bag Harlow had ever seen. "The girls were already jealous of you, and now they're boiling over with it—even if you did give your seat away. In fact, that only made it worse."

"Wait. What?" Harlow followed her.

"You didn't know?" Tarynn pulled out a flat iron. "The other women don't exactly like you right now."

Harlow perched on the edge of the enormous whirlpool. "Why?"

"You really don't know?"

"No."

"Because Blake has an obvious connection with you. Why do you think Dale had him wait to give you the last phone the other night?"

"What?" Serious confusion flooded her.

Tarynn hopped up on the counter, facing her. "You cannot be this clueless."

"Sorry." Harlow shrugged. "Afraid I am. I've never even seen a full episode of one of these shows."

"Come again?"

"Not one—well, I guess I did watch the last finale of *Gamble on Love*." She ran a hand along the white marble tile surrounding the tub. "Dale had Blake call me last?"

Tarynn nodded. "Better TV. There's a real chemistry with you, and Carmen is jealous, so you two were the last names. Draws out the drama."

So much for the real in reality. Not that she'd put much stock in it to begin with.

Tarynn studied her perfect heart-shaped face in the large mirror hanging over the tub. "Did your sister really nominate you for this show?"

"Yes."

"No one believes that story."

"Seriously?"

"Yes." She swung her long tan legs. What Harlow would give to have legs like that. "They all think it was a ploy to get on the show. Most of them doubt your sister is even sick."

Tears welled in Harlow's eyes. "I wish." She stood. All she wanted right now was to crawl into her bed and sleep.

"Hey, wait." Tarynn put a hand on her shoulder. "Hey. Didn't mean to make you cry. Your sister really is sick?"

"Limb Girdle Muscular Dystrophy."

"Wow." The word slipped past Tarynn's lips. "I don't even know what that is, but wow. Is she ... will she?"

"No." Harlow squared her shoulders. "God's going to heal her."

Tarynn's eyes softened. "Okay." After a few moments of awkward silence, she finished unpacking her toiletries. "I bet you'll get the first one-on-one date."

After their interaction over airport coffee, Harlow highly doubted it. Still, she hoped to corner Blake and ask about her upgrade. "Not likely."

"Care to bet on it?"

"No." She'd already wagered enough by coming on the show.

Tarynn grabbed a few clothes from her suitcase and returned to the bathroom. "I'm going to get cleaned up. A few of us are talking about exploring the town and grabbing dinner later. You want to come?"

Her nearly twenty-four-hour day was catching up with her. "No. I'm good. Think I'll take a nap."

"You sure? I hear the best thing is to stay up as long as you can."

"I don't think I could even if I wanted to at this point."

"All right." Tarynn closed the bathroom door.

A few seconds later the shower turned on, the patter lulling her to sleep. When she woke, the room was dark. She checked the clock. It was the middle of the night. Across from her, Tarynn snored softly. She'd never heard her leave or come back. Slept like a rock.

And now she was wide awake at four a.m. and hungry. She should have bucked up and gone with the girls. Maybe she could find a movie. Flicking on the TV she muted it and tried for subtitles. Except she didn't speak Hungarian.

No phone—other than the one Blake would call her on—and no laptop meant no scrolling social media to kill time. Her brain was too fuzzy to stare at all the numbers and unnecessarily complicated words in her books on marketing and business plans. She did have her camera though, and several SD cards yet to fill. Taking a few pictures might help clear her head enough, so she could at least brainstorm more creative ideas for raising money. Auctioning her wardrobe from the show wouldn't bring in dollars anytime soon—if it even worked at all. Who knew how they'd edit her? She might not even be around long enough to wear half the things Darcy had chosen for her.

She shoved her hands into her pockets and an edge of paper sliced her fingertip. Jerking, she tugged out Marty Pontelle's business card. She'd worn these jeans to travel to Malibu, then packed them in her suitcase, forgetting all about his card. His offer teased the corner of her mind. She shoved it away and tossed the card into the trash. The man wasn't worth her time or thoughts. Blake might not be her favorite person, but he didn't deserve someone playing him. Even if he was a player himself.

With incredible eyes. Great cheekbones. Tight jaw. One picture of that face *could* be worth—

She needed out of this room and an entirely different face to focus on.

Using the bathroom light to see, Harlow grabbed her camera, slipped on her Toms and scooted out the door.

She took the elevator to the lobby, then found the front desk. Her reflection in one of the mirrors stopped her cold. Yeah. Should have maybe changed out of her wrinkled clothes and possibly run a brush through her hair. She breathed into her cupped hand. Toothpaste would have helped too.

Luckily, she had Tic-Tacs in her camera bag.

Popping one, she continued toward registration, smoothing down her hair as she walked. No restaurants inside were open right now, but maybe someone could help her scrounge up something to snack on. It was The Four Seasons for cripes sake. They hadn't earned a five-star status by ignoring their guests.

One man stood behind the counter. He peered over the rim of his glasses, not a hair out of place. "How can I help you?"

"I wondered if there were any restaurants within walking distance that might be open all night?"

He raised his thick gray brows. "None that are a close enough for you to safely walk to at this time of night, miss." He put down his pen. "If you're hungry, I can have room service bring something up."

"I don't want to wake my roommate." Harlow swept her gaze around the lobby. "And I can't sleep, so I thought some fresh air would help me out."

The man nodded. "I see." He grabbed a piece of paper and handed it to her. "Then I suggest you pick a sandwich from this menu. I'll have room service bring it here, and you can take it outside." He pointed to the large glass doors off the front lobby. "There's a bench through there that is only steps away from our doorman and has a magnificent view of the Chain Bridge. Food, fresh air, and scenery you won't want to miss."

Harlow returned his smile and then quickly scanned the menu. "I'll take the avocado, bacon, and tomato sandwich. Only no bacon please."

He nodded and placed the order.

A scrolled mosaic pattern created the lobby floor, and one of the largest handblown glass chandeliers hung from the wide, open atrium. It was so quiet here. Harlow snapped a few pictures, following the pattern to the iron gate at the front. She studied each part of it, discovering tiny birds molded at the top. Every detail of the entire entry was breathtaking.

"Miss? Your dinner is ready." A gentleman held her plate and a bottle of water.

"Thanks."

Letting her camera hang from her neck, she took her snack and slipped toward the entry. Her hand didn't even reach it before the doorman swung it open.

"Thanks," she said again. In a place like this, she'd be using that word a lot.

She stepped outside and immediately discovered a different city than the one she'd fallen asleep in. During the daytime, the architecture of Budapest intrigued her. But this? This was breathtaking. The Chain Bridge lit up like a golden torch in the night. She'd never seen anything like it. Behind it, on the Buda side of the Danube, Buda Castle flamed into the black sky also. The two stood like buildings from a lost city of gold.

Entranced, Harlow set her food on the nearby bench and picked up her camera. She snapped off several frames, the beauty behind her lens unlike any object she'd captured before.

Movement to her left caught her attention. Illuminated by the city lights, the doorman handed off a brown bag to a crippled man who shuffled by. Without conscious thought, she captured the moment.

The very end of the opulent bridge. The tailored suit of the doorman. The red scarf wrapped around the old man's neck, his gnarled hands touching the softness of the doorman's.

Least of these.

That doorman catered to movie stars, debutantes, tycoons of all ages. Those same hands that grasped the affluent and received their riches, now freely gave to the poor.

She snapped again as the old man disappeared into the darkness. The doorman's gaze strayed her way. Harlow offered a small wave. He nodded and returned to his post.

Grumbling rolled across her stomach, and she put down her camera. Time to eat and enjoy being here. It still felt like a dream. One she'd desired for years, but it took Mae asking for it to finally be fulfilled.

And being here would allow her to help fulfill Mae's dreams.

She munched a bite, letting the cool breeze clear her mind, and finished her snack before returning inside. Clearheaded and full, she could start work on Wheels on the Ground.

Except Tarynn wouldn't be up yet. It was only nearing five. Guess she'd kill another hour down here with her camera before heading up for her things.

Harlow returned her dishes to the front desk, then studied the lobby. Down the hallway a large wooden door opened to—she had no idea. She beelined for it and stepped inside. A large oval staircase circled the room and led to a stained glass-windowed ceiling.

And she thought the lobby's chandelier had been breathtaking.

Pulling her camera to her face, she snapped the intricate details of the handrail. Then she aimed up and grabbed a shot of it winding all the way to the ceiling. She checked her screen. Hmm ... not quite what she wanted.

She lay down on the mosaic floor and started shooting.

"That seems comfortable."

A deep voice broke the silence around her.

She gasped. Turned.

One of the cameramen leaned against the door frame. He was wiry and tall, though not as tall as Blake, with sandy blond hair messed to perfection. She'd seen him around but hadn't spoken more than two words to him.

"You startled me." She sat up and capped her lens.

"Sorry." He didn't move from the door. "I saw you come in with your camera. Interesting angle."

She stood and brushed her hands off. "I look at things differently, I suppose."

"Good mindset to have." He ambled closer, his dark brown eyes roaming over her. "I'm Tad, by the way."

"I've seen you around," she acknowledged. "I'm Harlow."

"Yeah. I know."

This close, she caught a whiff of him and wrinkled her nose. Apparently he'd visited the bar—or several—last night. "I think I'll grab a few more shots of the lobby."

He grinned, showing a row of perfect white teeth. Did everyone in Hollywood get their teeth done?

"I don't know," he said. "I like the view in here."

"It's great." She moved to step around him. "But I already have what I need."

He intercepted her step, coming closer. His breath could make kittens cry. "You sure?"

"Quite." She stood still. He seemed to like whatever game he thought he was playing. Rather than join him, she held his gaze, unblinking.

"All right." He finally relinquished, though his tone remained overly confident. "But there's a lot more here if you change your mind."

"Doubtful."

Tad didn't move until she did, then he adjusted his stance so she'd have to brush against him to leave. Harlow held in her shudder. He didn't scare her. More like repulsed her.

She exited the stairwell, Tad so close on her step she could still smell him. Made her stomach curl. A sign for bathrooms was on her left, and she executed a quick turn. "Need to use the facilities." She ducked inside.

"Night, Harlow." Amusement lined his words.

She didn't even answer him, just let the door shut on his voice, then leaned against it for good measure. Apparently creeps were everywhere, and could hide their personality well, because she'd never have pegged Tad for one. He could try and blame the alcohol, but she wasn't biting. All it did was loosen inhibitions, not change who you were.

After counting to sixty, she slowly opened the door and peeked out. Clear. She slipped through and started toward the elevators.

"Evening."

She jumped for the second time tonight, but this voice had her blood pumping for completely different reasons. Which bothered her even more.

"Blake." How had she missed him? "Apparently no one's able to sleep."

He pushed off the wall he leaned against and advanced on her, hands in his pockets and jaw tight. "That's what I thought when I saw you and Tate together. You two seem to have found quite the cozy rendezvous."

She stepped back. "Excuse me?"

"You and Tate—"

"You mean Tad?" What was it with him and names?

"Right. Tad. I saw you two coming out of the stairwell." Blake's low laugh rolled across her nerves. "You do play the innocent well."

"Maybe because I am."

"Sure." He looked over her shoulder, as if she wasn't even worth a glance. "But I should warn you. You're playing a dangerous game. If Dale finds out you're seeing one of the production crew, he'll throw you off."

She hadn't done a blessed thing. "I'm not lying." That he even questioned it. "I *don't* lie. So go right ahead and tell Dale whatever you'd like."

Blake leaned into her face, cool eyes now squarely focused on her. "Maybe I will."

Several words came to mind, most of which she'd never even wanted to use before. But one she could say rose to the top. "Sad."

"What is?" Blake straightened but didn't loosen his stare.

"That you are so willing to believe the worst in people." She turned. "Tell Dale what you want to, Blake. I have a feeling you wouldn't believe me even if you'd actually asked for the truth." Harlow left him standing by the bathrooms.

She walked across the lobby to the elevators. No way she'd check behind. Not that she cared if he was following her. Okay. She cared a little. The elevator dinged, and she stepped on, alone.

Fire lit through her.

Only problem was she didn't know where to aim it.

Blake for assuming the worse about her.

Or herself, for caring.

Chapter Thirteen

Blake perched himself on the massive stone base of one of the statues in Hero's Square. A column stretched from the center of the base nearly one hundred feet into the air, topped with a statue of the archangel Gabriel. Encircling that column were seven men on horses—more like Clydesdales on steroids—who were meant to represent the tribes that had settled the area. Over time, all the bronze statues had oxidized into a greenish hue.

The place was impressive, he'd give them that. About fifty feet behind the column ran a stone section filled with fourteen more statues, not that he had a clue who any of them were. Still, made for a unique place to people watch. Something he was currently doing while waiting for whoever Dale had chosen for the first one-on-one. In the distance, he and the production crew discussed the best shots for her arrival.

Sunshine beat down on Blake from the cloudless sky, and he shifted into the shade of the statues. Darcy would kill him if he started to sweat. She'd already seen to it that his forehead wouldn't shine and now was somewhere working on whichever woman was on her way here.

Dale sauntered over. "We're going to have the car drop her there." He pointed to a spot in front of the Museum of Fine Art. "We've already grabbed a few wide shots. Charlie and Alex will be with you. Tad's already with her."

"Are you going to tell me who 'her' is?"

"Nope." He held out a thick ream of papers. "You read the shooting script for today?"

"I did." Blake nodded. "We're starting here, grabbing lunch in the park as we walk through to the Széchenyi Baths for a swim, and then dinner tonight at the Budapest Zoo."

Dale's cell rang, and he grabbed it, listened for a second, then hung up. "Sounds like they're a few minutes out. You better get in place."

Showtime.

Blake waited in the center of the large stone area for the black town car from The Four Seasons to arrive. Within minutes, it pulled up. The back door opened, and Tim—no, wait, Tad—stepped out, followed by a pair of skinny jeans filled with shapely legs. That was the only glimpse he had before Tad blocked his view.

It wasn't until the car pulled away, and Tad took a few steps backwards, that Blake could see who he had a date with.

He tightened his jaw.

Harlow.

Bet she enjoyed her ride over with the man.

"You okay?" Charlie asked from behind his camera.

"Fine." Blake approached the two, his gut churning. He could do this. He'd had years of practice at putting on the right face.

Reaching them, he plastered on the smile that had landed him in *People's* Most Sexy and engulfed Harlow in a hug. "Great to see you."

She stiffened in his arms, not returning the embrace. Probably awkward for her in front of Tad. "I was surprised to find my name on the envelope this morning," she said as she extracted herself from their hug.

"I was surprised to see you step out of the car."

Tad moved in close, and Harlow shifted away. She was smart enough to know Dale was watching too. But then she cut Tad a glance from the corner of her eye and scooched closer to Blake.

"So where are we going?" Tension wrapped her words.

Blake scanned from Tad to Harlow. "We're starting in this square and then—" Wait. It suddenly became crystal clear why Dale put her on this date, and that reason bothered him more than his suspicions—ones he now questioned—over her and Tad.

"Then what?" She peered up at him, shading her eyes from the sun.

"The baths." Because Dale knew she couldn't swim.

Her jaw tightened, but as Charlie's camera shifted, she unclenched it and added a grin. "Sounds fun."

He knew a fake smile when he saw one. Hers didn't even wobble.

He dipped to her ear. "I didn't know."

"Sure you didn't." Her tone wasn't even close to convincing. "Why don't you lead the way?"

"Harlow." Suddenly it was important she believe him. "I didn't pick you for this date."

An emotion clouded her eyes. Disappointment? Sadness? Either way, she blinked it away. "I'm not sure if that makes it better or worse."

What did that even mean?

She wasn't offering him the chance to find out, just slipped her hands into the pockets of her jeans and repeated, "Now, please, lead the way."

"All right." He sighed. This date was off to an awesome start.

They strolled the perimeter of the square, Harlow's attention on the statues while his rested straight on her. She had those dark skinny jeans that fit her perfectly and a simple white tank. Over that she wore a scarf swirled with several colors. The greenish blue in it matched her eyes like it was made for them. Her soft hair fell against her shoulders in a few loose waves. At least he assumed it was soft.

He reached out and snagged a strand before thinking through the movement.

She stopped and raised a brow.

"You had a bug," he lied.

Charlie coughed, and Blake silenced him with a look.

They completed their circle without another word between them. Harlow gazed one more time around the square. "Well, it's definitely a large area."

"It is."

"With several big statues." She tapped her finger against her teeth.

So. He wasn't the only one underwhelmed by Herald Square. He jumped on the common ground they'd uncovered.

"Not much more to see here, is there?"

"Not really." She grimaced. "Is that completely awful to say?"

"No. It's honest." His own words shifted inside. They seemed to fit her, and that realization supplied more answers to his questions over last night. "Want to take a walk? See if there's more to see?"

"I'd like that."

She didn't offer him her hand. Didn't lean into him. But she kept pace, even with her short stride. When she wasn't in heels, the top of her head barely even reached his shoulder. If he ever kissed her, she'd need a step stool.

Blake shook his head.

She peered up at him, squinting against the sun.

"Didn't you bring sunglasses?" he asked.

"Forgot them."

He pulled his off and handed them to her. "You won't make a fashion statement in these, but they'll keep you from getting a headache."

"No. You keep them, or you'll get one."

"Doubtful. I mean, we're on a date which requires us talking. I look down to do that. But you, Shorty, have to look up. That's a lot of time spent staring into the sun."

Would she take them, or would she only care about her appearance?

Harlow cocked her hip and stuck her hand on it. "You're assuming you'll keep the conversation interesting enough for me to participate in it."

"You doubt my charm?" He kept his voice light.

She grunted, but the first true smile he'd seen from her today lit her face, and it nearly blew him away. Taking the sunglasses from him, her soft fingers brushed against his. "Thanks." She plopped the oversized frames on her face. "Where to?"

She was going to wear them? Without even a glance at the cameras or a request for a pair that fit? He swallowed his amazement. "Uh, this way."

Blake pointed to a walkway that led to a park-like area. "We can cross here." Dale had given him a map to study earlier, and this would take them to the baths.

Which now made such perfect, sick sense.

Harlow couldn't swim, and Dale was sticking them on water. Blake clenched his fists and slowed his pace. No reason to rush.

They crested the hill and a lazy river came into view. Small paddle boats painted like race cars made their way up and down the area. Even a few gondolas floated nearby. He nodded to the stone bridge that covered the small river. Harlow joined him and they leaned over, watching the other couples paddling their boats.

"Are you enjoying Budapest?"

She turned to face him. "I haven't seen much yet. Still can't believe I'm actually here."

"What are you most looking forward to seeing?"

"All of it."

"Come on. There's got to be something specific rolling around in that head of yours that you're itching to take a picture of."

She hesitated a moment. "People."

Not the answer he expected, nor the one he wanted. "People?"

He obviously hadn't hidden the heat in his voice, because she tensed. "Yes, people. I want to show the side of Budapest so often overlooked."

"Which one? Buda or Pest?"

"I meant the poor side. The rich is so evident."

Her answer set him further on edge. "Something wrong with being rich?"

"Not at all." She straightened. "Unfortunately, many of the poor are seen through very judgmental eyes, if they're even seen at all."

"Same could be said of the rich."

Her eyes softened. "I wasn't intending my comment to be taken personally. It's just ... I see the world differently through my camera lens, and it often lands on the people I feel are most forgotten. For me, that tends to be the poor. I guess I never thought about the rich." Her hand slid over his and squeezed. "But anyone can feel a little forgotten at times."

The tenderness in her voice swept his earlier annoyance away and pulled his gaze toward hers. "I was referring to the judgmental part of your statement." He flicked his eyes to the cameras and back to her. "I *wish* I could feel forgotten at times."

"Trust me, it's not all it's cracked up to be."

He didn't miss the way emotion so tightened her throat that she had to clear it. Yeah. He knew what that was like, answers slipping off your tongue while you thought they were still swirling through your mind.

Dale's voice came over Blake's earpiece "Push her on it, Blake. Get me the tears, then comfort her." While Blake might want to know what caused her hurt, the idea of manipulating her to share it for better ratings made him as nauseated as suggesting they eat from one of the vendors he'd seen earlier selling insects on a stick. Neither was going to happen.

Instead he chose his own topic. "Tell me more about your photography."

Pure joy replaced any lingering heartache.

He could get used to that.

And patiently wait to uncover the root of the sadness she'd nearly exposed.

Apparently Dale couldn't.

"Not what I asked for, Blake."

Enough. He twisted down the volume of his earpiece and then started walking. "So, photography? You seem pretty attached to your camera."

Harlow fell in step with him. "I don't really know how to explain it, except to say I feel like I see people the way God intended when I pick it up. I'll catch a moment, and a word will click in place with it. Like the other day I watched an old homeless man take a little boy by the hand to lead him back to his house, and I thought, *found*. Like that's what God does for us. We're wandering around lost, and he takes our hand and leads us back to our home, which just happens to be with him."

"And you'd like to capture moments like that here, in Budapest."

"I would."

"Your faith sounds important to you." He kicked at a stone.

"Faith is important to me. It's not to you?"

"I've seen a lot of scripted things in my life. Faith is one of them." He looked down at her. "I won't downplay people who believe, but for me, it rates right up there with fairy tales."

She frowned. "Then you've been around the wrong people. God is very real."

"If he is, he's never introduced himself to me."

"Have you ever asked him to?"

They took a few more steps. "Can't say that I have."

"Maybe you should try."

Charlie kept his eyes trained on the camera, but Blake saw the grin. Probably in cahoots with Harlow. Beside him, Alex held the boom, and both of them walked backwards. How they never tripped, he didn't know. Tad was behind their group, which was good, as Harlow seemed to relax when he wasn't around. A theory he suddenly wanted to test.

"You won't be going out on your own to take these pictures, will you?"

"I don't see why not." She shrugged. "You don't expect me to sit around the hotel waiting for you to call, do you?"

"Funny." He directed them toward the bright yellow awning of a restaurant next to the canoe rentals. "Seriously though, Harlow, you shouldn't be wandering these streets by yourself." Not with that deep red hair of hers—when the sun caught it at the right angle, it came alive like fire—and how petite she was. She'd make an easy target for pickpockets or worse.

Especially when she lost all sense of her surroundings with that camera in her face. He'd proven as much when he startled her back in Abundance.

She stopped at the restaurant entrance. "We're here to have lunch, right? Not get on those things." She pointed to the gondolas.

"You're not going off on your own to take pictures."

"We're not getting on those boats."

She was impossible. Before he could think through his actions, he gently reached out and grabbed her chin, then tilted her face to his.

Charlie zoomed in close, but Blake ignored him. They weren't scheduled to ride the boats, but Harlow didn't need to know that. "I'll make you a deal. You don't go off taking pictures around the city, and I won't make you get on one of those canoes."

She smiled. "Again, you're assuming an awful lot." She pulled her chin from his hand. "Mainly that you have the power to make a deal with me."

Blake didn't have to see Charlie to know the man was grinning again. Tad, however, wore a large scowl.

Blake straightened. "How about I have production send someone with you?" He nodded at Tad. "You wouldn't mind, would you?"

Tad's scowl turned into an easy grin. "Not in the least."

"No." Her eyebrows rose above the frames of his Aviators. "I was only giving you a hard time."

And he'd just learned two things.

One, Harlow had no interest in Tad.

And two, Tad was entirely too interested in Harlow.

"Let's eat." He placed his hand on the small of her back.

She tipped her gaze up at him. "No gondolas?"

"You really want to?"

"No."

"Then no gondolas. Besides, if I was going to take you on one of those, I'd do it in Venice." He steered her away from the restaurant.

"I thought we were going to eat lunch."

"We are, only not here." He led her over another stone bridge and to the castle. "You really haven't seen one of these shows before, have you?"

She laughed. "I watched one episode."

"This season I hope you'll be around for more than that."

*

They strolled over the bridge and through the castle grounds. Violin music floated on the air, and as they rounded a corner, an arbor of trees created an intimate setting for their lunch. White linen draped a small white table with two iron chairs side-by-side. On top, silver domes covered what she assumed was their food, and a couple of large wine glasses stood beside them.

Blake escorted her to the table, his hand warm on her back. This morning had been all over the place. From awkward tension to laughter. She still wasn't sure what she thought of him—or what he believed about her—yet they seemed to have found their wobbly footing, and it headed in a direction she suddenly wanted to explore, because it looked like territory where they just might get along. He'd immediately put her at ease. It felt natural. Her defenses didn't feel quite as strong as she'd thought.

He pulled out her chair, and she sat down.

"Thanks."

"My pleasure."

And it probably was. To him, this was all old hat. According to his reality, dates like this were the norm, along with what they led to. Women fell for his charm, and none of it was real. Real people went to Applebee's, not a private table in the middle of a castle in Budapest.

And real people didn't have cameramen following them everywhere. Ever since she opened the door and found Tad on the opposite end of today's camera, she had to fight the tremor up her spine. It was bad enough to feel his stare on her last night, but knowing he could watch her, zoom in on her, film her from behind the comfort of that camera gave her the creeps.

Blake's distaste for photographers clicked into crystal clear focus.

"Want to take a peek?" He pointed to her platter.

Harlow placed her hand on top and pushed the thoughts of Tad out. "Count of three?"

He nodded. "One, two, three."

They pulled the tops off and found a gourmet meal underneath. Lamb, baby potatoes, asparagus. Whatever spices they used tickled her nose in a good way.

"No onions or garlic I'm guessing." The edge of his lip tipped up.

She set the silver dome to her right. "There you go assuming again."

"That they'd skip those ingredients?"

"That you'd need them to."

His rich laughter echoed around them. "Nice."

She sliced into her lamb and took the first bite. Never in her life had she tasted something so flavorful. It would take all her restraint not to inhale the entire plate full. And that flourless chocolate torte covered in raspberries sitting on a crystal stand in the center of the table? Sigh. She missed chocolate.

"Wine?" He held up the bottle.

"No thanks."

He set it back down, leaving his glass empty. "Okay. What gives? You said you drink, and I've yet to see you take a drop."

"I do drink." She lifted her shoulder. "Water, tea, coffee ..."

"Nice play on words." Laughing, he uncapped the water and poured her some.

"Thanks." She nodded to the other bottle. "You can have some wine if you'd like."

"I'm good."

After dealing with a drunk Tad last night, Blake's answer was a relief.

Tad moved in closer, his camera aimed on her face. Nearly made her skin crawl. Made it itch to say the least.

"What's wrong?" Blake scooped a bite of potato into his mouth.

Harlow shook her head. "Just hungry."

He looked at Charlie and then at Tad. Finally he settled his gaze back on her. "Eat up then."

Lunch was one of the most delicious meals she'd had in years. It didn't hurt that their conversation flowed easy now, even with the cameras around.

Still, she needed to remember this wasn't real. Today was the first in a week-long line of dates. He was probably handed a script this morning covering key points of interest to keep them dialoguing. Either that or someone was feeding him questions. She might not see them, but somewhere out there was a production crew who watched everything being filmed. She squirmed under their attention, the afternoon wearing on her. How did Blake live like this?

She sipped the last of her water and pushed away from the table. "Do you know if there's a restroom close by?"

Charlie pointed to an area at the foot of the castle. "By those double doors."

"If you'll excuse me." She hurried for them.

How long was too long to comfortably stay in a bathroom without embarrassing herself? She didn't even need to use it, but took advantage of the moment and then waited five minutes. The coolness of the stone wall steadied her as the second hand on her watch clicked down the minutes.

At the five-minute mark, she slipped into the corridor, following its narrow path back to the castle grounds. Three feet from the opening, someone snagged her arm and pulled her behind a wall. She gasped but immediately recognized the limey scent.

Blake's fingers brushed against her back, and she flinched. "What are you doing?"

"Having two seconds to really talk to you." He pulled his sunglasses off her face. "And I'd like to see your eyes when I do this."

"Do what?"

A chuckle escaped before he stopped it, his jaw tightening. "Apologize."

She pulled her thoughts from the fact she made him nervous to the word he'd uttered. "Apologize?"

"For last night."

Her face heated. "Oh."

"I was completely out of line, and I'm sorry." His eyes in this light were such a deep blue they were nearly black. And they watched her intensely. The man confused her. Rude yesterday, but uncharacteristically kind right now. Which side was the true Blake?

"It's okay."

He leaned down. "It's not, and I apologize." His warm breath touched her cheek. "Tad gave you a hard time, right?"

"Nothing I couldn't handle."

"If he does it again, let me know."

Charlie stepped around the corner. "You need to flip your mics on and get moving."

Once again, Blake's touch ran along her back.

She startled. "You turned my mic off?"

He smiled and fidgeted with his own next.

"Why didn't they ..." She nodded at Charlie. "Let me guess, your accomplice?"

"A man needs a few tricks up his sleeve."

"I have a feeling you've got more than a few."

Blake offered her his arm. "The day's not over yet."

Chapter Fourteen

Széchenyi Baths stood tall and ornate, its columns and white stone carved into an impressive structure. If Harlow didn't know what was inside, she'd want to explore it. Unfortunately, she knew what awaited her.

"Beautiful, isn't it?" Blake's calm voice tickled her ear.

"From this spot, sure." She attempted to smile up at him.

He grabbed her hand. "Come on. It'll be fun. Promise."

She didn't even bother to call him on the lie.

Darcy waited for them on the front steps along with a crew. "I have your swimsuits inside." She pulled open the front door. "Come on with me."

Harlow edged inside, taking in the expansive circular stone lobby with hallways shooting off in several directions. "We have this whole place to ourselves? It's huge."

"You have no idea." Darcy started down the hall to the right. "And we only have it for a few hours, so we need to get you changed fast."

"Where are we starting?" Blake followed them.

Charlie, Tad, and Alex broke off to meet with Dale while Darcy pointed Blake to a large wooden door. "You start in there. Get your suit on and someone will escort you where you need to be." She opened the door opposite and waved to Harlow. "I'll be in here with Harlow."

"Hey. Aren't I supposed to be the one who—"

"You already look great." Darcy silenced him with a grin.

"And I don't?" Harlow paused.

"I certainly have no complaints." He coated those words in that low caramelly baritone that oozed through the cracks in her defenses.

Luckily, Darcy pushed her through the door before he witnessed the flame in her cheeks. "Wait till I'm through with her."

They left him standing there, and Darcy directed Harlow through her dressing room to a wooden bench on the other side. Laying on it was the smallest bikini she had ever seen. The sight of it cooled the heat Blake had just stoked. "Um. You don't expect me to wear that, do you?"

Darcy picked it up. "You have the body for it."

"Not everyone needs to see it, though."

"I'm sure Blake wouldn't mind."

Harlow crossed her arms over her chest. "I would."

Darcy laughed. "I'm teasing you. I have a few others I thought you might like better." She dropped the turquoise string bikini. "That one's standard issue, but I had a feeling you'd prefer something with a little more to it."

"Oh, bless you." She snatched the black tankini Darcy held out.

"You're welcome." She pointed to the other door. "There's a changing room through there. Then we'll take care of your hair and touch-up your makeup."

Harlow quickly changed and returned to sit for her hair. Darcy hauled out her brush and started.

"Hey, you're trembling." She put a hand on Harlow's shoulder. "It was wrong of Dale to put you on today's date, but Blake will watch out for you. He's a good guy."

Harlow was starting to see that.

She peeked up at Darcy. "Thanks."

"You're welcome." She fidgeted with a few more strands of Harlow's hair and then spun her toward the mirror. "Not too perfect, but cute."

Twisted into a knot at her neck with a few wisps that framed her face. "I like it."

"Then get out there." Darcy pushed her through the door.

"What about my mic?"

"Alex has a different set-up because we're shooting in the pool. He'll take care of it."

"Oh. Okay."

Blake waited in the hall, his face pulling into a full, warm smile when he saw her. "Beautiful."

"Thanks." Her stare latched on to the large scar puckering a line from the right side of his collarbone up and around his shoulder.

"Get a good look?" His dark brown brows raised as his lips twitched.

A good look, yes. An answer, no. And she desperately wanted to know how he'd gotten hurt.

"Come on." He placed his hands on her shoulders, stepping in front of Tad's camera, and gently pushed her down the hall. "There's a room down here for us."

Apparently she wasn't going to get an explanation—or the chance to ask.

They stopped at a large wooden door and slipped inside. Charlie stood with his camera—small mic attached—blocking Tad's entrance. "It's a tight squeeze in here. How about you set up the outside shots?" Charlie instructed over his shoulder.

Tad didn't budge until Charlie started to turn his wide frame. Something passed between them that had Tad backing down.

Harlow barely registered their stare-down though. She studied Blake.

"Sauna instead of the pool?" Her nerves started to settle and warmth flitted through her—and not because of the steam rolling out of the room. "Did you do this?"

He shrugged. "I don't plan these dates, remember?"

She stood on her tiptoes and reached her lips as close to his ear as she could. "Thank you."

His bicep tensed beneath her palm. "You're welcome."

He shifted slightly, his nearness coupled with the look in his eyes tempted her more than the chocolate dessert at lunch. Both hinted at delicious promises— ones she'd committed to avoid. Snapping out of it, she backed away to the long wooden bench and sat, beads of sweat already dripping between her shoulder blades. No matter. It was a hundred times better than the pools outside.

Blake joined her. So much for putting a little distance between them. "That suit was made for you," he said.

She tugged at the fabric around her stomach. "Um, thanks."

They sat in comfortable silence, the steam providing privacy. Still, Charlie was filming, so she remained quiet.

Blake didn't.

"Why can't you swim, Harlow?"

His face was hidden behind a cloud of steam, but his leg brushed against hers, shooting heat through her of a different kind. Between the physical attraction sparking and the tenderness in his voice, something was shifting

121

between them. She wanted to be daring enough to follow the change. To trust him with her honest answer. But putting herself out there with a guy again freaked her out. Not to mention, Charlie sat across from them recording every word. So she gave the easy answer instead.

"I guess I never got around to learning."

"That's it?"

"No big mystery."

"Oh. I don't think it's a mystery." He bent his elbows on his knees and called her out. "I do think you're not willing to share with me the reason. Which makes me wonder why."

"There is no reason."

But he didn't let her brush him off. "You told me you don't lie."

Her words collided in her throat. She cut her eyes to the door.

"Charlie?" Blake shifted a glance toward his friend.

Charlie stood and opened the door. "Getting too hot in here for this old boy. I'll be right outside the door."

The door clicked shut, and Blake refocused on Harlow. "Shoot."

"You don't waste time when you want something, do you?"

"Time isn't something anyone should waste." He watched her. "Now spill."

She broke his gaze. It was already hot enough in here. The silence stretched, proving he was willing to wait her out. Finally, she released the complicated truth.

"I never learned because of Mae."

"Hmm …" His foot tapped against the bench. "Did she ask you not to learn?"

"What?" She stiffened. "Of course not."

Her parents had.

After a minute, he stood and held out his hand. "Come on, then."

She sat on her hands. "Where?"

"I'm going to teach you how to swim."

*

Blake waited for Harlow to take his hand. Thirty seconds later he was still waiting.

"Harlow?"

"I'm not going out there."

He sat by her. "Why not?"

"Because."

"You don't trust me?"

"I don't know you well enough."

He leaned in and wiggled his brows. "We can fix that right now."

She pushed him away. "Not what I meant."

"I know." He chuckled. "But do you honestly think I'd let you drown? On national TV?"

"They can edit it however they want. I wouldn't be here to tell them any differently."

Standing up, he offered his hand again. "Come on. I actually used to be a great swimmer. Nearly made it to the Olympics."

"Used to be?"

He pointed to his scar. "Might not be Olympic material anymore, but I'm still pretty good."

"About that. What happened?"

"Take a swim with me, and I'll tell you all about it."

"That's okay," she said. "I'll sit in a lounge chair. You go relive your glory days."

There'd been too many nos in Harlow's life. Self-inflicted or a habit someone else created, he couldn't be sure. What he did know was she deserved more. He brought his nose level with hers. "Come on, Harlow. Live a little."

The words seemed to spark something in her. "I live a whole lot."

"Really? Then how come you wouldn't have any cake after lunch—a lunch you barely touched? No cream in your coffee. No pastry at the airport."

"I don't need the sugar."

"You had to be shoved into taking this free trip."

"I've got a lot on my plate."

"You gave up your first class seats."

"Someone else needed them more." She stopped. "So that *was* you."

"Moot point." He waved his hand through the air. "The one I'm trying to make here is that you need to live life."

"I do. Mine might not be as exciting as yours, but I live."

She actually believed that.

"You exist. There's a difference."

That had her out of her seat.

"You don't have any clue what you're talking about." She went toe-to-toe with him. "What you consider living, most people consider a fairy tale."

123

He'd give it up in a heartbeat for a taste of something nonfiction. A little voice whispered Harlow could offer that to him.

He caught her arm as she brushed passed him. "If you're scared"—he leaned in—"I won't let you get hurt."

"I'm not scared." The heat in her soft words puffed against his chest.

"Then prove it."

She studied him. "Exactly what Dale wanted, me in the pool, right?"

"No. Dale wanted you scared. I don't plan on letting that happen."

Something flickered in her eyes. "I'm sure he'll go for the boredom factor."

"I could always get handsy." He grinned.

Harlow glared at him.

"Or maybe ask for a kiss as payment."

Her glare deepened, but the twitch of her lips stole its power.

The door opened, and Charlie peeked in. "Time's up. You guys ready?"

A war raged behind her eyes, then she blinked and it ended. "Fine. Teach me to swim."

"I thought you'd never ask."

She pushed past. "I didn't. I instructed."

"And here I thought that's what I was about to do."

Charlie had the camera rolling, but for once Harlow didn't seem to pay him attention. Either she'd finally grown used to him, or fear kept her preoccupied. Judging by her quickened breathes and fidgeting hands, he'd bank on the latter. Something about her relationship with Mae may have prevented her from learning how to swim, but he suspected that through the years her anxiety over water grew and became the defining factor in keeping her away from it.

They slipped through the glass sliding doors into the bright sunshine, and Harlow stopped. In front of them, three aqua pools engulfed the space, the late afternoon sun glistening across their clear waters.

"Happy we have the place to ourselves?" Blake asked.

Dale sat in a shaded corner. Tad was to their left on a camera; Charlie stood in front of them. Various other people held screens and lighting equipment, and Alex extended the boom.

"This is your idea of all to ourselves?"

"Guess you get used to it."

"Maybe after you teach me how to swim, I should teach you what it really means to be alone."

"You can have a million people around, Harlow, and still feel alone." The words escaped his lips. That was the only word to use, because he had no idea how he'd let them pass from his thoughts into hers.

His height and nearness cast enough of a shadow over her that she didn't need to squint as she held his gaze. Lines of near navy ran through her blue-green irises. And while blue so often meant cold, all hers held was warmth.

He jerked away.

First the confession, now the sappy thoughts? What was wrong with him?

"Feeling alone doesn't mean you are, Blake."

"Not sure I believe you on that score."

Her soft fingers touched his cheek and pulled him back to her. Searching his face, she tipped her head toward the pools. "How about you teach me one impossible thing, and I'll teach you one?"

"Which is?"

"That despite what you think, you're not alone."

The way she said it, he nearly believed it.

He reached up and covered her hand with his. "That's a deal."

She smiled. "Ah. So you're a gambling man."

Turning into one at least. But with Harlow, he worried if the stakes were too high.

Chapter Fifteen

The black town car stopped not even a mile down the road from where it had picked Harlow up at Széchenyi Baths. Outside the window, Blake and the camera crew milled around a stone archway. Steps away, several tourists snapped shots. But what caught her attention was the sign over the arch.

The Budapest Zoo.

She was in a short, snug dress and heels. Three-inch spikes. What were these people thinking?

Blake strolled to the car, Charlie and Alex on his heels, and opened the door. He leaned down and tugged on a lock of her dry hair before offering her his hand. "I wondered if Darcy would be able to dry you out."

"Me too." She let him help her up. "I've never spent that much time in the water. I thought I was permanently wrinkled."

"Wouldn't know it by looking at you." He scanned her from head to toe. "That dress fits even better than the bathing suit."

"Thanks." Warmth filled her from the inside out. "And thanks for all your help today. I doubt I'll win any races, but at least I won't sink anymore."

"Oh, I don't know. You do a pretty mean doggie paddle now."

She laughed. "Let me know when they enter that into the Olympics. I'll meet you there."

"Deal." He escorted her toward the stone entrance. "Did I mention you look great?"

"You did, but I don't think I returned the compliment."

"Really? I hadn't noticed."

"I figured you already knew you looked great."

With his flat front black pants and white button-up open at the collar, every lock of hair perfectly messed up, and those Aviators on ... yep, even better than great. But she didn't need to feed his ego any extra tidbits.

She pointed to the arch as they walked toward it. "Are we really going in there?"

"Yep. They closed it for us."

A woman with a headset scurried over to them. "Blake?"

He turned. "Yes?"

"Dinner isn't ready. We need you to take the walk first, dinner last."

"Not a problem, Ma—" He coughed. "—*darling*. Thanks."

Cheeks pink, the woman walked back to a van and climbed in.

Harlow studied Blake. Thought back through his interactions. How he stumbled with names. Called all women sweetheart or darling …

"You ready?" He swept his hand toward the entrance.

She let her thoughts go. "You do know we aren't exactly dressed for the zoo."

"I know you think I'm out of touch with reality, but yeah, I know." He offered his arm. "Unfortunately, I didn't get to pick our wardrobe."

She wound her arm around his. "I don't think you're out of touch with reality."

He lifted an eyebrow.

"Okay. I do." She held her thumb and forefinger out. "A little." She pointed again at the entrance. "But come on. Nothing we've done today even remotely resembles a real date."

"I didn't pick any of this."

"If you had, how different would it be, really?" She nodded to the town car. "Would you have picked me up? Taken me to Applebee's? Worn normal clothes?"

"Yes to the picking up, no to the Applebee's, and yes to the normal clothes."

"What kind of car?"

"BMW."

"Restaurant?"

"Depends on where we were."

"Your hometown."

"Scarpetta."

"Never even heard of it." Her neck hurt from looking up at him, even in these stinking heels. "Clothes?"

"Jeans and tennis shoes."

Probably brands she couldn't even pronounce.

"Did I pass your test?" Blake took off his Aviators. "Because the crowd out here is growing."

Beside them, Charlie filmed, and Alex's boom mic hung like a dead cat next to Blake's shoulder. More tourists had stopped, snapping away on their cameras. Steps inside the entrance, Tad stood ready.

"How do you ever get used to this?" she asked.

"It's not so much getting used to as accepting this is how things are." He walked them under the arch.

Tad smiled from behind his camera. "Gorgeous tonight, Harlow."

"You're here for the scenery, Tad," Blake responded.

"Exactly."

Beneath her hand, his arm tensed. "Ignore him," she said. "I am."

"You shouldn't have to."

"What was that you said about accepting how things are?"

"Some things you don't just accept." He directed her down a long path. "I'll speak with Dale later tonight. I've had enough of Tad." A monkey howled from the trees ahead. "So you haven't enjoyed today?"

"I've completely enjoyed today, but it isn't normal. And if the goal of this show is to be relatable to the general public, then you're sorely missing it."

"The goal is to give the public entertainment. Help them escape from their world for an hour."

She shrugged. "I don't know. I think I'd like to be entertained within the realm of possibility. I mean, I get that they have to be over-the-top with these shows, but mix in a date that someone could actually take me on. Give me something possible within all these crazy-impossible dates. Stray too far from reality and you lose me, but a story that could actually happen to me? Now that's romance I could tune in for."

That answer had him zeroing in on a little man standing beside a red cart a few feet down the path. The salty scent of popcorn wove through the air. Red and white boxes filled the top of the cart. He tugged her to it. "Two please."

The old man grabbed two boxes and handed them to Blake, who held the first out to Harlow. The top of the kernels glistened with butter.

She waved him off. "I'm good."

"What's more normal than popcorn?" Blake shook the box. "Wait. Don't tell me you don't like popcorn?"

"I do. Plain."

She might as well be speaking a foreign language. "Plain?"

She nodded.

He popped a buttery nugget into his mouth. "You really have a problem with indulging, don't you?"

"I indulge in popcorn all the time. The plain kind."

"Living on that edge."

"Living healthy."

He pointed to the fresh popcorn popping in the glass container. "Can we have one with no butter?"

The little man nodded, a gold tooth showing in his smile, and made another box. Again, he handed it to Blake, who gave it to Harlow.

"Tell me more about Mae. Do you have any memories of her being healthy?" he asked as they resumed walking.

She did, and they raced by like the gazelles behind the fence. "A few. We used to do everything together. Then, when I was five, the doctors' appointments started. I wound up staying with my aunt while Mom and Dad dragged Mae all over." That was when she first heard how special Mae was. How God had chosen her to be used. And right then she'd started to slowly fade into the background. "It took about a year, but we finally received a diagnosis." In front of them, elephants lumbered into view.

"Which was?"

"Limb Girdle Muscular Dystrophy."

"That couldn't have been easy for any of you."

"It was hardest on Mae."

He watched her. "I doubt that."

She stopped and leaned against the wall, looking out at the exhibit. It went on for miles, at least it seemed that way. Rolling hills, golden grass, a few massive trees that spread out instead of up. Elephants munched, their tails swishing off flies. Stretching over the wall, Harlow peered across the hills to the left where giraffes and zebras mingled. The cobblestone path they were on wove that way, eventually taking them closer to that portion of the exhibit.

Even with all the beauty around them, Blake's focus remained on her. "How's she doing now?"

"She has her good days and bad days."

"And you?"

"I'm not the sick one. What do I have to complain about?"

"Everyone has problems, Harlow."

"Even you?"

"Even me."

She aimed for the small crack in his veneer. "Like always feeling alone?"

He smiled, sealing the crack. "My turn for lessons?"

"It was our deal."

He glanced momentarily at Charlie, then continued walking. "Pretty sure I've already heard the lesson you're about to teach, though."

"Ahh, but have you learned it?"

"With God I'm never alone." He munched more popcorn. "Am I close?"

"I'm not talking head knowledge, not that I think you even believe what you're saying. I'm talking heart knowledge."

A breeze tickled her face, and she wrinkled her nose. This zoo could use one big air freshener.

"Hearts don't store knowledge, Harlow. They store feelings. And my experience with feelings is that they're easily manipulated and often manufactured."

"But don't you want to experience something real?"

"Desperately." His voice caught, and he cleared his throat. "But after everything I've seen in life, I'm not sure it's out there."

"You've only got to trust." They stopped beside the zebras and giraffes. She pointed across the grassy field. "It's beautiful, isn't it?"

He leaned on the wall. "It is."

"Yet you know it's fake, right?"

"Looks real to me."

"Looks real, but it's not the real savanna. It's manufactured. Made to fool people into feeling they've been to Africa. But simply because someone built this fake one and you've experienced it, do you suddenly doubt the real one is out there? Would this"—she waved toward the dry grass flowing over man-made hills—"stop you from jumping at the chance to experience the real thing?"

He didn't answer, but his blue eyes held such intensity, she kept talking.

"You may have been handed a lot of fake things, Blake, but the real deal is still out there. Sometimes the fake stuff is ugly, sometimes it's beautiful, but it always pales in comparison to the real thing. I mean, how can something fake ever compare to what's genuine?"

Blake studied her. "I'm beginning to wonder the same thing."

*

131

How did she do that? Get under his skin in such a good way. Her simple answer started to kindle a small ember of trust. Or faith. Who knew which, but something was stirring. He couldn't even pinpoint what was happening, only that she was different from anyone he'd ever met. The more time he spent with her, the more time he craved.

And he was stuck dating seven other women—who'd have thought that would be a negative?

But for the rest of today, Harlow was the only one.

"That popcorn didn't fill me up. How about we find a shortcut to our dinner?" He pushed away from the wall and held out his hand.

She took it. "Sounds great."

They walked past lions and tigers and bears. He chuckled. Tin Man and Dorothy. Or maybe she was a redheaded Glenda. Good definitely defined every part of her he'd encountered.

He pulled his head from the sap it had landed in and pointed to a lemur swinging in a tree. Beside him, Harlow stumbled. He grabbed hold of her before she could fall, and her nose bumped into his chest.

"Sorry." She peered up. "Like I said, heels and the zoo don't mix well."

"Seem to mix fine to me."

Pink tinged her cheeks and deepened as she caught sight of Charlie. She pushed off of Blake. "How far to dinner?"

He motioned to a small man-made rock about twenty feet away, not even bothering to conceal his grin. Good to know he wasn't the only one unsettled. "On the other side of that."

She clasped her hands together and started for it. He strolled beside her. Her presence even made the quiet bearable.

They reached the table, and Blake pulled out one of the chairs. "Have a seat." He waited while she tugged her skirt over her toned tan legs before pushing her gently to the table. As he sat, it hit him. He'd just checked her out. No way he could miss those legs stretching up from the black heels she wore or all her curves when he'd stopped her from falling, but he wasn't working a plan in his head to take her home after all this.

Kissing her, yes. But those thoughts hadn't gone any farther.

Every feeling she unearthed in him was new. This entire date enticed him and freaked him out all in one breath, because Harlow gave him a glimpse of a future full of vulnerability.

It could be beautiful.

Or a disaster.

Either way, it would be real.

And that was a realm he knew nothing about.

From behind the rock, a waiter arrived with two plates. "Enjoy." He placed them on the table and disappeared.

Harlow full-on belly laughed.

"What?"

She pointed at her food. "Somebody must have been listening to our lunch conversation."

He looked down. Roasted garlic studded his potatoes, and onions and mushrooms covered his steak. He was going to throttle Dale.

Harlow dug into her potatoes. "These are phenomenal."

There'd better be mints coming with the dessert.

With a grin, she pushed aside her potatoes and dipped into her salad. "So, were you really going to try for the Olympics?"

Normal conversation. Nearly made it feel like a normal date, even with Charlie filming and that boom mic beside him.

"I was." Blake rolled his shoulder. "But I messed up my shoulder pretty badly. Knocked me right out of the running."

"I've been itching to hear about that scar all day. What happened?"

His fork stopped midway to his mouth. "Have you never watched *ET* or *Access Hollywood*?"

"Not really."

"Read the gossip magazines?"

"I have better things to do with my time."

He believed her.

He set down his fork. "I was out at Vail for a ski weekend with a few buddies. Decided to see if my Porsche could handle the snow. It couldn't."

"Ouch."

"You live, you learn."

His biggest lesson? Mom preferred a son on the Olympic trail—and in the spotlight—to one at home recovering in privacy.

"Your turn." Because he'd rather talk about her. "Tell me something I don't know about you yet."

She shrugged. "What do you want to know?"

"More about your family, photography, nursing. Any and all of it." What kept her from experiencing life.

She swallowed the bite she'd just taken. "My family you met, and I told you about Mae. Photography—as I've said—is a great hobby, and I've been an ER nurse since graduating college eight years ago."

"I guess now that I know everything about you, I can take you home."

"Ha." Harlow pushed aside her plate. "Okay. I'm terrified of spiders."

"That's a start. What else?"

"I love the color orange but hate the fruit."

"What a paradox." He feigned surprise. "Another."

"I've watched the movie *Never Been Kissed* seventeen times."

"And have you?"

"What?"

"Ever been kissed?" His fingers found hers.

"You are the king of cheese. You know that, right?" She grabbed her water. "What about you? What don't I know? Things I can't pick up and read in a magazine—"

"Thought you had better things to do with your time."

"You know what I mean." Her voice held a hint of censure. "What's your biggest wish or dream?"

His knife slid like butter through his pink steak. "That's easy. I don't have any."

"You have to have a dream. Everyone has at least one."

Easy for her. Wheels on the Ground was a noble cause.

And what was his? A lasting relationship? To know that love was real? Might as well stick a skirt on himself and roll lipstick over his lips if he let those words past them.

"I'm living the dream. Ask anyone around." Except pity wasn't what he wanted coming from her eyes. He sipped his water, then set it down, his fingers still on the thin stem. "Guitar."

"Really?" She leaned on her forearms. "You've always wanted to learn?"

"Yes, but I never found the time."

"You should make the time." She smoothed her napkin. "So what else do you like to do?"

"Surf."

"California boy."

He grinned. "Through and through."

"What else? I mean, what do you *do*?"

"As in, do I have a job?"

"Or a passion. A cause."

"A purpose?"

She gave a simple nod. "Yes."

No one had ever asked him that before. Sure, they'd written plenty about his aimless life, but he discounted those people. Harlow wasn't the discounting type.

"Nothing."

She didn't back away from his stare. "That's sad."

His nerves bristled. "Let me guess. Like a dream, everyone needs a purpose."

"No. Dreams are given. Some are even made by people themselves. But your purpose?" Her eyes softened around the edges. "God wove that into you when he created you. You only have to ask him to help you discover it."

"Not everyone believes that."

"Doesn't mean it's not true." She grinned. "You may not believe in the law of gravity, but it's still holding you to that chair."

Behind him, Charlie chuckled.

"You're full of analogies today, aren't you?"

"I see the world through pictures. Some I can put words to, some I capture on film." She shrugged. "It's how my mind works."

And it was working on him. Unlike anyone else, Harlow was cracking through his hard places. Making him think, not simply discard.

"So you really believe everyone in life has a purpose?"

"Definitely." Not even a blink. "Otherwise we're all just walking around here, adrift. Your purpose helps focus you. It gives you something to concentrate on other than yourself."

"Makes you feel whole?"

"No. Only God can do that." She didn't miss a beat. "But it does keep you fixated outward rather than inward. And there's something to be said about helping another person. Knowing we're not all in this alone."

"Like you help Mae?"

Those words seemed to hit a pause button on her, and she dropped her gaze to her water glass. "Some people have big purposes while others have smaller ones." Like other times before, the words seemed to escape rather than her willingly sharing them. Then she cleared her throat.

135

"Point is, we all have a purpose"—she directed her gaze back to him—"including you."

Her eyes might be fixed on him, but he got the feeling most of that last part was aimed at herself.

"You really believe that?"

With the way she studied him, it was as if she could see through him. And every hidden nook along the way. "Yes." Her entire countenance softened. "But that's not why you were created. There's only one reason for that."

"Oh, really?" Wasn't sure how, but he'd held his words steady, even though his heart beat wildly through them.

"Nope. You were created simply because you are loved and wanted." She touched his fingers. "You weren't an accident. You weren't a mistake. You were envisioned and crafted together by a God who loves you infinitely more than you can imagine. And if no one's ever told you that before, then I'm sorry. Everyone needs to hear it."

Her words were soft, yet they impacted him with the force of a heavyweight punch. All his life people had given him lines, but whatever Harlow offered sounded like a truth he wanted to explore.

He squeezed her hand, trying to control his pounding thoughts and pulse. "And I thought we were done with the deep end."

"Trying to maintain my side of the deal."

"Thought that was by the zebras earlier." He chuckled.

Yeah. There. Her smile deepened. She knew she was making him nervous.

She pulled her hand from his and sipped her water. "Hey. You made me jump in more than once today. I'm returning the favor."

Only it was more than a favor. It had the taste of freedom.

"Thanks." Did she understand the depth attached to that one small word?

Alex shifted the boom mic.

The moment was gone.

Blake wadded up his napkin and tossed it on his plate. "Between the two of us, I think we've provided them with enough drama for the day."

Her smile disappeared. Suddenly she was incredibly interested in pushing the food around her plate.

"Don't like it?" he asked.

"No. It's good." Her gaze stayed on her mound of potatoes.

"Then why the sudden loss of appetite?"

She peeked up at him. "For a split second I'd forgotten you were Blake Carlton and this was a game show."

"Seeing as how you're not winning a cash prize if you're picked, I don't think you can call it that."

He'd attempted to coax out a smile with his light tone. If anything, she grew more tense.

"Right. If I'm picked." She pushed back from the table. "Reminds me of gym class as a kid."

"Not a very athletic child?"

"Always picked last." Her cheeks pinkened, and she fidgeted with her cloth napkin.

Stupid kids.

Well, he could give her a different memory.

"You do know you're my first date, so that makes you my first pick."

"Except you didn't choose me for this date. Dale did."

Right. He'd forgotten she knew that.

Drumming his fingers on the table, he watched her as an idea formed. He smiled and pulled out his cell phone. Curiosity and confusion flitted across her face.

He scrolled through his contact list until he found the one he wanted, pressed dial, then waited while it rang. Covering the mouthpiece, he addressed Harlow. "If a guy asked you on a second date via voicemail, would you go?"

She laughed. Except it sounded like a snort, which made her eyes widen.

His turn to look surprised.

On the other end, her voicemail picked up. "So?" he prodded.

"Guess it depends on if I liked the guy."

"And do you?"

She hmmed. "Jury's still out."

"Think I'll take the chance." He kept his gaze steady with hers as the line beeped. "Harlow Tucker, this is Blake Carlton. I had an amazing time today, and it would make me deliriously happy if you'd go on another date with me."

Her easy grin made his next move possible. Sliding his free hand across the table, he grabbed the silky skin of her wrist and ran his thumb in circles along the base of her palm. "I might not have picked you for today's date, but asking you for another is all me. What do you say?"

"You really want to date me?" She nibbled her lip. "I'm … not exactly your pace."

She wasn't. But something about her tugged at him.

Blake set the phone down but kept holding her stare and her smooth wrist. "Maybe not, but I'd like to try. Would you?"

Not removing either of his connections, he waited for an answer. Judging by the way Charlie shifted, so was he, but for once it didn't matter what the person behind the camera wanted. It only mattered what Harlow said.

The thought continued to shoot possibilities and promises through him, darting around, daring him to grab for one.

She broke their stare first, looking down at his hand holding hers, the touch more natural than any he'd felt in … forever. Her breath quickened, and her gaze flicked back to his. He inched closer.

Scooting back, she twisted from his grasp. She absently rubbed her wrist, staring out into the night sky.

Defeat slammed against him. He'd moved too fast. Thought she'd wanted—

"Okay." Her acceptance was nearly a whisper.

"Okay?"

Pink-cheeked, Harlow reconnected their stare and nodded.

And right there, the tiniest possibility dropped at his feet and turned into reality.

Chapter Sixteen

Her fourth morning in Budapest, and her fourth morning waking up before the sun. She should give in to it. It certainly would make acclimating when she got home much easier.

Harlow placed her feet on the floor and stretched. The clock glared five a.m. Beside her, Tarynn slept soundly. Let her sleep. It meant not having to hear about her date with Blake.

She tiptoed to the bathroom and flipped on the light, using it to quietly scour the room for her things. The weather was supposed to be warm and dry, a welcome relief from the rain that had kept her inside all yesterday. Luckily, she'd managed to find a quiet corner of the hotel and worked on the business plan for Wheels on the Ground. If only she could call Mae and see what she and Jack were up to, but that call wasn't scheduled till the end of next week. Jack volunteering to help was a godsend, but Mae shouldn't have to be bothered with these details.

Nothing about this felt right.

Staying home would have disappointed Mae, but leaving had placed responsibilities in her sister's lap she didn't need to spend energy worrying over. The situation tore Harlow in two, and if life were fair, she could take those fractured pieces and be in both places at once. That wasn't how things worked though.

One hot shower later, Harlow wiped steam from the mirror and stared at her reflection. The bonus to being first on Blake's date list meant the rest of the week was hers.

She refused to think of the drawbacks in that statement. All seven of them.

After tossing on comfy clothes, she threw her hair in a loose braid and slapped on some lip gloss. The goal today was to catch the sunrise and explore the town with her camera. The perfect escape from the mind-numbing effects of spreadsheets, ledgers, and an entire glossary of terms she didn't understand. Maybe after a breather, she could dive into them again and a few would make sense. Most of the stuff she wouldn't be able to tackle until she was home again, but hopefully with even a little jump start, Jack wouldn't think she was utterly helpless.

With Tarynn still asleep, Harlow left her things in the bathroom and snuck downstairs for breakfast. It was nearly six. The conference room for their group would be open with a small buffet.

Two other women sat in the room, chatting. Carmen and Jillian. Their tight smiles didn't exactly scream "good morning."

Harlow grabbed a cup of coffee and a small plate of egg whites and fruit, then crossed the room to an empty table.

"You don't want to join us?" Carmen's silky voice beckoned.

Not really. But she changed course anyway.

"I didn't want to interrupt your conversation," she said, joining them.

"No interruption. We're talking about my date tonight with Blake." Elbows on the table, Carmen cupped her chin. "I'd love to hear how yours went."

The woman wasn't nearly as interested as she pretended. Not with those cold eyes.

"It was nice."

"That's ... nice." Carmen cut a glance at Jillian. "I plan on my date tonight being real *nice* too."

Jillian giggled.

Oh, Blake was going to love her. She swallowed. Since when did she know or care what he'd like or not?

"Morning, gals." Tarynn strolled into the room, pink pajama bottoms still on and her hair in a messy bun. She snagged coffee and sat beside Harlow. "You were up early again."

"I was in bed early again."

Tarynn sipped her coffee. "Yeah, you were conked out when I came in." She glanced at her over her cup. "Snoring."

Harlow sat straight. "I don't snore."

"You do." Tarynn scrunched her nose. "No worries though, it's pretty minor. You only sound like a truck driver once in a while."

Carmen's smooth laughter grated her sore nerves.

Harlow pushed her near-full plate away.

"So," Carmen said to Tarynn, "how'd your date go?" She looked her up and down. "Think you'll get a call today?"

Harlow's thoughts drifted to the voicemail Blake had left, his eyes studying her. She could still feel his thumb making circles against her wrist.

"I will." Tarynn's voice dragged her back to their table. "Our date was amazing."

This was proving to be too hard. The time she'd spent with Blake had felt … special somehow. Like she was the only one. His phone call nearly melted her heart.

Now listening to Tarynn? And knowing Carmen had a date tonight? Jillian later this week? This whole thing nailed every tender place inside because she might have been picked first, but she wasn't the only one playing. And most definitely wouldn't be the only one chosen.

Not that she even really wanted to be. Blake Carlton was nowhere near the man she'd always looked for. On her list of qualities in a mate, he didn't even hit one of them.

Okay. So he was pretty easy on the eyes, but that was far down on her list.

He'd also made her laugh.

Treated her like a lady.

Listened to her like her words mattered.

"Harlow? Are you going to tell us?"

She snapped out of it. Three pairs of eyes stared at her. "Hmmm?"

Tarynn laughed. "Did Blake kiss you?"

"More like did she kiss Blake?" Carmen mumbled.

Harlow speared a strawberry. "No, we didn't kiss."

"Really?" Tarynn's deep brown eyes widened.

"Yes, really." She didn't want to hear what was coming next.

"Because the man is an amazing kisser." Tarynn touched her lips. "You definitely missed out." She leaned in. "Your next date, kiss him. You won't regret it."

Talking about kissing the same man and being okay with it? This conversation was surreal.

Carmen stood. "I, for one, plan on having no regrets. Along with no plans to go home." She nodded at Jillian who jumped up and followed her from the room.

141

Harlow blew out a breath. Refocused.

Tarynn pointed at Carmen's backside. "She's not lacking any confidence."

"Uh, no. Definitely not." Harlow met Tarynn's gaze, and they both burst out laughing. After catching her breath, she finished her breakfast, stood, and picked up her camera from the back of her chair. "I'm going to explore the city."

"When you come back, do you want to grab lunch and shop?"

"Sure."

Tarynn took her coffee back up to their room, and Harlow crossed the lobby. Outside, the sun tinted the morning sky pink. It would make for gorgeous pictures.

Holding her camera, she couldn't stop the smile. After the frustration of yesterday's business plans, this was something she knew she could do. Something she was good at. Something that lit her from the inside, slashing color through her as effortlessly as the sun painted the morning sky in front of her.

"You sightseeing today?" Tad somehow materialized beside her.

She took a step back. "I am."

"I'd love to join you, but duty calls." He pointed to his video camera, as if she could miss it, then shifted nervously. "And, uh, I wanted to apologize if any of my comments have made you uncomfortable."

Words completely deserted her.

Tad cast a glance behind, then returned it to her. "Sometimes I think I'm being funny, and apparently I'm not. But don't worry, I won't cause you any more trouble."

"Oh-kay." The words slipped out slow. She half expected to see Blake standing behind him, forcing the apology from him. No way he was making it on his own.

"We good then?" he asked.

Good was stretching it. "Sure."

He nodded. "I'm going to grab some coffee before the day gets too crazy. Glad we're all right."

Glad because of job security.

Another presumption of Blake toppled. As much as she tried to convince herself to not fall for him, it was proving hard. Especially when he kept finding some pretty great ways to surprise her.

Harlow nodded to the doorman as she stepped outside. A light warm breeze brushed her skin, and she closed her eyes, inhaling deeply. With an exhale, she let go of the chaotic morning and opened her eyes to the beauty around her. Across the Danube, the Buda side of the country held history to walk through. Buda Castle, Fisherman's Bastion, Matthias Church, even the Hospital in a Rock—whatever that was—invited her to visit, but today was all about the Pest side. Buda was later in her week's schedule.

After one more glance at the bridge, she started off toward Váci Street, the shopping center of the town. If she wanted to find people from all walks of life, this was the place to go.

Setting a fast pace, she relished the strain on her muscles. She'd been blessed with a healthy body, and it was her job to make sure she took care of it.

As she reached the shopping district, she slowed. Several streets convened together, and a large fountain bubbled in the middle of the intersection. Around it, people congregated, one of them playing a guitar. Movement farther down the street caught her attention. Numerous young women huddled around a man who was handing them groups of leather belts. Their long brown hair was pulled back, and they had on skirts and thin shirts. They fanned out to line the streets. Intrigued, Harlow snuck closer and zoomed in on the closest young girl, then snapped her picture.

The action caught the girl's attention. "Hello, lady." She invaded Harlow's space. "I have nice leather belts." Her hand shook as she held them out. "You buy?"

Though her face never turned, her gaze tracked to the man up the street. Was this the only way she stayed off the streets and away from selling herself in place of these items? Budapest was one of the largest cities for sex trafficking. Harlow had overheard people talking. Now seeing the desperation on this young woman's face, her heart broke.

She reached out and touched the belt. "May I see it?"

Hope inched into her face. Down the street the other girls watched the transaction.

"How much?" Harlow held the belt up.

"One thousand forint."

She did the math in her head. That only amounted to about five dollars. She scanned the others along the street. How much did they need to sell today to be safe? How much to keep them from having to possibly sell themselves instead?

"Okay. I'll take it." Harlow reached into her camera bag slung over her shoulder and pulled out the bill. It still amazed her how this money was marked. Most likely the only time she'd hold currency with 1,000 stamped across it.

The woman made the exchange, a small smile now on her face. The street was rather quiet, but later it would be full of people shopping. Harlow prayed they'd buy from these women, but most would pass over them.

Mind set, Harlow stepped to the next young woman and purchased a belt. She continued on down the street until she'd purchased a belt from each of the seven girls. Satisfied, she packed up her camera and returned to the hotel. The indoor market would have to wait, because she'd spent all her free cash here.

The Four Seasons came into view, but Harlow wasn't ready to slip inside yet. Instead, she perched on her favorite bench out front. An old couple strolled by, and she picked up her camera. She focused on their wrinkled hands holding tight to each other. Zooming in, she could see their small gold wedding bands and how the man's hand covered the woman's. She pressed the shutter button.

Everlasting love …

"Let me guess, you didn't ask their permission?" Blake stood beside the bench, his hands on his hips. He nodded to the older couple. "Even being on the opposite side these past few days, you still don't get it."

She lowered her camera. "I only took a shot of their hands."

He snorted. "Justifying again."

"Not justifying, simply stating my rights."

"And that couple doesn't have a right to privacy simply because they wanted to take a walk?"

"Just because I carry a camera, Blake, doesn't make me like the people who follow you around. If you can't see that—if you didn't believe anything I shared with you on our date—then why did you keep me around?" She waited a full minute, but he remained silent.

Fine.

She stood. "I should get back inside."

He finally looked at her. With a sigh, he ran a hand across the back of his neck. "Away from the grump you mean?"

"If the lens fits."

"I'm a tad sensitive when it comes to photographers."

"I hardly noticed." Harlow scooped up the belts she'd purchased. "But like I've said, this is a hobby, not my profession."

"Judging by that camera and lens, it's quite the hobby." He took it from around her neck and peered through the view finder. "Nikon D750 with an 18-

200 lens. Nicer than the 610, but not quite as good as the 850." He twisted the barrel. "I'm surprised you allowed yourself the treat."

"And I'm surprised you strung all those words together."

Blake grinned and held her camera out to her. "I grew up with cameras in my face. It became a game to know what each person held, and then it kind of grew from there."

She regarded him, wanting him to know she was so much more than those people who chased him. To see her heart like she was starting to see his. "I'm not like those people. I hope you know that."

"No. If you were, you'd have the D5 and the 300 lens." Even with all the noise and traffic, he kept his focus squarely on her. "But something tells me it's still more than a hobby to you."

She wanted it to be.

"Remember those dreams we talked about the other night?" she asked.

He nodded.

"This is mine." She held up her camera. "But not so I can hide behind bushes and snap pictures of people who already have their faces plastered over every screen and magazine." She hesitated, running a finger over the indentations on one of the belts she'd purchased, unsure what to say next. She'd never let even this much of her dream out of her head. "I'd like to use it as a ministry."

Blake's brow wrinkled.

"What?" Was her idea so crazy?

He pointed to the belts she was rubbing. "Buying your souvenirs in bulk?"

Seriously? She finally outted her dream, and he breezed right by it.

Fine. Sharing her heart with him would only lead to it aching.

"They're pretty belts." She tightened her grip on the leather. "And shouldn't you be more worried about the trouble you'll get in for talking to me out here?"

"Only if they see me."

"I thought you always had a camera on you." She leaned in. "Isn't that why you hate them so much?"

He matched her lean. "Oh, they definitely annoy me, but like I said, I know how to avoid them when I want to."

"And you felt like it this morning?"

"I feel like it every morning." He shrugged. "This morning I just chose to give in."

"Why?" The question came out before she had the good grace to hold it in.

He didn't answer immediately, but held her stare. Slowly that grin of his spread over his face. "I saw something out here that snagged my interest."

Her heart rate edged into a slow jog. She refused to let it race. Blake Carlton knew this game all too well, and if any part of her was going to start beating fast at that smile, it was her feet against the pavement. "I need to get inside. Coffee is calling."

But his chuckle was faster than her feet.

*

Good to know he unsettled her too. It leveled the playing field a little, because *unsettled* barely covered what she did to him. Strong and soft, the woman held a camera in one hand and her heart in another. Using photography as a ministry? He hadn't even known what to say, so he pretended he hadn't heard.

Real nice.

She'd shared her heart. He'd ignored it.

"Thought you wanted them running toward you, not away." Charlie's voice came from behind Blake.

He turned to find Darcy with him. Still didn't know what those two saw in each other. From size to eating habits, they were such opposites.

Darcy swatted Charlie's chest. "Leave Blake alone."

"Yeah. Leave me alone." Blake settled onto the bench Harlow had vacated.

Charlie nodded toward the hotel entrance. "I like her."

"Blake does too." Darcy sat beside him. "Don't you?"

"I barely know her." He focused on the Danube in front of him.

"Doesn't mean you can't like her."

"Doesn't mean I'm going to fall in love with her either." He nudged her. "You women always want to bring romance into everything." And he was nowhere near ready to talk about the prickly feelings poking up.

"Right." She patted his knee. "I keep forgetting how I fell madly in love with you."

He picked up her hand and kissed the top of it. "Took you long enough to admit it."

"Hey. Hands off my woman." Charlie squished his large frame in between them.

Darcy kissed his cheek. "You've got nothing to worry about, darlin'." She tucked herself into him, and he draped his arm around her shoulders. "Seriously, Blake. Harlow seems like the real deal."

146

The same intriguing and terrifying thought plagued him. After wanting something for so long, it freaked him out to reach for it. To believe it was finally in his grasp. What if he was wrong?

"Time will tell if she is or not." But with this game, he didn't have the luxury to think about it. "Right now, I need to concentrate on getting through my date with Carmen today."

Charlie rumbled beside him. "Be careful. That woman would have you for her main course if you let her."

Blake ran a hand through his hair. "At least with Carmen I know what I'm getting. She's in it for the screen time and notoriety." Unattractive, but relatable.

"And she can't hurt you." Darcy peeked across Charlie's wide chest. "But she also can't love you, Blake. You'll miss out if you never take a chance with someone who could."

Taking a chance on a person didn't worry him. Believing love was real provided the true challenge. Harlow's words from the zoo filtered through his mind for about the hundredth time, but he wasn't ready for the leap. Not when he couldn't see the other side yet.

"Don't you ever get lonely?" Darcy asked.

He did.

And hollow feeling.

Except that hole filled a little each time he was around Harlow.

It enticed him and scared the snot out of him all in one breath.

See? Unsettled.

Darcy arched a brow at him. "You okay?"

He pulled his perfect smile and spoke before she could call him on it. "Of course. I've got you guys."

"But you need more than us." Charlie wasn't falling for the smile. "We can point you in the right direction, but we can't change your heart. And without a heart change, doesn't matter how great Harlow is, you'll never find what you're looking for."

"You're talking God."

He nodded.

Blake stood and faced them. "This is about to get too deep."

"Maybe it's time *you* learned how to swim." Charlie dipped his chin, both brows raised.

Blake absorbed the bull's-eye shot, his mind swirling. He'd come on the show wanting to escape loneliness, wondering if it was even possible to feel. Never expecting that rousing his heart, his spirit—he didn't even know what it was—would mean needles and pricks, like waking a part of his body that had been asleep too long. The tingling hurt, but it also sparked hope.

And fear. Because the ground beneath him was too unsettled to stay, and the chasm in front of him, too large to cover.

Time to take a deep breath and regroup.

"I've got a date I need to prep for. I haven't read the shooting script for today. Any idea where I'm going?"

Charlie waited a beat, nodded, then pointed across the Danube. "Up there."

Thankful Charlie let the conversation stall out, Blake shielded his eyes and glanced over his shoulder to a large, creamy-white stone structure carved into the cliffs. "Fisherman's Bastion?"

"Yep." Darcy added. "And to Buda Castle. They're setting it up for dinner tonight." The two structures stood within walking distance of each other. Probably meant they'd be filming in the streets tonight. "I'd better get inside and grab some breakfast, probably chat with Dale too."

"We're going to sit out here and enjoy the view for a little while longer." Charlie pulled Darcy close to him. "I'll catch you at the top of your date."

"Looking forward to it." He didn't bother to inject enthusiasm. It'd never pass with them.

Darcy squinted up at him against the bright morning sun. "Of course, if you run into a redhead with a camera, we could help you make a break for it."

He walked away from her impish grin and teasing offer because rather than make him laugh, it tempted him. For all their talk this morning, and for all Harlow unsettled him, Blake couldn't shake the gut feeling that being with her could take him one step closer to discovering what he was searching for after all.

Chapter Seventeen

Harlow checked her camera screen. The card was nearly full. Served her right for not changing it, but having lunch and returning to Váci Street with Tarynn had turned into nearly a full-day event. If she'd gone back to their room when they'd returned, it would have.

How anyone spent four hours shopping on one street still perplexed her—even if she had tagged along for the entire mind-numbing event. Taking pictures, sure. But shopping? Harlow would have nailed that in under an hour. Tarynn? Not so much. If her purchases hadn't finally outweighed what their hands could carry, they'd still be out there. When they returned to the hotel, Harlow gave the bellhop the bags, Tarynn a hug, and herself a fast exit.

She strolled the streets until the top of St. Stephen's Basilica beckoned her. Now the sun dipped low over the Buda side, casting its soft light over a group of children playing soccer in the large stone square in front of the massive cathedral. She sat on the steps, snapping away. A small boy's toe caught on the uneven rock and he fell, skidding across the rough pavement. Movement stopped. As he stood, blood rolled down his knees as fast as tears poured from his eyes. Harlow hurried toward the boy, but a man reached him first and scooped him up. The boy's blood and tears smeared on the man's clothes, but he didn't notice. He leaned the boy against his shoulder and soothed him.

Peace.

Picking up her camera, she clicked through several frames.

Father, you soothe us in the same way. Doesn't matter how messy we are, you pick us up anyway.

She captured the shot from different angles. Satisfied she had transferred the idea from her mind to her camera, she stilled and simply watched the two. Setting the boy on the ground, the father took his hand, and they walked into the fading light.

Her head snapped up.

Fading light.

Beyond the square darkness was falling quickly. The hotel was a straight shot up the tiny streets, but she'd lost track of time. Her short legs wouldn't move as fast as the setting sun.

Sure enough, by the time the side entrance to the hotel came into view, it was nearly black out. Even better, halfway between her and the entrance, a group of men leaned against the stone wall of another building. Holding her breath, she faced forward, shoulders up, and hands on her camera bag. She cut them a glance from the corner of her eye, but they didn't even acknowledge her. Three steps past, she released that breath in a slow hiss only to quickly suck it back in as another two men materialized from the darkness in front of her.

Trapped. Or at least that was how she felt.

Again she squared her shoulders and continued forward. These guys could be completely innocent, like the men she'd just passed. All hope of that disappeared as one of them blocked her path. Clothes as black as his hair, he crossed his arms and turned into a virtual wall of muscle.

"You lost?" he asked.

"No. I'm staying at The Four Seasons."

His slow grin chilled her. "Expensive hotel."

Wrong answer. "I'm with a group that's filming. They're paying for it."

"You some kind of star?"

Maybe she should keep her mouth shut. She stepped forward, but he mimicked her move, cutting off her escape.

He reached a hand out and ran a finger under her camera strap. "Mind if I take a look at your camera?"

Inching backwards she landed on a toe. "Actually, I do." She didn't even want to check behind her. Didn't need to. No doubt the men she'd passed earlier were there. "If you'll excuse me."

The lead man raked his gaze over her, steadying it on her bag. That was better than other places it could have landed.

Heavy footsteps pounded from behind the men. "There you are." Blake's deep voice broke through the human barricade surrounding her. Harlow pushed up on her tiptoes, but couldn't see him past the men boxing her in. The footsteps grew louder, then the top of Blake's head along with Charlie's and Jace's came into view.

Harlow peered around the men and caught Blake's deep blue gaze. He reached a hand toward her. "You're late."

The men didn't step aside. Charlie pulled himself to full height. "Everything okay here?"

The one who'd reached for her camera held his cold smile. "We were worried the lady was lost. Glad to know she's all right." He nodded to the other men, and they dispersed. Glancing at Harlow he issued a warning as he walked away, "You should be more careful on these streets."

She exhaled, then swept her gaze past Charlie and Jace before finally settling on Blake. "Thank you." She stilled her shaking muscles.

His eyes hardened. "Were whatever pictures you took worth your safety?"

"I—"

"—was lucky I saw you." He let out a sigh, except it sounded more like a growl. "Couldn't simply have a night at the spa with the other women, could you?"

"I didn't come all this way to be pampered and shop. I came to see the real Budapest."

Gripping her arm, he practically dragged her to the door. "Was that real enough for you?" His words were low but with enough force that he might as well have been shouting.

She yanked free, ignoring the way Charlie and Jace tried to hide their grins. This wasn't humorous at all. "Aren't you supposed to be on a date?"

He jerked open the door. "I'm on it."

"Could have fooled me." She stomped past.

"We came back to change while they set up the dinner shots." Red ran up his neck and into his cheeks. "What if we'd gone back out the front entrance instead of this side?"

"I guess I would have lost my camera then."

He exhaled. "And what else?"

His words weren't ones she hadn't already asked herself.

Jace cleared his throat. "We need to get moving, Blake."

Blake's stare remained glued on her. He didn't move. After a moment he leaned down. "You're staying in the rest of the night?"

"Heading to my room right now."

"Stay there."

Harlow rolled her eyes. She had no intention of going back out by herself tonight, but not because he'd told her not to. "We'll see."

"Harlow—"

"She'll stay," Charlie spoke up. "Right, Harlow?"

"I'm not your pet, guys."

Charlie and Jace chuckled. Blake didn't release his glare.

She needed to stop needling him. He'd helped her out of a tight spot. Tugging her camera strap further up her shoulder, she conceded, "The only place I'm going is to bed." Then looked Blake directly in the eye. "Promise."

His jaw relaxing was the only thing he offered in response before facing Charlie and Jace. "Let's go then before Dale has a coronary."

They disappeared around the corner, and she stood there. What just happened?

"Shouldn't you be heading upstairs?" Blake's voice startled her.

"I thought you left."

"I thought you were going to your room."

The challenge in the tilt of his head warned he'd carry her there himself if she didn't start moving.

"I'm going."

Going straight to crazy. That's exactly where the man was sending her.

Judging by his face as she cast one last look over her shoulder, apparently the feeling was mutual.

*

Blake stared out the window of the town car, no interest in seeing Carmen tonight at all. The day had been long enough. She'd thrown herself at him in every way possible, and he didn't need any more claw marks.

Dale loved her though. He was pushing for some heat tonight, but she had Blake so iced over he didn't know if he could produce even an ember.

Harlow, however, had already ignited an inferno in him—and for all the wrong reasons.

"You've got steam coming out of your ears, bro." Charlie sat across from him in the limo.

Jace slammed back whatever he'd poured himself. "She sure knows how to get under your skin."

"Anyone who'd put themselves into a situation like that gets under my skin." All for a stupid photo.

He knew she did it for other reasons, but as the memory of the group of men surrounding her came back with full force, so did his anger. He didn't even remember his feet touching cement as he raced across it. Hadn't worried that they were outnumbered. His focus had been on Harlow.

And he didn't like the way it twisted his gut. The way he'd thought of her all day. The way he'd smiled when Carmen had dragged him through the shopping district and passed all those young girls selling knives and leather belts. Belts he'd seen Harlow carrying that morning.

Carmen hadn't been able to pass them fast enough. Harlow had stopped and bought a belt from each of them. He knew because he'd counted. Seven girls. Seven belts.

The woman confounded him.

"You in there?" Jace handed him a drink.

Blake pushed it away. "I am." He didn't need alcohol to cloud his judgment tonight.

Jace downed the glass himself.

"You've had enough," Charlie admonished.

"I'm not on camera tonight."

"You've still had enough."

Jace had always loved his drink, but it was growing worse this past year. Apparently Blake wasn't the only one to notice.

Jace held up his hands. "Fine. I can stop."

Charlie cast Blake a look. Blake shrugged. They couldn't do anything about it now.

The limo reached its destination, and the men climbed out. Bright lights lit the castle in front of them, casting their glow into the inky night. Three full stories of stone walls boxed in the castle grounds, and a carved archway provided entrance. In the middle of the cobblestone center was a small table covered with a red tablecloth. Candles lined a path to the table and stood in all sizes around it. Beyond that, more lights that would allow them to film in the black of evening illuminated the area.

Charlie hauled out his camera. "Ready?"

Alex waved from beside the table. Every time Blake saw that boom mic he thought of a dead cat.

"I'm going to the van." Jace made for the make-shift control room.

Darcy exited another van. "What took you guys so long?" She hauled out a sponge and went for Blake's forehead.

"Blake needed to play Superman." Charlie set down his camera.

Darcy's hand stilled. "Excuse me?"

"Nothing," Blake said.

Charlie smiled. "I'll fill you in later."

"You better." She nodded to a third van pulling in. "That's Carmen. You better get in position."

Blake strolled down the candle-lined path and met up with Dale heading his way, who pointed at him. "Remember. Heat."

"You've got your candles for that."

Dale drilled a glare into him. "People don't tune in for the candles."

"Maybe I'm trying to give them new reasons. Better ones."

"Not on my watch."

"It better be on your watch. The whole point is for me to wind up engaged at the end of this to only one of these women. Faking chemistry with all of them will only alienate your audience."

"Chemistry is what drives the audience." Dale rubbed his palms together. "Wondering who will win. Rooting for different women like you would for a sports team. If there's a clear-cut front runner with no chemistry or conflict, no one watches. You don't connect with the women, no one tunes in."

"And by connect, you mean physical."

"Lust. Sex. Hands all over each other." Dale nodded to the vans. "Yes. I mean physical. Deliver."

In other words, manufacture it.

Carmen slinked from the van in a red gown with a slit that—if he had to guess—she'd made a few inches higher, three-inch nude heels, and her black hair flowing on the light breeze.

At one time, she would have been exactly what he sought, but nothing about her chipped at the emptiness inside of him. It all felt fake. And while he wanted to deliver the ratings he promised Mom, there had to be another way. A way that involved the one person who wasn't provoking fabricated feelings.

Even if most of the ones she evoked drove him crazy.

He grinned. Carmen saw it and thought it belonged to her.

She was wrong.

That grin belonged to a petite redhead who loved to take pictures.

Chapter Eighteen

Harlow's hand skimmed against a cool, silver railing as she and Tarynn ascended the short gangplank attached to the Poseidon Rivulet, one of the many river boats floating along the Danube that she'd snapped pictures of this week.

Last night in Budapest. How on earth had time flown by so quickly?

"I still can't believe we're spending the next week on this thing." Tarynn's voice wobbled. "I have to admit, I get seasick."

"I doubt you will on this boat, but if you do, I'm sure they have Dramamine someplace around." She spied Tad filming their entrance. True to his apology, he'd left her alone ever since that morning. Still gave her the heebie-jeebies to think he was watching her from behind that camera.

She shivered.

Tarynn brushed her chestnut hair over her shoulder. "Nervous to see Blake again?"

It had been five days since the alley incident. Five long days without a glimpse. It wasn't apprehension that twisted her stomach; it was anticipation.

She'd rather have the apprehension.

Two glass doors slid open, allowing them entrance. "I'm not. You?"

"I'm more worried about all us women in one room."

Harlow laughed. "Tell me about it."

They were having a party with the remaining women to celebrate the beginning of their voyage down the Danube. At least that's how it was billed. More like Dale needed to stir up more drama.

They stepped inside, and Tarynn's gasp covered Harlow's. "Oh my." She turned. "Who knew a riverboat could be so beautiful?"

Dark wood trim ran throughout the entryway, crisscrossing in large beams on the ceiling. A chandelier dripped crystal from the center of the room, splaying its light in bursts around the entryway. To the left, a walnut staircase spiraled up toward the next level. Marble coated the floor beneath her silver heels, and to their right a glassed-in room provided views of a rosy-orange sunset slipping through the skyline.

Within that room, nestled among a cluster of off-white chairs, Carmen sat with Blaire. Acknowledging Harlow and Tarynn with cool grins, the two dismissed them almost in the same instant.

"Nothing like a warm welcome," Tarynn groused. "But did you notice it wasn't Jillian hanging on Carmen's every word?" Craning her neck, she peered around the room. "Pretty sure she had one of the half-day dates yesterday. Looks like she didn't make it." She headed for the walnut bar in the corner.

Harlow searched the room, counting bodies, and tried to figure who else was missing. The idea that some of the women went home produced a mixed bag of emotions. Her count landed on Gina Morley, a model-tall platinum blonde. Harlow hadn't spoken more than a "hello" to the woman since their first night.

Gina strolled across the room, her turquoise dress tight across every ample portion of her. "Harlow, right?"

She nodded. "And you're Gina?"

"I am." She bit into a small cracker slathered with something gray. "You had the first one-on-one, didn't you."

"I did."

"I know I'm supposed to hate you, but I figure I'll try to get to know you first and then make my decision." She smiled around another bite. "So where did you and Blake go?"

Her honesty was refreshing. Nice to know that at least one other woman here wasn't letting them write the full script for her. "We started at Hero's Square, had lunch in the park, went to Széchenyi Baths, and then dinner at Budapest Zoo."

Gina eyed her. "You didn't have fun?"

"We did." More than she'd like to admit.

"You don't sound too enthused. Not that I'm complaining." Another gray-stuff bite. "The less competition, the better."

Tarynn and Peyton joined them.

"What are you two chatting about?" Tarynn sipped Chardonnay.

"The weather," Gina scoffed. "What do you think?"

"Don't let her sarcasm bother you. It's how she talks." Peyton leaned in. "Did you notice both the half-day girls are gone? Amber and Jillian?"

"Amber had a half-day too?" Harlow surveyed the room.

"Yep. Keep me on the full dates, please." Peyton swirled the ice in her glass. "So, Tarynn tells me you had an amazing date."

Harlow swung her stare back to the group around her.

"Not what she told me." Gina snorted.

Tarynn leaned forward. "Harlow may downplay it, but she's had a permagrin since her date."

"No I haven't." She lowered her voice. "And before you all ask, no, I didn't kiss him."

"Why not?"

Did Gina even realize how loud she was?

Carmen and Blaire peered at them from their spot on the couch, and Tarynn wiggled her fingers in a wave.

"You had an entire day with him," Gina said, "and you didn't even kiss him? Not once?"

"Not once."

At least they hadn't asked—

"Didn't you want to?"

Scratch that.

Heat built up the nape of her neck. She hated lying, but couldn't admit that yes, a tiny part of her had wanted to kiss him. When he'd leaned in close, that mix of lime and spice had tickled her nose, enticing her forward. Those deep blue eyes of his tracing every line of her face with an intense stare that waited for her answer. Would she go on another date with him?

The vulnerability in his look ... she doubt he even knew it was there. But it touched something in her. Let her know that even in this game, somehow they were connecting. Something a week ago she hadn't even wanted.

And now?

"See? Permagrin." Tarynn pointed at her and the three girls laughed.

"No need to answer my question," Gina said. "Your face already has."

Tad stepped closer to the group. Alex had his boom mic nearby. Her own mic dug into her spine. Too much exposure.

She spotted a set of outdoor stairs. Fresh air. Quiet. Space to reel in her thoughts.

She made it two steps before Jace joined the room.

"Ladies." He wore a suit that had to have been tailored specifically for him. Charcoal gray, it accented his trim waist and coal black eyes. She'd never met someone with eyes as dark as his, especially with his sandy blond hair. It was a unique combination. And he set those eyes on her and smiled. "Blake is here. Let the cocktail party begin."

Blake entered looking better in all black than any man ought to, and her entire body tingled. Traitorous nerve endings.

She rejoined Tarynn, Peyton, and Gina, using them as a shield. Would do her good to remember they were all here for the same reason: Blake.

Carmen helped the cause by latching herself to his side. Lips pressed to his ear, she whispered something and kissed his tightened jaw before sashaying off toward the bar. Instead of watching her, Blake's gaze found and held Harlow's. He stepped forward, but Blaire reached out and grabbed his arm. Harlow retreated into the crowd with a mixture of relief and disappointment.

See? Traitorous nerves.

He might have asked her on a second date, but by the count in the room, he'd invited five other women on second dates too. Five.

Her relationship with Peter ended over only one other woman. Logic told her the situations were different, but it sure didn't *feel* like it.

"You want a drink?" Tarynn asked.

"No. I'm good."

"Suit yourself." Tarynn snagged a champagne flute as a waiter walked by. "I think I'm going to go and relieve Blaire." She sauntered off.

Blake and Blaire—sounded like a set of matching tea towels.

Sucking in a deep breath, Harlow went the opposite direction. Nothing in the rules said she had to stay in this room, so she exited through the glass door that led to the stairway she'd spied earlier. She took off her heels and climbed them.

At the top, Budapest spread out on either side of her, its lights firing to life in the darkening night. Absolutely breathtaking. Her hands itched to hold her camera, but she'd had to pack it with her things. Someone would deliver it to her room with the rest of her items later tonight.

The deck ran the entire length of the boat, a perfect place for walking out her mixed emotions since she couldn't calm them with her camera. Halfway around, her skin chilled. With the sun long gone, the breeze had turned cool. She should have worn the wrap that went with this dress.

Long and flowy, the rose colored material brushed against her skin in the light wind, but she wasn't about to go back inside until forced to.

She walked two laps before slowing at the back of the boat. Leaning over the rail, she watched traffic cross the Chain Bridge.

"For someone so short, you've got a fast pace." Blake's deep voice brought out goose bumps.

Rubbing them away, she kept her focus pinned to the bridge. "I needed some exercise."

"In an evening gown?"

She peeked his way. "I took my heels off."

He chuckled. "I see that." Coming closer, he towered over her, but she didn't feel threatened. "I could use you for an armrest, I think."

"Never heard that one before." She softened her sarcasm with a grin. "Dodging the cameras again?"

"Among other things." Blake leaned against the railing and crossed his arms, facing her. "You bought a belt from each girl along that street, didn't you?"

She straightened, her mind stretching to reach where his was. "Excuse me?"

"On Váci Street. I saw the women later that day." He brushed a lock of hair from her cheek. "Why?"

His fingers against her skin ruined her concentration. "Um … because they needed me to."

"It's that simple?" He removed his hand.

She blinked. Refocused. "Does it need to be more complicated?"

*

It should be. Life was always more complicated. Always had a hidden agenda. Except Harlow's blue eyes held an honesty he'd never seen and didn't know how to trust.

Each date this week was like a hurdle in a race to get back to her. And she'd missed him too. She tried playing it cool, but he'd caught how her breath picked up the second his fingers touched her.

"No, Harlow. I don't think it does."

She searched his face. He may not be physically touching her, but something in her look connected them more deeply than any touch they'd shared before. Beckoned him. All week he'd raced toward this moment, now he slowed, needing time but still sure of his destination.

He straightened. "I saw Tad downstairs. He hasn't bothered you again, has he?"

She watched him for another moment, then sighed. "Not since you made him apologize." Resting her forearms on the railing, she stared out at the night. "Thanks for that, and for helping me out the other night."

"You didn't go out again?"

"I gave you my word."

That answer didn't mean much in the circles he traveled. Strangely, he trusted her.

He leaned against the railing with her. Boats drifted past, rippling the amber lights reflecting off the onyx water. Budapest definitely knew how to do illumination. The city rose on either side of the Chain Bridge, bathing the night in its golden hue. Between the buildings and the bridge, there had to be millions of twinkling bulbs. Downriver, the Parliament building shimmered like liquid gold as its lights flared on, a sight that had entranced him all week.

He tapped Harlow on the shoulder. "Look."

She gasped.

"It's beyond words." Her hand touched her neck. Probably reaching for her camera. She spun in a circle, taking in every landmark around them. It was as if they'd stepped into Midas' kingdom and Parliament was his crown jewel.

Every angle produced beauty, but that building took his breath away.

So did the woman standing in front of it.

Harlow.

The glow of the lights engulfed her, their soft hue showing off all her curves. He reached in his pocket and tugged out the item he'd purchased earlier that week. His fingers traced over the smooth metal. "I have something for you."

She turned. "You do?"

He held out the pin, battling back the laughter that wanted out. One nervous chuckle pushed past, and she smiled, then reached out and took the small golden pin, a perfect replica of the Parliament building.

"It's beautiful."

"I figured you needed something more than a simple pushpin for places you've actually been. Especially since you learned how to swim here. Too bad we're headed to Vienna instead of Venice, or you'd get your gondola ride."

"It's okay. I've gotten pretty good at imagining things." Her deepening smile was worth every penny that pure-gold pin had cost him. "Thank you for this."

She studied it, her fingers caressing the dips and valleys of the small trinket, completely entranced by such a simple gift. She hadn't even asked if it was real.

"Why are you here, Harlow?"

Her head tilted. "My sister signed me up for the show. You know that."

"But you didn't have to come." He leaned close. Told himself it was to catch her words, but as he inhaled her clean jasmine scent, he knew better.

She didn't answer right away. Her hair lifted on the wind again, and this time he restrained himself from grabbing it.

Finally, she spoke. "I suppose not, but it was important to her. And I can't lie, I have always wanted to travel. I knew this might be my only chance."

"You planning on some big catastrophe or something?"

"No."

"Then why would this be your only chance?"

Her focus shifted to the Danube. "Not everyone has endless amounts of money available to them, Blake."

"But you work, don't you?"

Her laughter popped out along with a snort. She slammed a hand over her mouth. Wasn't the first time she'd done that. Laughed at his money or snorted. He wasn't sure which he wanted to address more.

He opted to play it safe. "You really think I'm out of touch with the world."

"Because you are." She nudged him. "But it's not your fault, it's simply how you were raised. Most people work to pay bills. You never had to think about either of those."

"Is that why you chose nursing over photography?" A boat's horn trilled in the distance.

"A big part of it. I needed the income."

She could sell the right picture for thousands, yet the fear she would had dispersed. He wasn't completely sure when, only that it was gone. "You said you thought of your photography as a ministry."

Her eyes widened. "You caught that?"

"I did." He nodded. "Don't really understand it, but I'd love to hear more."

She tapped her tooth. "I don't even really know how to explain—"

"Mind if I steal Blake for a moment?"

Harlow startled as light from Charlie's camera found them, along with Peyton. He hid the glare he wanted to throw Charlie. They'd agreed to ten minutes. No way it had been that long.

"He's all yours." Harlow stepped away from him.

Blake held up one finger. "I'll meet you downstairs, Peyton." The woman pouted but returned downstairs. No such luck with Charlie. There was only so far he could stick his neck out—he needed this job.

"I really want to finish this conversation, but duty calls." He hooked a thumb over his shoulder.

"Is that what I am too? Your duty?" Hurt laced her teasing words.

He couldn't have that.

"Far from it." He moved closer, blocking out the light from Charlie. Hopefully blocking out his very presence. "You're pure enjoyment." She inhaled sharply, and Blake reached for her, but she twisted away and looked out over the water, one of the largest sighs he'd ever witnessed escaping her lips.

Made his stretch into a smile.

Kiss him. She wanted to kiss him, and it bothered her.

He loved it.

Blake slipped his mouth inches from the place her jaw and neck collided. He struggled not to place a kiss there. "A little secret," he uttered the words softly, letting them tickle that silky area behind her ear. "You unsettle me too."

Her gaze stayed firmly on the Danube. His stayed on her, waiting. If she turned, he'd have full access to her lips, and he had every intention of taking the advantage.

Behind them, a throat cleared. Female. If it had been male, he'd do more than glare at Charlie later.

Blake turned, his shoulders slumping. Peyton apparently wasn't the patient sort.

Harlow stiffened. "You better go. Peyton's waiting."

And the last thing he wanted to do was leave this very spot.

Unfortunately, the choice wasn't his.

"Enjoy the rest of your night." Unable to resist any longer, he pressed his lips softly against her cheek. In all his years, he'd never shared a first kiss with a woman on her cheek.

And he'd never been more affected by one.

A puff of air escaped her, the tiniest of moans on it. If he hadn't been so close, he would have missed it.

Blake stole one last look and then stepped away. Peyton claimed his arm, but his thoughts were already taken by the woman still leaning against the rail. Harlow could hold that frigid stance all night, but she was just as affected. And he couldn't wait to further warm her heart.

Chapter Nineteen

Harlow woke to the gentle sway of the boat and soft sunlight drifting through her window. She burrowed deeper under her covers, her sight catching on the golden pin settled on her bedside table where it had sat for two nights now. Reaching out, she grasped it, bringing it close to study. Not that she hadn't stared at it for a good part of the night once again.

Or replayed in her mind the way she'd nearly kissed Blake that evening.

She couldn't figure him out or the effect he had on her, but there was no denying he did have an effect, and that fact posed a problem. This attraction hurled her toward a world of hurt. They couldn't even get ten minutes alone before another woman carted him off, and in those private moments, who knew what Blake said to them.

Had he bought them all special trinkets? Was it part of the game?

If so, he was a skilled player. Everything about him seemed honest and vulnerable when he was with her, like he rolled down a portion of the tinted window that separated him from the world and gave her a glimpse of the real Blake Carlton.

Pushing the thoughts away and herself out of bed, she headed for the bathroom. At least here they each had their own rooms. Not that she didn't enjoy Tarynn, but she needed space. Her conflicting emotions kept her crowded enough. Even yesterday, when they'd had a down day in Bratislava, Harlow had taken her camera and avoided everyone. Her hope had been to bring her wandering feelings into line. It didn't happen.

After getting ready, she climbed the stairs to the top deck. With the warm morning, they were serving breakfast outdoors. The venue provided her first glimpse of Vienna since they'd arrived in the middle of the night.

Vienna.

Unbelievable.

Tarynn waved her over, and Harlow crossed to where she sat, noting each of the women still there. She might need space, but she also needed to see these women, because each interaction with them helped keep her head on straight. Reminded her that none of this was real. Even if she *did* possess the ability to peg Blake, to glimpse a part of him not normally seen, none of that meant he was going to pledge his undying love.

Or that she even wanted him to.

Okay. She needed coffee.

Harlow flipped up her cup and went to grab egg whites and fruit from the buffet. When she returned, Tarynn smiled at her. "Any guesses on who gets today's date and where it'll be?"

Not a game she wanted to play. "No idea."

"How'd you like Bratislava?"

"It was nice. I toured the castle." She dug into her eggs. "You?"

"Shopped—not that there were many stores—and saw the castle too."

"How's the seasickness?"

"Nonexistent." Tarynn bit into her croissant. "This boat has nothing on the big cruise liners."

Floating down the Danube with the capacity of two hundred cruisers, this vessel didn't even fit the same category.

Charlie and Tad walked on deck, the red lights gleaming on their cameras. Alec followed with his boom. Jace joined them, picked up a champagne flute, and dinged it with a spoon. All attention swiveled his way.

"Ladies, I hope you slept well. We're in Vienna today. Five of you will be getting a guided tour of the city this afternoon while one of you"—his gaze perused their tables—"is going on a one-on-one with Blake."

Unbidden, Harlow gazed at her phone. Then she peeked at the other women. Apparently she wasn't the only one checking her device.

"Willing it to ring?" Jace teased even as a shrill sound broke the quiet. He zeroed in on Tarynn, who held up her ringing phone. "Lucky woman."

Harlow's heart bungeed off a platform she hadn't even realized it was on.

They didn't need the sun today—Tarynn's smile lit the sky just fine. She slid her finger across her screen. "Morning, Blake." Whatever he said made her giggle. "Of course, I'd love to join you." With a breathless goodbye, she hung up, nervous energy rolling off of her.

"Well?" Gina asked.

"A day fit for a princess. That's all he'd say." Tarynn stood.

Jace offered her his arm. "Shall we go get you ready?"

"Definitely." *Oh my gosh*, she mouthed as she walked away with her fingers tucked in the crook of his elbow.

"Have fun." Harlow tried for legit happiness. Her voice might have reached it, but her heart didn't. This entire thing was messed up, and the fact that she'd let her heart get involved made everything worse. No way she would have ever wished Opal good luck with Peter. And here she sat in the same situation.

What had Mae been thinking?

Wanting to center her thoughts, Harlow headed for her room, lobbing prayers against the jealousy that edged in. It wasn't a fully grown green monster, more like a toddler version. Still, it toddled around when she had no business thinking of Blake as anything other than the playboy he was.

She needed him out of her system. Peter had done a number on her heart when he chose Opal over her. Willingly putting herself into the same situation would be about as smart as taking a long walk off a short pier. Blake held her in no higher regard than any of the other ladies here. He played the game well, but that was the problem. She was a pawn, and she couldn't allow herself to be manipulated.

No matter how cute his smile.

Lost in thought, Harlow rammed into someone as she descended the stairs. "Oof."

Blake's citrusy spiced scent hit her senses even as his hands wrapped around her arms, steadying her. So much for flushing him from her system.

His warm baritone met her ears. "Harlow."

How'd he do that? Convey he missed her and was happy to see her all with one word?

"Morning, Blake."

"Sorry." His foot tapped her shoe. "Did I land on your toes?"

"Nope." She stood one step above him, and he was still taller than her. Deep lines furrowed his forehead. Concern quickly replaced any worry over controlling her emotions around him. "What's got you so upset?"

Surprise lit his eyes before he hooded it. "What makes you think I'm upset?"

"Your forehead."

His brows hiked. "Come again?"

"The lines there rival the Grand Canyon."

He watched her for a long moment, and then laughter burst from him.

A production assistant stopped at the bottom of the stairs. "Blake?"

He turned. "Stacey."

She emitted a long sigh. "Sarah."

"Right. Sorry."

Her eye roll could win awards. She pointed down the hall. "Dale wants to see you."

Blake nodded. "I'll be there in a moment."

With a huff, she walked off.

He turned back to Harlow. "I've got to go."

"I figured." Without a second thought, she laid her hand on his forearm. "You're okay though?"

"I am."

Except she'd didn't believe him, not when his voice shifted to that practiced tone, but now wasn't the time or place to push him.

"All right," she said. "But so you know, I'm not buying that answer."

"No?"

"No."

He stilled, studying her. "Then what are you buying?"

That was the problem. Buying any part of Blake came at a steep price she didn't know if she could afford. The last time she'd stood here, she'd paid with heartache. Was still paying.

"I don't know." Painful truth laced her words, and she raced past him.

*

Blake smiled and nodded at Tarynn, not filing a word she said. Not that she wasn't sweet. Not even that she was boring. She simply wasn't Harlow.

All afternoon, two scenes rolled through his mind, stealing his attention. His near-kiss with Harlow on the top deck as they left Budapest, and their conversation this morning on the stairs. Both impacted him and tied another knot in the string tethering him to her.

On deck, she'd turned from his kiss, a first for him.

And on the steps she'd been able to peg him with one look, because he *had* been upset this morning. Dale had sent Mom the first week of footage, and she wasn't happy. Wanted more conflict and heat.

But how was he supposed to stoke a flame with women he wasn't interested in?

A chuckle escaped. One month ago he wouldn't have asked that. Even two weeks ago.

"What's so funny?" Tarynn slowed their walk. "Do I have a bug in my hair or something?"

Blake peered down at her. Not that he had to look far. She was nearly as tall as him. "Sorry. Stray thought." Her lips turned down, and he reached for a suitable answer. "About how you tried asking that man for the anise tea—"

She laughed. "And didn't exactly pronounce it correctly." Her fingers laced through his, and she leaned against his shoulder. "I'm glad you're enjoying today, because I thought it was perfect."

He caught Charlie's gaze. No way he was fooling him.

They finished their hike up the large hill at the back of Schönbrunn Palace, the once summer residence of Vienna's royalty, where manufactured Roman ruins reached into the sky. Apparently creating a space that mimicked ancient crumbling buildings was the thing to do when the palace was built. Behind them, Vienna stretched across the skyline in an impressive display of red-roofed houses, tall stone buildings, and one lone steeple in the distance. Trees lined the pin-straight streets and provided the perfect green to contrast today's brilliant blue sky. Harlow would have a field day with her camera. Had they come this way today? Charlie mentioned the rest of the group was scheduled for a guided tour of the city.

"I'm going to use the restroom while they set up our picnic." Tarynn squeezed his arm, then walked away.

The tension building in his shoulders loosened.

Charlie started his way, but Dale beat him. "Thought you heard me this morning."

So much for relaxing.

"I did."

"Then start acting like it." Dale paced beside him. "You aren't giving me anything to work with. Harlow's the innocent. Fine. Play it up. Keep stringing her along. Off-camera time with her only pushes the rest of their buttons. But if I'm going to look the other way on that, you need to give me something with the rest of them. I can't edit what's not there."

"I'm not stringing Harlow along." He clenched his jaw tighter than his fists.

"Honestly, Blake, I don't care if you are or not. Just give me what you signed up for, or I won't have a show to lead into your mother's." He stormed off.

The man certainly knew where to throw his punches.

Blake kicked the dirt.

Darcy stepped over. "Reverting to our childish days, I see."

"Not now, Darce."

She took the sponge and dabbed his forehead. It wasn't the sun that had him sweating. After a moment, she stopped. "Your mom's happiness isn't your responsibility, Blake."

Maybe not his responsibility, but he wasn't about to pull it from her like he had his dad. Not when he could hand it to her with one simple show.

She squeezed his arm. "And yours won't come from trying to give it to her." Then she walked away as Tarynn rejoined him.

Production pointed them to a blanket spread out in a roped-off area to the side of the ruins. As they started filming again, he and Tarynn strolled over and dug into the picnic basket. He handed her a turkey and Havarti sandwich.

She unwrapped the wax paper around it. "So tell me what's it was like growing up in Hollywood."

"It's surreal. Like its own little world."

"I bet it's hard to know when people are being authentic with you."

"Sometimes."

"Probably feels like you're in a fish bowl."

"It can." He grabbed a bottle of water and handed it to her, ignoring the wine that sat at their feet.

She twisted the top off hers. "My father was the mayor of the town I grew up in, and then I went on to cheer for the Oilers. Nothing like the scale of your celebrity, but in my little town, we were like the Kennedys." She sipped. "I think that's why I'm so used to the cameras. I grew up with them too."

"You do seem at ease." He plucked a grape from the bunch beside them.

Tarynn leaned back. "Toss it."

He chuckled and aimed it toward her. The grape bounced off her nose and rolled down to her lap. She picked it up and crunched it. "Did you have many friends growing up?"

"Not many."

A sad smile slipped across her face. "Me either." Her long legs stretched out next to his. "At least not many real ones."

"Exactly."

"It makes it hard to trust people. And when you've been burned enough times, it makes it hard to trust your own judgment."

She was right. Which was probably why he'd felt comfortable with her from night one. No sparks. But a kinship of sorts.

Her fingers found his on the blanket. "You can trust me, Blake. I think we're a lot alike. I could be good for you, if you'd give me the chance."

She studied him, her lips slightly parted.

He knew what she wanted. What Dale wanted.

What his mother wanted.

So he brought his lips to hers She wrapped her arms around his neck, pressing into him. She pushed for more in the kiss.

And all he could think of was Harlow. How one kiss against her cheek brought more alive in him than having Tarynn plastered against him. More alive than anything he could remember feeling.

Tarynn scooted closer, nearly toppling him over.

He braced his palm against the blanket and pulled back. She kissed the corner of his mouth. "You're amazing."

He broke out his practiced smile. "And you're sweet."

The way her entire face softened pricked his conscience. Since when did a kiss mean more than physical? He had no answer, but there was new understanding. That kiss meant something to Tarynn. If Harlow found out, it would to her too. And he didn't want to hurt either of them, for completely different reasons.

Straightening, he reached for an apple, unsure of his next move with Tarynn. Unsure of his next move on the show.

But sure of one thing.

Harlow.

His lips hadn't touched more than her cheek, but she'd set an electrical current buzzing through him he'd never felt before. It crackled between them even when they weren't touching, and sparked when they did. If he really kissed her ... He shook his head. No telling what would happen. All he knew was she was the only woman he wanted to kiss from here on out.

And when he did, it would mean something real to both of them.

Chapter Twenty

Exhaustion pulled Blake to his pillow, but his nerves prevented his brain from shutting off. This show was turning into one big round of that old game Operation. Trying to hold things steady while pulling some sort of network hit from the hole he'd sunk himself into, without upsetting one of the women, Dale, or his mother.

Without upsetting Harlow.

He used to love that game. Colburn would play it with him most days after driving him home from school, and Blake always won. Except this time he wasn't sure he could. He sat up in bed, rested his elbows on his knees, and held his head in his hands. Today's date was a group one with three of the remaining women. And he'd thought yesterday's dynamic was tough.

He stood and grabbed the water bottle from his desk. From the bedside table, his phone rang. He grabbed it, checked the caller ID, and answered. "Hey, Mom."

"Dale said yesterday's date went much better."

Guess he had picked up a strand of her acting gene.

"It was all right."

"He said you gave him good footage to work with, but he thinks you can do better." Mom sipped something, but at least she sounded happier than she had yesterday morning. "He also said he thinks you're becoming attached to Harlow Tucker."

"And if I were?"

"She's sweet, and she certainly fits the role we cast her for, but I don't think you're compatible."

They weren't compatible. They came from two separate worlds. Ha! He could even use the woman as an armrest.

173

But she sparked something in him.

Challenged him. Awakened him.

He blew out a long breath. "I like her, Mom."

Silence strung over the line.

"I understand her draw, Blake. She's different from any woman you've been with before, so I'm sure it's refreshing. And I'm sure America will love her. It's why we picked her, and it's also why you need to tread carefully. If you break her heart, America will hate you." She paused. "And if they hate you, they won't want to watch my show."

"I'm not going to break her heart."

"Not on camera you aren't."

"Come again?"

"Just keep giving Dale what he needs on film, and you can do whatever you want off camera. Have your fun with her, but in the end, I need you to pick the right woman."

"What if that's Harlow?"

Mom laughed. "You honestly think she's cut out for this?"

If anyone could withstand the pulls of Hollywood, it was Harlow. She possessed a strength he'd never seen before.

Ice clinked as Mom took another sip. "You promised me this, Blake."

"I know." He paced the room. "But I need you to at least be open to the possibility of Harlow at the end."

She took a moment to answer. "I suppose I could be wrong about her."

She was. He'd show her that Harlow could handle it. The cameras. The invasion of privacy.

But could he ask her to?

"I should go," he said. "I need to get ready for today's date."

"And I need to get ready for mine as well." A smile filtered through her voice. "Carl invited me to dinner again."

If he had to guess, it was someplace they could be photographed.

They hung up, and Blake pushed open the wall of windows. Sunshine and a fresh breeze spilled into his room. The boat cruised down the Danube in the middle of the Wachau Valley. Hills filled with lush green trees climbed the bank of the river. Supposedly, the other side of the boat held the same scenery. From what Dale had told him, for today's group date they'd bike straight through the Valley with several stops at local wineries. Three girls were manageable. Three girls on wine … not so much. Probably why Dale picked it. At least group dates made this process go that much faster.

Blake stretched. Time for a shower. Darcy had laid out his wardrobe last night. Simple cargo shorts and a gray T-shirt. He donned it after his shower and faced the mirror. He liked his clothes fitted, but this was ridiculous. The thing molded to his body like it was made from Spandex, not cotton. Had she ordered it small on purpose?

Probably. He scruffed a hand through his hair, then grabbed his key, and headed to the dining room reserved for the production crew and himself. Fresh coffee, warm croissants, and jam filled a table.

Darcy glanced up from buttering her pastry. "Morning."

"Morning." He nodded at the waiter with the coffee carafe but waved off the one with pastry platter.

"Not hungry?" Darcy asked as the waiter filled Blake's coffee.

"No. I don't have room to eat with this shirt you put me in."

She grinned over the lip of her mug. "The ladies love it."

"Someday I'm picking an outfit for you."

"No way." She set down her coffee. "How'd you sleep?"

"Didn't."

She flicked a gaze around the room and then leaned toward him. "I think today's date is going to go much better."

His heart jump-started. "Harlow will be on it?"

Darcy shrugged as Charlie set his plate down and joined them.

"Heard anything on your mom?" Blake asked him.

"She's settled in the new Alzheimer's wing at Sunset."

"It has everything she needs?"

Charlie nodded. "It does. Thanks for putting me in touch with them."

"You'll let me know if there's more I can do?"

"You've done enough." He salted his eggs. "Getting my foot back in the door with production, finding the place for my mom"—he smiled at Darcy—"letting me steal your best friend."

"Share. Not steal."

"I get the better end of that bargain."

"Guys." Darcy's cheeks flamed a deep red. "I'm sitting right here."

"Couldn't miss you if I tried." Charlie kissed her cheek. He dug into his breakfast and pointed to Blake's plate. "You're not eating?"

"Blame your girlfriend."

Darcy glowered at him.

"Nah. I'm thanking her." Charlie chomped a bite of bacon.

Blake put down his coffee. "Huh?"

"Biking and wine tasting on an empty stomach, my friend. You're gonna give me a gold mine of video."

The man had a point. Blake grabbed his plate and headed for the buffet.

*

Harlow grabbed a light sweater and slipped into her Toms. She had no idea where the date was today, but based on the clothes Darcy had left for her last night, they were doing something active. Short shorts and a fitted tank. Harlow fought the urge to tug on the hem of her Daisy Dukes for the millionth time. They weren't getting any longer. While she'd helped choose her outfits for Malibu, Darcy had filled in the rest—with Dale's input, no doubt. For the most part she'd done a good job, but this ensemble pushed her limits. Oh well, Darcy had prevented the bikini in Budapest. She'd roll with the tiny shorts here.

Stepping into the hall, she ran into Tarynn.

"Hey. You look great, Harlow."

"Thanks. How was your date yesterday?" She didn't want to know, but the question tumbled out anyway.

"Wonderful. We went to both of the palaces. At Schönbrunn there was a private picnic on the hill by the ruins. A blanket, bottle of wine, Vienna in the background ..." She brushed a hand over her lips. "The man is an amazing kisser."

Harlow's gut clenched. She needed to get over it. It was the game she'd been signed up for. Blake could kiss every one of them before this was over.

Everyone except her. She refused to be simply another kiss to him.

"So you had a nice time then?"

"You could say that."

Harlow didn't even want to think of how far that kiss could have gone. "I should get going." She took off down the hall.

Tarynn waved. "Have a great time."

Harlow walked out the sliding glass entry doors and down the gangplank. She joined Carmen and Blaire, the other two on today's date.

Okay. Maybe her own outfit wasn't all bad. Carmen's pockets hung longer than the hem of her faded jean shorts. Her fitted shirt stopped above her belly button and dipped into a low scoop neck. The largest thing Carmen wore was her smile.

Jace met them in the gravel. "Good morning, ladies."

Everyone's attention swiveled to him. Charlie, Tad, and Alex followed along with Dale.

"Morning, Jace." Carmen and Blaire flanked him.

"Where's Blake?" Carmen asked.

"He's coming." Jace motioned for them to follow him and waved at Charlie. "You want them over here?"

He scanned the area. "Right by that tree."

"Dale?" Jace's gaze landed on him next. "Everyone look okay to you?"

The producer scanned the women one by one. "They're good."

"I'll go get Blake, then, while they're miked."

Jace disappeared into the ship while Charlie and Tad spread out. A production assistant started putting mics on them. Once she had hers, Harlow slipped to the end of the group. A few minutes later the glass doors on the ship slid open, and Blake stepped out.

Blaire and Carmen made a beeline for him. Harlow stayed by the tree.

Carmen grabbed him in a hug. "So where are we going today?"

He pulled himself from her only to wind up in Blaire's arms. It was going to be a long day.

Disengaging himself again, he took a large step back and clapped his hands together. "You love this beautiful countryside?"

Matching yeses.

"Good." He nodded toward the bikes. "Because we're going to ride through it with a few stops at local wineries."

A vice gripped her stomach. The wineries would have been bad enough. But bike riding? She retreated another step. How was she going to explain this one?

Blake crossed the grass. "Let's go pick our bikes."

Ten minutes later Harlow stood off to the side avoiding the bikes and hiding her laughter at Carmen's anger. The woman did not want a helmet, but no matter what she pulled, the guide wasn't budging. Seemed like the first time someone was immune to her charms, and steam billowed from her ears.

"Hey." Soft breath tickled her neck as Blake leaned in. She spun directly into his chest. Okay. Wow. The T-shirt Darcy dressed him in showed off his muscles. A throaty chuckle cut through her haze. Yeah. He knew he was hot. He didn't need any help from her. She looked into his amused face.

"If I didn't know better, I'd think you were trying to avoid me," he said.

Rather than lie, she nodded to the aqua bike he held and ignored the fear that he'd rolled it over here for her. "Cute. It complements your outfit."

He sighed and wiggled the handlebars. "It's yours. Mine is the black one." With his foot he pushed out the kickstand, then he picked up a helmet from the basket on the front. "Come here."

She held out her hand. "Pretty sure I can put that on myself." Not that she had any plans to use it. Let them all get started, and she'd hold back and explain to Dale she had no clue how to ride a bike. Blake and his questions would be long gone by then. Probably wouldn't even miss her.

Even though she kinda wished he would.

He grabbed her hand and tugged her close. "Pretty sure I'd rather do it for you." He tucked her hair behind her ears, his fingers lingering against her jaw.

Harlow sucked in a deep breath. Yep. She wanted him to miss her because, suddenly, she was missing him—and he hadn't even left yet.

Blake held her stare, his eyes crinkling around the edges. It was too easy to share these moments with him and feel like they were the only ones.

One of the cameras swooped in close, snapping her out of the moment.

They weren't alone, and this wasn't real.

Her inability to ride a stinking bike, however, was completely legit.

Harlow ducked from his touch. "I can do it."

Blake looked from the camera to her, and his grin fell. He shook his head and picked up his own helmet. "Fine." He left to join the group. One camera followed him, one stayed on her for another moment.

No doubt they'd edit it to show her initial reaction to Blake, not her pulling back. No one pulled away from Blake Carlton.

She twisted the straps of the helmet around her fingers. Problem was, she hadn't wanted to pull back. She'd wanted to lean into his touch. But she also wanted more than physical attraction with a man. She wanted to be his one and only. His forever. There was no scenario where she could even imagine that happening with Blake. He wasn't a Christian, didn't even understand what love was. And if they leapt those two huge hurdles? Their lives were still in two different places. She couldn't leave Abundance, and she'd never ask him to leave Los Angeles for her small town. Live in her guest house? Help take care of Mae?

Bottom line, any future she even tried to envision with Blake stood outside the realm of possibility.

A sad laugh escaped.

The lead guide, Marcel, introduced himself and outlined today's itinerary along with a few tips for the road. Harlow stood beside her bike, her fingers wrapped around the cool blue metal. Blake was at the front, followed by Carmen and Blaire. The second guide, Steven, pedaled up behind Harlow.

"Mount up," Marcel called out.

Harlow's feet stayed on solid ground.

"You ready?" Steven asked.

Time for truth.

"I'm not going." The rest of the group pulled out. "I, um, don't know how to ride a bike."

"Harlow. Steven. Move out," Dale called from the road.

Steven's thick black brows lifted. "Never learned or traumatic experience?"

"Never learned."

"Then I have just the thing." He leaned his bike against a tree and jogged over to a trailer.

"What's going on?" Dale huffed his way over to her. He spoke into a walkie-talkie, and the other bikers stopped along with the van.

Blake circled around from the front and pedaled back to them. "What's up?" His gaze caught on something over Harlow's shoulder.

She turned. Steven pushed a tandem bike her way. "You're kidding, right?" The dirt might as well swallow her.

Blake's brow furrowed for a split second before it relaxed. "You can't ride."

"Who doesn't know how to ride a bike?" Dale paced beside them.

"Harlow Tucker." A sigh escaped from behind Blake's grin as he put down his kickstand. "I've always wanted to try tandem."

Dale's *no* was quicker than Harlow's. "Steven can stick with her."

"Or I can stay back." She toed the ground.

Dale wasn't having it. "No. This is a group date, which means I need the entire group. So mount up."

"You okay with this?" Blake asked her.

"It's fine."

"I'll make sure you don't fall." Steven motioned her to the back seat. "It's a great way to introduce you to riding."

Blake hesitated.

"We need to get a move on." Dale tapped his foot in the dirt.

Harlow wasn't used to causing so many problems. She grabbed her handlebars and climbed onto the seat. "Then let's get going."

Blake held her stare for one more second, then mounted his bike and resumed his spot in the front of the group.

Steven smiled at her. "Ready?"

"As ever."

And then they were off. For the first half hour, Harlow gripped the handlebars so tightly her fingers tingled. But slowly the scenery and smooth pace of their ride calmed her. Vineyards stair-stepped up the side of hills and little towns displayed their maypoles. She'd only seen them in pictures before.

At the third town, she called to Steven, who'd been the perfect tour guide. "Where is their maypole?"

He half-turned. "It's a tradition for the boys of neighboring towns to steal them." He nodded in front of him. "Wösendorf nabbed Joching's and the bragging rights."

Ahead, the group slowed. Blake had spent the last hour taking turns riding beside Blaire and Carmen, but never Harlow. Watching him laugh and smile at the other women had tightened her nerves until the only thing to do was outright ignore him.

Didn't appear to be a possibility right now. When they arrived at the winery, he rode her way, his eyes on her.

"You two seem cozy." He stopped beside them, while everyone else leaned their bikes against the winery's brick wall. "Thanks for making sure she didn't wipe out, uh—"

"Steven." Harlow supplied, hopping off the bike.

Steven pushed down the kickstand and shook Blake's hand. "No problem. It's my job, though today was a pleasure." He winked and headed inside.

"Thanks for the save." Blake smiled at her.

"Anytime." She leaned against the wall. "I've noticed you have a hard time with names. That's why you're always calling women sweetheart or darling."

"Maybe I just like pet names."

"My theory's better. Makes you less of a player."

"I doubt America would agree."

"I doubt America knows the real you."

"But you do?"

"I'd like to think I'm getting closer."

"I'd like to think that too." He paused. "Sit by me inside? Unless you already told …"

"Steven."

"Right. Unless you already told *Steven* you'd join him."

"Nope. I'm on a date with you." She nodded toward Carmen and Blaire, who walked their way. "Not that you'd know it with two other women tagging along."

Blake wrapped his arm around hers and leaned close. "Maybe you're the only one I see."

He straightened so suddenly, she wasn't sure she heard him. Keeping his arm locked with hers, he faced the other two. "Ladies, Darcy is over by the van if you want to take a minute and get cleaned up before we head inside."

Blaire scurried toward Darcy, while Carmen grabbed Blake's other arm and leaned against his shoulder. She was tall enough to reach it. "How do I look? Should I see Darcy, or am I all right?" She trailed her fingers up his arm.

Like Harlow was going to stand here and watch this.

She pulled against Blake's hold, but he flexed his arm and held her in place. "Maybe a little powder on that forehead?" he said.

If looks could kill, she'd be dead right alongside Blake.

Carmen stalked off. Charlie peered from behind his camera at Blake, raised his brow, then turned and followed Carmen. If she didn't know better, Blake had just given some sort of hand signal to Charlie.

"Maybe I need to go work on my shine too." She pulled them toward the van.

Blake spun her in the opposite direction. "Or maybe you need to take a walk with me." He flicked off his mic, then ran his hand along the small of her back. His fingers brushed her skin as he turned hers off too. Her heart picked up. He ducked them behind a building. "Why are you trying to avoid me today?"

"I'm not."

"No?"

"Nope."

"Then why didn't you want me on the tandem with you?"

"You couldn't tie yourself to me. There's two other ladies on this date, and I wasn't about to be a third wheel on all those conversations."

The corner of his lip rose. "You're jealous."

"You wish." She tugged again at his hold.

"Give up. I'm not letting go."

She dug in her heels. "Why?"

"Because I like it when you're near me."

"Why?" The word whispered out.

Blake didn't answer right away. When he did, his gaze remained on the hillside. "Honestly?"

"Yes."

He shrugged. "I don't know."

"Not good enough."

"It's all I have." He started them walking again. Looked like he was taking them in a circle around the building. "I haven't ever met anyone like you, Harlow. I want to get to know you better."

"Little hard to do in this circumstance, isn't it?"

"I disagree."

"Seriously?" He could not be that clueless. "Forget the fact that the dates are surreal. Forget that cameras follow us nearly everywhere, along with mics catching practically every word. Let's talk about the fact that you're dating five other women besides me."

"It is a dating show, Harlow."

Women's laughter spilled around the side of the building. Harlow picked up her pace. "We better get moving, because your other *dates* are waiting."

He stopped and relinquished his hold so he could stand in front of her. "When I'm with them, I only think of you."

"You just met me."

"I know."

Quiet wrapped around them. Blake didn't take his gaze from her. Didn't blink. She gave in and dropped her head against his chest. He wrapped his arms around her, and she breathed in his familiar mixture of spice and lime.

"Harlow." His lips brushed the top of her hair. "I don't get this. I know physical attraction, but this is something more."

"There hasn't been time for more." Her words muffled into his chest. "And I can't get passed the fact that you're out there with other women."

"What if I told you I wouldn't get physical with any of them?"

She peeked up at him. "Not even with any of that physical attraction you mentioned flying around?"

The smile on his face she'd never seen before. Not on any magazine. Not on the TV. And not directed at any of the other women on this show. "All that attraction toward other women seems to have disappeared since I met you."

"But you kissed Tarynn yesterday."

His smile deepened and reached farther into his eyes. "Which is how I know it's gone. The only woman I want to kiss is you."

Her breath caught.

He slid his hands up her arms, across her shoulder, and then along her neck, eliciting a ripple of goose bumps in the wake of his touch. Cupping her jaw, he dipped his face so that his breath caressed her in its own kiss. Leaning closer still, he nuzzled his nose against hers before the rough skin of his lips trailed a whisper-light path against her cheek and his mouth hovered over hers.

"Harlow?"

"Hmmm?" At some point she'd closed her eyes.

"Can I kiss you?"

She couldn't speak. Could barely nod her answer.

Footsteps clomped behind her. "Incoming."

Charlie's deep voice penetrated her haze, and she jumped back.

Blake's chest rose and fell in deep breaths that matched her own. He grabbed her hand and glared at his friend. "What are you doing?"

"Preserving your privacy." He held up his camera.

Tad appeared from the other side. "There you two are." His hot gaze went from Blake to Harlow. "Dale thought we were missing something."

"You weren't." Blake squeezed, then let go of Harlow's hand. He placed his against her back, drawing her close and turning her mic back on before reaching for his own.

"Right." Tad watched Harlow. "Her face tells a different story."

Blake edged in front of her. "Thought you were grabbing shots of the winery."

"I was, but Dale noted Harlow's and your mics were on the fritz. When he couldn't find you with the other ladies, he wanted me to check it out."

Dale knew right where they were. It was his job. The only reason he pulled that stunt around Carmen and Blaire was to cause more drama.

"They're working now." Blake nodded at Tad. "Head on back. We'll be right behind you."

Tad disappeared around the corner. Charlie peered out from behind his camera. "Shall we?"

"Give us a sec." Blake shared a look with Charlie.

"I'll walk slow, but when I get to the edge of the building you need to be moving."

Blake nodded. As soon as Charlie turned, Blake leaned down to Harlow. "I have something for you."

"Again?"

He chuckled and dug in his pocket, then pulled out another gold pin, this one in the shape of St. Stephen's Cathedral from Vienna. He handed it to her. "I know you saw the palaces that day, but I thought this pin was beautiful, and—"

"It's perfect." Her fingers ran over the edges. "I could kiss you."

"At least you're finally admitting you want to."

"I must be delirious." She smirked at him.

He ran a hand over her forehead and cheek. "No temperature, but you're definitely hot." He wiggled his eyebrows then leaned to press a kiss to her cheek. His mouth slid to her ear, his voice deliciously low. "I'm claiming the real deal sooner rather than later."

Not even on her lips, and her nerves were jumping.

If he decided to stake that claim, she was in real danger of losing her heart.

Chapter Twenty-One

B lake leaned his head back and let Darcy knot the silver tie she'd picked to go with his tailored charcoal suit for tonight. Another cocktail party meant he was down to four women. Peyton and Blaire hadn't received a phone call, and they should be on their way home right now.

After three full days of dates, he was more than ready for this to be done. The only bright spot to yesterday's tour of Salzburg with Gina and Peyton—complete with *The Sound of Music* reenactment—was that Harlow hadn't had to sit through it as well.

It still tore at his heart, the way the rest of the bike tour turned out. After his private moment with Harlow at the winery, Carmen and Blaire had been like piranha ravenous for him and ready to tear Harlow to shreds. Cutting comments and razor-sharp glares circled her the rest of the day. Dale's bid for drama played out perfectly, and Blake wasn't about to put her through that again.

Darcy patted his chest. "All set, chief."

"Thanks." He sat to put on his shoes.

"Holding up okay?"

"Be better if I only had to spend the night with one woman." Someone knocked at his door, and he rose to answer it. "Unfortunately, I'm a few weeks out from that happening."

Darcy packed up her tools, snapping her gum as she went. "You'll make it."

He wasn't concerned about himself.

Blake pulled open the door. Great. "Dale. Come on in."

The producer entered and remained standing. "Final four. How you feel about it?"

"Like I'm ready to be done."

Dale leaned against the wall. "You're coming in to the home stretch." He crossed his arms. "Just got off the phone with your mom. She watched this week's footage and is wondering why you didn't show a connection with anyone after Tarynn."

Blake shrugged. "Because there isn't one. I realized that as soon as I kissed Tarynn. I would have let her go, but Peyton and Blaire could at least salvage their jobs if I sent them home now. Tarynn already quit hers, so I figured she could at least use the rest of this as a vacation."

"What a gentleman."

"Trying to make the best of a bad situation."

Dale bristled. "Didn't seem to think it was so bad when you suggested it to the network."

"Things change."

They stared each other down, and then Dale looked at Darcy. "Give us a minute."

Her eyes widened slightly. "Sure." She scurried out the door.

Neither spoke for a moment.

"*Things* need to stop changing until this show is finished. Got it?" Dale pushed into Blake's space. "I've been lenient with the rules, probably too lenient, but my generosity is wearing thin when I receive nothing in return. And," he added slowly, "your mother is starting to worry."

It was like pulling on a marionette's string. He wanted to cut those strings, but every time he came close, the memory of Dad's lifeless body stopped him. If this show could save his mother, he needed to deliver, because he couldn't lose another parent to their own hand.

But he also refused to hurt Harlow.

He simply needed to find middle ground.

Blake met Dale's cool stare. "It's going to work out. I promise."

"The footage you've provided doesn't exactly inspire confidence."

"Then I guess you'll just have to trust me."

*

Harlow grasped a fistful of the gauzy yellow fabric that flowed from her strapless dress. The material darted in at the waist then fell in folds to puddle on the floor—even with her in heels. Crystals lined the sweetheart neckline. One of the most beautiful gowns she'd worn yet.

She found Darcy's stare in the mirror. "Do you have an entire room dedicated to wardrobe on this ship?"

"Try three."

"Seriously?" Harlow took a sparkling choker from her.

"Blake takes up most of it." She sat beside Harlow and helped latch the necklace. "He loves clothes."

"He does?"

Darcy handed her earrings. "I think it's because he grew up watching them tear his mom apart if she wasn't put together. So now he never steps out anywhere unless he's in the latest style. That way, they can never rag on him."

Each day she was here, another layer of Blake unraveled.

Darcy unzipped a small black bag and pulled out concealer. "I saved you for last, but we need to hurry. Dale's pushing everyone to start on time tonight." Ten minutes later, Darcy snapped her powder closed. "Okay. Take a look."

Harlow stood and faced the mirror. "You are a miracle worker."

Darcy packed up her things. "I don't do miracles. That's God's department. I only work with what he's given, and you've been blessed."

Cheeks warming, Harlow squeezed Darcy's arm. "You've been so sweet to me. Thank you."

They walked out the door and in opposite directions. Harlow followed the maroon carpet to the marble atrium where the stairway circled both up and down. She grasped the dark wooden railing and climbed to the glassed-in sitting room.

Only three other women greeted her. Peyton and Blaire hadn't made it beyond their last dates. By the time this ship docked, one more would be gone. Could even be her.

A waiter approached her with a tray of champagne. "Miss?"

"Oh, no thanks." She nodded toward the bar. "Do they have club soda?"

"Coming right up." He returned to the bar.

Carmen sipped her champagne. "Not drinking tonight?"

"Nope."

"Evening, ladies." Blake strode into the room. Harlow gave him a full smile, which he returned and then sauntered her way. "You look beautiful tonight."

"Thanks."

Carmen wrapped her tentacles around him. "Can I snag you?" She ran a finger up his arm.

The clock might have well struck midnight, because the spell was broken.

"I was talking with Harlow." Blake's jaw tensed.

"Too bad." The woman had muscles, because he stumbled under her pull.

"It's okay, Blake." Harlow injected lightness, even if she wasn't feeling it. "I'll catch up with you later."

Lines strained his face, as if he hurt for her, but he followed Carmen anyway.

"Harlow," Tarynn called from the bar. "Come join us for a drink."

"Thanks, but I think I'll head upstairs for a walk."

Tarynn shrugged and reached for her tumbler.

Before escaping to the upper deck, Harlow snuck to her room for her camera. She needed something to focus on other than the fact that Carmen carted Blake off to some private place to cozy up—even if he was probably fighting her off. The mental image still needed replacing.

Outside she switched to her 70-200 ED VR II telephoto lens—her real treat, if Blake must know—and started snapping away. They floated past another town with its maypole at the top of the town center, bright ribbons floating on the wind. In the foreground a crane spread it wings wide and skimmed over the surface of the river. Harlow grabbed several shots, then angled back up to the lush hills of the Wachau Valley and the evening rays of sun.

Footsteps rose up the stairwell behind her. "I figured I'd find you up here," Blake said as he pointed to her camera, "with that."

"I needed some fresh air."

"Did you get it?"

"I did."

"So are you coming back in?" His voice warmed her.

The thought of seeing him with all the other women? Not so much.

"Is the party over yet?"

"No."

Setting her camera on the ground beside the heels she'd removed earlier, Harlow squared her shoulders and turned to lean her arms on the rails, her focus on the sunset. "Have Jace find me when it is. I think I'll keep enjoying the fresh air."

"Avoiding me again?" He stepped closer, mere inches away.

She half-turned. "No. I'm avoiding you with other women again."

He didn't say anything for a moment. Waited until she fully faced him. He had to know she would. Then he turned off his mic. His fingers trailed against the skin of her back as he flicked hers off next.

How could he keep doing that without getting into trouble? "Blake—"

"I know this is hard on you." His hands skimmed her arms. "For a split second tonight, when you left the room, I wondered if..." He paused, capturing her gaze.

She didn't look away. "If?"

"If it might be easier to let you go." Tenderly, he cupped her face. "But I can't do it."

She refused to ask why not. Refused to let him rethink his answer. Because she wanted to stay.

His fingers drifted from her cheek to her nape, and with both hands he gently tugged her to him. She stepped forward, her bare toes touching the cold tips of his black leather shoes. His thumbs rested at her jaw as he tilted her face up. "One night without you in the room, and it was like the air had been sucked out."

That's how her lungs felt with each of his words.

He dipped his forehead to hers. "I have no idea what's going on. All I know is I want to try to grasp whatever this is. To believe it's real."

The warmth of his hands on her skin set her heart racing at speeds she didn't think possible. His words sounded so good. His touch felt even better. So why couldn't she forget the other women inside? She inhaled sharply.

"What's wrong?" he whispered.

So much, and none of it their fault. This situation pulled out all of her insecurities. No doubt it made for great TV, but it sure was lousy for the condition of her heart. "It's so hard to see you with the other women and trust this is all going to work out. After my last relationship—"

"You mean with the idiot?" His jaw tensed but he relaxed it. "I get it, Harlow, I really do. It's equally hard for me to believe you're here for the right reasons." He played with the hair that had fallen from her updo. "It's like we're playing that old trust-fall game. Both of us are fine being the catcher, but neither of us wants to be the first to fall."

He was right. Still it scared her.

Blake leaned down, held her gaze, and spread that slow, lazy smile of his. Only when he aimed it at her, there was a tender warmth in his eyes tempered with a hint of vulnerability crinkling around their edges. "You have my word, Harlow. If you give me your trust, I promise, I will catch you." His assurance soothed her raw nerves. "I haven't ever made that promise in my life. Nothing ever meant enough for me to try. But you, Harlow, you're throwing me for a loop." He paused. "You make me want to try."

Their breath mingled, but he made no move to kiss her. She wanted him to. Badly.

She tipped her face up, but he slowly shook his head. "I'm not kissing you. Not until I know I have your trust. I've always moved with physical first, and this time I want more."

Who was this man?

Suddenly everything in her wanted to know. They'd find a way to make it work, because if he was willing to try, then so was she.

He pulled back slightly. "So, do you trust me?" More of a plea than a question, his words came on a whisper.

She brought her hand to his cheek. "I do."

*

Those were the two sweetest words Blake had ever heard. He watched her for a moment, his eyes taking in every detail. This woman ... Not what he expected and still, here she was, awakening feelings that for so long he didn't even believe he had. They buzzed inside, more real than anything he'd experienced and daring him to match the trust he'd asked of her.

When her lips deepened into a smile, he leaned down to claim them.

Footsteps pounded up the stairs behind them, and she jerked back.

Both their pulses raced, hers obvious by her rapid breath as she turned to watch Charlie hustling toward them.

His steps faltered. "Sorry," he said as he brought up his camera. "Dale mentioned something about waning confidence and sent me up here."

Holding back a growl, Blake flipped his mic on. Fine. Dale wanted footage, he'd give him footage. Fill every frame with Harlow. America would fall in love with her—he was already halfway there himself—

Whoa. Hold up. Love? A chuckle escaped his lips.

Her head tipped. "Is it Charlie or me who's making you nervous?"

"You."

"Good to know," she teased.

"Don't get too cocky," he said as he trailed his touch over the bare skin of her back, eliciting goose bumps along the way, "because I think it's a level playing field." He flicked the switch on her mic.

She shivered and lifted her chin.

Man, did he want to kiss her. But their first kiss belonged to them alone, and he intended to protect that. Ensure she never questioned his motives behind it. So instead, he cast a quick glance at Charlie, hoping she'd understand, then pointed to a pair of chaise lounges. "How about we sit?"

Following his gaze, she nodded with a half-smile. "Sure." She grabbed her camera and heels from the floor and then plopped into one of the chairs.

Blake settled beside her. "Nice lens." He stretched out his palm, and she handed her Nikon over. "70-200 ED VR II. Really didn't expect to see that."

"I saved two years."

He stood and pointed it at her.

She blocked his shot with her hand. "No way. I stay behind that thing. Besides, you're too close with the lens."

"It'll work." He stepped back and tried to angle around her barricade. "Come on. Let me take one of you, and I'll let you grab a shot of me."

She peeked around her fingers. "You'll willingly be in a photo?"

"Working on that trust. I wouldn't ask it of you without giving a little in return."

His words created the smile he captured on film. He studied the screen and then returned her camera. "I want a copy of that."

She stood. "We'll see." She aimed at him. "Your turn." Her camera whirred, and then she lowered it, a new expression on her face. One mixed with tenderness and awe. "You gave me your real smile, not your Hollywood one."

"You bring it out." Simple but true. He patted the space beside him, and she settled onto it, then rested her head against his shoulder.

He reached inside his pocket. "I have something for you."

She peeked up. "You have to stop doing that."

He held out a golden bike.

Laughter rolled from her, quickly turning into snorts. She slapped her hand over her mouth.

Blake chuckled. "You *do* snort." He lowered her hand. "It's cute."

"Can we agree it's not and pretend you never heard it?"

Blake nodded to Charlie. "Sorry. It's on film."

Her eyes turned into saucers.

Another laugh escaped his lips. "Trust me. It's cute."

"Sure. Like a rhino." She took the pin from him, examining it. "You really need to stop buying me stuff."

"Do you like it?"

Her gaze shot to his. "Of course."

"Then I'm not going to stop."

"I meant I like this pin, not—"

He squeezed her hand. "I know what you meant, but I'm still not going to stop." She shivered, maybe from the breeze, maybe from him. Either way, he wrapped his arm around her shoulder. "Tell me about Wheels on the Ground."

With Charlie filming, this could be free marketing. She hadn't pressed him on it like he'd expected, but since the day they met she'd been turning his expectations upside-down.

"I thought you didn't want to hear about my charity."

"I never said that."

She twisted and looked up at him. "Not in so many words."

Blake let loose a long sigh. "I've been burned a lot of times, Harlow. Giving you a flat no was a knee-jerk reaction."

"And now?"

"Now I'm controlling that reflex." He pressed a kiss to the top of her head. "I'd like to hear about what's important to you."

"All right." She sat up. "Wheels on the Ground is a nonprofit Mae and I are trying to start."

"To get wheelchairs to children that need them."

"You were listening at our interview."

He nodded. "But you haven't secured funding yet. Which is why you wanted to do an auction."

Her turn to nod. "It seemed like a good idea." She studied him. "I truly didn't know she had nominated me for this show, but it came at the perfect time. Mae … we don't know how long she really has. This charity is important to her." She hesitated. "It's important to me."

"Because of her?"

"And because of all the children. Kids who blur into the background because of their disabilities." A mixture of a sigh and light laugh came out. "Mae's sickness kept her front and center around our place. I always heard how God had chosen her for something special. But those kids, it's like the opposite."

Blake clasped her hand. "Suddenly your pictures make so much sense."

Her brow wrinkled.

If she couldn't see it, he wasn't sure she could hear it. So he'd make it his job to start showing her she was as special as her sister.

"I hear we'll be close to Regensburg tomorrow. It has some great shopping and beautiful old buildings that might be perfect for pictures."

The confusion on her face gave way to intrigue. "Sounds fun."

"Want to check it out with me?" He fiddled with her pinkie.

"You're asking me on a date *in person*?"

"Looks like it." He released her hand and watched her.

"Isn't that against the rules?"

"It's not what was scripted, but someone keeps hinting that a little more reality will make the show." He brushed a strand of hair off her forehead. "And since what she thinks is becoming rather important to me, I thought I'd take her suggestion. So how about it?"

Heels tapped up the staircase, interrupting them before Harlow could answer.

"There you are." Carmen stood on the top deck, her gaze narrowing in on them. "You've been gone a long time, Blake."

Charlie stepped back to include her in the shot.

"Really?" He checked his watch. "Only fifteen minutes."

"Without me." She pushed out her bottom lip as she sauntered over. "That's a long time. Do I get fifteen minutes alone with you?"

Harlow stood. "Think I'll head downstairs and inside. It's getting cold up here."

"It's about to heat up." Carmen eyed Blake.

He fisted his hands. He was through being someone's main course. "Actually, Carmen, I'm ready to head inside too. It's been a long day, and I'm sure most of you are ready to turn in."

Carmen cocked out her hip. Her red mini and heels that could double as stilts elongated her legs. Yet they didn't hold his attention like Harlow did. "Is that an invitation?"

Harlow brushed passed Carmen. Blake made to follow her, but Carmen stopped him with her palm flat against his chest. "Trust me, you want it to be one."

He grasped her wrist and pulled her hand away from him, for once glad Charlie was catching this all on tape. He didn't want her twisting any words. "Coming on this strong is not attractive, Carmen."

Her laugh was low and—he guessed—her attempt at sultry. "I've been called a lot of things, but unattractive isn't one of them. Get me alone, and I'll change that opinion."

"Sorry, but not going to happen."

She pressed her body close to his and her lips to his neck. "When the sweet ones don't give you what you want, you'll change your mind. Men like you always do."

"Don't count on it." He pushed her off and bypassed her for the stairs. Harlow was already down them.

Carmen didn't move from her spot, but her words found him. "Oh, I'm planning on it."

Once upon a time, she'd have been right. But not anymore. Now he was banking on something bigger. Something real.

Chapter Twenty-Two

Harlow knocked on the guest-room door in front of her. The cocktail party had wound down a little before midnight. Blake was filming his confessionals, while Gina, Tarynn, and Carmen turned in for the night. Harlow was waiting for her promised phone call to check on Mae. It felt like a year since she'd last heard her voice, not seventeen days.

Dale opened. "Come on in." He motioned to a velvet green club chair beside a small black desk and phone. "The call is being placed. You get ten minutes. You can ask about how things are with them, but no talking about the show." He handed her the phone.

That wasn't a problem for her. She wasn't ready to share her feelings about Blake. Not until she had them better figured out and could field all the questions her family would ask. Questions she obviously didn't have answers to.

Which was the only positive in the constant interruptions of their kisses. Not that feelings weren't there—incredibly strong feelings. She simply didn't know what to do with them, and if Blake kissed her, she'd have to face them.

And right now, there were too many variables she wanted to ignore.

She needed a moment to think. To pray.

The ringing stopped and three voices answered, "Hello?"

Harlow pushed aside her thoughts and focused on her family. "Hey, you guys."

Mom, Dad, and Mae all started talking at once.

"Hold up." Harlow pulled the phone from her ear. "One at a time."

Laughter flowed over the line. Mom's voice stood out from the others. "We miss you, honey."

"I miss you too."

"What's Europe like?"

"It's beautiful. I can't wait for you to see the pictures I've taken."

"We'll have a huge party once you get home. When will that be?" Dad asked.

"I can't say, Dad."

"Then fill us in on what you can tell us about."

"I'm seeing some amazing things, I'm doing well, and I only get ten minutes." She shifted in her seat, tucking her legs under her. "So what's going on there? How're you feeling, Mae? How was your doctor's appointment?"

"Your turn to hold up," Mom said. "One question at a time."

"Sorry." Harlow sighed. "I'm used to being there for everything."

"Which is why you needed a break." Mae's voice was soft. "To see that you can miss a few things and life doesn't fall apart."

"That's good. I think." Harlow switched the phone to her other ear. "You sound tired."

"I am, but I've had a busy day."

"Your doctor appointment would have been two days ago. Did you have to go back today?"

"My life can exist of more than doctors' appointments, Harlow."

"I know."

"Do you?"

"Girls," Mom jumped in. "We only have a few minutes. Can we spend it getting along?"

They'd always gotten along. At least until this silly show. Harlow played with the black coiled cord of the phone. "Sorry if that came out wrong, Mae. I'd love to hear what you were up to."

"I had lunch with Jack and his father."

Harlow's pulse leapt. She shouldn't have left. It was her fault Mae was tired. "I knew if you tried to work on things with him, you'd get worn out. Let me deal with it when I get home."

"It was fine, Harlow. We actually came up with some good ideas."

Dale knocked on the door. He opened it and held up five fingers. Harlow nodded, then refocused on Mae. "You did?"

"Which we'll talk about after your trip."

Her heart dipped. She hated being out of the loop. "At least give me an overview."

"Harlow, don't worry about it." Dad joined their conversation. "Concentrate on having fun there."

While Mae worked herself to exhaustion.

"I should come home."

"Don't you dare." Mae piped back up. "If God wants Wheels on the Ground to happen, it'll happen whether you're in Europe or here in Michigan."

"But—"

"But nothing. Now please, tell me about Europe. After all the work I did to get you there, I deserve some details." Mae's words popped with laughter.

Was it genuine?

Harlow sighed.

"Come on, Harley. Paint a picture for me."

"I landed in Budapest ..." she started. By the time she got to the palaces of Vienna, Dale had returned.

"Time," he said.

Harlow squeezed the phone. "I have to go."

"Enjoy yourself," Dad repeated.

Right. She'd completely failed. Here she sat on a beautiful boat, and her sister laid in her bed, dreams on hold while Harlow touched the corner of hers.

"Sure."

"Harlow." Mom's and Mae's voices overlapped.

Harlow injected enthusiasm in her voice. "I'll have fun. Promise." In her peripheral, Dale tapped his watch. She gripped the phone. "Love you guys."

"Love you too."

The phone cut off on all their voices.

Harlow set her end in the cradle and stood. "Thanks for that."

"It was part of the deal." Dale walked her to the door, opened it, and looked both ways. "Better get to bed. Tomorrow will come early."

She nodded. "Thanks again." Then strolled down the hall to her room.

What a long night. What a long two and a half weeks. She'd left Abundance certain of so many things and now stood in the middle of Europe with a million questions.

And no answers.

She flopped on her bed and reached for her Bible, hoping to find one.

*

Blake strode up the gangplank. Never-ending night. By the time he'd ditched Carmen and returned to the party, Harlow was across the room, and Gina took her opportunity to snag him. When he unwrapped himself from her, Tarynn stood waiting, only to be interrupted minutes later by Carmen, round two. He'd spent the evening bounced between those three women like a ping-pong ball. He was about ready to pull the plug on this entire thing, grab Harlow by the hand, and make a run for it.

Best he could do was make sure she was on tomorrow's date like he'd invited her to be.

"I'm turning in." Charlie was steps in front of him. The light guys were still packing up. "I'm exhausted just watching you tonight. Can't imagine how you feel."

"Glad it's over."

Charlie chuckled. "Night." And disappeared inside his room.

Blake continued to the end of the hall and knocked on Dale's door. Hopefully, this would only take a second.

The door opened, and Dale sighed. "What do you need, Blake? It's late."

Blake tried to brush past. "Can I come in?"

"I'm not dressed. Give me a sec."

He shut his door, and then the bathroom door opened and closed. Dale reappeared, tightening his robe around him. "Come on in."

Blake stepped into the room.

"What can I do for you?" Dale asked.

"Tomorrow's date. I want Harlow's name on the card."

"I heard, but you know you don't get to pick that."

"I asked you to trust me."

"And yet tonight you went off with her. Alone. Again."

"Charlie got you footage."

"Of you chatting up her charity. Not exactly pulse-pounding. Frankly, her small-town charm isn't as alluring or interesting as I'd hoped."

Maybe not for him. "Put her on the date."

Dale tapped the table beside him, his eyes cutting to his bathroom door and back. "Fine. You can have Harlow tomorrow, but when you go on the other dates, you keep up pretenses. These are beautiful women, and you're a red-blooded man. Start acting like it."

"I'm not kissing any of them."

His harsh laugh was argument enough. Still, he added more, "The only thing you're not doing is declaring your love." A smile slithered out. "That includes with Harlow."

"I know what I signed." And it might dictate his words, but not his actions. Nothing said he had to be physical with the women.

"Good. So do I. Don't forget it, because even though I've allowed a few blurred lines, my memory's just fine." He opened his bedroom door.

Blake nodded, and returned to his room. Exhausted, he slipped inside and into pajama pants. He started to pull off his shirt and caught a whiff of the fresh scent Harlow wore—cotton with the underlying sweetness of jasmine.

He caught sight of himself in the mirror. Like looking at a new man emerging from behind the old worn one.

This man held on to a sliver of belief true love existed. Not a purely physical attraction or a scripted relationship. But something bigger. Something he'd only scratched the surface of.

Remembering Harlow snuggled in his arms nearly had him out the door and knocking on hers. She'd answer. He was sure. And her open door would be all he'd need.

Blake scrubbed a hand across his face. Except he was tired of doing the same thing and expecting different results. That was the definition of insanity, and his life was definitely insane.

It was time for a change.

Which meant a cold shower, not a trip to Harlow's bedroom.

The physical would come. Soon. But first he wanted the right beginning.

Before he could change his mind, he ripped off his shirt and headed for the bathroom.

A knock rapped across his door. He stopped. Held completely still.

Another knock and his palms slicked. Was she thinking of him? He swallowed. It was one thing to stay away from her door, but if she'd come willingly to his … He walked to the door, telling himself he wouldn't invite her in, knowing he didn't possess the strength. He opened it a slit.

That was more than enough to see the little Carmen had on.

Relief quickly turned to anger.

She grinned. "Turn down service."

"I'm all set. Thanks."

"Oh." Her hand slid into the open crack, preventing him from shutting it. "I think you'll like this service."

"Carmen, it's late." He tried to remove her hand. She was better than any cold shower would have been. "You should be in bed."

She chuckled low. "Exactly."

"Your own bed."

"Yours would be more fun."

"We settled this earlier tonight. I'm not interested." No way he was opening the door any farther. "Go to bed."

"You're really not going to let me in?" Her fingers didn't budge from the open space in the doorway.

"Nope. It's the rules."

"From what I've heard, you like to break them."

"You shouldn't believe everything you read."

"I've *watched* you break them for Harlow." Her voice held an edge; her words set him on one.

"I've never had her in my room."

"Why would you need to? You've found plenty of other places to be alone with her." Ice glinted in her eyes. "I'm only asking for my fair chance to prove myself to you. I promise you'll like what I have to offer."

Maybe once upon a time he would have. But he wasn't going for that story anymore. He wanted a new one.

"You've already proven everything I need to know." He pushed on the door. "You're going to want to move your hand."

"And if I don't?"

"Then you're going to need some ice."

Her eyes widened even as he applied more pressure to her fingers. Finally she removed them, and he closed out her glare.

"You don't know what you're missing, Blake." She pounded the door, paused, then pounded once more before stomping off.

Let her be angry. He was done with her. Dale may insist on keeping her around, but Blake would severely limit interaction.

He could make it to the end of this knowing Harlow waited at the finish line.

Chapter Twenty-Three

Mornings were Blake's favorite time of day. Possibly because breakfast was his favorite meal. When he was little, he'd wake to the smell of pancakes, hop out of bed, and find Dad waiting for him. Coffee in one hand, newspaper in the other, and a lopsided pile of buttery flapjacks in the center of the table. After his death, Colburn—not Mom—continued the tradition. It wasn't the same as his father, but it made those mornings survivable, and after time, something to look forward to again.

It had been years since he and Colburn had shared a pancake. Years since a morning had been this enticing, this genuine. He'd stopped believing in the possibility until Harlow, but with the way his nerves fired under his skin, that belief was being resurrected. She made him feel alive. Alive and vulnerable, because if this was real, then it would actually cost him to lose it.

And he didn't want to feel dead ever again.

Charlie should be here any moment, and as soon as they were set up, Blake could make the phone call to Harlow about today's date—make it official. Yep. This morning was shaping up better than any pile of pancakes he'd ever had.

He chuckled. No way he was letting Harlow know he'd just compared her to pancakes.

A knock rapped across his door. Blake stood and opened it, surprised to see Dale in the hall.

"Mind if I come in?"

Blake motioned him in with his hand. "Is the shoot running behind?"

"You could say that." Dale crossed the room.

"How long till we're on schedule?"

"Depends."

"On?"

"You."

Heat built through Blake at equal rates with dread. "How so?"

"If you're in a mood to argue, then this could take a while." Dale pointed to the phone. "Otherwise, it's just a quick phone call to Carmen, and we're set to go."

"Carmen?" Blake straightened. "I thought we settled this last night."

"Things change." Dale threw his words back at him. "Isn't that what you said?"

"Don't play games with me, Dale."

Dale sighed long. "Argumentative then."

"Definitely." Oh, he had no idea. "I want Harlow on this date."

Dale crossed his arms. "And I want a usable season."

"I told you to trust me."

"I've trusted you for over two weeks, and it's left me with barely usable footage." Dale smiled. "But then I watched last night's. You really have created something special with Harlow, listening to her talk about her sister, promising her today's date before you even called. Nice set-up."

"It wasn't a set-up."

"No?" Dale shrugged. "I guess it's all in the editing then."

Breakfast became acid in his stomach. "Don't do this, Dale."

Silence. Blake didn't move. Didn't blink, even when Dale's eyes narrowed.

"Here's the thing, Blake. I've let you flip that mic on and off and evade cameras like you were the producer, every bit of it going against your contract. And I allowed it because I thought you'd give me something in return. You haven't, and frankly I can't wait any longer. I see an opportunity, and I'm taking it."

Dale rubbed his fingernails. "You're going on this date with Carmen, and you're giving me heat—or at the very least, potential for heat that I can have an editing team work with."

"Not going to happen."

He continued rubbing each nail until he got to the last. Then he clasped his hands together and gave the slightest of shrugs. "Then Harlow will be leaving today, and Charlie's fired."

The shock wave rocked him. "What?"

"Harlow's contract specified no off-camera or off-mic time with you—"

"That was all me."

"Yet she was there." He relaxed, his lips spilling down while his brows arched. "And if I ask her for the truth, do you honestly think she'll deny it?"

Blake's blood pressure spiked. "You really want to do this?"

"What I want, Blake, is chemistry and continued conflict. Putting you on another date with Harlow won't bring either, which means no ratings." Victory twisted across his pompous face. "But you *asking* Harlow on a date last night, then ditching her today for another woman—now that's good conflict."

"I won't do this to her, not when I gave her my word."

And breaking it would hit her weakest spot.

"I'm aware. I heard it on last night's footage." And with that wicked grin, he knew exactly how much it would hurt Harlow. "So keep your word to her or explain to your friend why he's out of two jobs."

"Two jobs?"

"You don't think I'd keep Charlie on your mother's show, do you?"

Frustration licked through Blake. He kneaded the back of his neck and stared out his window, thinking of Harlow and Charlie. Sunset Homes wasn't cheap, and Charlie's mother needed the care.

Then there was Darce.

He might be able to convince Charlie to let him pay for his mother's care, but it wouldn't be indefinite. And there'd be no way Charlie would ask Darcy to marry him if he was unemployed. They'd already waited a year.

Charlie needed this job. It was his step back toward repairing his old reputation, and if Dale fired him, no one would be willing to take a chance on him. There would be a permanent domino effect.

And Harlow would be gone. At least with her here, he could explain. Even call her first, because it nearly strangled him, the thought of her sitting there, expecting her phone to ring, and hearing Carmen's instead.

Blake turned to Dale. "You win, but at least let me talk to Harlow first."

The man straightened. "No can do. They're at breakfast together, and it would ruin the authenticity of the moment."

"Too bad. I'll only agree if I can talk to Harlow first." There was no way he'd let her think he chose Carmen over her.

Dale got in his face. "I think you've forgotten who's really in charge here. You're lucky I'm even giving you a choice. Keep it up, and it'll be gone."

The words backed him into a corner, squeezing tight. His anger climbed.

"So?" Dale checked his watch. "Am I filming a date today or an exit?"

Charlie needed this job. All Blake could hope for now was damage control.

"I'll go on the date." He ran a hand through his hair. "Better let Darcy give me a touch-up first though."

Dale's smile was all sorts of egotistical. "Sure. After you make your call."

Blake picked up his phone, bitterness replacing the sweetness he'd been dreaming of this morning. He'd asked for her trust, and he was about to obliterate it.

With her past, she might not give him the opportunity to set it straight.

*

Sunshine spilled across the top deck, warming everything in its path. Harlow tipped her face and absorbed every ray she could, the heat melting her muscles and soothing her. She'd hardly slept all night, but at least she felt more settled. As the sun rose, things had finally started to click into place.

It was as simple as accepting the situation at face value.

She liked—*really* liked—Blake Carlton. And even though the deepest part of her knew it couldn't work, it didn't stop her heart from hurling headfirst into him. From hoping that maybe, just maybe, things could change.

Last night she'd given him her trust. Something she didn't offer freely since Peter. Yet somehow, Blake won her over even in the midst of a similar situation. But what she already felt for Blake was more intense than anything she'd shared with Peter. Already he saw more of her, challenged her, and evoked feelings Peter never had.

Completely crazy, yet true.

And today they were going on a date. Her smile took over, and she ran her fingers over her phone which sat on top of the tablecloth. Anticipation for its ring trilled through her. Even knowing the cameras were coming along didn't dim it. Blake managed to put her at ease in every situation. Funny, thinking back on how much he infuriated her that first time they'd met. But he was nothing like the egocentric she'd pegged him as. He hid it well, but he had a big heart and right now it appeared aimed at her.

She happily stood in the crosshairs.

Peeking her eyes open, she sought out the spot she and Blake sat last night before tracking to the railing where he'd nearly kissed her. Her fingers brushed against her lips.

"You look happy."

Harlow slid her gaze to Carmen's tight smile. The woman plunked her plate of toast down and settled into the seat beside her as if they were long lost friends.

"It's a beautiful morning." Harlow nodded at a waiter with a coffee carafe in his hands. She desperately needed that dark brew—and the distraction.

"If I had as much alone time with Blake as you do, I'd be happy too." She buttered her toast.

Holding back her nasty response called for a bigger distraction than coffee. "Know what? I think I'll grab some breakfast too." She hurried off to order an omelet. Maybe Carmen would be gone by the time it was ready.

Sighing, she passed the chocolate croissants to where a waiter stood beside his fry pan. "Can I have an egg-white omelet with mushrooms and spinach?"

He nodded and pointed to her chair. "I'll bring it when it's done."

"Thanks." She snagged a plate and piled it high with fruit.

Tarynn joined her. "Looks like you could use some company at your table."

"You think?" Harlow scooped up pineapple chunks. "I have no idea why she sat by me."

"To create drama and snag camera time." Tarynn rolled her eyes. "I'll come over and play referee between you two."

"Thanks."

Saluting her with a banana, Tarynn headed for the table. Harlow slipped some papaya onto her plate and then followed. She slid her phone over and set her fruit down, focusing on Tarynn and not Carmen. "Did you sleep well?"

Tarynn smiled. "Slept like a baby." She picked up her coffee. "You?"

"Perfectly."

Tarynn leaned in close. "Who do you think will get the one-on-one?"

Harlow shrugged. Carmen smiled.

The waiter delivered her omelet, and Harlow dug in, grateful for the distraction.

Gina showed up and settled at the table with them. She looked at Harlow's plate.

"You know, I haven't seen you eat anything other than fruit and veggies since we showed up. Are you a vegetarian?"

"I eat fish and chicken sometimes." Harlow sipped her coffee.

"You don't even add cream to your coffee." Tarynn added a large dollop to hers. "That's crazy."

Again, Harlow shrugged. "It's what I'm used to."

"You're telling me you don't ever get a hankerin' for one of those chocolate croissants?" The Southern was coming out of Tarynn this morning.

"Sure I do." Harlow bit into a juicy strawberry and finished it.

"So what are you, Superwoman or something?" Gina goaded.

"Definitely not." Early morning sun warmed her face. "I guess I want to keep my body as healthy as I possibly can." God might not think she was special like Mae, but he had chosen her to be the healthy one, and she refused to squander that role. Eventually he'd see how well she handled it and think she was enough for something, anything, else.

Laughter snuck from Carmen's perfect nose. "And you don't think cutting loose a little helps your mental health?"

Why did everyone on this trip think she didn't have any fun in life? She set down her fork. "I cut loose."

"Really? How so?" Carmen challenged.

This entire trip was her cutting loose.

"And no saying this trip." Tarynn smirked. "You only came because your sister nominated you. Not because you were searching for love like the rest of us."

But she still found it. At least the beginnings of it.

Which made her heart flutter. So totally cliché, but it was the truth. Crazy fluttering like it was going to fly from her chest. Of course, it could be nervous anticipation over seeing Blake later today.

"Morning, ladies." Jace stood on deck.

"Morning, Jace." Four voices blended to one.

"I trust you all slept well."

Apparently that was a safe topic because everyone seemed to be using it.

Jace's dimple deepened. "I know your excitement has nothing to do with my good looks." He waited on the chorus of light laughter. "So let's get to it. I see you all have your phones ready."

Anticipation buzzed across the deck.

"In a minute, one of you will receive a phone call. That lucky lady is going on a walking tour of Regensburg with Blake today. The rest of you are welcome to take one of the tours we have scheduled or explore the city on your own." He held up a folded paper. "The desk downstairs has several maps for any of you adventurers."

Harlow tried to clear her face of expectation and listen to Jace's words, but her focus kept flickering to her phone laying beside her plate. It was like a ticking time bomb, except she couldn't wait for it to go off.

And still the ring caught her breath.

Except it wasn't her phone that rang.

Carmen's smile was a perfect impression of the cat who'd eaten the canary. She slid her finger across the screen in front of her and answered. "Morning, Blake."

No need to dig any farther. Shock covered Harlow's face without even trying, stealing her breath and slashing through her racing pulse. Sweet anticipation turned to bitter surprise, a taste she'd swallowed before and swore she'd never savor again.

But somehow, Blake Carlton had swerved past her defenses and served her another heaping portion.

Only this time, it was more than she could consume. She pushed back her chair and hurried to her room before tears choked her.

Chapter Twenty-Four

Harlow sat at the front of the boat, the warm breeze blowing her hair. At least Blake had told the truth about one thing. Regensburg *did* promise to be a picturesque city. A sigh puffed past her lips. The day wouldn't be a complete loss. She'd still be able to snap some pictures. So what if he'd taken her trust and crumbled it like the castle walls they'd passed along the water.

Served her right. It had been crazy to play the game. To believe, even for a night, that he would pick her.

She was background material. Her entire life she'd tried to show she was worth taking a chance on. Worth picking for more. But if God couldn't even see it, why had she thought Blake would?

Ever since Mae's diagnosis, Harlow had diligently cared for her healthy body, along with watching over her sister. As good as Mae was in her disability, Harlow would be in her health. And she'd never flaunted her well-being in front of Mae or made her want for more—just like Mom and Dad had asked. If Mae couldn't do something, neither would Harlow.

Only she didn't simply strive to succeed at maintaining her fitness or caring for her sister. No. Any challenge God placed in front of her, she met, hoping at some point he'd see her and realize he could use her too. When dance and violin lessons were pulled so her parents could form a support club for Mae, Harlow spent hours coming up with crafts and snacks for the weekly meetings. When she was turned down for the out-of-state photography school but accepted to her local college, she went into nursing to help with Mae's at-home care. When Peter broke it off with her, she threw herself into helping start Wheels on the Ground.

When would it be enough?

When would she ever stand out?

Apparently never—which was why Blake was on a date with Carmen. She'd been crazy to allow herself to expect anything different. The only believable thing about this show was Blake's desire for it to secure high ratings, and he'd played her well. Setting up the narrative for a heart-tugging conflict America would tune in for. She'd been the idiot to fall for him and his charm, and she'd done it all with her eyes wide open.

She blew out a frustrated puff of air and stood. Enough of this pity-party. Time to grab her camera bag and explore the city. Get her head and heart focused on something else. She hurried to her room to change.

Soon she was off and walking. The double peaks of Regensburg Cathedral rose into the sky. Harlow approached the massive building, its beauty and detail only growing as she wound to the front. She spent nearly an hour inside, the sun fully up and warm when she finally exited.

Picking one of the narrowest streets, its blue flowerpots and yellow awnings calling to her, Harlow continued exploring. The beauty she'd seen during this unexpected trip was beyond what she could have ever imagined Europe to be like.

Three teenage girls caught her attention as did the door they walked through. After they strolled away, Harlow approached the opening. Massive. Wooden. Full of scars, yet oiled to a new shine. Its brass handle held dents but was clean in spite of the several deep marks.

Restored.

She uncapped her camera and snapped shots, making sure the light caught each of its blemishes and the beauty they only added to the door.

He will restore, support, and strengthen you, and he will put you on a firm foundation …

The word and verse were instant and so needed for her own heart today. Harlow capped her lens, and put a hand on the door. Such stories, depth, and meaning. Most people would pass by and only see a marred entryway, but she saw a stunning picture with God woven through every pixel.

Sliding her finger along the wood, she turned and strolled up the street feeling a tiny bit lighter.

Another hour later and her stomach growled. She followed the smells of fresh baked bread to the center of the town where tables flanked the entrance of a small restaurant. She peered at the menu posted in a little metal and glass stand. Salmon caught her attention, and she slid into one of the seats, waiting for the waitress to come her way.

Instead, a familiar figure waved.

"Mind if I join you?" Darcy asked as she approached.

"Sure." Harlow moved her things over. "Surprised to see you here."

"I have the afternoon off. Thought I'd check out the city." She sat. "Taking pictures?"

"A few."

They made small talk while the waitress took their orders and quickly delivered their lunch. Harlow bit into her salmon. The cook knew how to grill this fish. It melted in her mouth.

Darcy leaned back in her chair. "Did you get any nice shots this morning?"

Good. She wasn't going to bring up Blake.

"I hope so. It's hard to tell until I get them on my computer."

"What will you do with them?"

She shrugged. "Who knows. I'll be too busy to think about it."

"Work?"

"That and Wheels on the Ground." The breeze slowed. "It's where I've focused all my extra time for the past year."

"Because of Mae?"

"At first. She'd heard about something similar that Joni Eareckson Tada had done and wanted to start her own charity. I jumped on board to help, but once I started hearing all the stories of these kids, overlooked and forgotten … They touched my heart."

Darcy pushed her empty plate away. "You mentioned fifty thousand when we went shopping. Is that all you need?"

"No. I need a whole lot more than that, but in order for an agency in our hometown to consider us for a grant, they'd like to see us come up with seed money." She sighed. "Fifty thousand may as well be a million. I don't have that kind of money."

"Have you prayed about it?"

"Of course I have."

Darcy watched her. "And what direction has God pointed you in?"

"I thought it was to the Townsend Agency."

"As in Charlie's Angels?"

Harlow chuckled. "As in the agency in Michigan. They're friends of my family, and I thought for sure they were the answer."

"And they weren't?"

"Not if they want me to raise fifty thousand."

"Hmm." Darcy picked up her water. "I'll pray about it too. You're sure God wants you to start this nonprofit?"

"Why else would he place it on my heart?"

Darcy didn't answer straight off. Finally she zeroed in on Harlow. "Sometimes we can give ourselves tasks that God never assigned. They can be some pretty great things too, but that doesn't mean they're from him."

"This one is."

"What about your photography?"

"It's something I like to do, but it's not what I'm called to do. At least not right now." If it was, God would have opened that door instead of constantly slamming it. But once she proved to him her worth, then maybe he'd open it.

Darcy waited another beat. "And you're sure Wheels on the Ground is?"

"Positive."

"I'll be praying that everything works out then."

"Thank you."

Pushing away from the table, Darcy rested her hands across her stomach and people-watched for a few minutes while Harlow scanned through her pictures.

"What Dale did to you today, that was wrong."

Harlow's head whipped up at Darcy's statement. "Dale?"

"You do know it was Dale, not Blake, who put Carmen on that date."

Her heart picked up, then quickly slowed. Darcy was one of Blake's best friends. She either saw the best in him or was skewing things to keep him in a good light.

"If Blake really wanted me on that date, he'd have chosen me." She pointed to the table they shared. "But here I am, having lunch with you. Not that I haven't enjoyed it." She tried for a smile.

"You know he doesn't get to pick the dates."

"Yet he's found a way to bend or break the rules when it suits him."

"Dale's known about and allowed every bend in the rules, but he put his foot down on this one." She fixed on her. "I don't know why, and I don't know what exactly happened, but Blake didn't have a choice."

"We always have a choice." Harlow shrugged. "If I was important to him, he'd have kept his word."

Darcy opened her mouth, and Harlow held up her hand.

"My last relationship was with a guy who lied, cheated, and wound up engaged to one of my former friends. I swore I'd never put myself in the same situation, but I did it for Mae. And I wound up caught in the moment, falling for the romance of the show. Bottom line, that was on me. This morning broke the spell and now that I'm awake, I don't feel like dozing back off."

"I get this show has stuck you in what feels like the same situation, but it's really not. And you need to know that Blake hasn't kissed another woman since Vienna." She leaned across the table. "That was no fairy tale he was weaving. It was the real Blake. More real than I've ever seen him."

She wanted to buy those words. She simply couldn't afford to.

Could she?

A commotion to her right snagged her attention. Charlie walked backwards out of a small path between the buildings. He kept his camera focused squarely on Carmen, who snuggled against Blake's shoulder, her arm wrapped around his.

Harlow tossed some bills on the table. "I have to go." She raced in the opposite direction, away from the avalanche of emotions bearing down on her, threatening to bury her heart in hurt all over again.

*

Like a homing pigeon, Blake zeroed in on Harlow's retreating form. He pulled away from Carmen, tired of politely attempting distance all day. That politeness had cost Harlow too much. The pain across her face was bad enough.

That she ran from him so fast she forgot her camera only made the hurt and regret slice deeper.

Regensburg was big enough. How on earth had they run into each other?

Darcy picked up Harlow's camera bag and offered him a tight smile from across the courtyard. Then she turned and followed Harlow.

"Blake?" Carmen stood beside him. "What's wrong?"

"Just need a little space."

Her eyes narrowed and her lips pushed out. "Not a line I often hear from men."

He shrugged. "How about we go find our lunch?"

She smiled. "I'm definitely hungry."

213

Why was everything out of her mouth so physically charged? Had he once liked this game? Because he honestly couldn't remember. Definitely couldn't conjure up any desire for it right now.

Not since Harlow.

And things were beyond messed up there.

Would she give him a chance to explain?

Two hours later, lunch wound down and a car arrived. After a short drive, it delivered them to a spa. Blake bit back a word he hadn't said in weeks. No doubt about what Dale was up to here.

Sure enough, thirty minutes later, he was in a bathing suit in a tiny room with Carmen in an even tinier bikini. A mud bath took up one corner, while a rain shower for two stood in the other.

"This looks fun," Carmen purred.

Charlie coughed from the doorway.

And Blake brushed past him into the hall. Dale had pushed him too far. "Find Dale."

He slammed into the change room he'd come from and paced.

A moment later, the door opened.

"What's the problem?" Dale nearly growled.

Blake crossed his arms. "I told you I wasn't messing around with her. You may have forced the date, but you're not forcing anything else."

Dale pinched him, and Blake flinched.

"Just checking if you're alive."

Blake rubbed his arm. "Living and breathing."

"Then act like it." His cheeks were red. "Any honest man would be all over that woman."

"Not me." The words pushed through his clenched teeth.

Dale stopped and studied him for a moment. Then his shoulders relaxed, and he dug his hands into his pockets. "Look, Blake, you might think I'm the bad guy here, but I'm doing this for Harlow."

"Sure you are."

"Come on. She's not cut out for this world, and bringing her into it would destroy her."

"I'd leave before that could happen." Blake held out his hands. "Give it all up, because Harlow's worth it."

Dale stilled. "You'd do that to your mom?"

214

He'd figure it out. Somehow.

"I can make this work." Blake paced. "And I won't have to hurt Harlow or my mom in the process." He walked to the door. "Now I came on this date like you asked. I've smiled and flirted with Carmen, but you want to film a massage? Better make it a couple's one with separate tables and someone else's hands. That's as loose as I'm getting with her. So get your shots and get me back to the boat."

Blake stalked out the door in the opposite direction of the mud room. Dale could come find him once he decided what he wanted to do. Whatever it was, it wouldn't involve his hands on Carmen.

By the time filming at the spa and then a late dinner and dancing had finished, Blake was convinced he'd just endured the worst day of anyone's life. Carmen was in a foul mood, Dale wasn't speaking to him, and he still couldn't erase from his mind Harlow's face when she'd fled the small square in Regensburg.

All he wanted was to knock on her door, but even if she opened it, she'd most likely slam it in his face. She'd given him her trust, and he'd trampled it— no matter that he had no choice. She'd had an entire day to stew on it, to come up with her own reasoning. And knowing her, it'd be because she believed she fell short of the other women. That he'd chosen Carmen over her.

She couldn't be farther from the truth.

A car dropped him at the boat, and he hopped out. Movement on the upper deck caught his attention. Harlow?

He flew up the stairs, reaching the top out of breath.

Except it wasn't Harlow.

"Hey." Tarynn turned from the railing and smiled at him.

He waved and returned to the steps. "Sorry to interrupt your quiet. Think I'll head down for bed."

"Don't let me run you off." She leaned against the railing. "Stay. I promise I won't bite."

He hesitated.

"Aren't we supposed to be getting to know one another?" Her smile hinted at vulnerability.

He'd shut down enough women for the day.

Blake joined her at the rail. He leaned against it too, but kept a few feet between them. There was a fine line here he didn't want to cross. Tarynn was a sweet girl. She didn't deserve him ignoring her—but she also didn't deserve him leading her on.

"You've been thinking about hometowns?" she asked.

He nodded.

"I think you'll really like my parents." Her shoulder nudged his. "If you pick me, that is. No pressure."

Except there was. He felt it with each of them.

"Tarynn—"

She held up her hand. "No, seriously, Blake. I came into this with open eyes. All I ask is that you keep yours open too."

"I have."

"You sure?" No condemnation, just honest curiosity in her voice. "Because you attached to Harlow pretty quickly."

He had, and it felt nothing but right. Even when the connection freaked him out a little.

"I don't want to lead you on."

"You're not." She peered up at him. "Like I said, no pressure—unlike other women on this show." She chuckled. "Sorry, I'm not trying to be snarky but honest."

"I appreciate that about you."

"And you can trust it. Trust me." A speedboat passed them. "Bottom line, you have to keep three of us for hometowns. I know what I'm getting into." She hesitated, and nibbled her lip. "And if I'm being completely honest, Mom and Dad would be ecstatic if you showed up on their doorstep."

Blake chuckled. "I'll keep that in mind."

Her smile seemed genuine. "You do that." She squeezed his bicep, and before he realized what was happening, she'd stretched up and placed a soft kiss against his lips. "Night."

She slipped away, and Blake remained, watching the stars shimmer on the water. Not that he really saw them.

He'd had two women kiss him today. Two women offer themselves to him. At least Tarynn didn't come with claws, but he had no doubt if he followed her down those stairs, she'd open her door for him.

And all he wanted was the one woman who might as well be a world away right now rather than a floor below.

"You ought to be lost in thought." Charlie's deep voice rumbled from behind. "It'll take more than an 'I'm sorry' to fix this."

216

Blake turned to his friend. All afternoon Charlie had glowered at him from behind the camera. "Beating myself up enough, Charlie. I don't need your help."

"Don't suspect you do." Clouds passed over the moon. "What I can't figure out is why you did it."

And he wouldn't. If Blake told him the truth, Charlie would quit and today would have been a waste. "I didn't have a choice."

"There's always a choice, Blake. You made the wrong one."

His muscles tightened. "You have no idea what choice I made."

"Pretty sure I do." He straightened to full height. "My fate is in God's hands, friend, not yours. I know what my contract says. I know what I did." He nailed him with a glance. "And I know I'm covered, so if Dale wants to make waves, let him. I can swim."

Confusion swirled. "How did you know?"

"I've worked with Dale before." He shrugged. "And I overheard him talking to someone on the phone—your mom if I had a guess."

"Couldn't let him fire you."

"I appreciate what you did, but I'm not who you need to worry about."

Blake looked up. "No. I guess not."

"So how are you going to make it up to her?"

"Go and talk to her." He started for the stairs.

Charlie grabbed his arm. "It's after midnight."

"And my apology has waited long enough. I'm going crazy here."

"You're making it about you when it needs to be about her."

Blake tensed. Turned. "I'm not."

"Knocking on her door this late? You are." He let go. "Stop and think things through. You'll see her tomorrow."

"On a group date, with your camera rolling, and Dale's not in the mood for my off camera stunts anymore."

"We'll figure something out, but knocking on her door in the middle of the night isn't it. Neither of you are in the frame of mind to talk."

Blake slumped against the railing. "She's never going to trust me again."

Charlie mimicked Blake's stance, standing beside him and staring off into the night. "Maybe this time, instead of asking for her trust, you show her she has yours."

Blake's brow dipped.

"Come on, man. You cannot be this dense." Charlie zeroed in on him. "You can't ask her to take a risk you're not willing to fully take yourself."

"My hands are tied here. You heard Dale, there's only so much I can admit to Harlow while we're filming."

"I wasn't talking about words, I was talking action."

"You're actually suggesting—"

"Get your head out of the gutter." Charlie's face darkened. "If that's what you think will show her how much you care, then you're not worthy of her."

Heat built up Blake's neck. "I haven't even kissed her yet."

"Good." Charlie nodded. "Because if she's just a physical connection for you, then you need to back off."

"She's not."

"Then show her. Get those wheels of yours spinning and come up with an idea that shows her she not only means something to you, but that you trust her."

Wheels?

Blake grinned. "I think it's time to get to know her sister a little better."

Chapter Twenty-Five

Harlow pushed her breakfast away as Gina joined her table. Not that she had anything against her, but she was so not looking forward to today's group date.

Not when yesterday was supposed to be her one-on-one with Blake. Then she'd had to see him with Carmen plastered against his side. She still couldn't believe she'd run so fast she left her camera sitting there.

Thankfully, Darcy had brought it back to her without a word. Which was good, because she didn't want to think about how much Blake meant to her. Not when he'd chosen someone else.

And to add insult to injury, Tarynn was getting the last one-on-one tonight. It stung.

No matter. Tomorrow she was headed home, and she was under no delusions that Blake would follow. She could thank Mae for the wonderful vacation and get on with her life. She was through playing games.

"Ladies, we're ready for you," Jace called from the steps.

Harlow didn't stand until Gina started across the deck. Whatever they were doing, it involved a hike, judging by the boots laid out with her shorts this morning. At least they'd agreed that she could bring her camera. She could lose herself in taking pictures and let Gina enjoy all the time with Blake she wanted.

They slipped down the stairs to the gangplank. Against her intention, her eyes drifted to Blake standing at the bottom, waiting and watching, as if he knew she'd be looking for him.

His eyes held questions and that same openness—almost insecurity—that she'd seen in them before. Except this time she wasn't falling for it. He'd made his choice, and it hadn't been her.

Gina hurried down the gangplank and threw herself into Blake's arms. Harlow glanced the other way. Charlie stood to her right and offered a tentative smile.

Blake disengaged from Gina and stepped to her. "Hey."

"Hey."

He pushed his hands into his pockets. "Glad to see you came."

"I made a promise to my sister."

"To show up on this date?"

"To film this show." She crossed her arms. "And I'm someone who keeps my word."

He flinched, but right now, she didn't care.

"Ladies, Blake." Dale stood in front of them. "We're going to hike up to that castle," he said, pointing to the hillside behind them, "and have a picnic at the top. If you're ready, we'd like to start."

Harlow marched toward the trail. Her mic pack dug into her back. Not sure why they wanted her to wear it, she had no intention of talking today.

Footsteps clomped in the gravel behind her, and Gina's and Blake's voices mingled with the sound. Let them have their privacy.

She pushed her pace, remaining just shy of a jog. Soon their conversation faded, replaced by the wind gently whistling through the trees and a few birds chirping. Harlow allowed the noise to relax her, right up until the moment she found a small table set for three.

Only today. She only had to make it through today.

Moving her gaze from the offending table to what was left of the castle walls, she started forward to inspect them. Let Blake and Gina enjoy the picnic. She wasn't hungry.

The rough beauty of the ruins captivated her; the yellowed stones jagged beneath her palm as she traced the broken wall. She followed it around to where an old set of crumbling steps rose up to another floor with two of the walls still attached. Above was a turret that appeared to still be intact. Up on this hill, it had to provide a beautiful view.

Securing her camera around her neck, Harlow grabbed the stone and hauled herself onto the first stair—which originally had to have been the third—and tested her full weight to make sure it was secure. She gingerly stepped to another. Most of it was there. Eight more and she'd be at the second floor. Except the next step gave out under her.

Scrambling for balance, she grabbed air. This was going to hurt. Twisting to protect her back from the rocks beneath, she squeezed her eyes shut and anticipated pain.

Warm hands caught her around her waist.

Harlow peeked open her eyes to find Blake's blazing blues.

He set her on her feet and nodded to her camera. "That thing causes more trouble than it's worth."

"You're biased."

"I'm speaking from evidence collected."

She brushed a scrape on her arm. "Biased evidence."

"You could have broken your neck."

"But I didn't."

"Because once again I saved it."

Heat rose into her cheeks. She swallowed her snappy retort. He *had* just saved her neck—literally. Even if she was angry with him, he deserved her thanks. "Thank you."

"You're welcome."

They stared at each other. Nothing more to say, at least as far as she was concerned. After a long minute, she turned. "You should get back to Gina. I'm going to take pictures."

"Not up there you're not." He gently grabbed her wrist.

She tried to twist her arm away from his grip, but he tugged her closer. The sparks his touch sent aggravated her. "Please let go."

"You won't try and climb up there again?" He nodded to the second floor of the ruins.

"I make no promises."

"Then I'm not letting go."

She glared at him.

"Sorry, Harlow. But I'm not letting go of someone I care for only to watch her get hurt again." He stepped closer.

Oh, she wanted to believe those words. Wanted to let them burrow into her heart …

She stared at her toes. "It's too late, Blake."

"We barely got started. It can't be too late."

His thumb rubbed the inside of her wrist. "Have lunch with me? Please?"

It was impossible to concentrate with his touch against her skin.

221

"You need to eat, right?" He pressed.

"Where's Gina?"

"Already eating."

"Then why do you need me?"

"Because you're the only one I want at that table."

"Know what?" Harlow tried to tug away again. "I've never really been one for repeat stories."

"Not a repeat. Just the same one continuing."

"Right." She gave another tug.

"Say you'll have lunch with me, and I'll let go."

"That's not fair."

He shrugged.

"Fine." Anything was better than his thumb making those circles, flaming something in her that she was trying to keep dead. Because when this was all over, he would return to his world and leave her in hers. He'd already proven as much.

And watching him flirt with another woman—no matter how it might hurt—would cement the truth, hardening it around her heart.

He released her arm, then leaned in, a breath away and not breaking their stare. Her breath caught as he tipped her chin, bringing them even closer. "I am so sorry I hurt you, Harlow. I was in a situation where my back was against a wall, and I'm sorry I betrayed your trust because of it. Know this though, I will make it up to you. I promise."

And then he let her go.

And darn her all, she missed his touch.

"Come on." He pushed his hands back into his pockets. "Lunch awaits."

Her jelly legs nearly gave her away. Judging by the tug of his lips, they had, but he wasn't calling her on it.

*

Blake waited for Harlow, giving her a moment to catch her breath. Or for him to catch his own. He'd wanted to kiss her. To pour every emotion into touching her so she'd know he meant each word. But she was more than a physical connection. In her he saw the potential for his future. That he'd nearly messed it up scared the living daylights out of him.

But he could still make it right.

Because he hadn't missed the way her breath caught or how her pulse raced under his thumb as he held her wrist.

She wasn't as immune to him as she wanted him to believe.

Gave him hope and a desire to be patient. To take things at her speed. Because she was worth the wait. Worth his trust. Which is what had kept him up all night, working on a way to show her she had it. Time he gave something rather than always taking.

Her footsteps dug into the gravel behind him, and he slowed for her to catch up. They needed to get back to the table. Charlie should be about done filming Gina, if he wasn't already.

"You need to switch your mic back on." Blake flipped his own.

Harlow scrambled for hers. "How'd you …"

"When I caught you."

They rounded the corner and saw Charlie. "Good timing," he greeted them. "Just finished Gina's solo interview."

Blake owed his friend, big time.

"I was wondering where you two wandered off to," Gina said.

"Pretty sure Blake did the wandering, not me." Harlow slipped into her seat beside Gina—who'd taken the middle.

"I hope you don't mind, but I checked out the picnic basket while I waited."

A bowl of pasta, a huge loaf of fresh french bread, a platter with assorted meats and cheeses, and two bottles of wine sat on the table. Gina's glass was already full.

"No problem." Blake dug into the basket. "Anything else to drink in here?"

"I may not drink, but that doesn't mean you can't," Harlow offered.

"I know." He pulled out a bottle of water and handed it to her.

"Thank you." She took it from him, avoiding his touch.

Gina dominated the conversation while Harlow played with her food. Nearly ten minutes in, Gina stood. "My turn to steal Blake for a while."

Harlow remained focused on the table. "Be my guest."

He hadn't even formed a response before Gina snagged his arm and pulled him toward the castle. As she snuggled in, her head on his bicep, Blake glanced over his shoulder. Charlie followed them, and Harlow sat alone, arms crossed at the table. As if sensing his eyes on her, she looked straight at him. So many emotions in that one glance, but the hurt shouted loudest. With a blink, she shut him out.

That was it. The last thing he wanted was to hurt Gina, but this date had lasted long enough. Dale wanted to be upset, he could be upset. Blake had given him enough footage to work with.

He waited until they were farther down the path, unwilling to break up with Gina in front of Harlow. She might not have his heart, but that didn't mean she didn't deserve some respect.

"Gina." He tugged her to a stop.

She leaned into him, obviously thinking he'd stopped her for a completely different reason. "Yes?" She inched up on her toes.

He put his hands on her arms and gently pushed her down. "I'm sorry, but my heart is somewhere else."

Her brown eyes widened, then filled with tears.

"I'm so sorry," he said.

She held up her hand. "No. It's okay. I just thought"—she waved her hand between them—"that what we had. I thought you felt it too."

He'd never even kissed her. Okay. He had back in Malibu, but not since then. How was this coming as such a huge surprise? "You're a really great girl."

She hiccupped. "Sure. But not great enough for you to want." Then turned. "I ... I think I'd like to be by myself."

"Do you want me to walk you back?"

She shook her head.

He waited with her until a production assistant showed up. Gina gave him one last look. "It's Harlow, isn't it? You're in love with her."

He wasn't allowed to say. And when he was, Harlow would be the first one to hear the words.

"It's okay. I know you can't say." She walked away with the assistant.

Blake inhaled deeply and caught Charlie's stare. "Not fun."

"Sorry."

All he wanted was for this whole thing to be over. To walk away and start his future with Harlow—if he could convince her to have him. Because he knew what he wanted.

And she was sitting at the table on the other side of this castle.

Blake rounded the corner.

At least she had been.

The table sat empty.

224

He took off at a jog. She couldn't be that far in front of him.

He crested a small hill on the trail, not checking if Charlie was keeping up with him or not. Thirty feet ahead, Harlow's coppery hair bounced as she sped-walked down the trail. He didn't call out. She'd only move faster.

Ten feet from her she must have finally heard him because she whirled around, and he stopped.

"Trying to ditch me?" he asked.

"You ditched me first."

Unable to help it, he laughed. "What? Are we in first grade?"

Her eyes narrowed. "Your nervous humor isn't very funny right now."

"No?" He reined in his smirk. "I guess not." He edged closer. "Harlow. I screwed up, and I'm sorry."

"Yeah. I got that earlier. But here's the thing, Blake. I've been down this road before and I'm not going back."

"We barely got started. That's hardly having been down this road."

"I'm not referring to you. I'm talking about my ex, Peter."

He stiffened. She'd yet to tell him any of the details. The little he knew he'd heard from Mae's audition video. But Harlow hadn't been able to hide her scars from the relationship. "I'm not him, Harlow."

"Really? So you didn't stand me up to take Carmen on a date?" She waved her arms. "And you don't have two other women besides her that you're also dating?"

Another chuckle escaped him. "Actually there's only one other—I sent Gina home."

"Again. Not funny."

He held it in. "Can't help it. I'm nervous. I have a lot to lose right now."

"Can't lose what you don't have."

Blake grasped her wrist and drew her to him. "So tell me you don't have feelings for me too." His eyes searched hers. "And remember, you don't lie."

"My feelings don't matter, Blake." She sighed. "I won't stick myself out there again. It hurts too much."

"I promise I won't hurt you, Harlow."

"You already have." She pulled away.

But he wouldn't let her distance herself. "Dale may have my name on a dotted line, but you have my heart. And I'm going to prove it to you."

"Nice words. Forgive me if I don't believe them."

"Which is why I'm adding actions to them."

Her brow rose and then dipped. "Going to take a bit more action than chasing me down a trail." Her face darkened. "Though it sure makes great TV, right?"

He turned. Charlie stood filming from behind him, an apology all over his face.

But Charlie wasn't his concern. Neither was Dale.

"I don't care about the ratings, Harlow. I only care about you."

"Right." She turned. "I'm going home."

"Want me to walk you back?"

"That'd be quite a walk."

It took a moment to sink in. "Abundance?"

She nodded. "This was our last date, right? I'm free to go?"

Might as well have punched him. Air hissed through his lungs, leaving him completely deflated. "You've always been free to leave."

A sad smile lifted her lips. "Then goodbye, Blake."

Two steps, and he couldn't let her go any farther. "But this wasn't our last date. And you promised Mae you'd stay as long as I invited you."

She spun. "No fair."

"Nothing about this situation is fair. So for once, I'm using it to my advantage."

Her hands fisted at her hips. "You want to come to Abundance?"

"Already have my ticket."

"Fine. Come. But don't plan on me falling in love with you."

He grinned. "Wouldn't dream of it."

Except he already was.

Chapter Twenty-Six

"You're home!" Mae squealed from her bright pink wheelchair lodged directly at the end of the security gate. Amazing that any other passengers made it past her.

Harlow dropped her bag and ran for her sister, swallowing her in a hug. "I missed you so much!"

"Ditto."

Dad tugged her away and embraced her. "My turn."

Then Mom.

Harlow welcomed each hug. "You'd think I was gone for a year."

"Felt like it." Mom held her face. "Let me look at you."

And Mae bumped her with her chair. "How was Europe?"

"I fell in love with it."

"And with anything else?"

Harlow's cheeks heated. She'd fought the entire two plane rides home to rid herself of the feelings still bubbling inside, but they wouldn't loosen.

Blake wouldn't loosen.

She grabbed her carry-on. "Let's get my luggage and go home. I want a shower, my pjs, and that bowl of soup." Her mouth had been watering ever since she touched down in Chicago and phoned home.

"And I want the story you're not telling us." Mae rolled with her over to the luggage carousel.

"I'm not hiding anything."

"Then why'd you turn red back there, and why's Blake coming to Abundance?"

Harlow stopped. "How'd you know that?"

"A few production assistants already showed up. They wanted to scout out our house and a few places for dates."

At least this time he'd told the truth. Though he'd yet to show up.

Dad and Mom helped with her luggage and then pulled up their van. The frigid spring had changed into an early summer in the few weeks she'd been gone. Didn't matter, she still wanted her chicken noodle, and an hour later she snuggled in the middle of her parents' couch with a big bowl of it.

"This is what I've needed." She inhaled the steam rising over the bowl. "Pure comfort."

"Homesick?" Mom settled beside her.

"Yes."

"How many pictures did you take?" Dad took the oversized blue chair across from them.

"Too many. I'll sort through them and then share." She dug into her soup, then focused on Mae. "Where are we at with Wheels on the Ground?"

"No way. Spill about Blake first."

Unable to swallow past the sudden lump in her throat, Harlow started coughing. Mom grabbed her bowl from her. "Maybe we'll save that conversation for later."

Or never. She needed him completely removed from her heart before he showed up on her step. Otherwise, she'd fall farther and hurt deeper when he walked away from her at the end of this. Having him pick Carmen for a date was bad enough. Watching him choose her as his partner when all was said and done would be worse than seeing Peter's engagement ring on Opal's finger.

"Did something happen?" Mae pushed closer. "I figured it had to go well if he's showing up here. Am I wrong?"

The last thing she wanted was for Mae to worry. This had all been her idea. Being on the show had brought a smile to her face. There was no way she was going to take that from her now.

"No. It's all good, but I can't talk details."

"Oh. Right." She nodded. "You at least had fun, right?"

"I did." That wasn't a lie. "I can talk about the grant, though. How are things coming with it? Did you and Jack work on the auction at all?"

A look passed between Mae and her parents so quickly, Harlow nearly missed it. "We did," Mae said. "Jack was very helpful."

"Great. I can't wait to compare notes." She reached for the bag she'd brought from her house. "But first, I got you all some things." She handed over the belts, scarves, and nesting dolls, and while they oohed and aahed, she pulled out her notebooks. "Okay. I jotted down ideas as they came to me. I have a lot of thoughts about the auction. Like maybe contacting a few local businesses to see if they'd be willing—"

"Harlow, stop." Mae held the pieces of her nesting doll. "Jack and I have it all under control. I want to hear about your trip. The story behind all these things you bought. The grant can wait."

Her fingers gripped the black leather cover of her book. "But I'm home now. I can take it back over. You don't need to be worried about it."

"Who says I am?"

"I mean you don't need to put your energy into this." Beside her, Mom shifted in her seat, but stayed silent. "I wanted to share my ideas, and let you know I've got things covered. Then I'll get together with Jack, and we'll get the ball rolling."

"Getting things rolling is kind of my specialty." Mae pointed to her chair with a smile.

Harlow didn't see the humor. "I'll handle this, Mae."

"And I can help. Jack and I work well together."

"Jack works well with everyone." Harlow opened her notebook. "And I appreciate that he'd work with you while I was gone, but I'm back."

Mae clenched her jaw. "Harlow—"

"Who wants some pie?" Mom stood.

Mae watched Harlow for one more moment before turning and smiling at Mom. "Thanks, but I'm full. Think I'll take a nap, since that's all I'm good for." She wheeled away.

"Mae." Harlow called after her, but she didn't stop.

Mom sat beside Harlow and ran a hand down her back.

"I really messed that up."

"She'll calm down. She knows you have her best at heart."

"And I do."

What was that comment? Only thing she was good for? Mae *was* the good one between them. The special one. She had nothing to prove.

Dad leaned forward, arms stretched over his legs. "She and Jack make a good team."

"I'm sure they did, but Mae should focus on keeping strong. She nearly landed in the hospital the day I left."

"And she's doing fine. She's stronger than you give her credit for."

"I want her to stay that way."

"That's not up to you, Harlow."

Mom continued rubbing circles on Harlow's back for a few minutes. Then her hand stilled. "So tell me about Blake. You like him, don't you?"

Her stomach flipped, or maybe it was her heart. "Doesn't matter." She reached for a reason to stack bricks around the wall she was building. It was going to take a lot. "We're from two such different worlds it would never work."

"Two different worlds like Hollywood verses Abundance, or two separate worlds as in you're a believer and he's not?" Dad asked.

"Both."

"But only one should be a deal breaker."

It should. It should be a big enough brick to form an entire wall.

She tossed it on top.

And sighed.

Because even that brick didn't make her wall feel very secure.

*

"Back at the lovely Tipton Hotel." Charlie flopped onto the bed in Blake's room.

"Don't get comfortable. This room is too small." Blake reached for his car keys and stepped to the door. "And I've got stuff to do."

"Isn't your stuff just making phone calls?"

"And checking with your girlfriend to make sure everything's set up."

"It is. I've already been out to the site." Charlie stood and followed him out the door. "You've made a lot happen in just a couple of days."

"I had a lot to make happen."

Harlow was expecting an auction. She was getting so much more.

And he'd received so much more.

In the past two days, he discovered a passion for helping people. A strength in himself he wasn't even aware he possessed. Okay. So maybe his wheels had been turning since Harlow pushed him to find a purpose beyond his smile. But digging his hands in and putting together something that was going to benefit others, well, it made him value something beyond himself, and it felt good.

They stepped outside where the rented SUV waited for them. "Think Mae will be able to keep it a secret?" Charlie asked.

"Jack assured me she would." Blake unlocked the doors. "Apparently she's more stubborn than her sister, if you can imagine that."

"Their poor parents." He rounded to his side. "And how 'bout you? You think you can keep things on the down-low?"

Blake laughed. "Who uses that phrase anymore?"

"I just did."

"All right then." He climbed in the car. "I'll do my best. I'm like a kid at Christmas, except this time I'm doing the giving."

The car shuddered as Charlie slammed his door and then grinned at him. "You know it's good to see you so happy. Focused on something other than yourself and realizing there's a world beyond your own."

Blake started the car but left it in park. "But?"

"You know what my *but* is."

"Seriously, dude, you need to listen to yourself before you talk."

"And you need to drag yourself out of the second grade."

Blake shook his head. "Fine. I know what you're butting me about, but come on. I'm not planning to seduce her."

"Lack of planning won't stop you from winding up in bed with her." Charlie didn't even bat an eye. "It tends to have the opposite effect."

"What are you talking about?" He jerked the car into reverse and took off.

"You two aren't lacking in the attraction department. Only one place that leads to, unless you're both on the same page."

"Right now she's barely speaking to me, so I think we're safe."

"Don't fool yourself."

He wasn't. "Enough of the preaching."

"Sermon ended." Charlie held up his hands.

Blake took a sharp corner, frustration building. He was doing things differently this time. Didn't that count?

He glared at his friend. "For once in my life I'm not jumping right into bed with a woman, and you're still on my case." The car in front slowed, and Blake ground into his brakes. "I haven't even kissed her yet."

"But you will."

"Of course I will." They drove another mile in silence. "You think I'm playing her?"

"No. I think you honestly care for her." Charlie's voice kept calm. "I also think you're searching for something, and you believe she has it."

"She does."

"No. You see something she possesses that you want."

His anger boiled over. "She's more than another bed notch."

"That isn't what I was referring to."

He clenched the steering wheel. "You're not making any sense."

"You didn't want another sermon, remember?"

"Fine. One shot. Make it quick."

Charlie stayed silent for a long moment. Probably praying.

"You've been looking for something real, Blake. That real thing is God. A relationship with him. It's part of what attracts you to Harlow, because she has him, but no one else can fill that spot for you." He paused. "You might be able to convince her to try, because I honestly believe she cares for you too, but you'll only wind up hurting her in the process if you don't settle with God first."

"You were right. I don't want another sermon." Blake flicked up the radio. Charlie leaned his chair back and closed his eyes.

The patience of the man normally soothed him. Today it infuriated him. Why did he get to be so peaceful after making Blake's life so turbulent?

They drove for another ten minutes to the auction site. Tents were going up. Food trucks lined the parking lot. Off to the side, workers readied a baseball field.

Charlie might think he wasn't taking things seriously with Harlow, but he was. In the last few days his brain hadn't shut down. Mom wanted him on her show, but he wanted to be here with Harlow. He'd come alive helping out with Wheels on the Ground, finding a purpose and skill set he never knew he had. Harlow had been right, helping others grounded him in a way he'd never felt before.

When he arrived in Catalina, he needed to convince Mom the ratings she wanted were here, in Abundance. They could cover the efforts to get the charity off the ground. Make it feel-good TV. Something families truly could watch together and get behind. There was a niche for that. It could be a win all the way around.

Now he hoped Mom would jump on board.

Of course, none of it mattered unless Harlow was willing to take the leap too.

Chapter Twenty-Seven

Harlow flipped through the pictures on her laptop, pulling out her favorites from the past three weeks. Mae wanted to see every moment she could, but that didn't mean she had to see all thousand-plus photos. Though narrowing it down proved near impossible. There were so many great shots Harlow envisioned using. But where? What would she ever do with any of these?

She flicked across to another file and couldn't help but grin. The picture of Blake stopped her. Hands-down the most handsome man she'd ever met.

She traced his smile.

He'd fully taken hold of her heart that night.

And she struggled to pry off his grip.

The clock over her desk ticked away another fifteen minutes before she closed up her computer. Darcy should be here any moment to help her get ready.

Harlow shuffled into the kitchen to brew a strong, dark-roast coffee. She added an extra scoop for measure. The last drip filled the carafe when her doorbell rang.

"Coming." She opened the door, and jerked. Marty Pontelle? She hadn't thought of him since tossing his business card into her trash can that first night in Budapest. And now he stood on her front step, slimy as ever? "Um, hello."

If he heard the disgust in her voice, he ignored it. "I heard you were back in town. Wondered if you've given any more thought to my offer?"

"How'd you know where I live?"

"Public knowledge."

Sure it was.

Another level of understanding for Blake grew.

"I have no plans on selling you pictures, Mr. Pontelle."

233

He held out another card. "You haven't even let me quote you."

"I don't need you to." Even if basic integrity would allow for it, she wasn't about to hurt Blake in that way. Didn't matter if things between them hadn't worked out. Everyone was entitled to their privacy—and Marty Pontelle didn't simply want her to violate Blake's. He wanted her to snap a picture he could manipulate. No one deserved that treatment.

Behind him, a car pulled to the curb and parked. Darcy jumped out and started up the walk.

Marty wiggled the card. "One picture alone would be better than that grant you're applying for. Get me the right shot, and I could set your charity up for years." He dropped the card into the metal mailbox attached to her house and left.

Darcy looked him over as they passed, but Marty kept his face forward, whistling an off-key tune.

"Who was that?" she asked as she jogged up the steps.

"No one." Harlow pushed her door fully open. "Come on in."

Darcy walked to the center of the room and dropped her fifty-pound bag of tricks. "You ready to see Blake again?"

If she could get her warring emotions under control. "I guess."

Snapping her gum, Darcy twisted her mouth to the side before blowing out a long sigh. "Look, Harlow. Blake's my closest friend, and I want the best for him. And I truly think you're it."

Harlow opened her mouth, but Darcy held her hand up.

"But I'm not sure he's the best for you." She squeezed her eyes shut. "At least not until he gets right with God." She popped her eyes open. "There. I said it. Now I'll step back and bite my tongue."

Harlow smiled. "I appreciate your concern, but it's unnecessary. Blake and I are over. He needed a number three for hometowns, and my story makes good ratings."

"You know that's not the case." Darcy started to say more, hesitated, then clamped her mouth shut. She hauled her bag onto the counter and unzipped it. "All right. Let's get started."

An hour later Harlow was camera-ready. Charlie stood outside, waiting to film Blake's arrival, and Darcy hovered by the door with her hairbrush. "Just want to touch up—"

"This is hometown dates, so let me look a little hometown."

Darcy relented. "That's one of the reasons you're so good for Blake."

234

She didn't have a response for that.

Or for the nerves that spiked when tires crunched over her gravel driveway. She looked. White SUV. Blake.

He hurried up the front steps and knocked. Casting a glance at Darcy, Harlow sucked in a deep breath and opened the door. His baseball cap and Aviators brought back the first day she met him. Only now her heart tripped for a whole host of other reasons.

Darn heart.

"Hey," she said.

"Hey yourself." He offered his arm. "Beautiful, as always."

"Thanks." She busied herself closing her door and ignored his arm. "Just flannel and jean shorts."

"You wear them well."

Her cheeks heated. "So. What are we doing today?"

"Hopefully having fun." He smiled and led her to the car.

Okay. So she needed to loosen up a little. They'd shared some laughs. If she took the day at face value, kept her emotions in check, they could at least enjoy the afternoon. No reason to be miserable.

She settled in and pointed to the dash after he climbed into the driver's seat. "No camera? And I noticed no mics yet."

"Nope. They'll mic us when we get to our next location." He turned onto the main road. "The deal was by the time we got to hometowns, I'd get more alone time with each woman."

Each woman. Harlow swallowed the thought away.

"Bet it was good to see your family." He looked over at her. "How's Mae doing?"

"Really well, actually." Their conversation from last night still pricked at her. "Apparently she and Jack made progress on the auction."

"Did you have a chance to share any of your ideas?"

"Not yet. I plan to tomorrow though."

Blake slowed for a stop light. "Hmm ... I don't think tomorrow will work for you."

"Really?" She eyed him. "Why?"

"I planned a date for us."

"You and your assumptions."

He chuckled. "I call it being hopeful."

He was nervous. Meant he still cared a little, right?

A sliver of hope wedged itself in, smack dab in the middle of the wall she was trying to erect. She didn't want it but couldn't dislodge it.

They chatted while Blake drove another twenty minutes toward the lake. Finally he pulled off into a sandy lot and parked next to a small tan building. King Dunebuggy Rides was painted in blue on an old white sign.

"I have it on good authority that you've never been on one of these."

"You do, huh?"

They got out and walked toward the stocky, bald-headed gentleman strolling their way. Charlie and Alex pulled up in their van, and Alex miked everyone while Charlie readied his camera. Then they shook hands with the owner of the store who led them to a big red buggy.

"Climb on in." He motioned to a bench behind the driver. A camera was already attached to the dash. Charlie and Alex climbed in as well. The owner stood and smiled. "Pull that seat belt over you both. We're ready as soon as I hear it click." He sat down.

The man wasn't lying. No sooner had two clicks sounded before the buggy jerked alive.

Sand stung her cheeks as they raced to the top of one of the dunes and down the other side. They careened around corners and shot up another hill. Laughter roared from all of them. This was better than a roller coaster—not that she'd ever ridden one.

They came to a stop at the top of the tallest dune. "Everyone out," the owner called.

Blake helped Harlow down. "You have a bit of sand, uh, everywhere."

Somewhere back there, sliding through one of the sandy tracks, she'd not only lost her breath but loosened her reticence. Blake's arm around her, his laughter in her ear, the smile on his face—she genuinely had fun with him. Liked his company. And if this week held her last memories with him, she wanted them to be good ones.

If they kept things in the friend zone, they would be.

Her smile came easy. "You too."

She brushed back a few loose strands of hair. No wonder Darcy had secured her mess into a braid for the afternoon. It'd be in knots otherwise.

The owner gave a short spiel about the dune and its trees, then encouraged them to explore. Harlow dragged Blake to a small lookout.

"You seem more relaxed." He grabbed for her hand.

She wouldn't let him take it, but didn't push him away. "I've decided friendship with you won't kill me."

"That's a place to start." The glimmer in his eyes rivaled the lake below.

"So. What do you think of our lake?" It sparkled about three hundred feet beneath them, stretching for miles into the horizon.

"It's nice, but it doesn't compare to the ocean."

"Excuse me?"

He shrugged. "I have a thing for salty air. Tasting it on my lips. Big waves."

"California boy."

"Thought we already settled that." His grin was all Hollywood.

A thought took hold. She might have never been on a buggy ride before, but she'd definitely been on these dunes. Running down them was exhilarating. Climbing up a killer workout.

"Come on." She tugged him forward. "You may think your ocean is better, but you've got nothing on these dunes."

Throwing her arms in the air, Harlow took one giant leap, her feet burying into the warm sand as she landed in a puff and started running. An oomph came from behind as Blake followed. They sounded like a couple of kids, their speed increasing until their top halves outpaced their bottom ones. Giggling, Harlow gave in to gravity and let it topple her down the rest of the dune, Blake rolling behind her. They came to rest at the bottom, her hard breaths mixed with laughter.

Blake leaned over her. "Okay. That was fun."

"Told you."

He stilled above her, his intense stare and calmed breath keeping hers ragged. His eyes darkened to near black, and he leaned in.

She rolled away. Sat up.

"Harlow." Such gentleness in his voice. But it was the gravelly emotion that kept her back turned toward him.

She couldn't give in. Wouldn't. Which was exactly why she couldn't look at him.

Standing, she brushed the sand from her arms and legs. "We've got a long walk."

He jumped in front of her. "What was that? One second we're having a great time, the next you're closing me out."

She sighed. Took a deep breath. Then went for honesty. "I need to close you out, Blake. Don't you get it?"

"Not at all."

And he couldn't because he'd never stood where she had. For that, she couldn't blame him.

"Can we just enjoy today?" she asked softly. "As friends?"

He scrubbed one hand over his jaw, his focus on a point over her shoulder. The war in his eyes mirrored the one ramming against her heart. Then he nodded and held out his hand for her to step in front of him.

She began their hike up the dune, her feet digging into the soft sand. For every two steps up she'd slide another one backwards. If she had any breath left to spare from the crazy-hard workout, she'd laugh, because this trek perfectly illustrated their relationship. Thing was, she'd end up at the top of this physical hill, winded and a little sore, but happy she'd taken the leap.

If only her heart had the same guarantee.

*

Harlow had been relatively silent for the remainder of their dune buggy ride. Of course, the walk back up had taken most of their breath away. Still, with the great physical shape she was in, he couldn't blame her silence on being out of breath from that workout. She resurrected her wall as fast as he could tear it down.

Not how he wanted things to go on their one week alone.

Maybe telling her about tomorrow would loosen whatever remaining fear was holding her back from him. But Mae had worked as hard on the surprise as he had, and he wasn't about to steal her portion of the thunder.

He waited while Harlow changed in the small bathroom of the dune buggy rental shop. Darcy had arrived with their change of clothes while they were on their ride. Harlow stepped out of the bathroom in a white sundress that showed off her tanned skin and perfect curves. Her red hair hung in loose waves, and he knew it would be impossible to keep his hands out of the silky strands.

"Hungry?" he asked.

"Starved." She brushed past him as he held the door open. Charlie filmed them from the parking lot. "Climbing that dune gave me an appetite."

"Yeah. You neglected to tell me what a workout that would be when you launched me down the thing."

"Thought you and your muscles could handle it."

"My muscles, huh?"

They crossed to the boardwalk that stretched down to the beach in the distance. Along one side of the walkway stood a row of shops, while on the other side, a channel ran from a marina to the open waters.

"Oh, don't pretend like you don't know you have them."

"I know I have them—I've worked my tail off for each one. Didn't know you took notice though."

She blushed and suddenly found great interest in the wooden slats beneath their feet. "So where's lunch?"

Her hands remained in her dress pockets, and she kept space between them. But at least she was talking again.

A sailboat puttered along the channel. "It's still early. I thought we'd walk and catch a snack first. Curb that starvation you're feeling."

A rainbow of awnings colored the area, beckoning them into the stores whose doors were propped open. People milled all around them, enjoying the sunshine and shopping. Blake caught the photographer from his peripheral vision before the young man spoke. Out of reflex, he stiffened and stepped in front of Harlow.

The sandy-haired kid smiled. "Could I get a picture?"

He actually asked. Blake swallowed his surprise and shook his head.

"Sorry. I'm on a date." He kept walking, anticipating the click of the camera anyway. When it didn't happen, he stopped. Turned. And smiled. "Okay. Go ahead."

The young man's grin was priceless, and he snapped off a few shots. "Thanks." He hurried to his car.

"Is that normal?" Harlow peered up at him.

"Want the honest answer?"

"Always."

He tossed her a grin. "Even when you have on a crappy outfit?"

"Even then. But I'd suggest honesty with finesse in those situations."

"I'll remember that."

"Smart man."

Mom never wanted honest answers. Only ones that stroked her ego. Harlow did. And kicker was, she meant it.

"Well, no worries today, because you look beautiful."

Her cheeks pinkened.

"As for the cameras, it's usually worse."

"Sorry."

"Don't like it, but I can't change it." He shrugged. "Believe me, I've tried." He nodded to the kid photographer driving away. "If more people were like him, I think I'd have an easier time handling it. But no one ever asks if they can take my picture or stops following me once they have one. And there's usually multiples of them. If I was with my mom in LA, they'd be chasing us."

"Apparently I'm not that interesting then."

There was so much wrong with that statement. "More like no one's wondering if I'm taking you for plastic surgery or Botox."

She snorted.

"Cute snort."

"Shut it."

This woman truly captured him.

They walked a little farther, Charlie filming their every step. Harlow fiddled with her mic pack. "You'd think by now I'd be used to this thing."

"Strange for me too. I'm used to the cameras but not the recording devices."

"And we're supposed to act normal."

Blake squeezed her hand. "I've had more normal moments with you caught on that camera than I have behind most of the closed doors in my life."

She blinked up at him. "Not sure whether to say thank you or I'm sorry."

He leaned down. "I think I'm the one who should say thanks." The desire to kiss her was so strong, he could nearly taste it. His gaze flicked to her lips.

Harlow ducked away and nodded at Lake Michigan. "So, our lake really doesn't compare with your ocean?"

He'd never had to wait to kiss a woman, and he was nearly at the end of his rope.

Good thing she had him tied in knots so he could hang on.

"Nope." Her mock glare was adorable. "Hey. You asked for honesty."

"Because I honestly thought you'd love the lake."

"I like it, but I don't love it. Big difference." Up ahead, a yellow and white sign caught his attention. "Speaking of loving something." He pointed. "Let's grab some ice cream."

Harlow let him tug her along. Charlie and Alex went in first, waiting for them to join. Two employees stood behind the counter and greeted them with anxious smiles, eyes darting from the camera back to Blake and Harlow. So much for appearing natural.

"Welcome to What's the Scoop." The teenage girl gave Blake a full-wattage smile.

"Thanks."

"What can I get you?"

"Harlow?" Blake motioned for her.

"Oh, you go ahead and order first."

"Okay." He stepped to the counter. "Key lime in a waffle cone."

"Single or double?"

"Double."

The girl made his cone and handed it to him. He bit in. It was amazing. "You guys make this here?"

The other worker nodded. "All of our flavors are homemade."

"Great stuff." He held his cone out to Harlow. "Care to try?"

"Not a key lime fan."

"Missing out." He took another bite and nodded toward the counter. "You gonna order?"

"No. I'm good."

He stopped, mid bite. "You're not going to get anything?"

"Nope." She was already by the door.

"Then why didn't you say something before we came in?"

"Because you wanted ice cream."

"So?"

"So, it didn't kill me to stop and wait two minutes for you to get some."

He eyed her. What was it that kept her from indulging in life? He knew the answer was somehow wrapped around her sister, and he had no idea how to unwind it.

"What's your favorite flavor?"

"My favorite flavor?"

He nodded slowly.

"I don't know. Vanilla?"

Of course it was.

He strolled the case, reading each flavor as he nibbled his key lime. Then grinned. He looked at the young employee. "I'd like a double cone of that one." He pointed at the perfect flavor.

The girl scooped out two heaping mounds of the light tan ice cream and handed him the cone. "Enjoy."

"She will." Blake marched the treat to Harlow. "Coffee toffee." He waved it under her nose, but her stubborn hand didn't reach for it.

"Can't make me eat it." She crossed her arms.

He always had loved a challenge.

Meeting her stare, he smushed the soft ice cream into her lips.

*

The sweet taste of coffee and cream slipped past her lips and onto her tongue. The last time she'd tasted ice cream, she was ten. Had they even made coffee ice cream then? Whoever put the two together had been a genius.

Her joyful taste buds only made her angry.

She licked the cold treat from her lips, narrowing a glance at Blake. Who did he think he was? Making her want things she'd given up on wanting. Conquered the desires with her steel will years ago. And here he came, someone she'd never even asked for, and somehow cracked open those doors.

"Looks like you just ate some ice cream." His tone was as smug as that look on his face. He held out a napkin.

She took it and wiped her mouth. And chin. "Are you happy?"

"I will be once you take the cone." He wiggled it again. "Or do I need to—"

Harlow grabbed it. "Fine. I'll take it."

Blake paid, and they waved at the two employees before returning to the sunshine. He went to town on his ice cream, and she nibbled at hers. Once upon a time, ice cream had been her and Mae's favorite treat. Daddy would take them out after every one of their Little League games. Until Mae couldn't play anymore.

Then there was no time for Harlow to play either.

She dumped her cone into a trash can.

"What'd you do that for?" Blake ground to a halt.

"I was finished."

"You'd taken two bites."

"More than enough."

He licked a smudge off his lips, stepping toward her. "I can't figure out whether you feel guilty for being the healthy one or if you're trying to prove something."

His near bull's-eye freaked her out. Her gaze bounced between him and Charlie. "Come again?"

He bit into his cone and munched rather than answering her. Then he swallowed, pitched the last bite, and brushed off his hands. "Don't worry. I won't Dr. Phil you." He started walking.

She grabbed the relief and followed. He slowed until she caught up. "So how often do you get out to the lake?"

"As often as I can. There's a really great set of trails that connect the beaches all the way from Mackinac Bridge right on down the coastline."

"You walk them?"

"Not that entire way." She laughed. "But yeah, I do. Well, jog them actually."

"Of course you do." She stayed in near perfect shape. "Bet you get some great pictures too."

"I do."

"What do you do with all the ones you take?"

"Keep them on my computer."

"That's it?"

"I made a book for my parents once. Made a few for myself too." Sent some queries out for publication. Got rejected. "Mainly I keep them on files and play around with them."

"How do you play with a picture?"

"Edit it, fiddle with the color, add a border. Lately I've been adding a verse."

"So you put what you see in your head onto paper."

"Try to."

"Can I see a few sometime?"

A group of teens passed them, jumping and waving at the camera.

"Maybe."

"I'll take a *maybe* over a *no* any day."

They reached the sandy edge of the beach and slipped off their shoes.

"Not going to make me swim again, are you?" she asked.

"Maybe."

"See, now I'd rather take the *no*."

He chuckled and led her down to the water's edge. They strolled for a while, the water dipping over their toes until the sun reached its peak. He turned her around, and they retraced their steps, a comfortable silence between them as they strolled to the car. So comfortable that Charlie finally took his camera off his shoulder.

"I think we're boring him," she whispered to Blake.

"Are you bored?"

"No."

"Then that's all that matters." His hand reached for hers and before she thought it through, she slipped her fingers around his. She caught his smile from the corner of her eye.

Holding hands could be casual. Right?

Sure. With her sister. Not with Blake. And yet she couldn't bring herself to break the hold.

They reached the car, and he tucked her inside before climbing in himself.

"Where's lunch?" she asked, her stomach growling.

"At a cute little Italian spot up the road. Marie's. I heard it's your favorite."

A tiny smirk pulled up her lips.

Both hands on the wheel, Blake turned. "What's that smirk for?"

Should she own up?

His raised brow prodded her to.

"Can you keep a secret?" she asked, and that darling brow inched up farther. Stifling a laugh, she admitted, "I hate Italian."

"You hate ..." He shook his head. "Italian is Mae's favorite?" When she nodded, he spoke. "So spill. What's yours?"

"Thai."

He started the engine. "You know, the more I see of you, the more I like." Putting the car in gear, he drove the opposite direction of Marie's.

"Marie's is the other way."

"But Thai Me Up is this way."

"And you'd know this how?"

"Thai's my favorite too."

Chapter Twenty-Eight

Blake stood on the deck of a beach house Dale had scouted, waiting for Harlow to meet him for dinner.

"You seem rested." Charlie leaned against the railing with him.

"It's been a good day."

"It was." Charlie rolled a quarter between his fingers. "She's a special woman."

"You're not gonna get an argument from me."

"Didn't think I would." He caught the quarter. "And speaking of that special woman"—he picked up his camera—"she's here. You ready?"

"More than."

Light bathed the entire inside of the house, illuminating it behind the glass wall that opened to the deck where he now stood. Gave him the perfect view of Harlow as she walked through the front door. Earlier today, with her hair whipping loose from her braid as she ran the dunes and those darkening freckles on her sun-kissed nose, he'd been blown away by her easy beauty. Women never let themselves be so untouched around him. Harlow hadn't thought twice about it—she never did.

But the woman who walked through that door tonight stole his breath in a whole other way.

Her midnight-blue dress poured over each curve as smoothly as the waves rolling off the lake today. The fabric ended mid-thigh, and heels extended her legs, shimmering with whatever lotion Darcy used. He needed to buy stock in the stuff and make sure Harlow always used it. Her hair swept up in a loose bun, exposing the soft curve of her neck, practically begging him to bury his face in her creamy skin and inhale her sweet scent.

He took complete advantage of the darkness that hid him, watching every move she made. If he'd just met her, he'd feel some attraction. Having spent time with her, it was more than that. Every day with her made him crave another.

She crossed the room and came out the back door, squinting into the dark night.

"Hey." He stayed by the railing, not trusting himself to keep his hands to himself.

Her face lit brighter than the inside of the house. "Hey."

"You look great."

She fidgeted. "All Darcy."

"She had a natural beauty to work with."

Harlow ran her finger along the edge of her hem. "Thanks."

He motioned to the table on the deck. "Hungry?"

"Starved."

He held her chair and then sat in his, keeping a small space between them. They had dinner, conversation flowing as easily as it had all afternoon. The camera and boom mic didn't even register. With her ease, Harlow seemed to ignore them for the night too. As a waiter cleared their dishes, Blake took her hand. "I had an amazing day."

"It was fun, wasn't it?"

"Seems that's becoming the norm when I'm with you." His fingers ran along her wrist. "I'm more thankful every day that you agreed to come on this show with me."

Her smile dimmed, and she rested her hands in her lap. "The things I do for my sister."

They may have had a great afternoon, but she was still skittish. He couldn't blame her after their ending to Europe, but he hoped by the end of the week to be back where they once were.

With her trust placed firmly in him.

A waiter arrived at their table with a heaping piece of chocolate cake four layers tall. This was a good place to start. Blake dug in and brought his fork to her lips. "First bite?"

"I'm good."

"There's always room for chocolate."

She pushed the fork away. "I haven't had chocolate in years."

"Years?"

"Like since I was twelve."

"Allergic?"

"Nope."

"I figured." He put the fork down. "Spill it."

"There's nothing to spill. I just don't eat chocolate."

"I've never met a person with more *nos* in life than you." And frankly, he was tired of it for her. Wasn't she? He picked up the bite of cake. She shied away. "I'm not asking you to eat the entire wedge, Harlow. A bite, that's all. Life is meant to be enjoyed."

"I do enjoy life."

He raised a brow. "Are we circling back to this?"

She shook her head.

"Good," he challenged, "then prove it."

She sighed. "Fine. One taste."

He couldn't stop his internal fist pump over another small victory. He'd keep piling the wins on until she was living free from whatever kept her so bound. "Prepare to be amazed."

She sucked in a deep breath and for a moment he thought she'd change her mind. But then she bit in, eyes closing. A small crumb clung to the corner of her lips. He brushed it away with his thumb and slowly traced her silky mouth.

Her eyes fluttered open.

She looked out at the inky night. After a moment, she spoke. "Sometimes you make me forget this is all pretend."

"Because it isn't." For the first time in his life, he believed that. Why couldn't she?

"I know you say that, but what happens when you leave here? When you've got a beautiful woman who's willing ..." Her gaze dropped before fixing on him.

"You're thinking about what happened with Peter."

She nodded.

"I'm not him." He'd keep saying it until she believed it.

"But you're still a man in the same situation."

"He was on a TV show too?" A low chuckle. The look she leveled at him said neither his attempted joke or nervous laughter were appreciated.

"You really need to learn how to control that."

Blake capped the laughter but kept on his easy smile. "Sorry."

"It's okay."

Behind him, boats motored along the lake shore and seagulls called. Perfect setting, but across from him, Harlow was hurting. And he'd had a hand in that pain.

"It's not okay. I'm sorry Peter hurt you." He softened his voice. "And I'm sorry I did too."

She'd come on the show, willingly stepping into a similar situation to the one that had broken her heart, and he'd hurt her in much the same way. Still, she sat across the table from him right now. Said it was for Mae, yet he'd caught glimpses of her heart throughout the day. Somewhere in there, he retained a corner.

He didn't deserve her. Probably never would. But he'd never stop trying. Never stop doing whatever it took to make her smile. Keep her happy. Help her truly enjoy life like she'd helped show him love could be real.

He leaned in close. The breeze brushed a strand of her hair against his cheek.

"Harlow." He touched her cheek, but she didn't look at him.

Instead, with one huge sigh, she pushed her chair back. "What?"

"I'm not going to hurt you," he whispered.

It took her several seconds to answer. "I honestly believe you mean that." One shoulder lifted. "But that doesn't stop me from being terrified that at the end of all this, I'll end up heartbroken."

His fingers stretched for hers. "I promise. You won't."

She placed her fingertips against his, not fully linking their hands but bridging the space nonetheless. "I want to be courageous enough to trust that, but it might take me a while."

"Take all the time that you need. I'm a very patient man when it comes to what I want." He waited for her full attention before adding, "And just so we're clear, that's you." He laced his voice with every inch of his confidence, intent on transferring his to her. Then, just for good measure, he stood and placed a kiss against her neck.

He might be a patient man, but that didn't mean he wouldn't pull out every trick in his arsenal to win the heart of the woman who already held an iron grip on his.

Chapter Twenty-Nine

The next morning dawned with cloudless blue skies. Harlow had tossed and turned most of the night, her heart and mind still arguing over whether to run away from or straight into Blake's open arms. It exhausted her worse than training for the one marathon she'd ever run. That race at least came with a guarantee that if she crossed the finish line, she'd receive a medal. But this one? There was no assurance that Blake's arms would remain open and waiting for her.

While that thought had slowed her pace, it hadn't stopped her from barreling towards him. And all the anxious energy building inside kept her wide awake.

On a positive note, her lack of sleep provided time to work on a business plan. The Townsend Agency would be making a decision soon, and she needed something to show them. Since the clock wasn't magically growing extra hours, she might as well use the ones she typically slept through.

She rinsed her coffee cup and leaned against her counter. Blake would be here any minute for another date, and for once Darcy hadn't preceded him. Apparently she'd taken the request to let Harlow look "a little hometown" fully to heart. She was on her own today.

Which meant ponytail, black leggings, and her favorite white T-shirt. She'd throw on a bright scarf when Blake showed up. He wanted reality, he was going to get it.

Her front door reverberated with a knock, and she went to answer it, smile in place without even consciously putting it there. Blake and his baseball cap stood on the other side.

"Morning." He held out a cup of coffee.

Harlow took it. "My third."

"Good thing I know you can handle it." He stepped inside.

She draped her aqua infinity scarf around her neck and grabbed a purse, barely noticing Charlie and Alex. They'd become staples in this crazy life of hers. "So what are we up to today?"

Blake shrugged and motioned her through the door, closing it behind him.

"Was that an *I don't know* shrug or an *I'm not telling* shrug?"

He grinned and shrugged again.

"Just so you know," she said as she slipped into the passenger's seat, "I don't like surprises."

"You seem to have liked all of mine."

She had. But his smirk was already big enough.

They drove for fifteen minutes, exiting off the highway and into the outskirts of Abundance. They wound through the streets until they came to Willis Park. Candy-striped tents, bouncy houses, and food trucks filled the area.

"What's all that?"

He didn't give an answer. Unless his teasing grin counted as one.

They stopped at the back of the parking lot. A few local news crews were near the festivities. Blake stepped out and offered her his hand. "Coming?"

The sun shone in the clear blue sky, temperature nearing seventy. A perfect day for a fair she didn't even know was happening.

Mae met her at the park entrance. "You made it."

Harlow looked down at her sister. "What's going on?"

Mae grinned at Blake, then back to Harlow. "Blake helped set this all up."

Confusion cluttered her brain.

He pointed to a sign attached to the ticket booth. "Look."

Town Fair and Auction to benefit Wheels on the Ground. "You did this?"

"With a little help from Mae and your family."

"But I thought you never—"

"I know what you thought. I know what I said." He squeezed her hand. "And I figured it was time to put action behind all the words I've been telling you. Extend some trust instead of asking for it."

His words—what he'd done—it was like the fuel her worn-out emotions needed. With a burst of speed, her heart hurtled closer to him.

Wait. The clothes!

"But I don't even have the clothes—"

"Darcy has it all covered." He pointed to a tent. "That's why she wasn't at your house this morning. She's even brought a few things I donated."

250

Darcy waved from beside Charity.

"I ..." Harlow's thoughts spun in circles. Not only had Blake put this all together, but he attached his name to it. Donated personal items. Trusted her. "I'm speechless."

He leaned close. "I'd rather kiss you speechless, but I guess this will work."

Her gaze dropped to his lips and back up. "That'd work too." The tease slipped out. By his widened eyes, she wasn't sure which of them was more surprised.

His shock gave way to an easy grin that stole her breath while his hands circled her waist, drawing her to him. He leaned down.

Shivers ran along her spine.

"Blake. We're ready for you."

He stilled. "You have got to be kidding me." His whispered words breathed across her lips, and his gaze still held her captive. He didn't turn. "These interruptions are getting old."

She smiled. "There's always tonight."

"I'm holding you to it." He pressed a kiss to her cheek and then turned to the man standing there.

Was that Mayor Williams?

Blake shook his hand and took the microphone he held out. Then he climbed the steps to the small stage there. "Glad to see everyone who's turned out. I'm Blake Carlton."

The crowd erupted in applause.

"And I want to welcome you to Abundance's Town Fair and Auction benefiting the charity of Wheels on the Ground. I'm going to pass off the mic and let Mae Tucker tell you a little about it."

He handed the mic to Mae, who started chatting, but Harlow barely paid either of them attention. She scanned the grounds, amazement growing with each new thing she saw. A Ferris wheel sat in the middle of the park and was surrounded by a dunk tank, bounce house, and several smaller rides and fair games. Along the other side, a full row of food trucks lined the edge of a baseball diamond.

She dug for words as Blake approached, starting with the most burning ones. "How did this happen?"

"Your sister, Jack, and I. Turns out I'm pretty good at organizing things. Calling in favors. Making things happen." He motioned for her to walk with him. "Not sure it's my purpose in life, but you were right, it felt good to focus on others."

"Thank you for trusting me enough to do this."

"Thank you for pushing me to see beyond myself." He leaned down, his gaze stripping the rest of the world away. "And for being someone I *can* trust."

Her cheeks heated. Strike that. Her whole body heated.

"Harlow!"

The heat slid to a chill. She turned. Peter and Opal approached from the cotton candy booth.

"You okay?" Blake leaned down by her ear, brow wrinkled.

"Peachy." She grinned and took Peter's hand as he held it out. "What a surprise, Peter."

Beside her, Blake stiffened.

"I told him we shouldn't come." Opal at least had the good grace to fidget.

"And I told her you wouldn't mind." He looked at Blake and then back to her with that smile that used to flip her stomach. Until she met Blake. His smile flipped her heart. "You've obviously moved on." Peter offered Blake his hand. "Thought we'd stop by and invite you both to the wedding."

Blake returned the quick handshake. "And you are?"

"Harlow hasn't told you about me?"

"Not a word."

She really could kiss him right about now.

"I'm Harlow's ex. Peter Eisler." He nudged Opal. "And this is my fiancée, Opal Berry. We all grew up together. Ran in a pretty tight-knit group."

"A little too tight," Harlow muttered.

Had those words actually escaped?

Judging by Opal's red cheeks …

"Sorry." Harlow squeezed Blake's hand to stop him from laughing. "I can't confirm if we'll be at the wedding or not. Can't even speculate if we'll still be together—"

"Oh, look. We're needed by the food tents." Blake interrupted, tugging her away. "Really nice to meet you, Paul."

"Peter," he called after them.

Blake didn't even acknowledge him. When they were a few feet away, he slowed to a stop. "He's a real catch."

"Shall we compare him to some of your exes?"

"Let's not." He peered over her shoulder to where Peter and Opal had stood. "I'll go to the wedding with you, if you want."

"It's not for another six weeks." *Call for Love* ended in three.

"I know," he said as if that tiny fact had absolutely no bearing on a thing. He pointed to a set of picnic tables. "I think they're having a hot dog eating contest later today. You game?"

"Uh ... no." What she was game for was him to expand on his earlier comment.

All she got was a grin.

"I figured." He passed the tents and walked out onto the baseball field. "I did sign you up for something though."

"What?"

He tossed her a red T-shirt from a box by the bleachers. "Team captain of the red team."

"And whose team are we playing?"

He held up a blue shirt. "Mine."

*

The day had been a great one. This must be what a small town felt like. It all culminated into the baseball game while the auction tally was counted. They'd announce it at the end of the seventh inning. For now, Charlie and Tad had set up cameras and fitted him and Harlow with mics. Her team was up to bat first.

And the girl knew how to hit.

She'd already knocked out a triple.

The base he just happened to be playing.

She grinned up at him and scooted toward home.

"You're not planning on stealing home, are you?" he asked.

"Me?" She batted her eyes at him.

"You're not nearly as innocent as you look."

Pink flickered across her cheeks. And she missed a perfect opportunity to steal.

She scowled at him. "Quit trying to distract me."

"Why, when it's working so well?"

She hunched down and focused on the plate. The pitcher tossed to first, trying to pick off her teammate but the first baseman wasn't ready. The ball sailed over his glove, and Harlow was gone. She slid into home like a pro.

Then she stood, dusted off the jeans Darcy had given her, and stuck her tongue out at him.

"Red team takes the lead."

Darcy was having too much fun playing announcer.

Half hour later, they were tied again. Harlow grinned at him from the pitcher's mound. "I'll toss you an easy one. I know Charlie's filming."

"I told him to pull in tight on your face when I hit this homer."

She narrowed her eyes and pulled both her hands in to her face, watching him as she prepared for her pitch. She hadn't played ball in high school. Shame. She seemed a natural.

Winding up, she arched her arm back and released the ball in one fluid motion.

He swung as it curved over the plate.

"Strike one."

That grin nearly made him decide to take another strike.

Her second pitch came in low and fast.

"Ball."

"Keep those coming," he called.

"You want the easy base then?"

Blake gripped the bat and dug in deep. He'd show her easy base.

She sent the ball flying over home plate, a little low again, but he could hit it up. It pinged off his bat, and he heard a collective gasp. He didn't stop, knew it was a strong hit. He ran.

"Harlow!"

The panic in her mother's voice pulled him around. Harlow lay out cold on the mound, the baseball in front of her. Blake changed course on a dime and slid through the dirt to her side.

"Harlow?" He gently touched her forehead where a welt already formed.

He'd knocked her out. Possibly cracked her skull. And for what?

He was an idiot.

"Harlow?" Blake ran his fingers along her cheek. "Someone call 911."

The last time he'd seen someone this still … He shoved the haunted thoughts away. Completely different situation. And those memories had no place here.

Charlie stood behind him, but he wasn't filming. "I've got you covered."

Translation: He'd field the mess at the ER that was sure to show up there.

She was so still. He ran his hand along her cheek. "Harlow, sweetheart, can you open your eyes?"

Her mother knelt on her other side. She squeezed Blake's hand. "It was an accident. Don't you worry, she'll be fine. It's only a bump on the head."

He'd taken out her daughter, and she was comforting him?

He'd entered a third dimension.

Within minutes, EMTs were on the field. They eased a neck brace on her and strapped her to a board. "Precautions."

One of them spoke to Harlow's mom. She followed them to the ambulance and climbed in with them.

Blake raced to his car, Darcy close by. "Want me to drive?" she asked.

"No."

By the time they made it to the hospital, a news crew was already there. So was Charlie. Nice thing about his friend's size, he made a great bodyguard. No one approached them. They headed into the ER and found Harlow's family.

"How is she?"

"They just brought her back. She's one of them, so there was a group with her."

Blake scanned the area. So this is where Harlow spent her days—or nights. Either way, she was used to being the one doling out the care, not receiving it. She wouldn't be happy when she woke.

He didn't really care. Because he planned on making sure she was all right.

"Mr. and Mrs. Tucker?" A tall brunette walked through the doors, then slammed to a stop when she saw Blake. A small crowd was already accumulating, but he wasn't going anywhere. "How about we take you to a private room?"

She ushered them through a set of doors and to a small, empty waiting room.

"How is she?"

He relaxed once the nurse smiled. "She's got quite a knot on her head. Our guess is it came with a slight concussion. To be safe, the doctor is sending her for a scan right now, but she looks okay."

Blake dropped into a chair.

"Can we see her?" her mom asked.

"I'll come get you once she's out of the tube."

Diane Tucker sat beside him and took his hand. "You're a little green. Can I get you anything?"

She was taking care of him?

"No. I'm good." At least he would be once he could get the images of Dad's lifeless form on his bedroom floor out of his brain.

Diane didn't let go of his hand. Instead she patted it. "It can bring back memories we don't want, can't it? Seeing someone we care for lying there on the ground."

His gaze snapped to hers. She offered him a comforting smile but no more words. Just her hand holding his.

So this was what it felt like to have a mom who cared.

That revelation watered the tiny seed of hope Harlow had planted. The things he'd long thought as fairy tale were turning into reality all around him.

Growing.

Like love.

Chapter Thirty

Harlow's head was going to explode. Mount St. Helens had nothing on her. She gingerly touched the knot on her forehead. At least she hadn't needed stitches. Though on second thought, she'd trade this headache for a few sutures. They could make the site numb. No go with her brain.

The door swished shut behind her co-worker, Nancy. They definitely would milk this one for all it was worth. No doubt a picture of her noggin graced the break room wall right this minute. At least they'd given her a private room to hang out in until they released her.

Leaning back on her pillow, she closed her eyes. The door creaked, but she kept her lids closed.

"Hey." Mae's small voice forced her to pop one open.

"Hey."

Mae wheeled closer to the bed, silent for a long moment. "So."

"So." No way she was making this easy on her.

Another long pause. "I should have told you."

"You think?" Harlow pointed to her head. "Would have been a lot less painful."

"Should have kept your eye on the ball."

"Should have told me you and Jack were an item."

"I didn't think you could see us from the mound."

"I could." Oh boy, could she.

Mae wrinkled her nose. "I'm sorry about that."

Harlow sucked in a deep breath. Knowing Mae hid their relationship from her stung. Knowing once again her sister was picked for something God seemed less inclined to give Harlow? That hurt even worse than the knock on her head. What was wrong with her that she constantly stood in the background of life?

"What I saw wasn't a simple peck on the cheek either, Mae. How long have you two been dating?"

"Officially?"

"There's an unofficial?"

She shrugged. "We've liked each other for a long time, but we didn't know how to make it work. More like I didn't."

"How long is a long time?"

"One year."

Harlow nearly came off her pillow. "A year?"

"A year that I knew he cared for me. I only gave in about six months ago." Her smile softened and grew. "He wore me down."

"Why didn't you tell me, Mae?"

"Honestly? I wasn't ever going to do anything about it, and by the time I finally changed my mind, you'd just heard about Peter and Opal's engagement. I didn't want to inject my happiness on your pain. Besides, I still wasn't sure Jack really knew what he was getting in to." Mae picked at her jeans. "Then we all started working on Wheels on the Ground, and I didn't want things to be weird if Jack and I didn't work out."

"You're obviously working out."

"We are." She looked at Harlow. "But I haven't had two seconds with you to tell you since you've been home."

"So you thought making out with him behind the scoreboard was a better idea?"

Mae's cheeks turned pink. "It was one kiss."

"Quite the kiss."

"Why are you so angry?"

"I'm not angry." She nibbled on her nail, caught herself, then settled her hand on her bed. "Try hurt and confused. I just don't get it anymore."

"Don't get what?"

This wasn't a conversation she could have with her sister.

"Harlow?"

"Never mind."

"I'm not going to never mind. Something is bugging you, so spill it."

"Leave it alone, Mae."

She set her brake. "I can sit here all day, sis."

Harlow stared out the window. They were an even match for stubbornness.

After a full five minutes of silence, Mae still wasn't moving. "You know your lack of words speaks pretty loudly."

Harlow kept her focus on the trees swaying outside.

"It tells me whatever is bugging you has to do with me. And whatever it is, you think it'll hurt me." Strength laced her voice. "News flash. I'm a lot stronger than you seem to think."

This loosened her tongue. "Never said you were weak."

"No. You just act like it."

"What?"

"Since the day I was diagnosed, you've treated me differently. Letting what I can't do dictate what you *can,* or simply hovering over me." She shook her head. "Limb Girdle may have changed my life, Harlow, but it never should have changed yours."

Her mouth dropped open. "You're kidding me, right?"

"No."

"I didn't ask for it to change mine. That just happened." She pointed to herself. "Little league? You couldn't play, so I was pulled too. Violin and softball lessons? No more time or money, but let's start a support group for Mae. Even normal things like swim lessons, riding bikes, skating—Mom and Dad said no to it all because they didn't want to upset you." Harlow fisted her blanket. "Over and over they chose you over me. At first I got angry, but how can you be angry at your disabled sister?" A harsh laugh. "Awful, right?"

"Harlow—"

"No. Let me finish." Like a dam burst, she couldn't stop until everything poured out. "So instead of anger, I decided if I could bear things as gracefully as you, maybe they'd pick me too."

Mae's lips parted, but Harlow still didn't let her talk.

"As good as you were with your disease, I've tried to be with my health. As peaceful as you were about each thing you lost, I tried to be about the things taken in my life. Whenever you needed help, I pitched in, and I never complained. But they never saw it. Never saw me."

"Harlow. I didn't know." Mae's eyes were wet. "Here I thought you always saw me as weak, and that's why you always stepped in and took over. It made me so mad." She hesitated. "It was like you were tossing your life away because you didn't think I could handle mine without you."

"I wasn't trying to take over, at least not at first, but with this last diagnosis—"

259

Mae interrupted her. "God's in control. Doesn't matter what the doctors say." The air kicked on, and Mae tugged her sweatshirt closer. "And I'm sorry for Mom and Dad doing that. I don't think they had any idea how it hurt you. None of us did."

Harlow swiped at her tear-filled eyes. "It wasn't just them. Do you know how many things I tried out for at school? I only got class secretary because no one else wanted it. My photography scholarship? They chose someone else. I have a pile of rejection letters at home from publications, sitting right next to Peter and Opal's wedding invitation."

"Oh, Harley."

A strangled sound escaped. "Even this stupid show. They didn't pick me, Mae. They picked you. It was your story that got me on. You're the reason Blake kept me. Then I go and fall for the guy while he has two other women waiting in the wings. What do I expect is going to happen? And all the while you're here falling in love with your best friend, picked again." Tears trickled as she finally dug to the bottom of her hurt, reaching for the roots. "I've tried so hard to hold my hand up and be noticed. Be chosen. But people keep passing me over." She nearly whispered the next. "God keeps passing me over."

Mae adjusted her chair, coming in parallel to the bed. "Harley, I can't speak to people and their actions, but I won't let you think that about God. He chose you the moment he conceived you in his heart and mind. Before the very foundations of this earth, God chose you." Mae took her hand. "His desire for you has nothing to do with anything other than his crazy, unfailing love for you. Nothing you do. Nothing you give up. Nothing. You can't earn it, and you can't lose it. It's just there."

"I know he loves me, Mae. He just doesn't see me as special enough to use. All my prayers have ended in a no."

"Tell me about it." She knocked her chair. "But I like to believe there are *nos* and then there are *not yets*, and sometimes our *not yets* contain a *no*."

"Because that makes perfect sense."

Mae laughed. "Growing and pruning, Harley. There's times you need to be stretched and times you need things cut off." Her laughter softened to a smile. "God's given you some pretty amazing talents. You care for people with more compassion than I've ever seen. You're loyal, and you love deeply with no strings attached. Those qualities didn't magically show up in you. He had to cut away selfish edges and grow your empathy—perhaps by having a sister in a wheelchair?"

A small smile wiggled Harlow's lips. Mae's words acted like someone twisting the barrel of her telephoto lens. Slowly a picture was coming into focus. "Perhaps."

"And your photography is amazing." She spoke as if she'd read Harlow's thoughts. "You've always taken beautiful pictures, but this last year, I've watched you start to tell a story with them. As you went through some deeply painful areas, you started to see God in different ways. He grew you through the hard places while he walked with you there, and it's showing."

"Doesn't feel like it." Life was still tender.

"Maybe not yet, but instead of going on your feelings, try looking at what he's done. He's been tending you, cutting off the places that would have gone astray and strengthening the areas that are going to produce beautiful blooms in the perfect season."

It was as if she had tightened the lens even farther. Harlow could nearly make out the shot, but ... She shook her head. "I'm scared to try again. To put myself back out there." It was why her photography sat in her computer now. Why she was holding back with Blake. "What if God says no again? Because, honestly Mae, I don't think I can handle any more pruning."

"His *nos* are always to protect us, Harley, never to hurt us."

"Not sure I agree with you there. Every door slammed in my face has hurt."

"In the moment, sure." Mae smiled. "But what if God hadn't closed the door on Peter?"

She'd be married to a cheater.

She hadn't looked past the pain of not being chosen again to see the beauty in God's *no*. Or the depth of his love for her when he'd protected her with it.

Her heart warmed.

"And when we wait for his perfect timing to open that door"—there was a knock on her hospital door and Jack and Blake popped in—"what we walked into is far better than we could have ever asked for or imagined." She grinned. "Come on in, guys." Then she leaned to her sister. "God's going to use you, Harley. Trust his timing and don't give up."

Harlow squeezed Mae's hand.

"And stop trying to show you're good enough to be used. He created you. Already chose you as his. You've got nothing to prove."

Jack hesitated inside the door. "You sure it's okay?"

261

Harlow held Mae's stare for a moment before a small smile worked its way out. "Definitely." She waved Jack in. "Come on."

He stepped inside, followed by Blake and the largest bouquet of mismatched flowers she'd ever seen. "I am so sorry." He set the flowers beside her bed. "How are you feeling?"

"Like I was smacked in the head with a baseball." And yet, strangely better than she had in a long while. Blake opened his mouth, but she waved him off. "Which was completely my fault, and I'm fine." She patted for him to sit. "Thanks for the flowers."

"Everything downstairs had roses, so Blake bought them all, tossed out the roses and made you a new bouquet," Jack supplied.

Blake shrugged it off. "Didn't think sneezing would feel too hot right now."

"Probably not." She wanted to kiss him. A real kiss. His smirk told her he knew it. She deepened her grin. Too bad they weren't alone. "So. How did the auction manage?"

"Don't worry about all that right now." He grabbed her hand. "Just concentrate on feeling better."

"Knowing how we did will help. Otherwise I'll go crazy wondering, and I can't spare the extra brain power right now."

Blake glanced at Jack and nodded.

Jack shifted beside her bed. "Between the proceeds from the fair, donations made, and the auction—which Blake was generous enough to add a few extra items too—we raised shy of twenty thousand."

Disappointment flooded her before she could fully stop its flow. Twenty thousand was not a number to be upset by. It was the additional thirty thousand that upset her. How on earth …

Her photographs came to mind.

Maybe it *was* time to try again. Go for it even if it scared her. No denying photography was a deeply rooted passion. Would God finally use it? Choose her?

"Sorry, Harlow." Blake squeezed her hand.

"Don't be." She ran her hand over his forearm. "We'll have the money come summer."

"How?" Mae and Jack asked together, already in unison.

"I'll donate it." Blake's voice spoke over theirs.

"You'd do that?"

He gave a slow nod.

"I may take you up on that, but I've got something I'd like to try first."

"But you don't have to, Harlow." Mae's warm voice reached her. "This is my charity. Whatever your idea is, I'll do it."

"I can honestly say this time it's not about protecting you, Mae. Things may have started out that way, but when I saw those children's faces and heard their stories ..." She swallowed the emotion clogging her throat. "No one should be forgotten."

Like the final twist of the barrel, things came into full focus. Every shot she'd taken in the last year, the constant theme running through each one, they made a perfect pairing for this charity.

She had work to do, because it felt like a door was cracking open.

Harlow slowly swung her feet out of bed and schooled her features. If they realized how badly her head throbbed, they'd likely petition for her to stay here overnight. "I'm ready to go home. Anyone here willing to drive me?"

"I've already volunteered." Blake gingerly kissed the top of her head.

If she lifted her lips, he'd kiss them too. She read it in his face.

Another cracked door.

And it was time to fully walk through it.

Chapter Thirty-One

"Which one first?" Blake stood in front of her, two movies in hand. *The Sound of Music* and *Mary Poppins*.

He'd obviously been talking to Mae.

Harlow looked around the empty room. Three full days of rest, and this was their first time alone. Their hometown week had gone nothing like they'd planned—it had been even better. They'd hung out on her sofa, played countless games of War, and caught up on her favorite shows, all under the watchful eyes of her family. While she appreciated their concern, she was hungry for some time alone with Blake. With him by her side these past few days, she hadn't just walked through the door, her heart had sailed through it.

And he was leaving tomorrow. She didn't want to think about it. Didn't want to share their last few hours with anyone.

"Where are my parents?" she asked.

"They decided to let me play doctor for the night."

"Really?" She raised her eyebrow.

"Yes, and Charlie and Darcy are stopping by later. He needs some footage." Blake waved the movies. "So are you picking, or am I?"

"Are we really alone right now?"

He smirked. "We are." Stepped closer. "We can always start the movie later."

"How about not at all?" She hated those movies.

"Sounds good to me." He tossed them behind his back. "I've been waiting all week to get you alone. No interruptions."

Harlow giggled and held up her hand. "Not so fast, Romeo."

"I prefer Casanova." He slid around her outstretched hand and onto the couch with her, then nuzzled her neck.

Her laughter turned to a snort and then a wince. He stopped. "You okay? I shouldn't be roughhousing with you. I thought—"

She kissed his cheek. "I'm good. Just sore."

He sat back. "Because of me."

"Because I got distracted and didn't duck." She traced his fingers. "We could go 'round and 'round on fault. It was a stupid accident. I don't blame you, so don't blame yourself."

He gave a small nod, but didn't agree. She settled against his chest, and he dropped his chin on top of her head. His response sparked questions she'd held in these past few days.

"Mom said you had a hard time seeing me knocked out cold. That it may have brought back some bad memories about your dad." A tremor ran through his hand. If she hadn't been touching him, she would have missed it. "I know he died when you were young, but I don't know the details. Mom wouldn't give them to me. Said I should ask you."

"You could always google it."

"I don't want detached details, Blake. I want your story."

He stayed quiet. After two minutes, she figured he would remain that way. Then he started talking.

"I'm the one who found him. He committed suicide."

She stopped rubbing his hand and gripped it instead. "Oh, Blake. I'm so sorry."

"It was a long time ago, but it's still there, you know?"

The way his voice cracked hurt her heart.

He cleared his throat.

"Mom had an affair with the owner of The Four Seasons. I walked in on them one day." He shrugged. "Thought I was doing the right thing by letting dad know."

She swiveled around to face him. "How old were you?"

"Seven when I told him." He looked at her, more like through her, as memories danced behind his eyes. "Eight when I found him."

She had no words. None that would suffice. Instead she hugged him, understanding another chunk of this man. Falling a little bit more for him. Unsure if it was love but sure of their connection.

He held her tight for a moment, then leaned back. "When the affair came out, the press wouldn't leave my parents alone. Dad never had time to grieve, the cameras were everywhere. The stories … all lies … and Dad broke apart in that pressure cooker."

Her heart hurt for the little boy trying to weather that storm. She ran her fingers along his arm in comforting circles. "What about you?"

"I did my best, but things only got worse after he died. I guess that depends on who you ask though. My mom never shed a tear in private, but she had buckets of them for every interview." A disgusted snort came out. "Along with me. We were a hot commodity, and she sold us to every bidder she could find. I told that story until I couldn't even feel anymore. All the news, every camera … Mom smiled and I'd try to hide, but there was no avoiding them." His chest shuddered.

Harlow brushed his cheek. "I'm sorry, Blake."

He shrugged. "That's when it hit me for the first time, the fact that I was merely a prop for her. Her love didn't extend beyond the camera. Her attention only lasted as long as I could propel her into the spotlight." He absently ran his thumb along the back of her hand. "She'd been distant before the suicide, then was around long enough to make the talk-show circuit. Once our story died down, so did her attention toward me. It picked up when I was cast for a few commercials and again when I started doing well in swimming—but the second that spotlight dimmed too, she was gone again."

"I'm so sorry that's the picture of love you grew up with." She played with his fingers. "But God's love is always there for you. Constant. You know that, right?"

He shrugged.

Oh. She needed—wanted—him to understand. To feel how much he was loved. Not just by her—

Whoa. Pull that thought back. Sure, she was falling for him. Was attracted to him. But love?

Was that what was taking seed?

"Harlow?"

"Hmm?"

Blake was watching her. "You okay?"

"I am." She shelved her thoughts until later when she could pull them out alone. "Your swimming career ended a long time ago. Has it been that long since you connected with your mom?"

"A handful of phone calls here and there, but … yep."

"Is that why you decided to do *Call for Love*? To regain her attention?"

"No." As he spoke, her cat, Ansel, stalked into the room. "I signed on because she needed me."

"How so?"

"Her career is washed up. The last few parts she auditioned for went to younger actors. I went to visit her a few months ago." He stopped. Swallowed. "She was passed out with a bottle of pills on her bathroom floor."

"Oh, Blake." He had to have seen his father all over again. She prayed for wisdom.

"I couldn't even take her to the hospital—it would've been all over the tabloids. So I called her doctor, and he came to the house. A few days later I suggested *Call for Love* to her. Said we could pitch it as a show that would spin off into her own reality series. Help her return to the limelight." He shrugged. "Her eyes immediately lit up."

Ansel jumped onto the couch, squeezing between her and Blake. "So she liked the idea," Harlow said.

"Loved it more than I'd anticipated." He rubbed the cat's ear. The two had become friendly over the past few days. "I planned to bow out after mine filmed, but she saw the immense popularity around other famous families and their shows. The pitch she took to her agent was slightly different than the one I'd suggested. Let America fall in love with me and my potential fiancée on *Call for Love* and then roll us right on to hers. Season one, plan our wedding. Season two, try for a baby. The studio loved it, and that approval brought her out of her depression. They green-lighted *Call for Love* but are waiting on numbers before filming hers."

"That's an awful lot to put on your shoulders. Feeling responsible for your dad's death and letting it pull you into your mom's world." It was enough to exhaust even the strongest person—and Blake didn't have a connection to the one who'd carry those burdens for him. "But all that weight isn't yours to lift. Do you know that?"

"Charlie and Darcy tell me it all the time."

"You should listen to them."

"I'm trying to."

It was a step in the right direction. "Can you also see life's not supposed to be scripted?"

Clouds chased from his eyes, and he softly smiled. "Each day with you I'm realizing it more and more. Seeing that life is incredibly real, and that's what I

268

want." He leaned close. "I know I screwed up in Germany, but I promise you, Harlow, it won't happen again. You are all I want."

Something settled inside.

She reached up for him.

Headlights bounced across them from her front window as a van pulled into her driveway.

Blake groaned, his forehead dropping to hers. "Seriously?"

Her thoughts exactly. "Interrupted. Again." She pushed off the couch and stomped to the door.

As her fingers skimmed the knob, Blake's arm snaked around her.

With one hand he turned her, with the other he flipped the deadbolt on her door. "Not this time."

Her breath caught, and then his lips were on hers. Such intensity and such restraint. His fingers gripped her waist as he backed her against the wall, his mouth making slow exploration of hers. His hold shifted, his skin warm against hers, sending shivers through her. He stopped. Gently released her and palmed the wall, encasing her in his embrace without an actual touch.

"Harlow." He cleared his throat, his stare roaming every inch of her face. "I don't want to just take from you. If this is too fast—"

Too fast? She'd wanted this kiss for weeks.

She stretched up toward him.

"Woman." The word growled out, and he emptied the distance, tugging her close. His hands tilted her head softly so his mouth could fully slant over hers as he deepened his discovery of her. She clasped his shirt, pulling him to her, letting herself be lost in the moment, in him. His lips trailed across her jaw and then back to her mouth once more, and this time she pushed into him.

*

He had plenty of practice kissing women, but when a moan escaped her and she pressed into him, he realized he'd never experienced this. The softness of her lips opening to him lit a slow burn through his body, but rather than a physical fire, this one stoked a deeper connection. One he wanted to explore farther, dip into, and hold on to. Her fingers crept up the front of his shirt and clenched the fabric tightly. He nudged her head back, whispering his lips over the soft skin of her neck. A tiny gasp, and her fingers released his shirt and slid up to roll through his hair.

Women had offered themselves to him before; he hardly had to try. But Harlow made him want to try. To be better.

He slowed their kisses, reaching for a calm he'd never needed to deploy before. Dropping his forehead to hers, he sucked in long, slow breaths. She slipped down his body until her head rested against his chest. She had to have been on her toes to kiss him the way she did.

He chuckled. "Next time I kiss you, I'll get you a step stool."

"You assume there'll be a next time?"

Big words for someone who barely could find her voice. He placed a finger under her chin, brought her gaze up to his, and let his smirk speak.

She turned an even deeper shade of red.

Her doorbell rang.

He dropped a kiss onto her nose, and she shivered. He wrapped his arms around her.

Now a knock.

"You better answer that," he grumbled.

"Do I have to?"

"Unfortunately."

Her flushed cheeks and huge eyes ... then she licked her lips. Blake dug his hands into his pockets before permanently flipping the lock.

Harlow unlocked the door and smiled.

"Interrupting something?" Charlie stepped inside, honing in on Harlow's face.

Blake couldn't even hide his grin when she peeked his way. Yep. The woman looked like she'd been thoroughly kissed.

Charlie shook his head and let Alex inside. "How are you feeling, Harlow?"

"Better." She followed them to the dining room table, which separated her living area from her kitchen. "I put on some coffee earlier. You two want some?"

"You sit." Blake led her to the couch. "I'll get it."

"Never thought I'd see the day." Charlie punched Blake's shoulder as he passed.

A few minutes later Charlie and Alex were set up, and Blake settled beside Harlow. He spied the movies he'd brought still sitting on the floor. He scooped them up. "Okay. Which one?"

"Neither." She checked out Charlie's camera, which was still turned off. "I hate those movies."

"Huh? Mae said—" He stopped. Sighed. "Do you ever tell them what you really like?"

"Julie Andrews is Mae's favorite. And she's had a lot of hospital stays and down days. It doesn't hurt me to sit through a movie with her if it makes her happy."

"But what makes *you* happy?"

"Seeing my sister smile."

"Other than that."

"Guest room. Curio cabinet."

Charlie started rolling film, pointing at them both.

Blake cocked his jaw and disappeared down the hall. A moment later he reappeared, two DVD sets in his hand. "You're serious here?"

"You have a problem?" Her lips twitched.

"That depends." He opened the first set. "Can you tell me the name Roddenberry used to market the show?"

"That's your idea of a hard question?"

"A true Trekkie would know it."

"And you'd know this how?"

He held up the Vulcan hand sign. "Now answer, or I'm stealing all your DVDs."

She returned it, her twitch switching to a full smile. "Wagon Train to the Stars. Easy. Now play the show."

He offered her a small bow, and she tossed a pillow at him. He caught it, popped in the DVD, and sank onto the couch. "Lay back." He patted his lap. "You need your rest still."

Harlow relaxed against him.

Two hours later, she was sleeping, and Charlie and Alex were packing up.

"Sorry if it was a boring evening, guys." Harlow slept peacefully in his arms. "Actually, no I'm not."

"Good to see you enjoying a piece of normal, friend." Charlie waved goodnight and slipped through the door behind Alex.

Blake ran his fingers through Harlow's soft hair. With the exception of the huge welt on her head, this had been the best three days he'd spent in a long time. Her family had welcomed him with open arms. He'd spent hours with them and Harlow, catching a glimpse of what most people's life was like.

271

Their time in Europe had been great. This had gone beyond. A part of him worried he was falling for the wrong thing and not Harlow. But when he thought about having to see Tarynn in a day, he felt nothing. Carmen in a week made him shudder. All he wanted was to stay on this couch with Harlow beside him.

Unfortunately, he couldn't.

The front door opened, and Harlow's mom peeked in. Her gaze landed on them. "How long has she been asleep?"

"About a half hour." He pointed to a pillow on the chair opposite them. "Can you hand me that?"

Diane brought it over to him, and he gently exchanged his lap for the pillow. Lucky pillow.

"Was she feeling any better?" her mom asked.

"Definitely." He walked to the door, wishing he could kiss Harlow goodnight but knowing she needed her sleep.

"I'm sorry you didn't get in all of the dates you'd planned." Diane followed him.

"I think this was even better."

"Me too." Harlow's sleep-laced voice reached him. She sat up. "You weren't leaving without saying goodbye, were you?"

"I didn't want to wake you." He retraced his steps to her. "You need your sleep.

"I need to say goodbye."

"It's not a goodbye, really. You'll see me in two weeks."

"I'm more worried about who you'll see in the meantime." She touched her forehead and winced.

"I'll go grab you some aspirin." Diane disappeared down the hall.

Blake settled back on the couch. "Harlow, you have nothing to worry about."

"You have to go?" She leaned against his chest.

"I do. But you'll be in Catalina before you know it."

"Then this will all be done."

"And we'll be starting."

She peered up at him. "On a new reality show?"

He hesitated. "I don't know."

Two lines deepened across her forehead. "We've got a lot to figure out."

He placed a soft kiss against her lips. When she snuggled closer, he drew the moment out. Slow and measured, he kept things gentle, breaking away as the urge to push for more nearly overwhelmed him.

"And we will," he promised.

"Here's your aspirin." Diane returned with a glass of water and Harlow's pill. She took it and swallowed.

Blake stood. "Walk me out?"

She took his hand and followed, pulling her front door closed behind her. A cool breeze rolled across them, and Harlow rubbed her arms.

What he would give to be the one to warm her up.

He took the first stair step, then turned, still taller than her, but her lips more accessible. He placed one more kiss against their sweetness. "Two weeks."

"Two weeks."

Time that would feel like forever.

Standing there, her hair in a messy ponytail and sleep still on her cheeks, she never looked more beautiful. He wanted to remember this night. These past few days. He hauled out his iPhone and leaned toward her until their faces were touching. "Take a picture with me?"

Her chin dipped. "You're certainly getting over your camera shyness."

"Only shy when people are trying to steal my private moments." He smiled with her. "This moment is just for us." Then he pressed a kiss to her cheek and captured the memory. "Number?"

"You have it."

"Not for the show phone." Surprise crossed her face before she rattled it off. Blake typed and hit send. "Texted the pictures to you." He pocketed his phone. "And now I have your number."

Her light blush nearly had him leaning back in for another kiss.

She beat him too it. Her lips a feather light touch, and then she was gone. "Night, Blake." She slipped back through her door.

Blake climbed into his SUV and turned to the Tipton Hotel. It felt like months ago he'd been there, meeting Harlow for the first time. In reality it had only been a few weeks, and what he'd found in that time was priceless. And he'd do whatever was needed to protect it.

He parked his car and walked inside, amazed that no one was filming him. No one waited in the shadows to get a shot of him coming from Harlow's house or walking into the hotel. They'd been at the hospital because that was actual news. Otherwise, they left him alone. Abundance was unlike any town he'd been to.

His phone rang as he opened his door, and he fished it from his pocket. Mom's face filled the screen. Swallowing a sigh, he answered. "Hey, Mom."

"Dale's sent me the footage from the past few days."

Not even a hello.

He perched on the edge of his bed, elbows on knees, free hand gripping his forehead. "Still too boring for you?"

"No, darling, it was perfect." Her voice nearly sang. "Have you googled yourself lately? Someone from that sleepy town put up a shot on their Facebook page of you kneeling over Harlow. It's gotten nearly one million likes, and it's been up one day."

Which meant this sleepy little town wouldn't be so sleepy soon.

"We were right about her after all. America loves her! Dale's going to start letting out promos for the show from footage already shot." Pure excitement laced her voice. "Knocking that girl out was one of the best things that could have happened."

He straightened. Tensed. Yes, he wanted her on board, but that crossed a line. "Mother."

"Making lemonade from lemons."

Probably spiked with vodka.

"I'm glad Dale had the foresight to keep Carmen." Mom continued on as if she hadn't just rejoiced over someone's pain. "With Harlow taking a front-runner spot before the show even airs, people will be rooting for her. Carmen's her complete opposite, so it's a natural rivalry. And it will drive up our numbers."

There was nothing natural about it. "If everyone likes Harlow so much, how about we skip right to the end where I keep her?"

"Funny, dear."

Had to at least try.

"You can take it easy for the next week with Tarynn," she instructed, "but really play things up when you get to Carmen so Dale can leak a few of those shots. People love a good triangle."

"Unless you're the person in it."

"These girls signed up for this, Blake."

"Harlow didn't."

"She'll still benefit."

"She's not looking to benefit."

Mom's laughter trickled over the phone. "Everyone's looking for what's best for them. You know that."

He did once. Then he'd met Harlow. She showed him things could be different.

"I'm not going to do anything that will hurt her."

Silence crackled. "You've really fallen for her."

"I have."

More silence. "By all means, I'm not advocating hurting a woman you've known all of one month. Not if you really love her."

"I didn't say love."

"But you think you love her?"

"I don't know. All I know is she's special to me." He creaked open the door toward the conversation he knew he needed to start. "And I've started to think I want to get to know her off camera."

Nothing. Then, "As in not on my show?"

Her voice was so thin. This was going to take more than one phone call.

"I'm not sure of anything right now, Mom, other than I want Harlow to be happy." He hesitated. "And you."

"All right then," she acquiesced. "I don't want you to do anything you're uncomfortable with. I won't force you to compromise your budding relationship with her, but you do have to finish the show. And as you know, Dale maintains final choice of the women. I'm afraid it's Carmen, so expect her to stay until the end."

Of course.

Mom continued, "Get through the next two weeks, then come out here to Catalina. I'd love to finally meet this Harlow."

"You'll like her."

"I'm sure I will."

He could only hope, because if it came down to it, would he be willing to sacrifice his mother's happiness for his own?

Chapter Thirty-Two

The house appeared the same, all seven thousand square feet of it. The town car pulled through the front gate, one of the few cars allowed on the island. With a clank, the black wrought-iron bars slipped back into place, and the car continued to the main entrance. The tan and brown stone façade looked like Mom recently had it painted, and a few of the paved walkways were new. Important to be camera ready.

Blake was anxious to put this all behind him. The past two weeks had been a form of torture he didn't want to repeat. Two large cities full of noise, people, and cameras. Two women he had no connection with. While Tarynn had been sweet, there was no chemistry no matter how hard she'd tried. At least she'd realized it and backed off. Pretty sure he still had claw marks from Carmen, who kept coming back for more. That woman either couldn't read signs or didn't care that all of his clearly said *back off.*

But he'd endured the days and, finally, this one arrived. Everything in him buzzed with the anticipation of seeing Harlow. Like a couple of teenagers in love, they'd burned up the data with FaceTime, selfies, and texting late at night during his downtime. She hadn't seemed to mind the crazy hours—he definitely hadn't. But he was ready to have her in arm's reach. The past two weeks served to cement his resolve. Finish filming and take Harlow back to Abundance. They could date like normal people and work toward their future.

Colburn opened the car door, and Blake stepped out. "Thanks again for picking me up." He hugged him one more time. "I've missed you, Colburn."

"The feeling is mutual." The old man returned the embrace. "I'll make sure your suitcases are brought to your room."

Blake nodded and strolled up the steps to the main door. "Mom?"

No answer.

He slipped inside and crossed through the wide-open interior. A bank of windows created the rear wall and overlooked the deep blue waters of the Pacific. He pushed open the slider and stepped onto the stone porch. Shielding his eyes, he scanned the pool area. There she was.

"Hey, Mom," he called.

She remained on her lounge chair under the huge umbrella, not even standing to hug him as he joined her. Just peered up from behind sunglasses that seemed three sizes too large for her face. "You're here."

"Yep." He lowered onto the lounge chair beside her. "How are you doing?"

"Wonderful. Dale is scouting our stretch of beach and the yard, trying to figure out the best place for your proposal."

"If I propose." He hoped that's where things would end up, just not this weekend.

"*When* you propose." She sat up. "I've already hired a wedding planner."

He didn't want this argument right now.

"When do these girls show up?" she asked.

"Within the hour."

"I've put Harlow in the east wing and Carmen in the west."

"My room is in the west."

She waved her hand through the air. "I've been renovating the east wing. I couldn't fit them both there. Does it really matter?"

He tried to gauge how much of this was to cause tension. He wouldn't let that happen again.

Blake eyed the empty tumbler beside her. "You'll be ready for dinner with Harlow tonight?" The thought of the two of them together, alone, while he was out with Carmen nearly undid him. If they could make it past tonight, though, it should be smooth sailing.

"I'm having it catered in. You said Harlow likes Thai food?"

"Yes."

"Perfect."

"And you'll be kind?"

"I'm always kind."

Apparently they had different definitions of that word. "I should go unpack."

"Colburn can do that for you."

"I'm good." He stood.

"Oh, Blake." She stopped him after a few steps but didn't bother to look his way. "Dale said something about a surprise tonight. Thought you should be aware."

"You don't know what it is?"

"Afraid not. I told him as long as it was good for ratings, I was fine with it." Of course she had.

Blake headed to his room and unpacked in under ten minutes. He had a few hours yet to kill, and the beach outside called his name.

He strolled down to it, the last few weeks running through his mind. The ocean was expansive. Powerful. Always moving. It was a force that could bowl a person over. It's what he always pictured his mom as. She'd swallow him whole if he let her.

And he nearly had.

Then he met Harlow. Over the past few weeks, what he felt with her had awakened something inside of him. Allowed him to believe that life was full of facets he'd never felt before. Ones that were incredibly real—like love.

And if love was real, then maybe God was too. Darcy and Charlie certainly thought so. Harlow definitely did.

But he still couldn't switch that story in his mind from fiction to reality. In front of him the massive sky touched the ocean, and Harlow's challenge from Budapest traveled back to him.

"I guess I'm going to ask that age old question. If you're real, show yourself to me. Make yourself real to me." A piece of driftwood floated in on a wave. That was him. Aimlessly drifting through life. And he wanted more. Thought he could grab more.

He just wasn't sure how.

*

Harlow unpacked her suitcase and then stepped out onto her balcony. This place was beautiful. She pulled up her chair and let the sunshine relax her frazzled nerves after a full day of travel. For nearly two weeks she'd itched to see Blake again. Their nightly chats hardly scratched that itch. If anything, they inflamed it. Then she'd arrived here to Dale waiting with today's shooting script. Not that he had a copy for her, he simply gave her the highlights.

She was scheduled for a one-on-one—with Blake's mother.

The warm air and crash of waves floating through her window helped settle her. Her camera in her hands rounded out the relaxing moment. She'd brought it and her laptop so she could fiddle with the photography book she was creating. Still not sure if she'd sell it on her own website, try and publish it, or offer it on the new Wheels on the Ground website being built, but she was pursuing it. She'd made a few contacts and was letting God open the doors he wanted opened.

Below, someone strolled the edge of the beach. With her camera, she focused in and her heart rate picked up. That wasn't just someone. It was Blake. She zoomed in and her brows drew together. Peeking out from behind the camera, she watched for a long moment, then looked back through the lens.

Lost.

The word dropped through her mind even as she snapped away.

"Lord, he needs you." As she prayed, he picked up a piece of driftwood and tossed it into the sea. "He's searching. Let him find himself in you."

Her heart hurt for him. Never in a million years did she think she'd find this connection with a man who'd blown into her life out of nowhere. She didn't know what to do with it. Impossible to fully give in to. Unable to let him go. So she continued to pray for him—for them both—until he finally walked toward the house. As he climbed the steps from the beach to the patio, he spotted her and jogged her way to stand under her balcony.

"I'm rethinking my choice of Casanova," he said.

She leaned over the edge. "Oh, now you want to be Romeo."

"If it means I get to kiss the girl standing on that balcony? Definitely." He perched one foot on the small stone wall near him. "How was your ferry ride over?"

She shook off the thoughts of him kissing her so she could find her voice. "Bumpy. How was yours?"

"Smooth." He nodded to her room. "Everything comfortable up there?"

"Perfect."

"You sure? I could come up and check."

Too tempting. Which meant she better decline. "I'm good, but thanks."

He stuck his hands in his pockets, seeming so unsure of himself. It melted her heart a little. "Don't let my mom mess with you tonight. She can be a handful," he warned.

"I'll be fine."

"That's what her last two husbands said."

Harlow laughed. "I'm not planning on marrying her, so I should be all set." He checked his watch. "I hate to say it, but I've got to get going."

"I'll see you tomorrow?"

"Wouldn't miss it for the world."

He disappeared, and she tried not to let it bug her where he was going. She'd made the decision to trust him again, and she was keeping it. Someone knocked on her door and she hurried over to open it.

"I need to get you ready for dinner." Darcy stood with her arms full.

"Can't wait." Harlow stepped aside.

"It's almost over." She walked into the massive bathroom and Harlow followed. "And the best advice I can give for tonight is to let anything Summer says go in one ear and out the other."

"She's really that bad?"

"Worse." Darcy hauled out her makeup. "She's done a number on Blake. I started to worry he'd never work his way out of it, then you came along."

"He doesn't need me, he needs God."

"Exactly." Darcy aimed a blush brush her way. "But you've reached something in him the rest of us couldn't. You've opened him to the possibility of God."

"Yet he's still not there."

"Not yet." Soft bristles tickled her cheek. "How are you doing keeping your distance until he finds him?"

"It's tough." Harlow sat. "I like Blake, Darcy. A lot. I think I may be falling in love with him."

"Oh." The brush stilled against her cheek. "That's playing with fire."

Harlow swallowed. "Maybe, but I can handle it."

It took a second before Darcy resumed. She finished the blush in blessed silence. Harlow was tired of arguing with her own thoughts, she didn't need Darcy's too.

Chapter Thirty-Three

With the way everyone spoke about Blake's mother, Harlow was fairly sure she was about to meet the executioner. So she wasn't prepared for the engulfing hug Summer wrapped her in as she stepped into the room.

"Harlow." Summer's perfume swam off of her. "I've heard so much about you, I'm sure I already know you." She took her by the hand and led her out to the small table on the patio. "Here, sit."

Harlow settled into a chair, and as she did, a waiter appeared over her shoulder. "Wine, ma'am?"

"Oh no, Harlow doesn't drink." Summer picked up the wine glass and handed it to the waiter. "Sorry. I've watched most of the season already in the clips Dale has sent me. I heard you tell Blake that on your first date."

Harlow simply nodded.

"You have an interesting chemistry with my son." She placed her napkin on her lap. "You seem to make him very happy."

"He's a great man."

"He is, isn't he?" She sipped her drink. Not wine, but something in a short glass with two ice cubes. "Such a blessing to me."

The waiter appeared again with their dishes. Rice noodles in a creamy yellowish-orange sauce that smelled heavenly for her. Salad for Summer.

"Oh. I had them prepare you a traditional Thai dish. Unless you'd prefer Italian." Her laughter bordered on a cackle.

"Let me guess, that made the cut too?"

"Raw footage. Who knows what will end up on the floor or on the screen." Summer cut her lettuce. "When you sign up for TV though, you must be willing for all parts of your life to become public. You do understand, don't you?"

"Of course."

"Has Blake told you about my new reality show?"

"Yes. He did." She wound a few noodles around her fork.

"So you know it's the follow-up to *Call for Love* and that Blake and his fiancée will be featured in the episodes. Moving to LA. Planning their wedding."

That was news. "Moving to LA?"

"Of course. Blake's home is here." She set down her fork. "He hadn't mentioned that fact?"

"No. But we didn't really talk too in depth about it."

"Oh dear. Then I shouldn't be prying."

The way she said it brought back Blake's earlier warning. Whether there was truth to all the aspects or not, this was a discussion she needed to have with him, not his mother. "No worries, Summer."

"So you wouldn't mind moving?"

"Like I said, I haven't given it much thought. But who knows? If we end up together, he might want to move to Abundance. That could make a great twist to your show—Hollywood moves to small town. I can see it now."

Summer's face paled. "We'd have to see what the network said."

"Blake and I could buy a farm. I bet they'd love to see you visit and help out." She spun another bite. "Now that would make for amazing TV, don't you think?"

Summer didn't say another word, just downed her drink. When dessert came, she pushed away from the table. "I feel a headache coming on. You go ahead and finish without me." She wobbled slightly as she stood. "It was so wonderful to finally meet the woman who holds my son's heart for right now."

For right now?

Harlow brushed off all the meanings those three little words held. "Hope you feel better."

She nodded and walked off toward her room. Not hungry, Harlow returned to her room too. She switched into comfy shorts and a tank, combed her hair into a ponytail, and snagged her laptop from the desk. The moon outside her window was so bright, she headed to her balcony to edit some photos.

Time seeped by, lost in creating pictures and attempting not to think about where Blake was. What he was doing. But those thoughts crashed through her mind until they became deafening.

She set her computer down and stood. Stretched. The waves rolling to shore made good imitators of her thoughts and beckoned her to the soft sand. Listening to their call, she put her work away and headed for the beach.

284

*

Blake pulled into the driveway with Carmen. To say she was miffed put it mildly, but he'd survived the night.

"You won't change your mind?" Her arms were crossed, and she pouted in the passenger seat like a petulant child.

He cut the engine. "No, Carmen. And I didn't see any reason to drag it out farther. This is the end of the road."

"One you haven't traveled." She ran her hand up his arm. "Give it one shot, and if you still don't want me after that, I'll go quietly." She slid closer. "One night, Blake. That's all I'm asking."

Her lips touched behind his ear, and he jerked back. "Made myself clear, Carmen. I think the best thing you can do is go inside and pack. There's a ferry leaving in the morning."

"No way. I'm here until the last day." She stormed out and slammed her door. Charlie walked her inside. Probably a good idea.

Blake loosened his tie, flipped off his mic, and leaned against the car. He'd made it. Broken things off with the last woman, even if she wasn't ready to accept it. The show was over.

He needed to find Harlow.

Stepping inside, he stilled as Jace greeted him. "Looks like that went well."

He was too exhausted for whatever this was. "What are you doing up?"

"It's not that late." He nodded to the deck. "And your evening isn't over yet."

By the french doors, Charlie stood filming. He shrugged at Blake. Apparently he was clueless too.

"I already told Carmen goodnight. Do you need my take on the evening?"

"No. We'll film that in the morning."

"So what then?"

Jace nodded toward the doors. "Head on out."

"That's it?"

"That's it."

His muscles tightened with each step closer to the door. No idea what was out there, but he had a feeling he wouldn't like it.

Charlie stepped through first. His jaw tensed, but he kept his camera focused on Blake. Walking through the doors, Blake first caught site of Alex and his boom mic, then a chestnut blonde in a short, summery dress leaning against the deck railing.

285

Tarynn. She appeared relaxed. No hint of a woman on the prowl. Yet when she stepped toward him, her brown eyes lasered in like he was her bull's eye.

"Tarynn," he greeted with caution.

Her footing faltered, and she stopped. "I know you're surprised to see me, but I hope it's okay that I'm here."

Loaded question. He'd hated hurting her in her hometown. Would like it even less in his.

Neither moved.

How incredibly awkward.

And then she covered the remaining distance between them. She clasped her hands in front of her, craning her neck to see into his face. "I asked if I could come back because I, well, Blake, I like you. A lot. And we have so much in common. I saw it, and my family saw it when you were with us."

They did. And in another world he could see them as friends. But that possibility was off the table in this situation.

"I get that your heart might be in another place, but I had to give it one more try." Her fingers twisted together. "I had to give you this."

Then her hands were in his shirt, pulling him toward her with a quick jerk that left him off balance. Out of instinct, his arms wrapped around her waist to steady them both. She slid hers around his neck, digging her fingers into his hair. She moaned and Blake pushed away, but she clung to him. He turned his head, and she ran kisses down his jaw and along his neck.

"Tarynn—"

Another gasp reached his ears. This one from behind.

Muscles taut, Blake twisted so fast this time Tarynn stumbled, but it wasn't her he tried to catch. It was the redhead fleeing in the opposite direction.

Chapter Thirty-Four

"Harlow!"

She didn't stop. Down the steps and onto the beach, thankful for every day she'd punished her muscles running the beach at home. Payoff was today, because she wasn't letting him catch her.

Behind her, Blake called again, emotion tearing from his throat. No way was it going to stop her. She'd been the fool too many times.

Fifty feet down the beach, his feet slapping the sand gained on her. Darn him and his long legs. She put on a burst of speed, but with another ten feet, his hand wrapped around her arm, halting her.

"Harlow. Stop."

She pulled against him.

He didn't budge, but turned her to him. "That was not what you think."

"Right." One tear slipped down and mingled with the ones already wetting her cheeks. "I am so stupid!" She jerked.

He held tight. "I had no clue Tarynn was here. I had no clue she was going to kiss me."

"You didn't look so clueless to me." Venom laced each word.

"You have to believe me."

She avoided his eyes. His vulnerability wasn't going to win her over anymore. "I have. Over and over. I don't think I can again."

Blake glanced at the ocean and then back to her. "Would you please sit here with me? Listen to what I have to say? Then if you want to leave, you're free to go."

She nibbled her lip. He had her heart, and she wanted it back.

"Please, Harlow."

She had to agree. Even if it was to disengage from his hold.

287

"Fine." She sat and bent her knees, wrapping her arms around them.

He lowered himself beside her. "I went out with Carmen. Told her it was over. When I got back, Jace was waiting for me. He brought me out to the back deck, and Tarynn was there. She came on to me, Harlow. Not the other way around."

She refused to look at him.

He brushed her hair behind her ear, then kept his touch right there against her skin. She struggled to hold her pulse in place.

"Harlow. When I signed up for this show, the last thing I expected to find was anything solid or true. Dreamed about it. But didn't expect it." The rough pads of his fingertips trailed down to her collarbone. "You've blown those expectations out of the water. You showed me love is real. Gave me more than dreams. You gave me hope." His thumb made circles against her neck. "I screwed up once and you trusted me again. Nothing, no one, is worth me losing that again."

She dared a glance at him. Saw the truth in his eyes and struggled to grasp it.

Blake didn't release her. "Think about what you really saw. Was I kissing her back?"

Her brows pulled together. "Your arms were wrapped around her."

"She'd pulled me off balance."

Harlow sighed. Thought again about the kiss she desperately wanted to forget. As it focused, she zoomed in on the details. Stopped. Looked back to Blake. "Your head *was* turned."

A lazy smile rolled across his face. Darn him for making her heart beat faster. "Because she's not the one I want to kiss." He leaned closer. "You're the only one, Harlow."

Putting pictures on replay helped slow her pulse. "That's why you had a date with Carmen, and I just found you necking with Tarynn?"

"No. That was this show." His fingers drifted to her cheek, spiking her pulse again. "This is me." His mouth hovered over hers. "I hate this show, Harlow. Loathe it. But if I have to play this game to win a future with you, then I will." Determination deepened his voice. "And I intend to win."

With an intensity she'd never experienced, Blake pressed in, sealing his promise with a kiss that eclipsed his words. She tensed, the air stilling in her throat as her thoughts splintered. His desire yanked at hers, pulling it from where she'd tried to keep it buried, but it was no use. She was falling in love with him. His touch igniting a wave of heat she'd never felt with anyone.

His stubbled cheeks roughed against her smooth skin. Touch him. The need more than she could control, she ran her palm against his jaw, drawing him to her. A low groan escaped as he let go of her lips and ran his mouth along her cheek, down her throat, and back up, heat from his lips lighting through her.

Every memory of every word he'd said. Every laugh they'd shared. The way he saw her. Challenged her. Cherished her. All came together in this kiss. This moment. Exploding inside her, every nerve pulsed to be closer to him. Her heart raced, her hands explored him, running from his jaw to his chest and down until they rested along his waist. Her fingers dug under his shirt until they found his skin again.

*

Fire raced up his back following the path of Harlow's hands. His lips, nipping at the edge of her ear, moved back toward her lips. He claimed them, wanting to claim her. Everything about this woman moved him. She spoke to all the empty places, filling them in ways he'd never imagined. He picked her up and pulled her to him, setting her on his lap. Her head tipped, and he kissed the skin along her neck, dipped to the edges of her tank, then back up along her collarbone. Her breathing sped up, and he returned again to her lips. He tugged on the lower one, and her hands left his back and ran into his hair. She pulled him closer.

Blake eased her onto the sand, his palms on either side as he held himself over her, kissing her senseless, exploring her skin. "Harlow." His mouth found the well of her collarbone. "You made this real." His lips slid to her ear. "Love. You saved me."

Her fingers stilled in his hair.

And a throat cleared behind them.

But Blake's gaze stayed on Harlow.

Her lids low, and her pupils full and large with desire, she stared at him with a depth of love he'd never seen ... and something else. Sadness?

Again, someone cleared his throat.

Harlow peered around him and those eyes widened. Blake turned. Charlie stood a few feet away with his camera in hand and eyes narrowed.

"Don't worry. I'm not filming." He worked his jaw.

Blake straightened and twisted away, moving off of her so she could sit up. Her hair was messed, and her cheeks were bright pink. Her lips swollen.

He reached for her hand and gave it a quick squeeze. "You should head up for the night." He pressed a gentle kiss to her temple.

She studied him, whatever he'd seen in her eyes a moment ago still there and growing. Then she blinked it away and leaned in, placing a soft kiss on his cheek even as she ran her hand through his hair. Her touch what he'd been missing for too long.

"Goodnight, Blake." She stood.

"Night." He held her fingers till they slipped from his.

Charlie waited until her form disappeared. Then he loomed over him. "Get what you wanted?"

Blake's gaze snapped to his friend's, and he stood. "She was a willing participant. And it was only a kiss."

"I'd say that was more than kissing going on."

"Then you'd be wrong."

"Fine." Charlie didn't let up. "Tell me where it was leading."

"It was only a kiss."

"And if I hadn't come out here?"

They'd be way beyond kissing.

"Exactly." Charlie sighed. "She'd have been a mess when it was done, Blake. I keep telling you, you keep saying you understand, but Harlow's not like the other women. But you can't get that because you don't understand God's playbook. And until you do, she'll be in a different league than you."

"I've built something more than physical with her." Blake pointed to the sand. "We didn't start here. Everything came first. We built a base, and I love her. Cherish her."

"What you were doing wasn't cherishing. It was taking."

No. No, he wasn't just taking this time. Not with Harlow.

"She was giving."

Charlie's jaw flexed. "She's still flesh and blood. Attracted to you. Connected to you. You manipulated her feelings and were about to take what you wanted, not even thinking of what it would cost her. Or yourself." He waited a moment. "You about ruined the second best thing that might ever happen to you."

"Really. And what's the first?"

"God." Charlie stood. "You finally get right with him, and then you'll be the man Harlow needs."

*

Harlow walked up the deck steps feeling every bit like she was taking a walk of shame. But she'd only kissed Blake.

"Who are you kidding?" she muttered.

It might have been just a kiss, but it was a kiss that crossed boundaries. A kiss where she'd been pushing for more and willing to give it.

And that scared her. Things never should have made it that far. Never had in any other relationship. But Blake touched something deep inside. Connected with her on levels she'd never shared with anyone. The intensity scared her.

She didn't know how to control it.

Didn't know if she could.

And what scared her even more was Blake had put her squarely where God needed to be in his life. *You saved me.* Those three words had slammed her back to earth. She wanted to shove them out of her mind, pretend he hadn't said them … but he had.

And if she let him, he'd consume her. She'd give everything she had to make him happy, and it would work—at first. But there was no way she could fill the hole in his life, and when he realized that, everything would come crashing down around them. He'd still be empty, and she'd be spent.

But oh, she wanted to try. Her head might know one thing, but her heart—her body—screamed for another. The past ten minutes on the beach proved that clearly. If she didn't make a change, this relationship would change her.

Which left her with one choice. She'd known it the moment she'd stilled beneath Blake's words on the beach.

She crossed the deck, focused on her feet, on her thoughts. A wall of person stopped her. She looked up, steadying herself against whoever she'd rammed. "Tarynn."

"Hey, Harlow."

Tarynn rubbed her hands across her arms. "Mind if we talk a moment?"

Keeping in the huge sigh, Harlow nodded. "Sure." But she didn't want to take the chance of running into Blake. "Come to my room?"

Tarynn nodded and followed. They went inside and upstairs. Harlow stepped into her room, already mentally packing. "What's on your mind?"

291

Awkward. But then, she seemed to be living awkward since stepping onto this show.

"I wanted to apologize."

Harlow hiked both eyebrows. "Okay."

"I shouldn't have come out here, but I really fell for Blake." She sat on the small chaise in the corner of the room. "I couldn't walk away without giving it one last shot. I thought … You know what? It doesn't matter because he didn't kiss me back. He chased after you." She laughed. "Tells a girl a lot."

It certainly did, but she already believed him. Still wanted him. Loved him.

Which was exactly why she had to leave.

She retrieved her suitcase from the closet. "I appreciate and accept your apology, Tarynn."

"So why the suitcase? Don't you feel the same way about him?"

"It's complicated."

Tarynn sighed. "Love typically is." She stood. "You're really going to leave?"

"I don't want to, but I have to."

"Is it Mae?"

Harlow tossed clothes in her bag. "No."

"You don't want Blake?"

She stilled, then retreated to the bathroom for her toiletries. "I want him, Tarynn. I'm falling in love with him, but until he makes some changes in his life, I can't be with him."

"You're talking about your faith?"

"I am."

Tarynn was silent for a moment. "But the falling in love, it's mutual?"

"Yeah." She came back and tossed her toiletries into the suitcase. Tarynn had already packed up the small desk Harlow had worked at and placed her computer and camera bags on the bed. "I need some distance. Need to give him time to figure things out. If this is what God has for us, it'll work out."

The irony wasn't lost on her. Finally. She'd been chosen—and she was walking away.

No. She was choosing God.

The one and only choice that mattered.

Warmth ran through her. Mae had been right. God had selected her from day one. It was time for her to secure her life to his and let him work out the rest. The *yeses*, the *nos*, all of it. To rest in his love for her and let it be enough.

A knock on her bedroom door stilled her heart. She had to leave without seeing Blake. One look, one word, and he could convince her to stay. She'd leave a note and call him once she was back in Abundance. It wasn't a goodbye.

She wasn't ready for the finality of that. God could grab Blake's heart, and she was believing in that.

"Want me to get it?" Tarynn asked.

Harlow nodded.

The door opened, and Darcy leaned inside. "Oh, hey. Should I come back?"

Tarynn waved her in. "No. I was leaving anyway." She hugged Harlow. "Thanks for listening to me, and if you need anything, let me know."

"I will." Harlow returned the hug.

Tarynn slipped out the door, and Darcy stepped in.

Harlow kept packing.

Darcy sat on the bed. "Leaving?"

"I have to."

"Charlie told me what happened."

Her hand stilled on her zipper, then she pulled it closed.

"You're in love with Blake."

She nodded and slumped to the bed.

"Which is why you're leaving."

"Partly." Unshed tears tightened her throat. "I don't know what else to do. I mean, look at how I acted with him." She dropped her head in her hands. "I went and fell in love with a man I can't have, and then I nearly …"

Darcy spoke into the silence. "So now what are you going to do?"

"I don't know." Her heart felt like it was tearing. "Force him to accept God?"

"I wish it were that easy."

"Me too." Tears welled in her eyes. "Darce, all that emptiness he's spent years trying to fill? He's sticking me right in the center of it. I can't be that for him, no matter how badly I may want to be."

Darcy didn't say anything.

Harlow grabbed a pillow and squeezed. "I love him. I want him to be happy, and I'm worried if I stay, that desire will take out my common sense." She looked at Darcy. "It nearly did tonight."

A corner of Darcy's lip picked up. "And that makes you every kind of normal, girl." She tucked her legs under her. "What's not normal is starting things up and not carrying through. That's why we're not supposed to start them without marriage protecting us."

"But I can't marry Blake." She swallowed back her tears.

Darcy squeezed her shoulder. "I know."

"If I stay, he'll never need to search farther for God."

"I know."

So did she. That was the whole problem.

Harlow sniffed, her heart shredding. "Why did I ever come on this game?"

"I don't think any of us figured it would end like this. I certainly didn't."

But even if she had, she wouldn't have changed a thing, not if it meant never having met Blake. That thought didn't stop the dam from bursting or her sobs from coming, because letting him go and trusting God to make them both complete was the hardest thing she'd ever done.

Chapter Thirty-Five

B lake woke early the next morning, the ocean calling him. He threw on his trunks and headed out for a swim. Clicking his door shut behind him, he turned toward the stairs and caught Dale sneaking down them. Blake looked across the hall to where Carmen slept; her door was slit open.

Had they been carrying on from the beginning?

He was more than ready to leave this make-believe world. Thankful that he'd finally found his something real.

His gut twisted. Had he ruined it last night? Memories from the beach crashed around him, heating and icing him all in one turn. Charlie's words came on the cusp of the memories. As much as he was falling for Harlow, could there be something larger beyond her? Something that would help him love her the way she deserved?

Something that would love him even deeper than she could?

Harlow had shown him love was real. Could God be real too? Did one exist without the other?

Another door in the hall closed. Blake startled. "Morning, Tarynn."

She had a bag over her shoulder. "Morning." She took a hesitant step his way. "I spoke with Harlow last night and set things straight, but I feel I should apologize to you too." She smiled. "What can I say? You're a great catch. If things hadn't worked out with her, I think we'd make a good match, but I can see your heart is taken." She hitched her bag up. "I'm out of here on the first ferry. Just going to hang out downstairs and have some breakfast. I'll stay out of your way. Promise." She moved to pass him.

"Tarynn?"

She turned. "Yeah?"

"You're a great woman. If things had been different—"

Her hand came up. "No apologies. It's all good." Then she walked down the steps.

Blake waited a minute, then jogged downstairs and made a beeline for the beach. Swimming always soothed him. The waves were calm this morning, the breeze light. He waded into the warm water. No rip current.

He dove. Swam until his shoulder started to ache. It didn't match the ache inside. So many moments in the past few months served as evidence to remind him that the world he lived in was full of counterfeits. Then there was Harlow.

He stopped and treaded water, watching the sunrise paint the sky. He sought something real, found a glimmer of it with her, but though he asked, still no word from God. Which meant the jury was still out.

Charlie's words added to the jumble of last night.

If he didn't believe, he couldn't have Harlow.

If he didn't believe, he'd never know true love.

And he desperately ached for them both.

But how could he believe in something—someone—that simply didn't exist?

Maybe he could try to live by the same principles Harlow did without sharing her convictions. It couldn't be too hard.

Slowly hope started rolling back in. Sure, he could do that. He could do anything for her, because the thought of her leaving left an immense hole. No way he could continue settling for Mom's idea of a relationship. Not when Harlow offered him so much more.

He started for shore, but after a few strokes, he was farther away.

He didn't feel a current pulling him out. But something was. No need to panic. He'd swim parallel to the shore and be out of a rip with a few strokes. He swam another minute for good measure, not worried when he was pushed even farther out. He was still at an easy distance. Turning, he tried for shore again. After about ten strokes, he was no closer.

No major waves or wind. The ocean was eerily calm. No reason for a rip current. It was almost like an invisible hand held him in place and—wait. That thought morphed into stunned realization, and he looked up. "Really? You pick now to show up?"

Unbelievable.

Anger curled in him, and he swam for shore. Except the shore got farther away.

All you have to do is ask me.

The words echoed from what felt like the depths of the ocean floor.

He pushed towards the shore, but no matter how much he worked or how badly he wanted it, dry ground stayed out of his reach. Except he didn't grow tired. A strange energy buzzed through him. Held him up.

All you have to do is ask me.

Seriously? "I asked if you were real. I've asked so many times, and you ignored me." He smacked the water. "I asked you to save my dad. I asked you to make Mom love me. I asked you to send someone, anyone to love me. You sent nothing."

My son.

It was both an answer and an endearment. It ripped through his core.

All you have to do is ask me.

"Ask you what?" Blake shouted to the sky.

To be the one to love you. To be your enough. To be your Father.

Blake looked toward the dry ground.

To be your Savior.

Swallowed in the inky water, still he felt no fear. No exhaustion. Right now he was held up by a strength that wasn't his own. Protected when he should be consumed, sinking beneath the silky blackness around him.

He stilled.

God had dropped him smack dab into a picture of his life. He'd been drowning for years in a sea of emptiness. Exhausted and hopeless from the repeated attempts to hold himself up when he was never meant to tread through life on his own.

Somewhere in the depths of his soul, he knew God was real. He was just too scared to believe it. Scared he'd ask for the strength, accept the love, only to have God leave him too.

I will never leave you or forsake you.

Adrift and lost, like that piece of wood floating through the ocean, he needed someone to save him.

Blake looked to the sky. "Will you save me?"

I have loved you with an everlasting love. You are mine. You are loved.

The words softly floated down to him, coating the strength that had filled his muscles, keeping him afloat. He stroked toward shore, this time making progress. Rough sand met his feet and he trudged forward, collapsing on the beach. Warmth enveloped him, and he laughed.

Joyous gulps of laughter.

This was real love. Overflowing. Drenching. Never-ending.

Abundant.

*

Blake raced up the deck steps, his mind on one thing. Harlow.

He thought he loved her. Thought he understood what that really meant.

Now he knew. And it bottomed out his stomach. Raced through his blood. Kept his heart from fitting in his chest.

He hit the top of the deck and flew toward the french doors. His mother and Tarynn sat at the breakfast table. He barely spared them a glance.

"Where are you headed in such a hurry?"

"To see Harlow."

His mother's face twisted. "She's not up there."

He stopped. "Where is she?"

"She left." His mother tried for a frown. It missed. "Tarynn just came and told me."

"Harlow left?" There had to be a misunderstanding here. But the look Tarynn showered on him said there wasn't. His blood stilled. "When? Why?"

"I'm not sure of the when, but last night, I think. And the *why* you'll have to ask her," Tarynn supplied. "I'm sorry I didn't say anything this morning, but she asked me not to. She said she was going to call you—"

He raced for her room.

"Blake!" His mother yelled, but he didn't stop.

He threw open the door, half expecting to see Harlow there. Waiting for the cameras to come out and Dale to say this was all for ratings. He could still smell her soft scent. His mind spun at the sight of her empty room. He stalked inside, memories of last night slamming into him. This was all his fault.

He needed to find her. Let her know what happened this morning. They could fix this.

Fear trembled against the peace he'd just found. He started for his room, but his mom blocked the door. "You can't leave."

He stopped. "I'm going after Harlow. Once I find her, we can figure out the show, but she's my first priority."

"You need to see something first, and then if you still want to go after her, I'll step aside."

She was still trying to manipulate him. He could see it in her eyes.

"I don't have time for games anymore." He tried to brush past her, but she didn't move. Tarynn, Darcy, and Charlie all stood in the hall. He looked to Charlie. "That important thing? I found it this morning."

Charlie's eyebrows punched together before he broke into a huge grin. He brushed past the rest and grabbed his friend in a bear hug, slapping his back. Darcy joined the hug.

His mother's voice broke the moment. "I have no idea what is going on, but Blake, you need to see this." She thrust her iPad into his face. "You want to know why Harlow left? This will tell you."

Safari was open to *Star Magazine*'s website. The selfie of Blake and Harlow on her front porch stared at him along with the headline: *Blake's latest love to sell tell-all book of their time together.*

A chill broke over his skin. He started reading, disbelief coating every word. "Photographer Harlow Tucker went on *Call for Love* to find more than love. With a sister in a wheelchair and a nonprofit starting up, Harlow knew Blake Carlton would be her ticket to the money she needed. She's given *Star* a sneak peek at the photos we'll find in her new book, *Snapshots of Love.*"

Blake held it up. "How'd they get this?"

His mother looked at Tarynn whose face crumpled with pity. She hauled out a small green business card. "He wrote the article."

"Marty Pontelle?" Blake took the card. He'd heard of the creep. "Half of what he writes is fiction, and I'm being generous."

"Sometimes. But this time he has a credible source." His mother slipped into acting. No way she felt the empathy injected into her voice.

Tarynn reached for his arm. "I found that card in Harlow's room while I was helping her pack."

Blake looked down at it. "I'm sure there's an explanation." Because the Harlow he knew wouldn't do this.

Darcy stepped forward, concern crinkling the corners of her eyes. She flicked her gaze to the card with Monty's ugly mug on it and inhaled sharply. Then eyes full and wide fastened on Blake. "I saw him at her house."

No. Not Darce—she'd never lied to him.

Pain twisted so deep he needed to sit down, but he couldn't. Had to stay strong. No way after all this, Harlow wasn't who she said she was. Nothing about her was fake. She'd fueled him with the ability to hope again. Pointed him to the God he'd just found.

She—all of it—had to be real. This had to be a colossal misunderstanding.

"He could have been fishing for information."

His mother tsked. "Looks like he got it." Then she laid her hand on top of his arm. "I'm sorry, Blake, but that's not all. I made a few phone calls. She has been in contact with publishers."

He still wouldn't believe it. Words could be explained away. Circumstances created. He needed evidence. He reached for his cell phone, remembered he was in swim trunks. He picked up the phone on her desk. Dialed Marty Pontelle's number.

"Marty."

Bitterness fought for his memories. Blake focused on the task at hand. "Blake Carlton here. I'd like to know where you got today's photos from."

"You're referring to the website?"

"I am."

"Harlow Tucker supplied them."

If he didn't hang up, he'd break the phone. "Thank you."

No way. Marty could say anything. This didn't jive with the Harlow he knew.

Darcy stepped forward.

"Not now, Darce." Blake picked up the phone and dialed Jack Townsend's number from memory. He barely let him answer the phone. "Jack. It's Blake Carlton."

"Blake! Did you do this?" The excitement brimming over his voice cut into Blake's nerves.

"Do what?" He didn't want the answer.

Tarynn squeezed his arm gently, as if to give him strength.

"The donation. One hundred and fifty thousand dollars." His voice trembled as he noted the amount. "Wheels on the Ground is a go. They don't even need the grant anymore. You have no idea—" He stopped. "Mae wants Harlow to give you a hug from her."

"Harlow's not here."

And now he knew why.

She'd gotten what she'd wanted and left, no more real than the love he'd thought he found.

Chapter Thirty-Six

Harlow followed the line off the plane, flicking her phone on and ready to use it. In the hours since she left Blake, she'd questioned her decision about ten thousand times. Her heart was ready to hop a plane back to him, but they needed distance.

And she was trusting God with the decision.

She glanced at her watch. It was still early in California, but he had to be awake. She wanted to talk to him right away. Let him know why she'd left and that her feelings were still there, stronger than ever. They were why she had to walk away.

Stepping off the jet bridge, she surveyed the terminal. Chicago was busy, but she had a long layover. She hustled through the crowd to a gate that wasn't being used, took a seat in the corner, and hit dial, Blake's number already on screen.

With each ring, her stomach tightened. Darcy had said she'd watch for him this morning. Talk to him and prep him, but until Harlow heard his voice, her heart would stay in knots.

"Harlow Tucker." Blake's cool voice slid across the phone.

She expected him to be upset, but something in his voice relayed more than that.

"Blake." Her voice shook. "Um. I guess you know by now I left."

A hard puff of air shot over the phone. "Yep. I got that." Silence hefted its weight for one long moment. "Nice article in *Star Magazine* this morning."

"*Star Magazine?*" The name wriggled in her brain. "Did something happen?"

"Aren't we past playing games, *sweetheart?*"

She stilled. "I thought so, but it sounds like you want to play one."

"I can assure you, I don't want anything of the sort." He nearly growled. "I'm sick of people playing me. You were the best though. Never saw it coming."

"What are you talking about?" She shifted. "I didn't leave as part of a game. I left because I'm falling in love with you and—"

"That's why you sold Marty Pontelle the pictures? Why you're publishing a book from your time on *Call for Love*?"

Breath pulled from her lungs. Marty Pontelle. That's why she recognized *Star Magazine*. "I don't know what he's told you, but I haven't given him anything."

"Funny, because he has pictures and quotes."

"Not from me."

"You're the only other person who had the shot, Harlow, besides me."

The picture from her front step.

"It didn't come from me."

"I'd like to believe you, but you happened to leave his business card in your room here, and Darcy confirmed seeing him at your house. And we both know Darcy doesn't lie."

"But you think I am." Frantic, she stood and paced. "Marty Pontelle approached me twice. Each time he gave me a card, but I threw them both away. One in Europe, one at my house. I never had any other contact with him."

Pure silence.

"As for any publisher I've contacted?" She had to make him understand. "I do want to make a photography book and use the proceeds for Wheels on the Ground, but it has nothing to do with you. I wouldn't do that." She sucked in a lungful of air, scrambling for solid ground. "If I'd sold a story to *Star*, I'd have money. I wouldn't need a grant for Wheels on the Ground. Check my accounts, Blake. I'll give you access and you'll see. I haven't sold a thing."

He was quiet so long, she thought he'd hung up. "Call Jack."

The line went dead.

She stared at her phone. Hit redial and got voicemail. Hit it again. Voicemail.

Tears tumbled from her eyes, and she frantically dialed Jack.

"Harlow! Did you pass on that hug to Blake?"

She could barely squeeze a word out. "No."

"Why not? After what he did, he deserves one." Jack laughed.

"What are you talking about?"

Jack quieted. "The money?"

"What money, Jack."

He must have heard the catch in her voice. "You okay?"

She clutched her phone. "What money?"

"The one hundred fifty thousand deposited this morning."

She hung up the phone and burst into tears.

Chapter Thirty-Seven

After a month, Harlow still didn't know where the money had come from. An anonymous check had been deposited in her name to an account for Wheels on the Ground. The letter attached to it thanked her for the photos she'd supplied to *Star Magazine*. And while the cover picture had been the selfie of her and Blake, the remainder were photos taken from her camera, but she'd never sold them. If she could, she'd return every last cent of the money. Only problem was she had no idea where.

Her first few days at home, reporters had swarmed her, and even though she tried to set the record straight, they thought her book had been put on hold due to the lawsuit Blake had slapped on her the same afternoon she arrived home.

In reality, there'd never been a book contract. A few publishers contacted, but nothing signed, and none of it had contained one shot of Blake. Not that anyone was believing her. Enough other people were lying.

What a mess.

That first week she'd tried calling him several times, right up until the day he changed his number. And she had no way to get in contact with Charlie or Darcy. Any call she placed to Dale went unreturned. The network too. No one was talking. But they were sure benefiting from the story.

So while she'd hidden out at home, she put together her photography book. The one she would publish herself if every publishing house sent her a rejection letter in the end. Last week, she uploaded her work to an online photo company to print herself a mock-up. A digital scrapbook full of all the photographic illustrations that had bubbled up in her heart this past year. And it was good.

It felt like her purpose.

And she was finally ready to follow it once things quieted some.

Settling onto her sofa, she picked the book up and let it fall open to a random page. A picture from Budapest stared at her. Next to the large fountain on Váci Street, a man stood with a puppet on a string. She closed her eyes, hearing the music as the marionette danced to a melody playing from a box at the man's feet. With each tug of a string, the puppet had moved. No will of his own. No thoughts of his own. His only lot in life was to fulfill the entertainment of the puppeteer.

Bound.

She opened her eyes and traced a hand over the photo, seeing Blake in place of the puppet. He was so tied up, and he didn't even realize it. The desire to find the biggest pair of scissors and snip him free hit her again. But that wasn't her job.

She looked heavenward. *It's yours.*

Still, even with all the silence on his end, she couldn't stop praying for his freedom.

Her front door popped open. Charity and Mae came in. "How you doing?"

"Decent." At least she'd made it to lunchtime without crying.

"Did it finally come?" Charity pointed to the large empty envelope on Harlow's coffee table.

Harlow held up her scrapbook. It wasn't perfect or the highest quality, but it was finished either way. Charity and Mae were the only two who knew about it currently, and they'd stopped by daily to see if it had arrived. At least that was their current excuse for checking on her.

Mae rolled over and took it from her hands.

"This is beautiful." She flipped through the pages. "The verses and words you chose. This will impact people in huge ways." She stopped on the page with Chet holding the little boy and the caption *Found.* "You're gonna make me cry."

Charity scooted in on the other side, flipping pages with Mae. They paused again in the center. One picture covered both pages. Set in sepia tones, the beach and lake spilled from the left side over to the right where a figure sat at the base of a rustic cross. Her knees bent, her arms hugging them, she faced the water rather than the camera, and a breeze caught a few strands of her hair.

"This is beautiful." Charity ran her hand over the matte pages.

"That's you, Harlow." Mae pointed to the shot. "How—when did you take it?"

Moisture built in her eyes. "When I came home."

With her fingertip, Charity traced the caption *Chosen*. "You are, you know. Even if Blake Carlton messed up big time."

"I know." Her smile trembled. "That shot had nothing to do with Blake."

That first day home she'd been a mess. But slowly moments and words from the last few weeks started to infiltrate her heart. God chose her simply because she was Harlow. That seed had sprouted and taken root. Her body was whole and healthy. Her spirit was messed up and broken. He loved every drop of her. Not because of anything she'd done or hadn't done. But because she was his.

He chose her.

She'd packed up her camera and visited the dunes at sunset. A broken old tree stood at the top of a small dune, beach grass blowing all around it. At the right angle, the tree formed a rugged old cross, beaten and blown but still standing. Felt a lot like her. The lake shimmered in the distance, the soft glow of sunset creating beautiful light. She perched her camera on a log, sat at the base of the tree, and looked out to the lake. Her camera's timer went off and the picture it captured said everything inside her heart.

It didn't matter who Blake Carlton chose. Didn't matter if her book was ever published. Didn't even matter if she was never picked for anything again in her life. She'd been chosen by the Most High since the moment he conceived her in his heart. And his all-encompassing love soothed the brokenness in her.

After captioning it *Chosen*, she'd written in scrolled letters across the bottom, "He chose us in him before the foundation of the world. Ephesians 1:4."

"I'm having that one enlarged for my wall." She pointed to the spot beside her desk where she'd hang it. "I think I'll need to look at it often."

Charity blew out a soft breath. "Can you make a copy for me?"

"Sure."

Her sister and friend continued flipping through the book, making comments. Harlow stood. "Coffee anyone?"

"I'd love some." Charity didn't glance up from the book.

Harlow disappeared into the kitchen. By the time she returned, they were on the last page. Should have thought about it before she let them see it. That book was just for her. The one on her computer—the one she intended to send to publishers—ended differently.

It didn't have the pictures Charity and Mae now stared at.

On one side was the close-up of the old couple's hands, their wedding rings blinking in the sun. Beside it was the picture of Blake smiling at her from the top deck of the Poseidon Rivulet. It was the first night she'd glimpsed her own feelings for him and seen the possibility reflected in his eyes.

She'd simply titled it, "True Love." Because it's what her heart still held for him. And even in the midst of all her pain, it's what she daily prayed he'd find.

Her cheeks heated. "I know I can't use that picture of him."

Charity looked at her. Smiled. And left the caption alone. "But this copy is for you. I'm sure it's okay."

"Have you heard from him?" Mae handed the book to Charity.

"Not a word, as long as you don't count the lawsuit."

She again fought tears.

Reminded herself of all God had blessed her with even in the midst of this chaos.

Wheels on the Ground could start. Her photography was moving from a hobby to something more. She'd floated down the Danube, for goodness sake.

All things she'd never truly imagined taking shape. Things she hadn't earned, but God blessed her with anyway. And slowly she was coming to realize that was his way. He loved blessing her because she was his. That's what love was, giving to someone simply because you loved them.

She looked at her book, open on Charity's lap.

Yes. That was love, and it was why she'd walked away from Blake.

The best gift she could give him was leaving him alone.

Chapter Thirty-Eight

Blake swam to shore, ignoring the figures waiting for him. If he wanted to talk to Darcy, he would have returned her calls. Unfortunately, she'd brought Charlie with her, and he couldn't be ignored.

"Good swim?"

"Decent." He took the towel Charlie handed him. "What do you two want?"

"Darcy wants to talk to you." Charlie crossed his arms. "I want you to listen to her."

It had been six weeks since he walked out of Mom's house and contacted his lawyers to send Harlow a cease and desist. Five weeks, six days since he told Dale not to plan on him for Mom's show. After that he'd gone home and unplugged his phone. Unfortunately, reporters knew where he lived, and they wanted to know if Harlow was the reason for his still-single state after *Call for Love* had wrapped. One day of that and he'd had all the questions about her he could stomach. Especially since they hit too close to the truth. So he packed and drove up the coast.

How Darcy and Charlie found him, he didn't want to know.

"Fine. Talk. Then leave me alone."

"You're an idiot."

"All right, I'm an idiot." He pulled on a shirt. "Is that all?"

Darcy shoved a small photo book at him. "You need to look at this."

He recognized the photography immediately.

"If there's one shot of me in there, she'll lose every penny of that advance and then some."

"Have you read it?"

"Don't need to. I was there for most of it."

"Funny, seeing as how most of the pictures were taken before she ever met you."

Blake stopped. "Come again?"

"She's not doing that cooked-up book someone sent to *Star*. I can't believe you even fell for that." Hands on her hips, fist tightened, she was like a cobra ready to strike.

Fine by him. He'd bite back. "You going to tell me now that you *didn't* see the guy at her house. That she didn't have money suddenly appear in her bank account?"

"No. But I am going to tell you I never actually saw her give Marty anything, and she still doesn't know where that money came from. Anyone could have deposited it in her account, Blake."

"But not anyone could have the pictures she took."

"If they ripped them off her computer, they could." Darcy tried to catch his gaze, but he avoided it. "I was as caught off guard as you were. But we got to know her. *You* got to know her. Somewhere inside you know she's not responsible for this."

"I got to know the role she was playing."

Darcy held out the book in her hands. "Fine. But at least read this."

He didn't take it. "If I do, you'll leave me alone?"

"Depends." She tossed the book on top of the bag at his feet. "You may not be trusting anyone else, but are you still trusting God?"

"I'm not sure."

"Why?"

"Because sometimes I think we can make ourselves want something bad enough that we convince ourselves it actually exists. Then we find out it doesn't." He picked up his bag. "I thought what I had with Harlow was legit. It wasn't. The entire thing was a set-up. I don't want to be set up by God."

"You haven't been by either of them." Darcy turned and started up the beach. "Read the book."

Charlie waited a long moment. "Try and discount God all you want; you and I both know he's real. As real as what you had with Harlow."

"How do you know?"

"You can't miss something that wasn't real." Charlie nodded at him, turned, and left.

Blake walked up the steps to the small beach house he was renting. He went inside, grabbed a drink, and settled on the back deck. He stared at the book on top of his bag. An hour later, he finally picked it up.

Chapter Thirty-Nine

Harlow watched the kids running through the fire hydrant they'd opened at Ford Square. Middle of summer, and it was a record breaker. She was half tempted to join them. As it was, she snapped pictures of their wide smiles.

For her next book she focused on one subject. Joy.

She'd had enough of pain.

A little boy ran through the water, his arms spread wide. She snapped the picture.

A blue shirt stood in her way and didn't move.

Harlow lowered her lens. "Excuse m—" Her words turned to dust.

"Let me guess. He doesn't know you're taking his picture?"

She saw Blake's grin, but didn't see his humor. Pushing to her feet, she grabbed her camera bag and turned to walk away. "I don't need this."

His strong fingers gripped her upper arm gently. With this heat she'd worn a tank, and she felt every inch of his skin on hers.

"I'm sorry. That was a poor attempt at a joke." His nervous laughter peppered her sore nerves.

She didn't look at him. "Yeah. It was."

He kept chuckling.

She peered over her shoulder. "That's really annoying."

"I'm really nervous."

"Why should you be? I'm the awful person who sold you out. Lied to you and used you. If anything, I should be nervous you're here to slap another lawsuit on me."

He pocketed his hands. "Deserved."

"What do you want, Blake?"

"To apologize."

She watched him through narrowed eyes, then spun in a circle, palms up. "Where are the cameras?"

"There aren't any."

"This isn't some strange ending that Dale's trying to tack on to the show?" She fisted her hands at her hips. "Confronting the woman who sold you out?"

He absorbed the hit, turning a shade lighter. "I made a mistake."

"Yes. You did." He wasn't the only one. She should have tried harder to keep her heart away from his. "We both did. Good thing you had two back-ups."

"I didn't pick either of them."

"I heard. Thought it was another tactic to amp up buzz for the show."

"Been keeping tabs on me?"

Kids' laughter in the background made an awful soundtrack for her mood. "No. I've had reporters here questioning me if I was the reason."

"What'd you tell them?"

"To check their local listings and watch the show."

"They may be checking indefinitely. As far as I know, the show isn't going to see the light of day."

"Neither of your back-ups wanted you?" She gave a harsh laugh. "I find that hard to believe."

"Because you still want me?" The intensity of his stare shot heat through her.

"Ha. Right." She stomped off.

His smooth voice reached out and grabbed her. "The entire thing turned out to be a disaster that even the editing floor couldn't help." He waited until she looked at him and then stepped closer, hands lazily in pockets, tentative smile tugging at his lips. "Apparently not enough chemistry. The bachelor they had was only interested in one woman."

"Well, he screwed it up royally."

"And he's here wondering if he can fix it." He reached for her hand, but she wouldn't let him take it. "I'm sorry, Harlow. For every mean word I said. For ignoring your calls. Changing my number. The lawsuit." His voice caught, and he studied the ground for a moment, then his blue eyes ripped back up to hers, his heart open and beating inside the look he held her with. "For all of it."

"How about for not believing in me?" The words barely squeaked past her tight throat, but she refused to cry. She'd given him enough tears.

"For that most of all." A long pause filled with more than silence. He puffed out a breath of air. "Believing in people. I'd started that journey about two seconds before my mom dropped that bomb on me. And it nearly broke apart the most important relationship I've ever known."

"I'd say it did a great job of that."

"I wasn't talking about us."

*

He held in his smile as she narrowed those perfect eyes of hers again. It was all he could do not to tug her to him and kiss her. But he'd prayed about this all morning. For the last three days. And he might be new at this prayer stuff, but he was pretty sure he knew he needed to get things right with her before kissing her.

"I was talking about God."

Her narrowed eyes widened.

"Charlie told me if I ever wanted to come close to being the man you need, I had to get that relationship right first."

"Charlie's a wise man."

"He is." Blake tried a step closer again. This time she didn't back away. "I have a ways to go yet, but I'm firmly on the right track now."

"I'm glad for you, Blake. And I accept your apology." She tapped her finger against her tooth. "I know how it appeared, but I didn't do all those things. I don't know who did—"

"Tarynn did."

Her hand fell from her mouth. "What? Why?"

"She wanted to end up with me. Slept her way to the final three with Dale. She's been pulling his strings for quite some time, trying to wedge Carmen in between you and me. From what I gather, she thought you'd leave, I'd ditch Carmen, and she'd be the last woman standing. Unfortunately, that didn't happen, and when I didn't invite her to Catalina, she upped her game." He shoved his hands into his pockets. "Tarynn had found Monty Pontelle's business card in the trash can when she roomed with you in Europe. She threatened Dale, and he brought her to Catalina to save his own rear end. She figured on causing you some trouble by herself, but then she found a willing partner in my mom."

"Your mother?" That pricked her heart.

He nodded. "We'd had a few conversations leading into Catalina. With each one she could tell I was getting closer to you. The last time we spoke, I hinted I might not be willing to do her show if it meant losing you, so she didn't want me with you." He looked to the park and then back to Harlow. "Tarynn

317

showed her Monty's business card, and my mom ran with it. Had Tarynn steal your pictures and send them to him. Then Tarynn waited around to pick up the pieces once I broke apart."

"She played the part so well. Except you didn't end up with her. Why?"

He held his hands to his side. Knowing he couldn't touch her yet, but having her this close was a test of his newly found patience. Especially every time the wind drifted her sweet scent to him. "Because I knew I didn't love Tarynn." He wanted to add it was because of what Harlow had shown him. Even before he believed in her innocence, he was still believing in what they'd shared. Even if he hadn't admitted it to himself.

But her crossed arms and squared shoulders stopped him. She wasn't at a spot to listen yet.

"And your mom?" she asked.

"I'm tired of being her prop. If she wants me around, it's going to be because she wants me. Not because she needs me as part of her set." He tried a smile. "I also finally realized I'm not responsible for her happiness. I can't be her savior any more than you can be mine."

Harlow blinked rapidly. People walked by, a few glanced their way, but no one stopped or interrupted. Answer to hours of prayer before coming here.

"I'm happy for you, Blake. You seem … content. And it means a lot that you'd come all the way here to make sure I knew the truth." She hesitated. "But what made you look for it anyway? You were pretty hung up on me being the guilty party."

He waited a beat, wishing he hadn't caused the hurt in her voice. "I read something the other day that made me realize I just might be wrong about you."

"What was that?"

"I'll get to it." A group of kids raced by, playing tag. Blake remained silent until their shrieks softened into the background. "But after that, I had someone check into my mom's accounts. It was pretty easy to track the check she'd sent to Wheels on the Ground in your name."

"No it wasn't. I tried for weeks to figure out who sent it. To clear my name that was being dragged through the mud."

Because of him.

He let out a long breath. "I knew the date it went out and the amount. All I had to do was look at her accounts. You didn't have that ability or the suspicions." He took another step closer. "And I'm sorry for all the trouble she caused you."

"It blew over."

"It still had to hurt."

"I've been hurt worse."

"By me."

She lowered her eyes. "Yes."

Nearly tore him in two. "From the bottom of my heart, Harlow, I am sorry."

Her eyes watered but not a tear fell. "I forgive you." She held on to his gaze for another long moment before hitching her camera bag farther up her shoulder. "I should get going. I have to work later today."

"Speaking of work." He pulled off the backpack he wore and dug in it. A huge, hardcover book sat in his hands. He gave it to her.

Her face was priceless. "Where'd you get that?"

"A friend." Her fingers ran over the cover, sparking joy through him. "Actually she gave me a different copy and then sent the file of pictures. I hope you don't mind that I took what was in it and had it bound a tad more … professionally. It's what amounts to a galley copy."

Confusion rolled over her face. "A what?"

"That means it's nearly ready for print."

"For print? I've never even signed a contract. I haven't even sent it anywhere yet. Only query letters."

"I took it to a publisher friend for you."

"Blake." She held out the book, and when he refused to take it she set it on the table between them. "You don't owe me anything, and I certainly don't expect you to use your connections to get me published."

"I brought it to him because I believed in you, not because I owed you anything. Your talent is what will get you published."

"What made you change your mind?" Her voice was so soft.

"About the pictures?"

"About me."

The corner of his lip tipped up. "Time. Space. A couple of good friends." Blake paused. Took a deep breath. "My whole life I wanted to believe someone could love me for me. Not playing a role, not needing anything. And then I found it—with you. That led me to God," he said with a step closer, "which led me back to you."

*

His eyes. That smile. She wanted to trust the tenderness there.

He started to reach for her, then shoved his hand into his pocket. "I'm sorry I let you go so easily. It won't happen again."

Her mouth twitched. "There you go, always assuming."

"Assuming?"

"That there'll be an again."

"Not assuming. Knowing." He shook his head as if he was giving in to a pull he no longer could resist, then reached out and cupped her face. "You love me, Harlow Tucker. Not my name, not my status, not what I can do for you. Just me."

She leaned into the rough skin of his palm.

His thumb stroked her cheek. "And I am crazy in love with you."

Yep. Her heart was about to burst. "You are, huh?"

He nodded, then leaned in, his lips hovering over hers. "I want to kiss you, but don't want to be accused of assum—"

She closed the distance between them, but he quickly took over. Digging her hands into his thick hair, she tugged him down closer, missing the home of his arms. He wrapped her into him, and all the hurt from the past month unfurled inside of her, replaced with a deep love.

"Charlie's on to something."

She peeked at him. "Charlie?"

"Suggested we double-date."

His breath trailed heat from her temple back to her lips where he placed a soft kiss.

"Might be a good idea."

His chest rumbled with laughter, and he rested his forehead against hers. "Definitely is. I don't want to cross any lines again. I want to do this right." He released a sigh and trailed his fingers down her arms before setting her a step away, then he ducked to look into her eyes. "I have something for you."

His words warmed the space between them, flip-flopping her stomach much like his kisses. "I told you to stop buying me things."

"That's an argument I'm afraid you're never going to win, sweetheart."

The love he wrapped around that term of endearment made it a completely new word. One she'd never grow tired of hearing him call her when he said it in that tender way.

He held out a gold heart-shaped pin, further melting her.

"To mark Catalina in?" she asked, taking it from him.

He touched the tip of the pin. "I thought this one could mark an even better location. It's not someplace you physically traveled to, but it represents a journey all the same. One it took us both some time to reach." His voice cracked, and he cleared his throat before continuing. "It's to mark where our story begins. Right here in Abundance." Her heart started racing even as he reached over and flipped the photo album open to the last page. "We'll need to change this though. That picture you had of me alone can't happen."

Her racing heart slowed. "I'd never have used it. It was only for me—"

His lips silenced more words from tumbling out. After a long, sweet moment, he pulled away. "I know. But I do think you had a great idea, it just needs a little tweaking, and the publisher happens to agree with me." The faintest hint of vulnerability laced his expression and slipped into his voice. "I'm hoping you will too." He nodded toward the album.

She followed his gaze. The book lay open to its final pages. The left side captured the old couple's hands grasped together with the caption "True Love" exactly like she'd drafted in her own copy. On the right where Blake's picture had once been, however, now was a blank space. "End on the couple?"

He softly chuckled. He was nervous. Before she could ask why, he took her hand in his and placed them on the blank page. "End with our hands." He tapped her third finger. "Except we'll need a ring here."

Her eyes flicked to his huge grin. No cockiness. No Hollywood. Simply Blake.

And he was fully focused on her. "Because you did, Harlow."

"Did what?" She couldn't tear her gaze from his.

"Love me, truly." Tenderness still filled his face, only now she dove into it. Trusted it.

"No. You're wrong." He tensed and started to pull away, completely missing the slight tease in her voice, but she held on tight. "Not past tense, Blake. Present. As in, I do." This grabbed his full attention. "Love you, truly." And she'd happily spend forever showing him how much.

He seemed to have the same idea. Wrapping her in his arms, he grinned slow and easy. "You do, huh?"

"Madly. Abundantly. Deeply." She punctuated each word with a kiss.

But it was Blake's addition that settled her heart into home. "Eternally," he whispered, capturing her lips fully, every ounce of his love flowing into her, each breath beyond what she could have ever asked for or imagined receiving.

Truly, indeed.

THE END

CPSIA information can be obtained
at www.ICGtesting.com
Printed in the USA
LVHW090006070121
675953LV00027B/373

9 781645 262350